CAN'T FIND MY WAY HOME

CAN'T FIND MY WAY HOME

Carlene Thompson

This first world edition published 2014
in Great Britain and the USA by
SEVERN HOUSE PUBLISHERS LTD of
19 Cedar Road, Sutton, Surrey, England, SM2 5DA.
Trade paperback edition first published 2015 in Great Britain
and the USA by SEVERN HOUSE PUBLISHERS LTD.

British Library Cataloguing in Publication Data

Thompson, Carlene author.
  Can't find my way home.
  1. Missing persons–Investigation–Fiction. 2. Children
  of criminals–Fiction. 3. Romantic suspense novels.
  I. Title
  813.6-dc23

ISBN-13: 978-0-7278-8457-2 (cased)
ISBN-13: 978-1-84751-556-8 (trade paper)
ISBN-13: 978-1-78010-603-8 (e-book)

All Severn House titles are printed on acid-free paper.

Severn House Publishers support the Forest Stewardship Council™ [FSC™],
the leading international forest certification organisation. All our titles that
are printed on FSC certified paper carry the FSC logo.

Typeset by Palimpsest Book Production Ltd.,
Falkirk, Stirlingshire, Scotland.
Printed and bound in Great Britain by
TJ International, Padstow, Cornwall.

PROLOGUE

Eighteen Years Ago

No one was home.

Brynn Wilder climbed the steps of her porch and turned to wave goodbye to her best friend Cassie Hutton and Cassie's mother, who'd brought Brynn back from a sleepover at their house. Brynn unlocked the front door, walked into the living room, then stopped and listened. Usually she heard kids stumbling through the piano lessons her mother gave on days off from her part-time job at Lavinia Love's boutique, Love's Dress Shoppe, or rock music coming from her big brother Mark's bedroom, or her father loudly opening and closing drawers in the metal file cabinet in his small office. Now there was only unnatural silence. Then she saw the note taped to the inside of the door:

> *Lavinia needs me at the shop. I canceled today's music lessons.*
> *I should be back by four. If Dad isn't here when you get home,*
> *he's fishing. Lock the doors. Be good and most of all, be*
> *careful.*
> *Love,*
> *Mom*

Brynn smiled. A miracle – a beautiful spring Saturday morning with Mom at Love's Dress Shoppe and her sixteen-year-old brother, Mark, on a school trip to the Maryland Science Center in Baltimore. For once, the house was empty and she could do exactly as she pleased.

Except that faced with this unexpected marvel, Brynn couldn't think of one thing she wanted to do. What a bummer, she brooded as she slumped upstairs to her bedroom, opened her canvas duffle bag and held it upside down over her twin bed. Out tumbled her nightwear, a plastic sack filled with a bottle of bright pink nail polish, a collection of cheap cosmetics, a curling iron and a travel-size can of super-hold hairspray. Last night, she and Cassie had worked for nearly two hours performing makeovers on each other. Satisfied with the results, they'd agreed they looked at least fifteen and no one would ever guess they were only twelve years old. After that, they'd watched a horror movie and finally fallen asleep at around one a.m.

Brynn now looked at herself in her dresser mirror, picked up her pink plastic brush – she'd been looking for her favorite silver-backed one since Wednesday – and ran it through her long, wavy dark cinnamon-brown hair, still sticky from too much cheap hairspray. She liked her thick hair, her straight nose and her long-lashed, almond-shaped hazel eyes, but she didn't like looking twelve, especially when people said she acted more mature than most twelve-year-old girls. Dad always told her that by eighteen she'd look just like her mother, who Brynn thought was movie-star beautiful. That was a long time to wait, but until then . . .

She leaned forward and looked closely in the mirror. Was that a *zit* on her chin?

Appalled, Brynn dabbed on a spot of acne cream, whirled away from the mirror, walked straight into the kitchen and opened the refrigerator. Food and drink usually helped her during bouts of oncoming depression caused by things like thoughts of zits.

Gazing into the refrigerator, she spotted a pitcher of sugarless iced tea and poured herself a tall glass, telling herself it was non-zit-producing, unlike Coke. Then, on the countertop, she saw a plate of fresh spice muffins covered with cling wrap.

As Brynn sat at the kitchen table sipping her drink and downing a muffin, she tried to think of something to do – something she wouldn't be allowed to do if she weren't alone. After a minute or so, her mind blank, Brynn sighed. She could *not* miss this opportunity and just sit here doing nothing. Besides, she felt weird. She frowned. Weird? Weird how? 'Weird, like something's wrong, spooky,' she said aloud, startling herself. Something wasn't right, but she had no idea what.

Then she knew. Last night she and Cassie had talked a lot about the Genessa Point Killer, the guy who'd murdered eight boys and girls around town in the last three years. They'd turned off the lights, lit candles, and in low, melodramatic voices discussed theories about who could be the killer. *Anybody*, they'd finally decided, shuddering, frightening each other. Then they'd creeped themselves out even more by watching a horror movie that was way beyond scary.

Brynn shivered. I can't stay in this house all by myself, even with the doors locked, she thought, suddenly nervous. Her friends often told her that she was the bravest girl they knew. She acted modest, shrugging off the label, although she considered it a tremendous compliment. Yet now she didn't feel brave – she felt afraid, and she wanted to get out of this silent house as fast as possible.

But Mom was busy at the store. Mom's boss, Lavinia Love, would get mad if she had to leave to pick up her 'little girl.' The Huttons had returned Brynn home over an hour early before they headed to the hospital to see Cassie's grandfather, who'd fallen down the steps and broken his hip this morning. She couldn't bother them and the nearest neighbors were gone for the weekend.

Abruptly, Brynn remembered the note she'd found on the door: *If Dad isn't here when you get home, he's fishing.*

Fishing! Of course Mom wouldn't have gone off and left her alone, especially with a killer running loose, she thought. Jonah Wilder went fishing within sight of the house every Saturday morning when the weather allowed. She would rush to his favorite fishing spot and surprise him.

Brynn grabbed the can of bug spray Dad always forgot and dropped a couple of muffins in a plastic bag for him. She didn't want to fish – she didn't even like fishing. She just wanted to be with her dad.

Jonah Wilder had been the principal of Genessa Point Middle School for four years and moved up to principal of the high school three years ago. Brynn knew how much the job meant to him and that he took his duties seriously. He put up with no nonsense at the school, seemed to know how every student was doing, and had no tolerance for troublemakers. Three-day suspensions had become common since he'd taken over as principal. Many students – and quite a few parents – thought he was strict, harsh and completely without humor, earning him the popular nickname 'Stone Jonah,' both for his stone-gray eyes and his austere manner.

But Brynn didn't know 'Stone Jonah.' At home he was a different man than outsiders saw. He treated her and Mark with love and understanding. He rarely raised his voice, and listened to their explanations when they got in trouble. He adored Mom. He always complimented a new outfit or a different hairstyle and looked fascinated when she rattled on about her days at Love's Dress Shoppe or teaching a special piano student. Sometimes Brynn had secretly watched them slow dance late at night to ballads. After two or three songs, during which they'd giggle and murmur, Dad would hug Mom, kiss her cheek and call her 'My sweet Marguerite.'

She dashed out the back door of the house that stood on a low rise above the Chesapeake Bay. Brynn loved her house at the end of Oriole Lane. Dad diligently maintained the modest, two-story beige home with rust-colored shutters, and Mom kept her summer flowerbeds bursting with a riot of colors. Warm summer air blew Brynn's stiffened hair and the sun glowed butter yellow in a washed denim sky.

She hurried through the yard and drew a deep breath, bursting into a run through the saltmeadow cordgrass to the wooden steps leading down to the beach where her father fished. The Wilders had no dock, boathouse, or fishing boat. Dad and Mom said they should save extra money for Mark's and Brynn's college funds, not spend it on excesses.

Halfway down the steps, Brynn spotted her father's orange and black tackle box, his rod and reel and his folding aluminum chair. But she couldn't see her father. The tackle box was turned on its side. His rod and reel lay in the sand. The chair was upside down.

Brynn slowed, almost stopping as her earlier uneasiness returned. Where was Dad? He'd never leave his fishing spot in such a mess. He was the neatest person she'd ever known.

A scream suddenly ripped through the beautiful, sun-filled scene. A girl's scream.

Brynn went stone-still, only her gaze moving to the river birches, sycamores and white oaks growing near the beach. Another scream came from the mass of trees: 'Please, God, no!'

Terror filled a girl's shrill voice. Brynn began to tremble. Her mind told her to run back to the house and lock herself inside, but her body wouldn't obey. She walked stiffly down the steps and mechanically through the sand toward the trees. Overhead, a sea gull shrieked as if alerting her to impending danger. The sun flashed blindingly on the water of the bay. Brynn blinked in surprise. The sun shouldn't be shining now, she thought distantly. Darkness should be descending – darkness to shut out what was happening in the woods.

'Dear God, no! Don't—'

She barely recognized her father's agonized voice.

'No more . . . no . . .'

'Help me!' the girl shrieked. 'Please, don't!'

Brynn shriveled into herself. She felt little and helpless and could hardly breathe. The gull screeched again. The sun glared unrelentingly.

The world stopped for Brynn as Jonah Wilder staggered from the trees clutching his neck, weaving, his steps dragging. He angled toward the bay, then turned. He seemed to look right at Brynn, but somehow she knew he didn't see her. Even from this distance, she could tell his sight had turned inward, the outside world lost to him as he slowly dropped to his knees then crashed face down on the sand.

Brynn stared at her father for a few shock-frozen moments before life flowed through her and she ran down the rest of the wooden steps. Almost immediately, a girl emerged from the trees – a teenage girl in jeans and a white T-shirt, her blonde hair garishly streaked with scarlet, a hand clutching a red patch spreading from her back to her side. Her gaze found Brynn's. She swayed. 'Help me,' she called in a weak, ragged voice. 'P-please . . . *help* me.'

Then she sank down, her slender body sprawling beside Brynn's father.

ONE

> *A cloud moved across the moon, the shadows deepened, and not far behind her, Evangelista heard a ferocious sound – not human, not animal, not like anything she'd ever heard before . . . or anything she'd ever hear again, she thought, because whatever was making that sound intended to*

Brynn Wilder paused and frowned at the computer screen. Intended to what? Rip her to pieces? Tear off her head? Paralyze her and take her back to its den? Critics called her novels 'a rich mixture of supernatural and fantasy, both poignant and thrilling.' They'd change that label to 'crude, amateurish horror' if they got a look at her latest effort.

'This is *awful*,' Brynn said angrily, hitting the delete button. 'Even *I* don't know what I'm writing about!'

She'd been working on her latest book all evening and she'd completed only four awkward, emotionless paragraphs. She couldn't get into the mood. The heroine's plight seemed contrived, her fear wooden, her actions stupid. No sensible reader would care about her. At this point, Brynn didn't care about her.

Brynn leaned back in her chair, rubbed her neck and glanced at the wall clock: 10:30 p.m. Definitely time for a beer, she thought, going to the refrigerator and grabbing a bottle. She twisted off the cap. A glass? Not tonight. She tilted her head and downed a long, cold swallow. She liked gulping beer directly from the bottle. Something about it made her feel blithe and bold, like a sassy woman who didn't have a care in the world. She knew it was a childish illusion, but it was better than the alternative: worrying about her brother, Mark.

Dammit, why was he obsessed with Genessa Point? Why did he have to go back to that awful place last week?

Because it was where their father had died. Died? Brynn laughed bitterly, nearly choking on her second gulp of beer. A teenage girl named Tessa Cavanaugh had stabbed Jonah Wilder to death. Tessa's father was the president of Genessa Point's largest bank. The Cavanaughs were the town's most affluent family and Tessa's older brother, Nathan, was a close friend of Mark Wilder, while Tessa had taken piano lessons from Marguerite. Yet based on all the evidence police found at the time, the town, and later the whole country, had labeled Brynn's father Stone Jonah Wilder, the murderer of eight victims under the age of fifteen.

At first, people had thought a fifteen-year-old girl couldn't possibly win a battle for her life against a grown man. Yet it seemed to be true. Although she'd suffered multiple lacerations and puncture wounds – the most critical barely missing a kidney – Tessa had survived. She'd told police that photography was her hobby and she'd gotten an early start that beautiful day. She'd been taking some photos in the woods behind the Wilder house for the last three Saturdays. That day, Mr Wilder had been fishing nearby and had good-naturedly posed for a couple of pictures. The police had later found the shots on the film in Tessa's camera. Afterward, she'd gone into the cluster of trees.

Tessa said she was bent over, taking pictures of the fairy ring mushrooms that flourished in the woods, when suddenly someone had leaped on her, slamming her face into the moist earth. Although she hadn't passed out, the attacker had ground her face into the dirt and begun stabbing her. He'd said nothing, so she couldn't identify a voice. Still conscious, she'd fought desperately, her lean, muscular body writhing away from him for an instant and digging in the dirt until her hand closed around her camera. With all her strength, she'd struck him with it.

'I don't remember much after that except someone grunted, the stabbing stopped and the guy rolled off me,' she'd told police weakly in the hospital. 'I was trying to crawl away and something cut my hand. I knew it was a knife and I grabbed it and stabbed him, over and over. But there was so much dirt in my eyes, I couldn't see who I was stabbing.' Through sobs, she'd asked, 'Who was it?' The police said when they'd told her the person was Jonah Wilder, Tessa had gotten hysterical. 'Not Mr Wilder!' she'd cried. 'It couldn't have been! Not Mr Wilder!'

No, there had to be a mistake, most people said. Tessa was traumatized, blinded by dirt and badly injured. Jonah Wilder *couldn't* have attacked her. His reputation as a hard-working, law-abiding, devoted family man had never been questioned. Sometimes he seemed stiff, humorless, even quaint, but he was always kind and polite and, over time, most citizens of Genessa Point had realized that he was merely serious and reserved, maybe even a bit shy. People didn't love him like they did his best friend, the outgoing, good-natured Dr Edmund Ellis, but generally they liked and respected Jonah.

The theory of a third person in the woods emerged almost immediately. Even Tessa said it was possible – she hadn't seen who'd knocked her to the ground and rubbed her face in the dirt before stabbing her. Most people believed the Genessa Point Killer, as he'd been named, had attacked Tessa. Jonah had heard her scream and rushed to her aid, but the man who'd terrorized the town for years fled upon Jonah's arrival after being hit hard with the camera. When Tessa grabbed the knife, blinded by the dirt in her eyes, she'd stabbed Jonah by accident. Jonah's death was tragic, they'd said, but it wasn't for nothing. He'd saved a girl's life.

For two days townspeople had brought food to the Wilder home, offered comfort and praised Jonah. Although Mark would seldom come out of his room, Brynn and her mother had accepted the food, the praise and the hugs, although Brynn knew they both felt numb.

Then the police found the knife.

According to the Wilders, when Mark was fourteen he'd bought a fishing knife for his father's birthday – a Buck 110 folding Hunter knife. He didn't have much money, so he'd bought a used knife he could get cheap because of a nick in the blade. He'd spent hours carving J.W. in the wooden handle to make up for the flawed blade. Marguerite told the police that Jonah was thrilled with the knife, especially because of Mark's carving of the initials, but the knife had disappeared almost two years before Tessa killed Jonah with it.

Marguerite said her husband had felt awful about the loss of the knife and bought a new one just like it, asking Mark to put J.W. on the handle, but Mark's feelings were hurt because he thought Jonah had just carelessly misplaced the original, and he'd refused to carve initials. Although police had not found the replacement knife the family claimed Jonah had bought, they'd found the supposedly missing knife with the blade knick and the initials near the site of Tessa's attack.

The police questioned Dr Edmund Ellis, Jonah's fishing companion, who'd said he knew nothing about Jonah losing the knife Mark had given him almost two years earlier, or its replacement. The family was stunned at Edmund's statement to the police. Then, after what seemed an infinity in the earlier days of DNA testing, finally the police had received the results. Under the hinge of the initialed knife, experts had found the DNA of Jonah, Tessa and three of the Genessa Point Killer's victims.

The news about the DNA results quickly leaked from the local police and spread like wildfire throughout town. Some people, who knew little about DNA, claimed someone was pulling a chemical trick with this stuff. What was DNA anyway? Many more people knew about DNA and thought it was the be-all, end-all of evidence. Jonah Wilder's knife – the knife he kept in his *tackle box*, for God's sake – had been used to kill innocent kids; probably all of the GPK's victims. It seemed impossible, but that quiet, polite man had killed children. Come to think of it, they whispered among themselves, hadn't Jonah Wilder been just a little too reserved, too unnervingly calm, yet too strict with students at the high school? And those sophisticated chemical tests at a place like the FBI didn't lie.

Within two weeks, many people were certain Jonah Wilder had been the Genessa Point Killer. Sheriff Dane, convinced of Jonah Wilder's guilt, closed the investigation.

Jonah's name had become a staple on television newscasts. Later, behavioral scientists studied him. Someone wrote a book about the murders called *Stone Jonah: The Genessa Point Killer*, and he became almost as famous as Ted Bundy or The Green River Killer. Worst of all, in the book some 'experts' conjectured that Jonah had not worked alone. They claimed that Jonah and his son Mark had often operated as a team, like Bianchi and Buono, known as The Hillside Strangler.

Now, eighteen years later, Mark still couldn't live with the horror of what had happened to his father or the suspicions about himself. He'd struggled emotionally with the disaster since the time of his father's death. Like Brynn and their mother, he'd refused to believe Jonah was a killer. They knew that the quiet, kind, patient man they'd lived with for so long did not have murder in his soul.

Still, they couldn't change what most of the world believed. The general population of Genessa Point had turned cold and most of their friends suddenly became aloof. Within three months after Jonah's death the family had escaped to Baltimore and never returned to Genessa Point. After the first shocked year, Marguerite had gone silent about Jonah, refusing to answer if Brynn or Mark tried to talk to her about their father, and getting angry if anyone mentioned the murders.

On the other hand, not a day went by that Mark had not zealously 'worked the case.' Convinced there had been a third person in the woods who'd attacked Tessa and then Jonah when he'd come to Tessa's aid, Mark had made hundreds of notes, drawn timelines, called the Genessa Point County Police Department with his new evidence and harangued the families of victims for details until the police had threatened to charge him with harassment. Although Brynn agreed with her brother – a third person had been responsible for Tessa's attack and their father's resulting death – her mother's days of obstinate silence and Mark's frantic activity had made Brynn feel constantly tense, exhausted and bleak.

When she was fifteen, filled with grief and depression, along with the belief that they would never discover what had really happened on that awful day, Brynn decided if she was to have any life of her own she had to close a door in her mind and refuse to think about the disaster that had destroyed the world she'd loved. She didn't try to obliterate beloved memories of her father, though, and at un-expected times the image of his tall, slim frame or the sound of his deep, slow, mellow voice flashed in her mind. Often she wondered what he would have done in a bad situation, what he would have been like as he grew older, how different Mark and Marguerite would be if he were alive.

Unlike Mark, though, she had never let herself dwell on the details of how her father died. Imagining his painful death filled her with a shaking horror that shut everything else from her mind and she knew she must focus on what needed to be done *now* because although she was the youngest in what was left of her family, she was the strongest. Both her mother and her brother needed her. Day after day, she'd forced herself to concentrate on them, not on sorrow about her father, not on her anger toward Genessa Point, the town that had turned its back on the Wilders. Finally, in her mid-teens, she realized the blinders she'd kept rigor-ously in place had allowed her to develop enough resiliency to move on and function successfully, even if it was hard for her to let anyone become close or important to her.

For Mark, the battle was longer. It wasn't until he was twenty-seven that he'd seemed to tiredly relinquish his own denial and rage about his father's death as well as the rumors about himself, and settle into defeated peace. Three years later, he'd married a pretty but shallow girl neither Brynn nor Marguerite liked. Nevertheless, Brynn had hoped desperately she'd be a good wife, they'd have a child and that a family could keep Mark grounded in the present.

Unfortunately, the wife had quickly grown bored and also announced she had no desire for children. Not long afterward, Mark had learned that she was having affairs with a string of men. Soon, he had begun talking about the old murders, at first occasionally, then incessantly. Along with his renewed obsession came increased impatience, irritability and, finally, drinking binges that led to liquor-fueled fury.

The rest had followed with heartbreaking inevitability. Within the past year he'd lost his wife, most of his few friends, and, a month ago, he'd been fired from his job as a bank loan officer. He'd sunk into despair as once again he'd begun obsessing about that little town on the Chesapeake Bay where his family had been so happy, then so devastated.

One evening, obviously drunk, he'd called to tell Brynn he was going to Genessa Point to clear their father's name and, before she could argue, he'd hung up on her. For two days, she'd told herself the plan for a trip was only the result of too much liquor. Still, when she'd ceaselessly called his apartment in Baltimore, his cell phone, and texted, he hadn't answered. That was eight days ago. Now, certain he'd been serious about revisiting their hometown with some crazy, hopeless and possibly risky goal, Brynn's anxiety had grown to a fever pitch.

'I should have believed him and gone to Genessa Point. He's a damned mess and he's going to get himself in trouble, I know it,' Brynn fumed, thumping down on the couch across from the wall of windows overlooking the brilliant city lights of Miami. Miami where no one seemed to sleep. Miami where the sun blazed and winter never came. Miami where she'd fled after her mother died eighteen months ago and where Brynn planned to spend the rest of her life – a city of fun, bone-warming heat. A place where she could forget the past.

Except that, even at age thirty, and in spite of all her efforts, she'd never been able to forget that horrible day when, as a twelve-year-old, she'd run toward the beach, expecting to find her father peacefully fishing and instead heard screams coming from the cluster of trees. Then she'd seen Dad stagger onto the beach and fall. Sometimes she'd wake in a sweat after reliving the scene in a nightmare.

Now the phone rang, jerking Brynn back to the present and her Miami apartment. She nearly pounced on it. 'Hello, it's Brynn.'

Silence. *Unknown caller* showed on the caller ID. Usually, Brynn would have hung up on someone blocking their identity. But then she wasn't usually so desperate to hear from her brother. 'Mark?' she almost shouted. 'Mark, is that you?' Nothing. 'Mark, dammit—'

She heard music, soft at first, then growing louder. Within moments, she recognized the introduction of Blind Faith's 'Can't Find My Way Home.' Although the song dated from the late sixties, it had been Mark's favorite. Jonah had liked it, too, and played it often. Brynn hadn't been able to listen to the song after her father's death, but now she sat mesmerized as Steve Winwood sang, 'I can't find my way home,' in a haunting, lost voice.

The song played all the way through. After a moment of silence at the end, someone sighed, long and lonely. The connection broke off.

Brynn stood still, barely breathing, gripping the handset. She pressed the off button and took a deep breath, hoping desperately that the phone would ring again. Although she waited fifteen minutes, with depressed certainty, she knew it wouldn't. She was also sure the call hadn't been just a prank. It had been a message.

Her hand trembling, she immediately called the police and reported the call, asking if it could be traced and answering a number of what Brynn considered maddeningly inane questions: had she been threatened; had she been receiving calls regularly; did she have any idea who'd placed the call? Saying she thought the call had come from her brother, who might be in trouble, did not raise the cop's excitement level.

'Do you have reason to believe your brother could be in trouble, miss?' he asked calmly.

'Yes. He went back to our hometown of Genessa Point in Maryland. It's on the Chesapeake Bay. Our father was murdered there.'

'Oh. When was that?'

'Eighteen years ago.'

'Was the murderer caught?'

'Well, yes, sort of. It's a complicated story.'

'I see.' Pause. 'Why did your brother go there?'

'He thought he might catch the murderer.'

'I thought you said the murderer had been caught.'

On and on. Finally, the cop ended with, 'If you continue to get these calls, Miss Wilder, let us know. Otherwise, I wouldn't get too worked up over one phone call with a song. Probably just kids trying to frighten you. Annoying but harmless.' The cop gave her a pleasant 'Good evening, ma'am' and hung up. Furious, Brynn tried to slam her handset back in the tilted base and dropped it. She picked up the handset and banged it against the table three times, muttering curses.

Trying to calm down, Brynn closed her eyes and drew another deep breath. Still, her chest felt tight. She picked up her bottle of beer, opened the sliding glass doors and walked out onto the terrace of her apartment. Even for late June in Miami, the day had been unusually hot. She stared at city lights bouncing off tumultuous clouds, predicting a fast-approaching storm.

She leaned on the terrace ledge, gazing at the clouds. For as long as she could remember, Brynn had loved storms. When one loomed close by she would stand outside, the wind blowing her hair, looking up at brooding skies while waiting to see shards of lightning and hear the boom of thunder.

As a child, Brynn hadn't understood her fascination with storms. She only knew that the electric crackle in the air and the sight of fiery spears against billowing clouds followed by the roar of thunder filled her with rapture. As an adult, she saw it all as a display of the anger and the power of nature, a tiny slice of universal force. Storms were unpredictable. Storms were exciting.

Except for tonight. Brynn watched white light flash inside the mist of a cloud. To her surprise, the fine hair on her arms raised in a nervous chill. Her spine tightened as a shiver raced through her. She turned away from the fire-streaked sky and hurried back into her apartment, not even waiting for the thunder. This storm seemed different than any storm she'd ever watched before. It didn't fill her with exhilaration. It seemed like a portent of disaster.

My God, who had called and played Mark's favorite song and hung up? she wondered. Even if Mark were drunk, he wouldn't do such a thing. When he was drunk – which wasn't often until this year – he ranted. He turned loud and defiant, usually sounding like a boisterous little boy having a temper tantrum. He wasn't quiet and tricky. He would never have made that anonymous, insidiously cruel call. Never.

Brynn closed the terrace doors, shutting out the sound of thunder.

Immediately, she remembered wrapping her arms around her dying mother. As Marguerite drew her last labored breaths, she'd whispered that she'd always loved her brave little girl. Then, with a rasping voice that ripped at Brynn's heart, she'd asked for a promise. 'Please, honey, always take care of your brother. He needs you so much. Promise me . . . promise . . .' And with heartfelt sincerity, not temporary comfort for the dying, Brynn had promised.

Now, the time had come for that promise to be tested. Brynn had sworn to herself she would never go back to Genessa Point no matter what the circumstances. For eighteen years, she'd kept that oath.

As a nearby brilliant burst of lightning lit the dim apartment, Brynn closed her eyes, reluctantly embracing the truth – it didn't matter that the memory of the town stabbed her with icy apprehension. She would not – could not – break her promise to Marguerite. Her mother was gone, but the brother she loved, the brother she'd vowed to protect, was still alive, and he was in trouble.

Mark needed her more than he ever had, and Brynn knew she had no choice – she must return to Genessa Point.

Later, Brynn lay in bed, hot and sticky although she'd set the air conditioner to a lower temperature than usual. She wished desperately for the sleep she needed but knew wouldn't come even though she felt weary to her bones, fragile mentally and physically.

When the bedside phone rang, though, she tensed, snatching it up and almost pleading, 'Mark?'

'Uhhh, no.' A light, hesitant, feminine voice. 'Brynn, it's Cassie.'

'Cassie!' Cassie Hutton, the one person in Genessa Point who had remained Brynn's friend during the last eighteen years.

'You sound exhausted, Brynn. I know it's too late to be calling you.'

'It's just midnight.'

'Oh, you were probably writing.'

Brynn knew Cassie had visions of her writing – by candlelight – half the night about haunted houses and tormented spirits. Cassie wouldn't call now unless something was wrong. A thought shot through Brynn's tired mind and she sat up. 'How stupid of me not to think of calling you earlier this week, Cassie! Do you know if Mark's in Genessa Point?'

'Uh . . . yes. I've seen him.'

'You've *seen* him? Is he all right? Why didn't you let me know sooner? He doesn't return calls—'

'Slow down. I'm the fast-talker, remember?'

'I'm sorry, it's just that I've been frantic. Mark's had an awful year,' Brynn rushed on. 'I told you all about it in the spring and things haven't improved. He's been in really bad shape and a week ago he called me, drunk, and said he was going to Genessa Point. He's fixated again on clearing Dad's name, only this time he's worse than ever. I haven't heard from him since he left. I've gotten so little sleep this week, I feel like the walking dead.'

'My God, no wonder!' Cassie's voice picked up speed and urgency. 'I should have called you Saturday, but he said you were fine about him coming and not to bother you because you were really busy.'

'He did? It's not true, dammit!' Brynn's anger surged. Mark had been lying to Cassie while causing his sister sleepless nights and stress-filled days. Still, she knew her feelings weren't important now. 'Just tell me what's going on with him.'

'Well, I didn't see Mark until Friday. He stopped in the store to say hello.'

Eight years earlier, Lavinia Love had died and willed Love's Dress Shoppe to Cassie, her great-niece. The dress shop had never interested Cassie's mother, but Cassie had always loved the store and had a college degree in business. Most important, Lavinia had wanted to keep the store in the family and not will it to Cassie's mother, who would have sold it.

'Mark didn't look great,' Cassie went on, 'but he didn't look bad, either – just too thin, eyes a little sunken like he hadn't been getting enough sleep, but still handsome. He said he'd driven down here for the festival.'

'The festival?' Brynn asked blankly.

'The One-Hundred-Fiftieth Anniversary Festival of the founding of Genessa Point. He came to the store on Friday and the festival started today. Monday. Or is it Tuesday now?'

'Officially Tuesday. Cassie, please. *Mark*.'

'OK. At first, I didn't believe him about coming for the festival, but he started talking about how he used to love them and he'd heard this was going to be the biggest one yet – it lasts two weeks now. Since you moved away, the tourism board has amped up the number of activities and the publicity. With it being on the Chesapeake Bay in the middle of summer, the festival draws about twice as many tourists as we did back when you lived here.'

Brynn went silent for a moment before saying dryly, 'Don't tell me the business people didn't add a little color to their publicity by mentioning that Genessa Point was the home of the famous serial killer, Stone Jonah Wilder.'

'Oh, Brynn—'

'Or that some criminologists believe Stone Jonah's son Mark was his accomplice. Oh, and his daughter writes *horror* novels. They always say horror instead of supernatural or fantasy.' She sighed. 'Don't try to spare my feelings, Cass. Just be blunt.'

'OK, that's all true, but we can't change it.' Cassie's voice toughened. 'Now, do you want me to tell you about Mark or do you want to go on being bitter?'

Brynn drew a deep breath, trying to calm down and concentrate on the present, not her rage over the past. 'I'm sorry. Tell me everything.'

Cassie continued as if there hadn't been a cross word between them. They'd always had the ability to overcome a squabble in a nanosecond. 'Mark invited me out to lunch. I thought he was just being polite – we'd grab a quick sandwich, he'd dump me as soon as possible and that would be the end. Instead, we ended up spending two hours at lunch.'

'Was he drinking?'

'He had iced tea. Anyway, he brushed over his divorce and losing his job and just talked about you, how proud he was of your success and how much he missed you since you moved to Miami. Then he asked how things were going at the store and for me in general.'

'Anything else?'

'Only general stuff but he seemed to be enjoying himself. He asked if I'd like to go for a drink that night. He was staying at the Bay Motel – it's a small, new place with a nice bar. That evening he still seemed to be in a good mood. We each had a couple of drinks—'

'He only had two?'

'Yes. Two gin and tonics, to be precise. He walked me to my car around eleven o'clock. I saw him going toward one of the rooms.'

'Did he say anything important?'

'No. He mentioned how Genessa Point had grown since he'd been here, asked about how my family was doing since they moved to California and . . . well, made a couple of leading remarks about how I liked divorced life, and asked if I was seeing anyone.

When I said I wasn't, he suggested we take a walk around town
the next morning. We met in Holly Park at ten. It was a beautiful
day and he took a lot of pictures. He seemed happy, Brynn. He
asked me to have dinner with him that evening. I couldn't believe
it. We've only seen each other a few times since you moved away.
I felt like he still pictured me as a twelve-year-old with a mouth
full of braces and a crush on him, so I was thrilled. Then he called
me late Saturday afternoon and asked if we could skip dinner.'
Cassie paused. 'He said, "I know this is late notice, but I've learned
something about my father's death."'

Brynn sat straighter on the bed. 'And?'

'And nothing. That's all he'd say over the phone.'

'But later . . .'

'There was no later,' Cassie said shakily. 'I haven't heard from
him since that call.'

'What? *Nothing?*'

'Not a word.'

Brynn's stomach twisted. 'Do you think he headed back to
Baltimore?'

'I tried to tell myself that, but he'd know I'd be upset after what
he'd said about your father. Maybe he didn't want to tell me what
he'd found out, but I knew he wouldn't have gone home without
another word to me, even if it was just "goodbye."' Cassie drew a
deep breath and rushed on. 'I didn't have his cell phone number,
so on Sunday night I drove past the Bay Motel twice. I didn't see
his car either time. I drove by again this morning. Again, no car.
I drove past the motel this evening around seven o'clock. No car.
I went to the office and talked to the night manager. He said Mark
had arrived last Wednesday evening and was registered until
tomorrow, but he hadn't seen Mark's car since Saturday.'

Brynn felt her neck muscles tightening, sweat popping out on
her forehead, but she tried to keep her voice steady. 'So we're now
very early Tuesday and Mark hasn't been seen since Saturday?'

'At least not by me or the motel manager. I've sat here for hours
wondering if I should call you. I thought maybe you'd heard from
him, but you haven't.' Cassie paused. 'Brynn, some people who
still live here believe your father was the Genessa Point Killer and
Mark was his accomplice. This is a dangerous place for him . . .'

'I know,' Brynn said tonelessly. 'That's why I'll be there this
afternoon.'

TWO

On the phone last night, Brynn had surprised Cassie by telling her that an hour earlier she'd reached the anxiety point of scheduling a flight to Genessa Point. 'There's a plane leaving Miami at eight twenty-five, arriving in Baltimore at ten fifty-five. I want to take that one, but I have a dozen things to take care of before I leave Miami. I'll be on the one forty-five flight and arrive at the Baltimore/Washington International Airport around four-thirty. I should be able to get my baggage, rent a car and drive to Genessa Point by six. I'll come to your house.'

'No,' Cassie had said quickly. 'I'll pick you up at the airport.'

'Why should you waste all that time?'

'Because . . . well, I just want to pick you up.'

Brynn had smiled. Cassie had always been maternal. 'You're afraid for me to drive because you think I'm too upset.'

'You *are* upset. You just won't admit it. Brynn Wilder still thinks she's the bravest girl in the world.'

'I *am* the bravest girl in the world, although I'm thirty – not a girl anymore.'

'Oh, well, I have an extra car here you can drive.'

'The one you bought for your snake of a husband Ray but never put in his name?'

'You mean my *ex*-husband for five months now and yes, the same car. It's nice – too nice for Ray. Think of the money you'll save by using it and not renting one.'

'Yes – all I've been thinking about this week is saving money.'

'Don't you get sarcastic with me!' Cassie retorted, her tone slightly lighter. 'I'm picking you up at the airport and while you're in Genessa Point, you're using my spare car, and that's final.' Cassie had paused. 'Brynn, I'm *so* glad you're coming. You're more capable and resourceful than I am.' Her voice had thickened again. 'I just feel like I should have done something earlier—'

'I swear, Cassie, if you start crying I'll hang up.'

'OK.'

'Take a sleeping pill or have a couple of drinks and get a good night's sleep. I'll see you soon and we'll find Mark.'

Brynn had hung up and curled into a ball, wishing she felt as confident as she'd tried to sound. She wanted to see Cassie tomorrow, but even more, she wanted to see Mark. Deep down, though, lurked the fear that she might never see him again.

'No. Don't. No more . . . no more . . .'

Pressure on her arm. Gentle shaking. The sense of someone bending over her.

Jonah Wilder's agonized voice filled Brynn's mind as she blinked against the sun on that beautiful beach she'd once loved. *Dad!* she called to the man staggering onto the sand then falling, face down. *Dad!*

'Ma'am?'

Brynn jerked to a sitting position, looking wild-eyed at the man seated beside her.

'You were having a bad dream,' he said gently. 'I'm sorry to disturb you, but we're at the airport and deboarding.'

Brynn blinked, her senses slowly sharpening. She realized her head had been lying on the shoulder of a good-looking older man to her left. She blushed furiously. 'I'm so sorry!'

'It's quite all right.'

Brynn stood up, pulled at her white jeans, a silky red T-shirt with three-quarter-length sleeves and a low-slung gold chain belt, and smoothed the long brown hair she'd pulled into a ponytail this morning. She retrieved her duffle bag from overhead storage and managed to get in front of a group who seemed hell-bent on stampeding to the door. I'm not like them, Brynn thought. I don't really want to get off this jet at all. I'd like to stay on here, go back to sleep for hours and have pleasant dreams. I don't want to face what might be waiting for me when I reach my destination.

But her immediate destination was not Genessa Point – it was the Baltimore/Washington International Airport where Cassie was waiting for her. She'd called her around eleven this morning and told her she'd already talked to the police. They'd promised to start looking for Mark and let her know if they found anything. So far, the police had found nothing.

Now, as soon as Brynn stepped from the jetway into the small waiting room, she saw Cassie Hutton, who rushed to her. 'Any news?' Brynn asked immediately.

Cassie shook her head. 'I called the police again ten minutes ago. Nothing yet, but they've only been looking for a few hours. They promised me the search would go on all night if necessary.'

'Oh. All night,' Brynn said desolately.

'Maybe not. Like they said—'

'It's only been a few hours.'

'Right. Have faith.' Abruptly, Cassie enfolded her in a hug, smelling sweetly of vanilla cologne. 'Oh, Brynn, it's wonderful to see you,' she almost whispered.

Have faith, Brynn thought. Don't expect the worst. She forced a broad smile. 'It's wonderful to see you, too. If I *could* see you.' Brynn pushed away and looked Cassie up and down. At five foot two, she stood only three inches shorter than Brynn, but gave the impression of being even shorter. She wore a blue tank dress and sandals, and she'd lost what looked like at least fifteen pounds since Brynn had last seen her just over a year ago. Her shoulder-length light brown hair now bore a reddish gold sheen and bangs that touched her brows and flattered her large, dark brown eyes.

'Cassie, you've always been pretty, but now you're downright gorgeous!'

Cassie tried to look nonchalant and failed. She grinned with pleasure – that little-girl grin she'd never outgrown. 'I'm not gorgeous, but I think I've improved. After my divorce, I lost the weight I'd gained during my marital misery. I started going to an expensive salon in Baltimore to get this haircut and they put a rinse on my hair to brighten it up. Also, these days I wear eye makeup, just like you always said I should.' She batted her eyes. 'And *you* look—'

'Don't even try to be gracious,' Brynn interrupted. 'I didn't sleep all night and this morning just threw on some clothes that were handy. Then I fell asleep on the plane and I'm sure the little bit of makeup I did put on is a mess.' Brynn sighed. 'I'm a wreck, but you look fabulous. You should have sent me a picture of yourself.'

'I was planning a vacation to Miami this summer to let you see for yourself.' Cassie hugged her again, then gazed at her seriously. 'I'm so sorry about all of this.'

'Thanks for helping me. Even back when Dad died, you did your very best to help.'

'Let's not talk about that,' Cassie said gently. 'It was a long time ago.'

'But it still haunts Mark and me.' Brynn sighed. 'Oh well, let's take care of this latest trouble. Then I want you to come on an extended vacation to Miami. We'll lie on the beach and drink piña coladas.'

'That sounds heavenly.' Cassie paused. 'You know what will be even more heavenly?' Brynn raised her eyebrows. 'When Mark joins us.'

Brynn smiled at Cassie although her mind said darkly, *if Mark is alive to join us.*

'There's my car,' Cassie pointed as they crossed the airport parking lot.

Brynn almost stopped walking when she saw a sonic orange Hyundai Genesis Coupé with a black hood and roof shining in the bright July sunlight. 'Cassie, what a cool car! What a great color! You always drove . . . well . . .'

'Boring cars in even more boring colors?'

'Well, used cars in muted colors.'

Cassie beamed. 'This was a gift to myself for divorcing that creep Ray and losing the weight.'

'Where is that creep Ray these days?'

'Don't know, don't care,' Cassie said briskly of Ray O'Hara, a moderately talented writer with delusions of grandeur, always hitting the road for research on the next *In Cold Blood*. 'Do you really like the car?'

'I love it. It's perfect for the new you.'

As they headed south toward Genessa Point, Brynn asked abruptly, 'Is Tessa Cavanaugh still around?'

'Yeah. I thought she'd go to college, but after high school she got a job at the library. She still works there,' Cassie said. 'She never moved away from home. Her mother died when Tessa was in her early twenties.'

'Mrs Cavanaugh died? Of what?'

'Cancer. It turns out she'd been sick for years but the family had covered it up.'

'Why?'

'Her husband said she was a very private person and also very proud. She didn't want people feeling sorry for her. Anyway, supposedly that's why Tessa didn't go away to college – she didn't want to leave her mother. After she died, Tessa stayed with her father.'

'I think she had a crush on Mark for a while. She started taking piano lessons from Mom. She didn't seem to have any real interest, though, and whenever Mark was around she couldn't hit one right note. The lessons didn't last long.'

'Well, Tessa wasn't alone. I had a crush on Mark, too. Poor guy. I actually thought I had a chance with him that last spring you lived here. I was twelve! Anyway, about two months ago, Tessa's dad died in a car wreck.' Cassie paused then said, 'I didn't tell you any of this because you said you didn't want to hear about Genessa Point people.'

'I didn't, until now. How did Tessa take her father's death?'

'I don't know. I don't see her much, Brynn. She came in the store at Christmas and bought a silk scarf. Occasionally I see her at some town event. She's what – thirty-three? She looks older. She's always polite, but not chatty. If she has any close friends I don't know about them. I don't think anyone holds her responsible for . . . well, what happened to your dad. She's a loner. Nathan is some kind of computer genius and he goes all over the world setting up computer systems that have something to do with ships,' Cassie went on.

'Computers aren't my thing. I hate them. I hardly ever use my home computer except to look at email every week or two. Anyway, Nathan only comes back to visit a couple of times a year. He's been married at least twice. I don't know his current status.'

'Did Mark ask you about Tessa?'

'No. He only asked about your dad's friend, Edmund Ellis, and his daughter. She died last week. Her funeral was on Tuesday.'

'Joy?' Brynn had a brief, sharp memory of a beautiful little girl with a buoyant spirit and a weak heart who'd taken piano lessons from Brynn's mother. 'Was it her heart?'

'Yes. She was only twenty-five.'

'How sad,' Brynn said quietly.

'Yeah. She spent her last few months at home with her dad. I saw them together a couple of times and she was very frail but always smiling and upbeat. She even came in to see the store since I remodeled it. Her dad bought her a beautiful designer jacket. She looked so pretty in it.' Cassie sighed. 'What a shame that she had to go so young.'

'I barely knew her, but I remember her as being adorable. My mom loved her. She usually didn't take on seven-year-olds as students, but she said Joy had talent.'

'Mark said he didn't know until after the funeral and he was going to visit Doctor Ellis.'

'How did Mark find out about Joy's death?'

'He had a subscription to the local newspaper for years, Brynn. You didn't know?'

'No. I never dreamed . . .'

'Oh. Well, he knew how much you hated this place. He probably thought you might not like him keeping up with things around here.'

'How I felt shouldn't have mattered. His feelings are just as important as mine.' Brynn sighed. 'I haven't been a great sister, especially this last year.'

'You did the best you could for Mark ever since your dad died. Now he's a thirty-four-year-old man, Brynn. Get real. You can't tell him what to do. As for him being missing for days, I'm more to blame than you. I wanted to think he'd only come back for the festival. But I didn't – not really. Face it – I was so concentrated on making him like me, I just tip-toed around trying to be charming and I missed something.'

Brynn could feel waves of anxiety shimmering off Cassie. She turned and smiled at her. 'You didn't do anything wrong, Cassie. I'm sure if you'd started asking Mark questions, he would have pulled away from you like a shot.'

'You really think so?'

'I'm sure of it. I know my brother.' Brynn paused. 'Sort of.'

'Well, if you believe I didn't do anything wrong by not following him, questioning him, or calling you sooner, then I do feel better.'

'Good. Because I think he told you about finding information about Dad because he'd come to trust you.'

'Really?' Cassie asked again, looking relieved, her hands relaxing on the wheel.

'Really.'

Cassie, now sitting less rigid in her seat, smiled at Brynn. 'I hope you stay a while. I don't want you immediately running back to Miami. I know you don't like Genessa Point, but you're here now and it's the festival and . . . well . . . maybe you can manage to have a little bit of fun. After we find Mark, that is,' she added quickly. 'And we will find him, Brynn. Don't you worry.'

Don't you worry. Don't worry about your brother being missing in the town that considers your father was a serial killer and perhaps your missing brother was his accomplice. Fat chance that I won't worry, Brynn thought. I'm more frightened than I've been for eighteen years, but I'll try to hide it. I'll try.

Brynn forced herself to smile back at Cassie, whose worry lines showed through her fringe of bangs. Poor thing, Brynn mused, and felt her eyes getting droopy; tiredness was catching up with her.

Brynn felt as if she'd only dozed for a moment when someone clutched her arm and shook her. 'Brynn, wake up!'

'Huh?' Brynn said fuzzily. 'What?'

'It's the police!'

Brynn blinked against the glow of an evening sun. 'What? The police . . .'

'We're home and the police are here!'

Brynn jerked wide-awake as Cassie turned onto her driveway and stopped. Brynn squinted at the officer walking toward them. 'Cassie, is *he* the sheriff?'

'Garrett Dane, yes. He's been the sheriff for three years now. I told him this morning I was picking you up at the airport and about what time we'd be back. I had to talk to him about Mark, Brynn, even though I know you didn't like his father when we were kids.'

'When Dad was killed, Garrett's father was the sheriff. William Dane. I hated him.'

'Yeah, but you liked Garrett a lot,' Cassie said. They stopped. Cassie swung open her door, jumping out of the car and demanding, 'What's wrong? Have you found Mark? That's Brynn in the car. You remember Brynn, Garrett. What's—'

'I remember Brynn,' Garrett interrupted. Brynn emerged from the car and stood staring, aware that she probably looked hostile when all she felt was fear. Garrett's light brown hair waved close to his scalp, the slant of the pre-evening light emphasized the strong lines of his long, angular face, and his sapphire-blue eyes seemed to burn at her, just like they had when he was a teenager. He nodded but didn't smile. Brynn could almost feel bad news quivering like a live electric wire between them.

'Miss Wilder, I'm sorry to tell you that we haven't found Mark.' His voice was level and steady, completely without practiced sympathy. 'However, about ten miles south of town, we found his car. It was sitting off the road, behind a cluster of trees. The trunk and glove compartment were empty and the keys missing.' He paused as Brynn's heart began to pound. 'We also found quite a bit of blood in the car.'

THREE

G arrett and Brynn sat on opposite sides of Cassie's living
room, staring at each other. Brynn couldn't speak, embarrassed because she thought he knew she'd once had a crush
on him, but also distrustful of him as William Dane's son. Garrett,
in turn, looked determined not to volunteer any information. Every
minute seemed like ten in the strained silence. She felt relief wash
over her when Cassie dashed back from the kitchen.

'I've put on a pot of coffee,' she said. 'You might want something
stronger. Brynn?'

'Coffee is fine.'

Cassie didn't wait for an answer from the sheriff. She sat down
on the couch next to Brynn, took her hand and demanded, 'Sheriff
Dane, have you gone mute? I was listening from the kitchen. You
haven't told Brynn one thing. You're scaring her!'

Garrett glanced at her in surprise. Cassie talked a lot but usually
in a light, girlish voice. His gaze shifted to Brynn. 'I'm sorry if I'm
frightening you even more, Miss Wilder. It's just that you looked
like you might faint. I was waiting for Cassie to come back.'

'I've never fainted in my life,' Brynn declared, insulted although
she didn't know why. 'Just tell me everything you know about my
brother's whereabouts.'

Garrett raised his eyebrows. 'I thought I made it clear we don't
know your brother's whereabouts. All we found is the car.'

Brynn suddenly felt furious – he sounded so calm, so uninvolved,
so matter-of-fact. 'You must have found *something* besides his car!
It didn't just drop behind that cluster of trees from the air. Didn't
anyone see anything, hear anything?'

'Not that we know of yet, but it's early. We just found the car.'

'Look, it's no secret you don't like Mark, Sheriff Dane,' Brynn
lashed out, 'but that's no reason to blow off a search for a man who
could be dying—'

'Whoa!' Garrett held up his hands, palms turned toward Brynn.
'Wait a minute, Miss Wilder.'

'And stop calling me that! It's Brynn.'

'OK! I didn't know if you'd want me calling you by your first name under the circumstances,' he said warily, as if not knowing what to expect next. 'Brynn, I'm not blowing off the search for Mark. Maybe you don't know how upset you are right now, but you are. I was trying to give you a few minutes to absorb the information about the car before I went on.'

Brynn grudgingly realized he was right. She was beyond upset. She'd had a week of fear and lack of sleep. Now hearing from the son of the sheriff who'd been vehement about her father being the Genessa Point Killer that the police had found her brother's car deserted and bloody was almost too much for her. Almost. She must pull herself together, she told herself, if she was going to be any help to Mark.

'I'm sorry,' she forced herself to say, aware that she didn't sound sorry at all. 'What you said about the car was a shock. I didn't mean to fly off the handle.'

'I understand. It's all right.' Garrett didn't sound any more sincere than she had. He looked at Brynn cautiously for a moment, and Cassie slipped out to the kitchen to check on the coffee. Apparently deciding she'd settled down slightly, he said, 'There are no houses or businesses near where the car was found. No one was around to see anything.'

'But people must have been passing on the highway.'

'There's not much traffic out that way at night. Besides, the car was about a hundred yards off the road and behind—'

'A cluster of trees. I got that much,' Brynn snapped.

After a moment, Garrett asked in a direct tone, 'Brynn, why did Mark come here?'

'Why do you think? He wanted to prove that our father wasn't the Genessa Point Killer.'

'Did he have a lead? Had he learned something new?'

'Not that I know of. He called and told me he was coming to prove Dad's innocence. He didn't say anything else and he wouldn't answer questions. The call was brief. Actually, when I started arguing with him about coming here, he hung up on me. I called right back, but he didn't answer. He also didn't answer the next twenty calls I made. That was over a week ago and I haven't heard from him. Cassie talked to the manager of the Bay Motel, who said Mark had checked in last Wednesday evening.'

'I already knew Mark was in town before Cassie came to

headquarters this morning,' Garrett said. 'Since last Friday, people have been telling me he was here. They were mostly older. I guess that's because according to Cassie, Mark hasn't been back for eighteen years. Young people don't recognize him or know about his relationship to your father.'

'These people who told you about seeing him thought he was a threat?' Brynn asked, trying to keep her voice even.

'Well . . . yes.'

'Did they want you to start keeping an eye on him?'

'Yes.' Their gazes met, Brynn's blazing with anger. Garrett paused, then said calmly, 'I asked them if he'd done anything wrong. They said no. Apparently, he was just sight-seeing and minding his own business. I told them it's a free country and sent them on their way.'

Brynn was surprised by his answer. 'Your father wouldn't have felt that way.'

'I'm not my father.'

'But you must be influenced by his opinion of my father and Mark.'

'Brynn, I formed my own opinions even when I was a teenager, even when Dad was the sheriff. Now that I'm a man, as well as the sheriff, I sure as hell don't rely on what my father thought. I think for myself!' He was angry and breathing hard. Brynn, startled, went silent. After a moment, Garrett seemed to calm down, drew a deep breath and said, 'Also, you've known me for twenty years. You might as well call me Garrett.'

Cassie arrived with a large, elaborate silver tray, three thermal mugs, a few packets of diet sugar, plastic spoons and a small container of skim milk. Clearly, she'd assembled her guest tray as quickly as possible. After she impatiently served everyone, she sat down on the couch and looked at Garrett. 'I heard you tell Brynn people came to your office to tell you Mark was here,' she blurted. 'Did they say they'd seen him with me?'

'A couple of them did.'

Cassie's eyes narrowed. 'Gossips! Not that I minded being seen with him.'

'They said they were worried about you.'

'Yeah, sure they were. They were just snooping. They don't know a damned thing about Mark!'

'It's all right, Cassie. I'm sure Mark's reappearance caused a sensation for some people,' Brynn said. 'Did you tell Garrett that Mark said he'd found out something about my father's death?'

Cassie flushed. 'Yes, and also when the motel manager said he'd last seen Mark's car.'

'Good. If Garrett's going to search for Mark, he should know everything.' Brynn could feel Cassie's relief. Knowing Cassie, Brynn was sure she'd worry that she'd told the sheriff too much about Wilder family business when Mark's sister should have been the one to decide what Garrett Dane knew.

Brynn looked at Garrett. 'You said people had come to you to report seeing Mark in town. Did anyone tell you anything else about what he'd been doing?'

'No. They said he'd just been wandering around like a tourist and taking lots of pictures.'

'No one said he'd been asking questions about my father's murder?'

'No.' Garrett sighed. 'Look, I know that back when my father was sheriff, Mark was hell-bent on proving his father's innocence. For years afterward he flooded headquarters with what he thought was vital information—'

'What he *thought* was vital information?' Brynn cut in. 'Did your father even look at what Mark sent to him? Maybe Mark had stumbled on important evidence. I don't think your father's heart was in the investigation.'

Garrett stiffened. 'Brynn, a police officer's *heart* isn't supposed to be involved in a murder investigation. He is supposed to be objective.'

'And thorough.'

'My dad was thorough.'

'It didn't seem that way to me.'

'You were what? Twelve? What did you know about police investigations? What did Mark know, for that matter? Only what you'd seen on television or read in books. Besides, do you think my father and the local county police conducted the investigation of Jonah Wilder by themselves? The state police and the FBI were here. Have you forgotten that? They went over opportunity, method, even DNA. Traces of DNA from three victims were in the hinge of the knife that killed your father.'

'I'm not saying that's impossible,' Brynn said. Garrett raised his eyebrows. 'It's possible because the knife used to murder those kids was the same knife used to murder my father. But *that* knife, the murder weapon, hadn't been in Dad's possession for years.'

'Brynn, I know what your family said, but—'

'Just one more time, listen to me on this subject,' Brynn said firmly. 'When Mark was fourteen, he bought a knife for Dad's birthday. Mark was terrible about saving his allowance. He didn't have much money so he had to buy a used knife. There was a nick in the blade. He spent hours carving J.W. in the wooden handle. Dad was thrilled with the knife – especially because of the work Mark had done carving the initials – but Dad lost that knife about two years before Tessa killed him with it. He bought a new one but Mark refused to carve his initials again.' She saw Garrett's face tighten. 'Or should I say she stabbed him with it. She could have meant to stab a third person, the one who attacked her.'

'I know this story, Brynn,' Garrett interrupted impatiently. 'It doesn't change the fact that the knife with your father's initials and the nick in the blade was the *only* knife found at the crime scene. There was no knife in your father's tackle box. His friend, Edmund Ellis, who he fished with every three or four weeks said he didn't know anything about your father losing the knife Mark had given him. In fact, Ellis said he thought your dad used it the last time they went fishing, about a month prior to the . . . incident.'

'Doctor Ellis made a mistake.' Brynn wanted to say something harsher about what Edmund Ellis had claimed, but she was determined to sound completely fair and rational.

'Maybe Ellis did make a mistake, but that doesn't change the facts, Brynn,' Garrett said. 'The knife that killed your father had his initials carved into the handle, a nick on the blade, the DNA of some of the Genessa Point Killer's victims, and it was the only knife police found within a radius of about two hundred fifty feet around where Tessa was attacked.'

'They just missed it or didn't look in the right place.'

Garrett's eyes narrowed. Brynn could tell he was getting mad. 'Do you know how big a radius of two hundred fifty feet is? It covers the property around your house, all of the adjoining beach and the patch of woods. The searchers also used metal detectors. Do you think your father went fishing without his knife the day he died? Or do you think Tessa somehow got your father's old knife, the one Mark gave your father years earlier, went into the woods with it, and then started screaming?'

'No. I'm saying there was a third person in the woods – the one who attacked Tessa. She didn't know who her attacker was.'

'The possibility of a third person in the woods wasn't dismissed, but there was absolutely no evidence of a third person being present, and believe me, that angle was investigated just as thoroughly as every other aspect of the case.'

'Are you sure?'

'Yes. After I saw Cassie this morning, I went over everything to do with this case. *Everything.* There were no mistakes, no shortcuts, whether or not you want to believe it or not. The investigation was run by the book.'

Garrett simply looked at her and Brynn felt like she was drowning, desperately reaching for a life preserver ring. Suddenly, something came to her. 'Was my father's blood or DNA on any of the victims?'

'None of the victims was found immediately. You know that. They'd been kept alive for a few days before they were stabbed in the heart. They suffered from dehydration, and toxicology screens showed barbiturates that must have been used to keep them sedated.'

Brynn felt queasy. If Mark had been kidnapped, maybe he was being treated the same way as those long-ago victims, but she couldn't give in to weakness now. 'Go on.'

'None of the victims had been sexually assaulted or tortured. After death, the bodies were moved to locations where they'd be found fairly easily,' Garrett went on. 'None was buried and, according to the FBI, when they were discovered they'd been thoroughly scrubbed with bleach. Bleach contaminates DNA. If your father left some of his DNA on a victim, it would have been compromised.'

'So you think my father went into the woods to kill Tessa, knowing I'd be home from Cassie's soon—'

'I believe you were over an hour early. Cassie's grandfather broke his hip or something? Your father—'

Brynn glared.

'The killer thought he'd have more time.'

'And how did this killer know when I was supposed to be home?' Brynn immediately realized she'd made a mistake. Who besides her parents would know what time she was supposed to be home? She gave Garrett a searing look. 'OK, let's pretend my father *was* the killer. An hour isn't a very long time. Was Dad supposed to have killed Tessa, hidden her body in the woods and cleaned himself up in just an hour? And after Dad supposedly scrubbed her with bleach, how do you think he was going to take a girl of her size and drop her at a visible dump site?'

'With his accomplice's help.'

'Who you think was Mark. He was in Baltimore that day!'

'I thought we were playing pretend,' Garrett said easily. 'We don't know for certain what was going on in the killer's mind when he attacked Tessa.'

'*We don't know,*' Brynn imitated. 'The police didn't know and it's a question that bothered quite a few sensible people in this town. Not *everyone* believed my father was the murderer because if he was, his method changed abruptly when it came to Tessa Cavanaugh. All of his victims were under fifteen. Tessa was fifteen.'

'She'd just turned fifteen. And she was so convenient. Maybe he was decompensating.'

'Oh, don't give me one of the favorite terms of the criminologists. Like hell he was *decompensating.*'

'Brynn, you can't know what he was thinking—'

'No, I can't. No one can, except for the killer.'

'Psychologists have studied serial killers for years—'

'And they're still just guessing.' Brynn's voice rose.

'That is not necessarily the truth.'

'Not necessarily? That qualification sounds to me as if you have your own doubts, Garrett.' Brynn took a deep breath. 'Tell me, if Dad used bleach to contaminate the DNA on the victims, why didn't he use it on the knife?'

'Maybe he did. Maybe he just didn't get all of the DNA, especially what was under the knife hilt.' Garrett looked at her solemnly and said softly, 'Brynn, after your father's death, there were no more murders.'

'No more murders,' Brynn said coldly. She wanted to fire a devastating question at him, make an irrefutable point, but she couldn't think of anything. She took two sips of strong coffee, marshaling her forces, deciding to change tactics, then said evenly, 'You said the victims were kept alive for days before they were killed and that the bodies were scrubbed with bleach then left in easy-to-find places. You seem very familiar with an eighteen-year-old case.'

'I told you I read all the files dealing with the case today. I wasn't completely honest. I've actually read the files several times over the years and not a month's gone by when I haven't thought about the case, partly because your brother used to be a friend of mine and he kept sending information, especially this year,' Garrett told her solemnly. 'You probably won't believe me, Brynn, but I read everything he sent.'

'Oh,' she said faintly, surprised. His father wouldn't have gone to so much trouble, she thought. He'd probably ignored everything Mark had sent to him. It had seemed to her that Garrett's father decided Jonah Wilder was the Genessa Point Killer from the day someone attacked Tessa Cavanaugh and nothing could change his mind.

Garrett's cell phone rang. He answered, then looked at the two women leaning forward, their eyes snapping with curiosity. He put a hand over the phone speaker. 'Personal call. Sorry.' Brynn and Cassie sank against the back of the couch and drank their coffee in silence. 'I'll be home in about twenty minutes, honey,' Garrett said. 'Yes. Half an hour, tops. OK. Love you.' He tucked away the phone and said, 'Sorry.'

'It's all right.' Brynn thought about a wife and probably children waiting dinner at home for him, a wife and children that didn't wait for Mark, Mark who lived a solitary life and probably subsisted mostly on TV dinners and fast food.

'I know Mark was obsessed with proving his father wasn't the GPK.' Cassie looked at Brynn. 'Sorry, but that's what they call the Genessa Point Killer around here,' she informed Brynn with soft regret.

Brynn mumbled, 'Oh,' Cassie's gentleness almost making her smile for the first time in hours. The murderer had been referred to as the GPK even eighteen years ago.

Cassie turned her gaze back to Garrett and went on emphatically: 'But I think you're wasting time talking about the past murders. This is about Mark and GPK wouldn't go after him. After all, there haven't been any more murders for eighteen years and GPK killed kids. Mark is thirty-four.'

'It's possible,' Garrett said. 'Unlikely, but possible, that Mark could be another victim of the same person. Maybe the Genessa Point Killer has been inactive because he moved and got away with more crimes matching GPK's when everyone blamed Jonah. Or he's been in prison for something else, served his sentence and came back to Genessa Point. In either case, Mark came here and found out something he thought was crucial. That's what he told you, right, Cassie?'

'He said he'd found out something about his father's death.'

'And you think he'd found the killer.'

'Well . . . yes. He didn't say that, but he sounded upset, or like he was trying to hide that he was upset or—'

'OK.' Garrett's blue gaze flashed to Brynn. 'And you also think he'd found the killer?'

'Yes. Don't you?'

'I don't think anything yet. I need more evidence.'

Brynn felt like grinding her teeth in frustration, but tried to act composed and, most of all, credible. 'There's something you don't know, Garrett,' she said. 'Last night, around midnight, someone called me. The caller ID said unknown caller. I usually don't pick up anonymous calls, but I thought maybe it was Mark so I did. Music began playing. "Can't Find My Way Home" by Blind Faith. Mark loved that song. He listened to it over and over, he played it on his guitar and sang. It was *his* song. At the end of the song on the phone, someone sighed. Then they hung up.'

'You didn't tell me that last night!' Cassie exclaimed.

'You were already upset. I didn't want you to lie awake all night like I did.' She looked at Garrett. 'Anyway, Mark wouldn't have made a call like that to me. Someone else did – someone who knew it had meaning for Mark, especially way back when we lived here. I'm sure the call came from the person who took Mark.'

Garrett leaned forward, his piercing eyes fixed on Brynn's. 'Did you hear anything else during the phone call? Any background noises?'

'I've thought about that a lot. I only heard the song. Then the sigh.'

'Is the sigh part of the song?'

'No.'

'You're sure?'

'Absolutely. The caller sighed, and no, I couldn't tell if it was male or female.' Brynn felt a chill tingle through her. 'Only that it was long and . . . dramatic. Haunting.'

'I've heard the song but not for a long time. I can get a video of it on the internet. I'll listen to it tonight,' Garrett said in a business-like tone, scribbling in his notebook. 'Who around here would know it was Mark's favorite song?'

'I don't know.' Brynn thought. 'Mark had a lot of friends. You, for instance.'

Garrett stiffened and looked up at her. 'Like I said before, we used to be friends. Then when he was sixteen, a few months before your dad's death—'

Brynn lifted her eyebrows.

'Well, it was just teenage boy stuff.'

'Like what?'

'Nothing important. Go on with who could have known Mark's favorite song.'

Brynn could sense that further questions wouldn't get her any more information about the end of Mark's and Garrett's friendship. 'Well, any of his friends. They could have told their friends or families. Mom gave piano lessons at our house. Some of her students probably heard Mark playing the song in his room before Mom made him turn it off. Those students could have told other people.' Brynn's voice fell. 'My God, I hadn't thought of all the possibilities.'

'Don't get depressed,' Garrett told her. 'The calls you got are what's important, especially if Mark's been taken.'

'*If* he's been taken?'

'I have to consider all possibilities, Brynn. I can't assume he was kidnapped and is being held for some reason.'

'You know he was kidnapped but it wasn't for ransom! We would have gotten a ransom demand by now,' Brynn said sharply.

'Maybe.'

'Maybe, nothing!' Brynn fixed Garrett with a hard stare. 'How much blood is in Mark's car?'

Garrett looked taken aback for a moment. Then he regrouped and answered in a business-like voice. 'The seats are vinyl. There was a wide streak along the back of the front seat, blood smears all over the back seat, and a patch about four inches in diameter on the back-seat carpet. It was still damp. We don't know how much blood there is altogether because we just found the car about an hour ago.'

'You're assuming it's all Mark's blood,' Brynn said.

Garrett gazed at her steadily. 'No. I'm not.' He paused. 'Maybe none of it is Mark's blood.'

His meaning was clear and anger again washed over Brynn. 'You mean maybe it's the blood of someone *Mark* took?'

Garrett remained silent.

'That's crazy.'

'I said I have to consider all the possibilities.'

'That's not a possibility,' Brynn snapped and rushed on. 'But maybe Mark wounded whoever attacked and took him. His blood type is O positive. Is all the blood in the car O positive?'

'As I said, we only found the car an hour ago. We haven't had time to collect all the blood, much less test it. But you may be right and not all the blood is from one person.'

You're not convinced, Brynn thought. You're seriously considering the possibility that the blood might belong to someone Mark kidnapped. You think Mark might have taken someone and killed them because the Genessa Point Killer really was a team – Jonah Wilder and his homicidal son, Mark.

Brynn stared at Garrett. Until today, she hadn't seen him since he was seventeen. In twelve-year-old Brynn's opinion, he'd been the handsomest of Mark's friends. He'd been polite to everyone, but he'd always seemed reserved, private without being furtive, confident but not cocky, more mature than Mark's other friends. And there had been something about his eyes – not just their striking azure color, but a perceptiveness and sensitivity she'd never seen in anyone else's gaze. When he'd looked at her, she'd felt as if he could read her mind and she could almost read his. It hadn't made sense to her at the time. When she was older and remembered Garrett, she attributed it to a romantic, adolescent fantasy, yet Brynn never forgot the feeling of having a bond with Garrett that went deeper than a crush, a bond she'd never mentioned to anyone, even Cassie.

Disturbingly, she still felt a link between her and Garrett. Somehow she could see through the careful inscrutability he tried to maintain and what she saw now was doubt. For a moment, Brynn and Garrett stared at each other just as they had when they'd first sat down. Then Brynn straightened her shoulders and said in a strong, definite voice, 'Garrett, neither my father nor my brother was the Genessa Point Killer. That man was never caught. He's still out there and I think he has Mark. I have a feeling you think so, too.'

Garrett's gaze didn't waver as he took a deep breath. 'I told you earlier that I depend on evidence, not feelings,' he said firmly. 'Mark is your brother and you love him. You can't see beyond your emotions, Brynn. That's why you have to rely on me. You have to believe that I will go where the evidence takes me, no matter how my father felt about Mark, no matter how I feel about Mark.' He paused, his voice deepening. 'You also have to believe that I will not stop until I find Mark, dead or alive.'

Brynn's cell phone rang. She answered immediately, to hear 'Can't Find My Way Home.' She stood up and frantically motioned to Garrett, who rushed across the room, holding his head close to Brynn's. When her slightly extended arm began to tremble, he put a steadying hand over hers. Finally, the song ended. After a moment, a distorted voice asked, 'Have a nice flight, Brynn? So glad you finally decided to come looking for your brother. He's thrilled that you're here. Too bad the two of you can't say hello, but you'll have another chance . . . *maybe*. Got to go now. 'Bye, pretty girl.' After a beat of silence, the voice added, ''Bye to you too, Sheriff Dane.'

FOUR

Brynn ran down the stairs to the first floor of Cassie's house. For the first time in over a week, she'd awakened feeling rested thanks to the sleeping pill Cassie had forced her to take around nine o'clock last night. The pill had not lessened her anxiety about the anonymous phone call, though, and she couldn't wait to learn what Garrett had found out about it. She'd hoped to catch Cassie before she went to Love's Dress Shoppe but on a small antique table near the foot of the stairway, Brynn found a note:

Good morning, Sleeping Beauty! I checked on you before I left, and you were out cold. I'm so glad you slept well. Wish I could spend the day with you, but I have a big shipment coming into the store today. I left the keys to the car on the kitchen table. If anything comes up, call me immediately! C

In the kitchen, Brynn found not only the keys to the car, but a foil bag of Costa Rica coffee, a fresh loaf of bread from the bakery and a jar of seedless blackberry jam. Brynn smiled. Cassie had remembered her favorite breakfast. Within five minutes, while the kitchen filled with the smell of fresh coffee, Brynn downed her first slice of jam-laden toast while planning her day.

After eating, she dressed in dark skinny jeans and a bright turquoise and green chiffon blouson top with long, pleated bell sleeves. She added her opal and gold dragonfly pendant and the matching, dangling earrings. She'd been fascinated by dragonflies since she was a little girl and believed they brought her good luck. 'And I need all the luck I can get,' she told herself, fastening an earring. She studied her image in the mirror. I look happy, cheerful, and optimistic, she thought, which shows how deceptive appearances can be.

Twenty minutes later, she climbed into the dark blue coupé that Cassie had loaned her for the visit to Genessa Point. Eight months earlier, Ray's frequent absences from home had extended from days to weeks; when he was in Genessa Point he spent most evenings in bars drinking hard, taking drugs, and Cassie had gotten proof of adultery. She'd divorced him and had seemed happier ever since.

Brynn pulled out of the garage, rolled down the windows and paused a moment to appreciate the warm, sunny morning before leaving. What a beautiful day, she thought. But she had no time to enjoy it. She had to get somewhere quickly: police headquarters.

She had been there after her father's death, but she thought she remembered little about the interior until she walked in now and saw how much it'd changed. In the last eighteen years, the building had been refurbished. The once-yellowed white walls now shone dove gray and white solar shades hung at the windows. Gleaming oak-toned vinyl covered the floor, and waist-high faux wood partitions placed throughout the main office gave deputies privacy for their desks. Several lush plants sat in sunny spots.

To a casual glance, the room looked entirely different than it had eighteen years ago. Some new paint and window treatments didn't change the atmosphere for Brynn, though. She remembered the old room as vividly as if she'd seen it yesterday. She also remembered walking in as she clung to her mother's cold, shaking hand and cringed under the hard stares of the deputies. Back then, she'd wished she could disappear.

Brynn straightened her back, reminding herself she was not that twelve-year-old girl anymore, and approached a middle-aged, craggy-faced woman sitting behind a counter. She gave her name and noticed the woman's face twitch slightly when she heard, 'Wilder.' In a deep, grainy voice, she told Brynn the sheriff was busy and she'd have to wait a few minutes. Brynn took a seat as the woman picked up a phone but, almost immediately, Garrett walked down the hall, talking loudly. He glanced into the main office and stopped along with his companion – a young girl holding onto the leash of a very large, beautiful reddish golden dog.

Brynn stood up. 'Good morning, Sheriff Dane,' she said, aware that the activity of two officers at the coffee machine came to a standstill as they listened. 'I know it's early, but I stopped by to see if you've found anything new about . . .' Brynn glanced at the girl. 'If you've found out anything new.'

'I'll speak with you in my office,' Garrett said expressionlessly.

The girl was a different matter. 'You're Brynn Wilder, aren't you?' she asked excitedly.

Garrett frowned. 'Savannah!'

'Well, she is,' Savannah insisted. 'I *know* it. I've seen her picture on her books and I saw her on TV doing an interview.'

Brynn finally took a good look at the slender, adolescent girl with long, slightly curly blonde hair and laser-blue eyes like Garrett's. A wisp of pale pink gloss covered her heart-shaped lips.

'This is my daughter, Savannah, who's obviously a fan,' Garrett said in a slightly apologetic tone.

'And this is Henry,' Savannah added, motioning to the dog who cocked his head at Brynn, as if curious. 'He's half Irish Setter, half yellow Labrador. He's a fan, too.'

'Hello, Savannah. Hello, Henry.' The dog sat down and raised a paw. Brynn smiled, stooped and shook his big paw. 'What a gentleman.'

'I really *love* your books, Miss Wilder,' Savannah gushed. 'I've read all of them.'

'Well, there've only been two,' Brynn said, smiling.

'And I've read them over and over. I read them to Henry. He loves them, too.'

'I'm glad both of you like them.'

'Oh, I *do*! They're *wonderful*! Aren't they making a movie out of the first one?'

'Yes.'

'I wish I was in that movie! There's a part in it that would be just *perfect* for me!'

'Let's see . . .' Brynn pretended to think. 'Evangelista!'

'Yes!' Savannah looked up at Garrett. 'See, Dad, I told you!'

'You're not an actress.'

'I'm going to be in the play.' She looked at Brynn. 'It's called *Genessa Point: The Beginning*. I don't think that's a great title, but I play second lead—'

'Savannah, Miss Wilder is here to talk to me about business,' Garrett said repressively. 'I thought you were going to help Mrs Elbert with her hot dog stand.'

'Oh, the hot dog stand,' Savannah said in a beleaguered tone. 'It's nine-thirty in the morning, Dad. No one's buying hot dogs.'

'Still, you promised to help her.'

'When you dumped me off with Mrs Elbert and drove away like something was chasing you, she told me she didn't need my help until three this afternoon. I had to walk all the way here to tell you.'

'And you have told me. Four times. You can start helping her at three.'

'What do you want me to do until then?'

'Go home.'

'Don't you remember? Mrs Miller's taking two weeks off because her daughter's having a baby and you said you didn't want me at home alone.'

Because of what's happened to Mark, Brynn thought. He's flashing back to the old days of the Genessa Point Killer when parents didn't want their adolescents unsupervised. But where is Savannah's mother? Maybe she has a job, like mine did.

'Just sit in the waiting room for a while,' Garrett told Savannah. 'We'll decide what to do with you after I talk to Miss Wilder.'

Savannah flashed another look at Brynn, who saw disappointment in her beautiful blue eyes. 'Oh, OK,' she said mournfully. 'But I want a cup of coffee and Henry wants a doughnut.'

'Fine, only make it decaf coffee for you and one doughnut for Henry. Now be a good little girl.'

Savannah closed her eyes, her face turning bright pink. 'Oh, Daaaad,' she moaned.

'What did I say wrong now?' Garrett asked Brynn as they walked down the hall and Savannah slumped into the main office, Henry trotting jauntily beside her as if he already smelled doughnuts.

'"Be a good little girl?" *Really*, Garrett? How old is she?'

'Just thirteen.'

'Thirteen is nearly an adult in her mind. You insulted her in front of about a dozen people.'

Garrett sighed. 'Raising a teenager is hell.'

'I believe that's the general consensus. I wouldn't know.'

'But I wouldn't trade her for anything in the world,' he added quickly.

Brynn couldn't help smiling. 'I didn't think so.'

They walked into his small office. Brynn couldn't remember what the office had looked like when Garrett's father was the sheriff, but the new color scheme continued here. He motioned to a blue and gray tweed chair, offered her coffee from the fresh pot brewing on a side table, then sat down behind his desk.

'You look a lot better than you did yesterday,' he said.

'Cassie talked me into taking a sleeping pill around nine o'clock and I got a good night's sleep for the first time in a week. Physically, I feel much better. Emotionally, I feel guilty for feeling better.'

Garrett smiled. 'You looked ready to drop on the floor yesterday evening. You deserved a good night's sleep.'

'I needed sleep so I could do everything I could to help find Mark.' She took a sip of coffee. 'Good. Hawaiian Kona?'

Garrett looked at her in surprise. 'How did you know?'

'I'm an addict. A gourmet coffee addict.' She smiled tensely. 'What did you find out about the call yesterday?'

'We know you received a call at six forty-five that lasted for four minutes and nine seconds. We don't know who called you.'

Brynn's mood dropped a few notches. 'But my phone showed the caller's number.'

'Which we called. The call to you came from an unlocked phone.'

'Unlocked?'

'I won't try to impress you with my computer knowledge. This is what our tech guys have told me. When you buy a cell phone from a cellular provider, the phone is usually configured or *locked* to work only on that provider's network. If you buy a phone for GSM carriers—'

'GSM?'

'Global Systems for Mobile communications. Phones for GSM carriers, like AT&T or Verizon, also come with subscriber identity cards that provide access to a network, but if you buy an unlocked phone you can use prepaid SIMs for any carrier. The number we saw on your phone led to a number of a prepaid SIM card.'

'So what it all comes down to is that you weren't able to trace the call we got yesterday.'

'Yes.'

'And what about any future calls?'

'I'd guess the caller would use the same method with a different SIM card. If the cards are paid for with cash, it's nearly impossible to trace them.'

'Oh, great.' Brynn took another sip of her coffee before she slumped in her chair.

Garrett got up and came around his desk to her, holding out his hand. 'I'm sure that coffee is lukewarm by now. Let me warm it up for you, bring some color back to your face.'

'I think it's going to take more than hot coffee to bring color to my face.' Brynn watched Garrett calmly pour the coffee. 'Garrett, whoever made that call had to be in sight of the house. They knew you and I were there.'

'Well, my patrol car was out front. And that's what makes the call interesting. Whoever made it wasn't just trying to scare you – they also wanted to show they knew I was involved and that I didn't scare them. They were just as willing to play games with me as they were with you.'

'Which means?'

'I don't know yet.'

Brynn sighed.

'I know you feel like we don't know anything, but you have to remember that I only found out about all of this less than twenty-four hours ago. We can't work miracles.'

'I know, but I feel like we're not doing anything.'

'You mean *I'm* not doing anything.'

Brynn said nothing.

'I'm doing all I can at this point,' Garrett said calmly. 'I've contacted the Baltimore police and told them everything about this case, including the fact that Mark was the son of Jonah Wilder, who many people think was the Genessa Point Killer.' Brynn noted with gratitude that he'd said 'who many people think' was the GPK, not stated that he *was* the son of the GPK. 'I've also notified the FBI. The information about Mark will be put in the National Crime Information Center as a missing person.'

'The FBI doesn't have all the information about Mark they need. I should talk to them,' Brynn said urgently.

'Brynn, after the phone call at Cassie's, I took all the recent stats on Mark – height, weight, coloring. Don't you remember?'

'They don't have a picture.'

'Yes, they do. Cassie took a Polaroid of him. She gave it to me.'

Brynn ran a hand over her forehead. 'I suppose I was more upset yesterday than I thought. I'm not losing my mind – I guess I was in a daze after that phone call. I thought a good night's sleep had cleared my head, but it doesn't seem to be as clear as I thought. I remember now, though. And I'm feeling better. Tell me what I should do next.'

'Nothing.'

'Nothing? I came here to find my brother or at least to help look for him, Garrett.'

'Brynn, when you came in here, you thought you had "it all together." You didn't. Now that you remember everything that happened after the call, you're back to thinking that your mind is perfectly clear. It isn't. That's why I'd like for you to just sit back and let us look for Mark.'

Brynn suddenly felt angry. 'I can't. I *won't.*'

'I thought you'd feel that way. I know how you are.'

'You don't really know me at all,' Brynn said stubbornly. 'Since you're the detective, though, do you have any news about Mark's car?'

'I'm not a detective. I'm the county sheriff. And the only news I have is that the blood on the back seat of the car is O positive.'

'The most common type and, of course, Mark's.' Brynn felt tears pressing behind her eyes, but she would not show weakness. 'Anything else of forensic value in the car?'

'It's still being processed. We don't have the lab resources of a big city police force.'

'I'm frustrated but I get it. In the meantime, I'd like to see Mark's motel room.'

'We haven't finished processing it, either.' He paused. 'I hate to keep saying no to you.'

Was he really sorry to keep saying no to her? Brynn looked at him closely. In some ways he resembled his father with his strong features and his rare, tight smile. She could tell that, like his father, he didn't trust people easily. If he was wary in general, he'd certainly doubt Stone Jonah Wilder's daughter. But the expression in Garrett's eyes seemed sincere and she reminded herself that Garrett was not his father. Yesterday, he'd made a point of saying so in a tone hinting he didn't want to be compared to his father.

'Maybe you can see his room this afternoon,' he went on. 'We're gathering fingerprints, which is hell in a motel room.'

'I'm sure it is.'

'You can take a quick look around, though. Are you familiar with all of Mark's stuff?'

'Not really. I haven't seen him for almost a year. Clothes are a loss. When he wasn't working at the bank, he lived in blue jeans. Cassie would know more about the shirts he wore when he was here. He's into cameras, computers, smart phones – all that electronic stuff. He probably has a lot of new things I haven't seen. On the other hand, I know money's been tight for him this year. He might not have much new equipment.'

'Well, you can tell us what items you remember when you see

the room,' Garrett said, already starting to rise from his chair. 'In the meantime . . .'

'In the meantime, I guess there's not much I can do.' Brynn stood up.

'Go sightseeing. Don't think about Mark. Just amble around and let your mind relax.' Garrett sauntered toward the door, looking relieved that she was leaving. 'The town's changed quite a bit since you lived here. You might be surprised by how it's grown, how much better it looks.'

I don't care how it looks, Brynn thought, but she didn't argue. Garrett walked down the hall with her. Brynn wondered if he was making sure she left the building. As they passed the main room, Savannah jumped up and rushed to them. 'Dad, have you decided what you want me to do?'

Garrett looked at her in near despair. 'I guess I could take you back to stay with Mrs Persinger.'

'Dad, she's a hundred! She wants to teach me how to crochet doilies! *Doilies!* I had to look in the dictionary to see what they are!'

'Well, you could stay here . . .'

'Until *three o'clock*?'

'I'm going sightseeing,' Brynn announced. 'I could use a guide.'

Savannah's face flashed from petulant to exultant. 'I can be your guide!'

Garrett's expression went stony. 'Oh, I don't know about you going off with Brynn.' Brynn turned an offended face toward him and he began to backpedal. 'I mean, I know Brynn doesn't want to drag around a kid and a dog.'

'I'm not a kid!' Savannah announced hotly.

Brynn knew she shouldn't interfere with Garrett's authority over his daughter. But at the same time, she felt bruised, desolate and scared. She was afraid if she had to leave this place by herself she'd simply sit down on a sidewalk bench and burst into tears.

Brynn said abruptly, 'I'd enjoy the company of a young woman and a dog like Henry.' At the sound of his name, the dog looked up, powdered sugar from a doughnut lacing his whiskers.

Savannah begged, 'Oh, Dad, *please*?'

Brynn looked at him pleadingly. She felt slightly underhand, knowing he didn't want Savannah to go with her. At the same time, she realized the girl admired her and wanted to spend time with her. 'We'll have Henry to protect us.'

Garrett looked like he was thinking, but Brynn could tell he was already caving in under the weight of a double whammy from two girls, not to mention Henry's dancing paws and wagging tail. The dog had picked up on the word 'walk.' Garrett sighed and said reluctantly, 'I guess I'm outnumbered. All right, but don't go far.'

'We won't. Oh, thanks Dad!' Savannah gushed.

Brynn smiled. 'Yeah, thanks, Garrett.'

Henry barked and Brynn and Savannah laughed.

Brynn, Savannah and the dog were descending the steps in front of headquarters when Garrett opened the front door they'd just closed and called, 'Don't talk to strangers.'

Don't talk to strangers, Brynn thought. How many victims of the Genessa Point Killer had been told the same thing before they left home?

'There's the Genessa Point Museum,' Savannah said, pointing to an old, stone building. 'Do you want to go there?'

'Not really. I was there a dozen times a long time ago. Besides, it's too nice a day to spend inside a musty old museum.' Brynn looked down at Henry. 'I doubt if they let eighty-pound dogs in there, anyway.'

Savannah smiled. 'He's closer to a hundred pounds. The vet says he needs to lose at least ten.'

'All those doughnuts he ate this morning won't help a diet.'

Savannah started laughing as the dog walked calmly beside her, his long, feathery tail swishing, looking up at the sound of her laughter. 'He did make a pig of himself, but he eats too much when he's mad. This morning we were both mad. Dad acts like I'm a little girl.'

'He just worries about you. Do you know why he didn't want you to be alone today?'

Savannah hesitated, then looked up with a candid gaze. 'Something's happened to your brother. I'm not supposed to know, but I heard Dad talking on the phone about him. Mark? Is that his name?'

'Yes. Mark is missing.'

'I'm sorry, but Dad will find him. Dad's a super-good policeman.' Savannah's gaze shot around eagerly, obviously searching for something to entertain Brynn. 'Oh, look!' she cried. 'There's your second book in the bookstore window!'

'So it is.' Brynn looked at the book that had seemed to write itself, unlike the book she now struggled over day after day. 'I'm afraid bookstores will be a thing of the past soon. So many have closed and not as many people read these days as they used to.'

'I love reading. The biography in your last book says you live in Miami. Can you see the beach from your apartment?'

'No, but I'm only a few blocks away. My place is on the seventh floor. I have a terrace that looks out over the city.'

'Oh, wow, that must be so exciting!'

'It's nice,' Brynn said, thinking she should enjoy it more than she did. 'I walk to the beach nearly every day, even though I usually don't go swimming.'

'I'd go every day, too.' Savannah studied her for a moment. 'I love your top. You look all floaty, like a butterfly.'

Brynn giggled. 'A butterfly? Is that good?'

'Oh, very. And your necklace and dangling earrings are . . . just to *die* for.' Brynn could tell Savannah was trying her hardest to sound sophisticated. 'Are those butterflies?'

'No, they're dragonflies.' Brynn bent slightly at the knees and let Savannah look at them and her necklace. 'I've been obsessed with dragonflies since I was about five. My dad read to me about them and I learned they have two sets of wings and can fly thirty-five miles an hour, forwards and backwards, up and down, or just hover like a helicopter. But I was especially fascinated that, according to myths, dragonflies were once dragons.' Brynn grinned at Savannah. 'You can imagine how that blew the mind of a five-year-old!'

Savannah grinned back.

'My brother even gave me a nickname – Dragonfly. He never called me that in public – it was our secret. I loved having a secret nickname. Anyway, I bought this necklace and the earrings three years ago. I almost always wear them, particularly when I feel like I need to be powerful. When I was a kid, I wore something similar, but much cheaper. Not much more than a trinket.'

'That is *so* cool.' Savannah paused, then burst out: 'You're just fabulous, Miss Wilder!'

Brynn broke into laughter. 'As long as you think I'm fabulous and not silly, I'm happy.'

'Oh, you're not a bit silly,' Savannah said earnestly. 'Did you always want to be a writer?'

'I guess so. When I was younger than you I used to write short stories sometimes, but I wasn't really trying and they weren't very good. It wasn't until I was about fifteen that I got serious and spent all my free time writing. That time I put my soul into my stories. I must have written about thirty of them before I decided that someday I'd write a book.'

Writing saved me, Brynn thought. She'd escaped her own sad reality by creating a beautiful world where good people never died and everything worked out in the end. But she wouldn't go into all that with this young girl she'd just met.

'I write stories, too, but I'm always disappointed in them when they're done,' Savannah said.

'Just keep working at your writing. Someday you'll be successful.'

'You think?'

'You'll never know unless you try and you try and you try. Don't give up.'

'That's what Dad says when I'm unhappy with one of my stories.'

'Does he want you to be a writer?'

'He says he wants me to be what I want to be, but after he read your second book, he said if I worked hard enough, I might get to be a really good writer like you.'

'Like me? Really? How . . . nice.' Brynn was surprised. She would never have guessed Garrett Dane would want his daughter to be anything like Brynn Wilder. Suddenly self-conscious, she looked around. 'There's Holly Park. I used to go there. Is it the same?'

'They've made lots of changes the last couple of years. Now it's even better than before. It's a good place for Henry, too.'

'Great. It's right across the street from police headquarters. If your dad gets worried, he can just look out a window and see you. Still, I think I'd better leave a message for him, telling where we are. Do you have a cell phone?'

Savannah dug in a pocket and held one up.

'Then call your dad and tell him where we'll be.'

Because he'll be mad as hell at me for taking you away, Brynn thought, her mind darting back to the phone call they'd gotten at Cassie's less than twenty-four hours ago. Someone is obviously watching me and I just swept his daughter away like she was my own child. How foolish—

'Dad said Holly Park's fine,' Savannah announced cheerfully, interrupting Brynn's spiral down the well of self-criticism. 'He said we should just stay in the park, though, and not go anywhere else.'

As they walked into the four-acre city park, Brynn remembered coming here with Mark, her mother and especially her father, who'd told her the names of all the trees and shrubs, which she'd promptly forgotten. She'd wanted to break free of Mom and Dad, to ramble on her own and meet up with her gaggle of friends. How the years change you, she thought. Now she'd be thrilled to stroll through the park with her parents and Mark, no matter how long her dad spent explaining the Latin names and proper care of all the foliage.

'Over there they built three little shops I really like,' Savannah said. 'One Henry can go in, the other two he can't.'

They walked over and Savannah looked up as one of the doors opened. The girl's face paled as she gazed at the woman with long, light auburn hair draped over the shoulders of a sleeveless, navy-blue dress that fit her tall, slim body as if it had been made for her. 'Hello, Savannah,' the woman said coolly. 'Taking a stroll with your dog?'

'Hello, Rhonda.' Savannah stood, looking unsure of herself. 'Yeah, I'm taking Henry for a walk. And showing Brynn around. Brynn Wilder. She's a friend of my dad's.'

Rhonda turned slightly. She had the coldest gray eyes Brynn had ever seen. They traveled up and down Brynn twice, almost giving her a chill. Finally she said, 'Hello, Miss Wilder. It is miss, isn't it?'

'Yes. Or Ms.' Rhonda continued to openly scrutinize her, taking in every detail.

'I'm afraid I didn't catch your last name,' Brynn said.

'That's because Savannah didn't properly introduce us. I'm Rhonda Sanford. *Miss* Rhonda Sanford.' Staring frigidly at Brynn, she asked, 'Are you here for the festival, Miss Wilder, or did you come to see Savannah's father?'

If she'd only asked about the festival, Brynn wouldn't have known what was wrong with this beautiful yet icy woman. But the overly curious, possessive way she said *Savannah's father* spoke volumes. 'I came for the festival,' she answered, feeling as if the warm summer air had dropped at least ten degrees. 'I'm staying with Cassie Hutton.'

'Really?' A perfunctory smile appeared on Rhonda's perfectly sculpted face. 'She's my employer.'

'You work at Love's Dress Shoppe?'

'Yes. In fact, I'm on an errand for Miss Hutton now.' Rhonda looked Brynn up and down a final time. 'I should be on my way. Goodbye, Lynn.' She didn't turn her head. 'Savannah.'

Savannah moved closer to Brynn as Rhonda took long strides in expensive high heels, heading for a small red car at the curb. She got in as if she were being filmed for a commercial, put on huge sunglasses and roared into the traffic lane. Meanwhile, Savannah's hand crept into Brynn's. It was cold and shook slightly. Brynn felt slightly alarmed by the girl's physical response to Rhonda but decided not to call attention to it.

'What's this shop?' Brynn asked with lively curiosity. As they continued walking they'd moved on to a large brick building called Painter's Cove. 'They sell good paintings.' Savannah paused and sniffed, pulling a tissue from her pocket and dabbing at her nose. 'They have *two* of Grams's paintings. She died about three months ago. I loved her so much and I miss her like crazy. She took care of me after my mom left Dad and me.'

'Your mother left?' Brynn asked, unable to hide her surprise. 'I thought . . . well, I didn't know—'

'You thought she died,' Savannah interrupted. 'Lots of people think that and I don't tell them different because she didn't love Dad *or* me and she just left one day with some other man when I was four. Dad never says anything about the man. He still thinks I don't know, but I used to sneak around listening to him and Grams talking. You know how kids are,' she said disdainfully, as if she hadn't been a 'kid' for years. 'Grams said Patty – that's my mother's name – wasn't meant to be a wife and mother and she wasn't surprised that Patty had run off with that "piece of trash who happens to have some money." That's exactly what she said. She also said when the money ran out, Patty would leave him 'cause he was a lot older than her.'

'Oh.' Brynn was so startled she couldn't think of anything comforting to say. 'That's a bummer,' she managed and could have kicked herself.

'It was for Dad. I don't remember a lot about it. Dad's parents are dead and Patty's mom lives in Montana. Her husband – Patty's father – is dead.' Savannah went on: 'That's how we ended up with Grams. She's Patty's grandmother. She has a big house and Dad told me she begged him to move in and let her take care of us.' Savannah finally smiled. 'She really loved me *and* Dad. She made him call her Grams, too.' She sighed. 'Once I heard her tell Dad that Patty was a real disappointment.'

'I'm sorry, Savannah. The same thing happened to my brother, Mark. His wife just left him and went off with another man.'

'Did they have kids?'

'No. They weren't married very long and after they got married, she told him she'd decided she didn't want kids.'

'Did he want kids?'

'Yes. Mark loves children.'

'I think Patty wasn't right for Dad and that girl wasn't right for Mark. Dad and your brother will both find the right girls someday, though.'

'I hope so.'

'They will.' Savannah's mood had definitely improved since their encounter with Rhonda. She looked around. 'Can I tell you something I can't say to Dad but I feel like I'll burst if I don't say it to someone?'

'Sure you can, if you think I'm the right person to tell.'

'You are. I can feel it.' Savannah took a deep breath. 'Just between us, I don't love my mom Patty one bit. I hardly even remember what she looked like. She ruined our family and she never calls or writes to me. Oh, she sends me a Christmas card – big deal – like I care. Sometimes she remembers to send a birthday card. I just throw them away and I *never* look at a picture of her. I don't miss her at all. Do you think I'm awful?'

'Of course not. How could you miss her? You barely knew her.'

'Yeah, but I miss Grams every day, sometimes so bad it hurts.' She swallowed hard. 'Now Dad doesn't know what to do with me. I can tell he worries about me and I don't want him to worry. I keep telling him I'm old enough to take care of myself, and I am, but he acts like I'm six.'

'I'm sure he doesn't think you're like a six-year-old. He's just trying to protect you.'

'From what? Or who?'

'Well, people can get lost or hurt . . .'

'Or taken, like your brother.' Savannah colored. 'Damn. I mean darn! I'm sorry I made you think of him.' She took Brynn's hand and squeezed it. 'I'm *sure* my dad will find him, Miss Wilder. He's super smart and a really good sheriff.'

'I knew your dad when he was still a teenager. He and Mark were friends. Your dad was really smart and dedicated to anything he decided to do. I have faith that he'll find Mark.' Brynn smiled and wondered if the beautiful, bright girl in front of her saw right through it. She had a feeling Savannah saw much more than she let on. 'I want your dad to find Mark and I want you to do something for me, too.'

'Oh, I'll do just about anything you want,' Savannah said eagerly.

'I want you to call me Brynn, not Miss Wilder. Friends call each other by their first names.'

'Really? You like me enough for me to be your friend?'

'You wouldn't believe how much I like you.'

Savannah looked dumbstruck. 'I can hardly believe it! Wait till I tell Dad!'

'You don't think he'll mind us being friends?'

'Gosh, no! He always says I need more friends.' She looked slightly to her right and softly said, 'Brynn.' Then, 'Brynn,' a bit louder. Finally, with airy abandon, 'This is my friend, *Brynn.*' She smiled. 'Do I say it right?'

'Just right. You sound like you've been saying it for years.'

'So Dad and I are both your friends. Dad longer than me because he's lots older.' She frowned. 'I'm really glad you have faith in Dad, 'cause I'm sure he'll find Mark. I wasn't just saying that to make you feel better.' Brynn felt the girl's gaze flash on her for a second. 'He's got plenty of time, even at night. He doesn't date at all now. Back in the winter he dated that woman, Rhonda.'

'Oh,' Brynn said carefully. 'She's very pretty.'

Savannah made a huffing noise. 'Grams always said, "Pretty is as pretty does." I don't think she's at all pretty because of how she is. When Dad dated her, Rhonda pretended to like me and Grams, but we could tell she was being fake. Dad hasn't gone out with her since Grams died. Well, really for a while before then. When he stopped dating her, she started calling the house for him all the time, even at two or three in the morning! He got our number changed. He said if anyone at headquarters needed him, they'd call on his cell. Rhonda doesn't have that number. He *really* doesn't like Rhonda anymore.'

'She doesn't sound very likeable,' Brynn said neutrally. She didn't want to pry into Garrett's private life.

'Oh, she's not! And I sure wish I hadn't said you were a friend of Dad's. She'll hate you because you're lots prettier than her and Dad likes you. She's real jealous, even though they don't date anymore. And even when they did date, I don't think Dad thought she was all that great.'

'Do you want your father to have a girlfriend?' Brynn couldn't help asking.

'For sure! He's hardly dated anyone that I can remember and I think he gets lonely sometimes. He had Grams and me. Now he just has me. He needs someone his own age. He's real stubborn about going out with women, though.' Savannah looked at Brynn, a twinkle in her eyes. 'I think he's like your brother, just waiting for the right girl. Someone pretty and nice and talented and who really likes me and Henry . . .'

You're a little matchmaker, Brynn thought in amusement, although she kept her face blank as they reached a wishing well and Savannah insisted on them both throwing pennies. They each leaned over the well, closed their eyes and dropped their coins into the water. As their pennies disappeared, they raised their heads, smiling at each other.

'A penny for your thoughts or pennies from heaven?'

Brynn and Savannah turned and looked at a woman standing a few feet behind them. She didn't smile or move her gaze. 'Hello, Brynn,' she said evenly. Then Brynn knew who she was . . .

Tessa Cavanaugh – the girl who'd killed her father.

FIVE

Except Tessa wasn't a girl anymore. Brynn hadn't seen her for eighteen years, and only just recognized her. Tessa would be thirty-three now, Brynn thought, but she looked much older: deep horizontal lines crossing her forehead, her lips pale and dry, and her gray-blue eyes bare of makeup as they gazed from behind wire-rimmed glasses. A narrow scar curved outward from above her right ear and ended halfway down her neck – a scar she'd received during her attack. She hadn't attempted to hide it. In fact, she didn't wear any makeup. Her long, sharp nose looked shiny in the sunlight and her sparse eyebrows were nearly invisible. Brynn guessed her to be about five foot seven. A shapeless blue linen dress covered her knees, she wore lace-up white walking shoes, and her long, thin, gray-streaked blonde hair was pulled back with a white ribbon.

'Hello, Tessa,' Brynn said woodenly.

As if sensing Brynn's body going rigid and her inability to say anything else, Savannah began chattering. 'Hi, Miss Cavanaugh. You probably don't remember me. I'm Savannah Dane. I come in the library sometimes. I'm taking a walk with Brynn. We're having the most amazing time!' Savannah seemed to be running out of breath, but she added, 'Henry's with us. He's the dog.'

'I guessed Henry was the dog,' Tessa said with a stiff note in her voice and a slanted smile. Henry took a step nearer to Savannah and sat down, staring at Tessa. No doggie handshake for you, Brynn mused.

'Henry goes almost everywhere with me,' Savannah said. 'Dad says we're nearly inseparable.'

'How nice. I've always thought you should keep what's important to you as close as possible.'

'Huh?' Savannah frowned. 'Oh, important. Well, Henry's real important to me. We love each other.' She paused. 'And he also loves Brynn.'

Tessa gave Savannah a tight smile. 'Of course he loves Brynn. Everyone loves Brynn. She was the most popular girl in middle school when she lived in Genessa Point, or so I've been told – I was three years older than her. Then Brynn went away to become a bestselling author. I've heard talk that people in Hollywood will be making a movie of one of her books.' Tessa paused. 'Brynn has always been a winner.'

'Oh, I wouldn't say that,' Brynn returned, trying to keep her voice easygoing. She wanted to shout at Tessa. She wanted to drive her away as if she were a breath of plague coming too close to Savannah and her. 'I've had my share of bad times, Tessa. And I wasn't popular at the school I attended in Baltimore. Not at all.'

Tessa dropped her gaze and clutched the brown bag she carried. Then she slowly looked up. 'I'm sorry about what I said about you always being a winner, Brynn. I'm sure you won't believe this, but for years, I worried about you.' She paused and took a deep breath. 'I ruined the lovely life you had in Genessa Point. Don't think I've ever forgotten that fact. I know saying I'm sorry after all of these years is meaningless, but I *am* saying it.'

Brynn softened slightly. 'You said you were sorry after . . . the incident. You said it over and over to the police. You even sent separate letters to Mom, Mark and me. I kept mine.'

'I meant every word I wrote.' Tessa twisted her hands, obviously feeling awkward, although she was trying to be sociable. 'Why are you here after so long, Brynn?'

'I came to visit Cassie Hutton.' Brynn couldn't believe how easily the lie rolled out. She certainly didn't want to discuss Mark with Tessa. 'Cassie's come to see me but I've never been back to visit her. I also wanted to see what she's done with Love's Dress Shoppe.'

'Ah. What's your opinion of the store?'

I haven't even been there, Brynn thought guiltily. 'I just got here yesterday evening. I'll see the shop this afternoon or tomorrow.'

'It's much lovelier than when her aunt – or great-aunt – owned it. Not that I do a lot of shopping. People don't notice what librarians wear, do they, Savannah?'

'Well . . . I'm not sure . . . maybe . . .'

Tessa laughed softly. 'I'm making you uncomfortable. Forgive me.' She gazed at Brynn. 'You look quite well . . . lovely, like your mother. And you've always had such beautiful dark cinnamon-brown hair.' Her pale eyes drifted almost sadly over Brynn's long, thick hair, her fanciful, bright top and tight jeans, making Brynn even more uncomfortable. 'I'm pleased about your success.'

'Thank you very much, Tessa.'

Tessa went on in her quaint, formal manner: 'When we were young, I was unaware you wanted to be a writer.'

'We barely knew each other.'

'I've always been an introvert. My brother Nathan inherited all the charm and charisma in the family. He had so many friends. Even your brother.' Tessa might as well have said, *Your brother whom everyone thinks is a killer like your father.* She rushed on: 'Now Nathan travels all over the world with his computer consulting business and I think he's comfortable everywhere. There are people like that, you know. The ones who are at home in the world. He keeps in close touch, but his job is important and he can't come home often. His work was at such a critical point, he couldn't even break free when Father died. I had to go through it all alone.' She looked mournful for a moment, then seemed to catch herself and said gaily, 'Nate's coming for the festival, though! He'll be arriving tonight. I'm so looking forward to having him around for a few days. He has such an invigorating presence. I haven't seen him for months, not since Daddy . . . Well, perhaps Cassie told you he died in a car wreck two months ago?'

'Yes, she did.' Brynn answered. 'I'm sorry.'

Tessa sighed. 'Sad times around here lately. I'm sure you heard about Doctor Ellis's daughter Joy dying less than two weeks ago. She was such a pretty girl. Did you know her?'

'Not well. She was five years younger than me, but she took piano lessons from my mother and Mom was impressed with her skills even though she was so young. I know her parents adored her.'

'Yes. Such a shame.' Tessa seemed to search for something to say, then pounced on Savannah. 'Have you been practicing your lines for the play?'

'Sure! I don't want to mess up on stage in front of all those people.' Savannah smiled nervously. 'I think I've got them memorized.'

'*Genessa Point: The Beginning*?' Brynn asked.

'You remembered!' Savannah beamed.

'After Father died, I was so sad I threw myself into writing this play. I'm called the assistant director, although I'm not good at directing,' Tessa said. 'Savannah won the second lead. I'd hoped she would be the star, but another girl's mother who dotes on her daughter and has so much influence around here got the part for her child. Unfortunately, Savannah didn't have a mother pulling strings for her.'

Another girl's doting mother. *Savannah didn't have a mother.* How tactless could Tessa be? Brynn stared hard at the woman. Savannah was silent. Finally Brynn said, 'Savannah doesn't need anyone to pull strings for her. She's capable of managing just fine on her own.'

'I really like my part better anyway,' Savannah ventured.

'Oh, well, if you're satisfied with that . . .' Tessa trailed off.

'Are you coming to the fireworks tonight?' Savannah asked politely.

Tessa cringed. 'No! I *hate* loud noises. I can't bear them!'

'Oh, that's a shame. They'll be pretty,' Savannah said. 'I didn't know about your noise phobia.'

Brynn almost started laughing at *noise phobia.* She knew Savannah was gently making fun of Tessa's violent reaction to the very mention of loud noises. Tessa didn't have a clue.

'I suppose you'll be here, Savannah.'

The girl nodded.

'Brynn?'

Brynn shook her head.

'Well, enjoy yourself tonight, Savannah.' Tessa gazed around, almost vacantly, then looked back at them and held up a paper bag. 'My lunch. In the summer, I always eat in the park and watch the birds. I throw bits of bread to them.' She gave them her stiff smile. 'Have a pleasant day.'

It wasn't until Tessa walked slowly away and sat down on a bench, opening her bag and pulling out a cling-wrapped sandwich, that Brynn realized the woman had talked about Nathan but hadn't asked a word about Mark.

'Are you OK?' Savannah asked tentatively.

Brynn drew a deep breath. 'Yes. I'm fine. It was just a surprise to see her, although I don't know why. This isn't a big city.'

'I think she acts like she's from another planet,' Savannah said emphatically.

'She's . . . off-beat.'

'Since I've been around her so much because of the play, I've noticed that sometimes she seems OK and other times she, like, has a *freaky* spell. That's what all the kids call it. One of Tessa's freaky spells. Anyway, I wish we hadn't run into her. We were having so much fun.' Savannah paused, then asked tentatively, 'Do you hate her?'

Yes, I think I do, Brynn felt like saying, but she lied. 'No.'

'I probably would if she'd killed *my* dad.' Savannah blushed. 'Oh, I'm sorry. I always say the wrong thing.'

'No, you don't.' Brynn paused. 'You were just being honest, so I'll be honest with you. Tessa said she killed my dad, but some people believed there must have been a third person in the woods. I think they're right.' Brynn was aware of her voice rising. 'Tessa was only fifteen and my dad was a grown man. He wasn't as big as your father, but he was bigger than Tessa. I'm sure she was attacked by someone else but was terrified and confused and . . .' Brynn took a deep breath. 'It must have been an accident. She was acting in self-defense and wasn't thinking straight. She didn't know who she was lashing out at. I shouldn't hate her for that. I mean, to be fair I *can't* hate her. It's just—'

'You don't have to talk about it anymore,' Savannah interrupted, her voice agitated. 'Your face is getting really white. I know you're upset and—' She looked at the street. 'Oh, great! There's my dad in the squad car! He's come after us. Come on. Let's hurry and get away from Tessa.'

'She's not doing anything wrong,' Brynn said weakly, but Savannah, who was pulled by the strength of Henry, had taken her hand. Brynn was no match for the two of them.

'I saw the three of you at the wishing well,' Garrett commented as he climbed out of the patrol car and opened a rear door for them. Savannah clambered into the back seat, Henry right behind her, and Brynn tried to squeeze in beside Henry. Garrett motioned her toward the front.

'I'm riding shotgun?' she asked.

'Yeah, but don't get carried away. You're not a deputy.'

'You could swear me in.'

'No way.' He got in the car.

'We had the best time, Dad,' Savannah chirped from the back seat. 'We looked in the bookstore window and Brynn's book is there. We threw pennies in the wishing well and . . . and Tessa Cavanaugh came up to us.'

'I know. I saw that she had you cornered at the wishing well. What was she doing there?'

Brynn kept her voice even, her gaze straight ahead as Garrett pulled away from the curb. 'She eats her lunch in the park during the summer. She was very polite.'

'Define *polite*.'

'"Hello. How are you? I'm happy for your success,"' Brynn imitated.

'There was more than that, but Brynn will tell you when I'm not around,' Savannah said cannily. 'Tessa's so creepy.' Brynn waited for Savannah to say something about Rhonda, but she didn't. 'Are you taking me back to headquarters now, Dad?'

'No, I'm taking you to Mrs Persinger's house. Before you start arguing, I'm telling you that you can bear one afternoon of learning to crochet doilies. Tomorrow you can help Mrs Elbert at the hot dog stand.'

Savannah groaned. 'A whole afternoon crocheting. Just don't forget that I have play rehearsal tonight. You said you'd take me to rehearsal and then the fireworks.'

'I didn't forget.'

'Are you taking Brynn back to headquarters now?'

'No, I'm taking her somewhere else – somewhere that's none of your business.'

The 'somewhere else' turned out to be Mark's room at the Bay Motel.

'I didn't think you'd really bring me here,' Brynn said.

'I said I would.'

'You said *maybe* I could see it this afternoon.'

'Well, *maybe* turned into *can*. But I want to say something to you first.' Garrett turned in his seat, pinning her with his gaze. 'I didn't like the way you ran off with my daughter this morning when you knew I didn't want her to go.'

'I didn't run off—'

'You know you encouraged her to go with you. I could see you knew you were doing something you shouldn't. You've always been determined to do things your own way—'

'You don't know what I *always* do! You haven't even seen me since I was twelve.'

'You were the same way at twelve. Anyway, I have to set some boundaries. You can help us a lot in the search for Mark, but you cannot take over, Brynn, and have me reporting everything to you. Some things the police need to keep confidential.'

'I don't see why—'

'Because I said you can't, that's why. And you can't override my wishes when it comes to Savannah.' Garrett paused. 'Have I made myself clear?'

'Crystal,' she snapped, although her face was burning and she couldn't look at him. She had interfered with him and his daughter this morning. She'd known it at the time. 'I'm sorry.'

'It turns out Savannah had a wonderful time with someone she just about worships. She'll never forget it. I'm glad for the time you spent with her.'

Brynn glanced at Garrett's face, which looked just a shade less than angry. 'But don't do it again.'

'I won't.'

'And you won't interfere with this investigation? You won't go barging off on your own? Even if you think you have a brilliant idea about something that should be checked, you'll tell me first?'

'I'll try.'

'Brynn, do you want to end up like Mark?'

Her emotional reaction was immediate. *No.* He was the only family she had left. If he'd been killed here in Genessa Point, she'd want to live. She would know she'd done everything she could for Mark, but she deserved a life of her own, even if she'd never get over the loss of her brother.

She looked at Garrett. 'I'll do my very best to follow your rules,' Brynn said formally. 'I promise not to give in to my headstrong nature.'

'Good. That's all I ask.'

'OK. I'm ready to look at Mark's room now.'

A deputy Garrett called Carder lingered near the door. His dark gaze swept over Brynn before he looked at the sheriff. 'She doesn't need to wear shoe covers,' he said. 'We didn't find any blood on the floor. No blood anywhere, actually.'

They hadn't found blood in the room. Brynn wondered if that should make her feel better. It didn't. What about the blood in his car?

Garrett took Brynn's arm and firmly led her through the doorway. This morning she couldn't wait to see the room. Now she was afraid to look at it. Garrett and Deputy Carder were waiting for her, though, and the last thing she wanted to show was fear.

Brynn stepped briskly over the threshold, stopped and scanned the room: a double bed covered with a synthetic quilted blue and gold spread; an oak veneer bedside table; a matching dresser with a tall mirror attached; medium blue carpet; blue and gold patterned thermal draperies; two vinyl chairs with a small, round table between them. Brynn walked to the table. Three generic magazines and two pamphlets about local sights were lined precisely in front of a white ceramic-based lamp.

'Has the maid been in here yesterday or today?' Brynn asked.

'Not since Sunday.' Brynn turned at the sound of a different male voice. 'Hello, Brynn.'

She looked at him for a moment, trying to imagine the face eighteen years younger. 'Sam? Sam Fenney?'

The tall, thin man with heavily gray-streaked black hair and a prominent nose smiled at her. She'd always thought he looked like Abraham Lincoln. 'You're as pretty as your mama. I knew you would be. Got a hug for an old man?'

Brynn had never been one for casual hugs and kisses as a form of greeting. However, Sam had been a close friend of her father and she didn't want to insult him. She walked toward him and lightly wrapped her arms around him. His arms circled her and squeezed hard.

'You're too thin, girl,' he said.

'Still a silver-tongued devil, aren't you?' she asked lightly. 'And you're one to talk about being too thin.'

'I've always been skinny as a rail.'

'What are you doing here?'

'I guess no one told you, but I'm part owner of this motel.'

'Really? What happened to your real estate business?'

'Oh, I still have it. My father started Fenney Real Estate and I've always felt obligated to hang onto it. I've never been the go-getter Dad was, but I've made a good living from the business and having a wife who never wants to travel or entertain has helped me save money – enough to invest in this place.'

Brynn nodded, although she used to overhear her father telling her mother how Sam's childless marriage to a woman who'd become a recluse by the time she was thirty made him feel resentful and thwarted. 'I'm proud of this place.'

'It's very nice,' Brynn said.

Sam smiled. 'Oh, it's nothing fancy, but it's a sturdy, well-built establishment scrupulously maintained and kept clean. Some people didn't like that it has a bar, but it's quiet, respectable.' His smile faded and he looked solemnly at Brynn. 'Honey, I'm so sorry about this trouble with Mark. You must be real worried or you wouldn't have come back to town.'

Brynn nodded. 'Sam, have you known Mark was in Genessa Point since the day he checked into your motel?'

'Not until the day after. Mark checked in Wednesday night. The man in charge after eight o'clock didn't know who Mark was. The next day, Mark came to see me. I couldn't believe it was him at first. I didn't think he'd ever come back here. He told me he'd driven past your old house. It's up for sale again and I'm listing it.' He took a breath. 'He wanted to see it. Inside.'

Brynn felt a moment of surprise followed by a longer moment of repulsion. She never wanted to see that house again. 'Did you show it to him?'

'Yes. I had mixed feelings about it, but I couldn't very well say no to him. We walked all through the house but he didn't say anything like, "We used to watch TV in here," or "This was my room" – just nothing. I thought it was unusual.'

'Did he tell you why he was in Genessa Point?'

'He said he wanted to see the town again.' Sam shrugged. 'To be honest, I didn't buy it, but I acted like I did. He didn't bring up the old business, Brynn. He claimed he just wanted to say hello, see how I am, and made a couple of comments about how much had changed around here. That's it. I've already told Sheriff Dane everything I know.'

'Brynn, do you want to look at the room more closely?' Garrett asked pointedly, cutting off Sam.

She was glad for the interruption. Sam Fenney had been a friend of her father and he'd been vocal about the impossibility of Jonah Wilder being the Genessa Point Killer. After her family had left town, though, they'd only heard from him five times, when he'd sent Christmas cards along with half-page, generic letters. True, the family had wanted to cut ties in Genessa Point, but seeing one of her father's old friends still shook Brynn, especially in light of Mark's disappearance.

Brynn stepped into the room. The curtains were open, letting in bright sunlight. At first she stood still, scanning the neat room. Then she looked at Garrett. 'Mark wasn't particularly tidy, to put it mildly. He wouldn't have left the room like this.'

'The maid cleaned it Sunday morning when we didn't know anything was wrong,' Sam said quickly with an anxious glance at Garrett, apparently worried the maid might have tampered with important evidence. 'She said a few of Mark's things were here. That's what made us think he hadn't skipped out on his bill.' He looked at Brynn. 'Not that Mark would do that, of course.'

'The room looks nearly unoccupied.' Brynn turned to Garrett. 'Did your people take away things as evidence?'

'There wasn't much to take. I have the formal inventory on file at headquarters, but I brought along a copy.' He pulled a folded piece of paper from his pocket.

She glanced at it, then walked farther into the room, looking at the long dresser. 'OK if I open the drawers?'

Garrett said yes and she pulled them out, noting some folded underwear, a pair of jeans and socks. On hangers, she found two long-sleeved cotton shirts. No other personal items remained in the bathroom.

'We took the razor, toothbrush and comb for DNA,' Garrett told her, consulting his list. 'Also toiletries and a trash bag holding his dirty laundry.'

'I know he had either a lap top or a notebook computer,' Brynn said. 'He wouldn't have taken a trip without one. Or a cell phone.'

Garrett looked over his list. 'No cell phone or computers were found in the room.'

'Cassie said he took pictures when they went out Saturday morning, but I don't know if he used a digital camera or a smart phone. I'll ask her tonight.'

'We didn't find either,' Garrett said, checking his list.

Sam Fenney had been wandering slowly around the room when he suddenly announced, 'I don't know what personal items of Mark's are missing, but something we put into every room is gone.' Sam paused. 'A Gideon Bible.'

SIX

'Mark used a digital camera with a zoom lens on Saturday,' Cassie said that evening as she turned steaks and slid the rack back under the broiler. 'I don't remember the name of the camera. Mark could take pictures at a distance and then adjust the lens, hold it out and take our picture. In fact, he took two of us.' She grinned. 'And three of just me. He said I looked beautiful.'

'I'm sure you did.'

'Oh, yeah.' Cassie shook her head, smiling. 'I was just really happy that day.' Her smile vanished as she leaned against a kitchen counter. 'The police didn't find the camera in his motel room?'

'No. Not a computer or a camera or a cell phone.'

Cassie frowned. 'I didn't see Mark use a cell phone.'

'I'm sure he had one with him, but I called every few hours so he would have turned it off when he was with you. Anyway, the police didn't find any electronic gadgets in his room or his car.'

'What about the call last night – did they trace it?'

'They couldn't. Garrett explained why, but I only got half of what he was saying. Just take my word that they couldn't.'

'OK. That's all I really want to know, anyway. Electronic stuff bores me to death. My home computer's in the shop. I can't remember what they said was wrong with it. I'm supposed to pick it up the day after tomorrow. I can always use the one at work. Go on about the motel room.'

'We don't know what Mark brought with him. The only thing Sam insists is missing is the motel Bible.'

'The Bible? I didn't know the Bay Motel put Bibles in their rooms.'

'They do according to Sam Fenney.' Brynn frowned. 'Cassie, I didn't know he was part owner of the motel. He came along to oversee the search.'

'Or to see you. Sam's asked me about you a hundred times the last few years. I think he always felt guilty that he didn't stand by your family after your dad's death.'

'He defended Dad to the police.'

'Talk is cheap, Brynn. Did he ever give your mother any kind of assistance?'

'He helped us move.'

'Did he offer your mother money?'

'I don't think so, but Mom wouldn't have taken it, especially because Fenney Realty never set the world on fire. She knew Sam didn't have money to spare.'

'He managed to save enough to invest in a motel,' Cassie said caustically.

'Almost eighteen years after Dad died. Today I brushed up on local statistics – the population of Genessa Point has nearly doubled since we lived here. Sam's business must have improved and, like he said today, he never spent money on trips and luxuries.'

'Because his wife won't leave their house. That's what he leaves unspoken but is understood by anyone who listens to him.'

'I only met her a couple of times even though Sam and Dad were good friends. She barely spoke and never smiled. I guess now she's a complete recluse. You have to give Sam credit for staying with her all these years.' Brynn reached over and picked up a carrot slice. 'Speaking of peculiar women, I saw Tessa Cavanaugh today.'

Cassie halted, knife in the air, and looked at Brynn with wide eyes. 'No way! Really? Your first day back?' Brynn nodded. 'Tell me all about it,' Cassie said, pushing aside carrot slices and grabbing a tomato.

Brynn started with her trip to headquarters and meeting Savannah. At the girl's name, Cassie's head jerked up. Then she grabbed celery and began chopping. 'Go on.'

'We were at the wishing well tossing in pennies when Tessa came up behind us. She said she always ate lunch in the park in the summer.'

'That's all?'

'Pretty much. I know it sounds harmless, but something about her is so strange. Maybe it's a combination of things: the way she dresses; the way she talks; how you feel like she's looking right through you. She seems removed from what's going on around her, but at the same time, completely aware of the effect she's having.'

'Well, she's had an unhappy life, to say the least,' Cassie said grudgingly. 'I don't know why she didn't leave Genessa Point after she graduated from high school. Her parents, I guess. First her mother dying, then her dad getting sick.'

'Earl Cavanaugh was sick?'

'About seven or eight years after you left I heard he'd developed Parkinson's, but he kept it under control with drugs for a long time. Last year, it got really bad and the drugs weren't helping too much. The rumor mill said he was going to lose his job as president of Genessa Point Bank. One night a couple of months ago he went out for a midnight drive. He rammed into a tree and died immediately. Maybe he lost control of the car or he might have done it on purpose. I heard Tessa took it really hard, especially since Nathan couldn't come home for the funeral.'

'She said he's coming home tonight. She sounded excited about it.'

'She's crazy about him, which isn't surprising. Nathan could charm the birds out of the trees, as my grandmother used to say. Not to mention, he's gorgeous.'

'Sounds like Tessa isn't the only one who's crazy about him,' Brynn said, grinning.

Cassie made a face. 'I just got out of a bad relationship. I'm not looking to get my heart broken again. Nathan Cavanaugh is thirty-five and I know he's been married two or three times. He's not a good candidate for my next romance.'

'I wasn't encouraging you.'

'Good. I'm determined to stay single for a while.' Cassie looked at Brynn. 'What about you? Anyone special in your life?'

'A guy? No. I'm too busy.'

'You always say you're too busy. How long has it been since you've even had a date?'

'Cass, I'm really hungry.'

Cassie sighed. 'Subtle as you are, I can take a hint.' She pointed at the refrigerator. 'Pick out a salad dressing you like. This gourmet meal is just about ready.'

As they sat down to dinner, Cassie said, 'It sounds like you and Savannah got along.'

'We did.' Brynn looked up from the steak she'd almost finished in record time.

'I'm surprised that Garrett let her go running around town with you. He's really protective of her.'

'Oh. Well, I did get a lecture about taking off with her and Henry, her dog. I deserved it, really. I was only thinking about how lonely and upset *I* was, not the fact that Garrett really didn't want her to go with me. He didn't actually say so, but I could tell he didn't. That was before he told me he didn't like it. I apologized to him. And I did have a good time with them. Savannah is a sweetheart.'

'Hmmm. I have an employee, Rhonda Sanford, who went out with Garrett for a few months,' Cassie said. 'He hardly ever dates. Then along came Rhonda. She's really beautiful. I heard they were seeing each other. Occasionally she'd say something about Garrett – how nice he was, what a gentleman, how much fun they had together – that sort of thing. She even hinted that they were getting really serious. Rhonda wasn't a fan of Savannah, though,' Cassie went on. 'She called her "the brat" or "that spoiled, smart-ass kid." Then, about three months ago, she stopped talking about Garrett, except when Savannah's great-grandmother died. She went into detail about how she was helping with the funeral service. I attended the service and she literally clung to Garrett's arm. He looked uncomfortable at first. Savannah was white as a sheet and every time he leaned down to say something to her, Rhonda pulled him closer. He started looking mad. Later, whenever I mentioned him, she'd barely say a word or she'd go silent. I haven't seen a genuine smile on Rhonda's face since that funeral.'

'I met her today,' Brynn said, and told Cassie about their encounter. 'Savannah said when Garrett stopped dating Rhonda she started calling him constantly, even in the middle of the night.'

Cassie looked slightly troubled. 'Rhonda's attractive, smart and great at her job. She can really work the customers – talk them into buying things they'd never shell out money for without her encouragement. In some ways I admire her. But there's something about her . . .' Cassie frowned, then shrugged. 'Maybe the things that make her such a good employee don't make her a good candidate for a friend. Besides, two or three customers have complained to me lately that she was impatient and snappish with them. I've noticed a change in her, too. She seems unfocused.'

'Depression over losing Garrett?'

'I think so. If she doesn't straighten up in a week or two, I'll have to talk to her. If Garrett is the problem, it indicates *I'll* have a problem – Rhonda isn't the type to accept rejection. I also think she's not the type to take the blame for losing Garrett. She'll find someone else to blame. Probably Savannah. Or . . .' She looked at Brynn. 'Another woman.'

Brynn's eyes widened. 'You can't mean *me*?'

'You're young, beautiful, successful, a damsel in distress that Garrett's daughter obviously admires and likes. I'd say you make a formidable competitor.'

'For Garrett? You must be kidding, Cass. I'm not interested in Garrett Dane.' Brynn refused to meet Cassie's gaze as her friend gave her a long, thoughtful look.

'Let's just hope Rhonda knows that.'

Just past midnight, Brynn and Cassie sat on the couch together, eating popcorn and watching Nicole Kidman trying to take care of her children in a huge, gloomy house full of ghosts. Although they'd each seen *The Others* before, they jumped and squealed at the same moments only to immediately burst into laughter.

'Just like the old days,' Cassie gasped between giggles. 'We haven't grown up.'

'I'm glad. After all, I specialize in the supernatural.'

They'd talked all evening about anything except Mark's disappearance, even though Brynn's head seemed to beat with the question, Mark, where *are* you? She was on the verge of developing a throbbing headache when the movie ended.

Cassie suddenly let out a huge yawn. 'Gosh, I'm tired. It's been a long day.' She'd been sitting with her legs curled under her and she groaned as she straightened them. 'I have to go to bed if I'm going to make it to the store at opening time. Do you want to stay up and watch TV?'

'God, no. I'm about to fall into a stupor.'

Cassie flipped off the television and two lamps before they both headed for the stairs. They were halfway up when Brynn's cell phone rang. Since coming to Genessa Point, she'd carried the phone with her everywhere. Now she pulled it from the pocket of her robe. 'Hello?' Nothing. '*Hello?*'

'Did you enjoy the movie, Brynn?'

Brynn froze. The caller again used a voice distorter, which made it even more chilling. Cassie had turned, looking at her and mouthing, *What?*

'Well?' the voice asked.

'Who is this?'

'Now Brynn, you know I can't tell you. Besides, you didn't answer *my* question. It doesn't matter, though. You looked like you were having a good time. *The Others* is a good movie. One of my personal favorites.'

Brynn lost her breath as she clutched the phone in a trembling hand. 'What do you want?'

'Not in the mood to chat? Oh, well. There's a surprise for you on the porch. A gift. Now listen closely. *If* your brother is still alive and you don't get the gift *now*, or you call your friend the sheriff to come to your aid, Mark won't be alive much longer. Understand?' Air flooded from Brynn's lungs and she went mute. '*Understand?*' the distorted voice demanded.

Brynn managed to inhale. 'Yes! Don't do anything to Mark. Oh, please, don't—' The connection broke.

Cassie shook her arm hard. 'Who was it?'

'I don't know. There's something outside on the porch. I have to get it.'

'What? No! You can't go outside!'

'I have to. If I don't . . .'

Brynn rushed through the dark living room toward the front door, Cassie running after her. 'Brynn, no! Do not open that door! Stop!'

But Brynn had already turned the lock and flipped the deadbolt. She flung open the door, pulling free of Cassie's frantic grasp on her arm, and crossed the porch to an ivory and gold gift bag sitting at the edge of the porch light's glow. Grabbing the thin handles, she darted back inside, pushing Cassie aside, slamming the door and turning the deadbolt.

'My God, Brynn, what are you doing?' Cassie gasped. 'Someone could have been out there waiting to grab you! Have you lost your mind?'

Brynn grabbed Cassie's arm and pulled her through the living room to the windowless downstairs bathroom. She shut the door and turned on the light. 'I don't want whoever's outside to see us.'

'Someone is out there?' Cassie asked in a strangled tone. 'I'm calling Garrett!'

'No! He said no police and he's *watching*.'

'The guy on the phone? You're sure?'

'He knew we were watching *The Others*.'

'Oh, God,' Cassie moaned, then looked at the bag. 'That's a bag from my store! Ivory . . . the gold design . . .'

Brynn peered into the bag carefully, as if she expected to find a poisonous snake. Instead, it held gold tissue paper wrapped around something. She lifted out the mass, judging that it weighed about half a pound. Carefully she removed the paper to see a slim, rectangular mother-of-pearl case. Her stomach clenched as she recognized it.

'What's that?' Cassie asked in a near-whisper.

Brynn couldn't answer. She pressed a button and the lid snapped up, revealing a mother-of-pearl comb, a gold lipstick container, a tarnished silver nail file and a small nylon mesh-covered compartment filled with musty face powder. On the inside of the lid was a mirror and a narrow gold plate with an inscription:

With Love
To My Sweet Marguerite

'My father gave this to my mother on their fifteenth anniversary. She cherished it,' Brynn whispered, thunderstruck. Then she looked at a huge-eyed Cassie. 'It disappeared right after Dad's death.'

SEVEN

'It's my mother's! It's been missing since my father died, but last night someone put it on Cassie's porch, all wrapped up like a birthday present!'

Garrett Dane looked at the woman across from him, her face a mixture of rage and anguish, her voice rising with every word. 'Brynn, stop shouting,' he said sternly. 'You're so worked up you can't even give me a coherent account of what happened last night.'

'I *told* you—'

'You were waiting on the steps when I got to headquarters. You followed me into my office, nearly slammed this thing on my desk and started ranting. Now if you want me to take you seriously you'll sit down, take a few deep breaths and start calmly at the beginning. Otherwise—'

'You'll throw me out.'

'Maybe,' Garrett answered, his voice steely.

Brynn glared at him for a moment, then sank onto a chair across from his desk. He fixed two cups of coffee. 'That *should* be decaf,' he said, handing one to her. For a few minutes they each sipped coffee and regarded each other warily. Finally, Brynn drew a deep breath and said, 'All right. Here's what happened.'

She told him about watching the movie with Cassie, the phone call and running out onto the porch to pick up the package. Garrett stared at her sternly. 'Why didn't you call me?'

'Because the voice said I was being watched. I was afraid to call you. He said if he saw the police coming to the house, Mark might be killed—'

'And you fell for that.'

Brynn felt as if she'd been slapped. 'Fell for it?'

'You thought the kidnapper had Mark with him and if you didn't dash out onto the porch to pick up this makeup case, he'd slash Mark's throat.'

Brynn stiffened. 'I didn't think Mark was with him. I thought if I called you, though, he'd go back to wherever Mark is and kill him.'

'And lose his only trump card? If he even has Mark, that is.'

Brynn felt like throwing her coffee in Garrett's face. She managed to reign in her impulse, though, and say quietly, 'I was afraid for my brother's life.'

'You were stupid, Brynn. Downright stupid.'

She held his steady gaze. 'Maybe, but I wasn't going to take any chances. Whoever took Mark is crazy. Who knows what he might do?'

A moment passed before Garrett said, 'Well, under the circumstances . . . I mean, Mark is your brother . . . you were panicked.' He sighed. 'Maybe I understand. A little.'

'Gee, Sheriff, thanks.'

'Don't get defensive. It was still a stupid thing to do. You could have gotten yourself killed and you know it.'

A small wave of spirit washed over Bryn. She raised her eyes to meet Garrett's. 'OK, I've been properly chastised for my stupidity and I've taken your judgment to heart. Now can we get back to the subject of the makeup case?'

Garrett's stare held. Then he looked back at the mother-of-pearl case. 'You're certain this was your mother's?'

'Absolutely. When I was a kid, I thought it was beautiful. I used to lie on Mom's and Dad's bed and look at it. I hoped someday someone would give me something so beautiful. The lipstick is the same shade my mother always wore. So is the powder. Also, you can't ignore the inscription, *To My Sweet Marguerite.*'

'That's not proof. Someone who saw the original inscription could have duplicated it on a different case.'

Brynn hesitated. 'Well, I guess so. But where has it been all of these years?'

'Did your mother know it was missing?'

'Not until after we moved. When we unpacked and she couldn't find it, she was in tears. We looked everywhere.'

'It could have been stolen when people came back to your house after the funeral.'

Brynn went silent for a minute before saying, 'Don't you remember that there was no funeral? After the police finally released Dad's body, Mom had him cremated. That had been his wish anyway, but his mother had always fought the idea. She didn't after he was killed. She didn't even come to Genessa Point. His own mother.' Brynn's throat tightened. 'Mom kept his urn until she died. Now I have it in Miami.' She managed to swallow. 'Only a few people came to help us pack – Cassie and her family, Sam Fenney, and Dad's closest friend, Edmund Ellis, made an appearance but didn't do much. No one else came near us.'

She caught a flash of pity in Garrett's eyes before he turned away his gaze, quickly picked up his coffee cup and concentrated on taking a sip. Finally he looked at her, the pity gone. 'You're sure no one else helped you pack to move away from town?'

'Pretty sure, but maybe if I think about it, I'll come up with someone.' She sighed. 'What should I do?'

'Leave the makeup case with me. We'll get your fingerprints so we can eliminate them when we process it. I'm certain whoever left it wiped it down, but sometimes no matter how thorough someone is they manage to leave a partial in some obscure spot. If we find anything, I'll let you know. Until then, I want you to forget about this.'

'Forget about it! How can I?'

'You have to try, Brynn. Worrying about it isn't going to help. I know that sounds like useless advice, but I have nothing helpful to tell you at this point, except that I don't want you to take any more chances like you did last night.'

'I don't know what else I could have done.'

Garrett tilted his head, his mouth tightening.

'All right. I could have stayed inside but even if Mark's life wasn't in immediate danger, we wouldn't have the cosmetic case.'

'Getting your mother's case wasn't as important as protecting your life. Besides . . .'

'I know, Garrett.' Brynn swallowed hard. 'Mark may already be dead.'

After Brynn left police headquarters, she wandered aimlessly down the street, looking in store windows although she didn't really see the displays. Her memory of last night blinded her. At the time, she hadn't given a thought to her own danger when she sped onto the porch and retrieved the bag. Now she had to agree with Garrett – she'd been beyond foolish, especially because she'd put Cassie's safety in danger, too.

Finally she passed a small cafe called Cloud Nine. For the first time that day, Brynn smiled. Who'd come up with that playful name? It appealed to her, as did the pretty, flower-bedecked terrace, and she took a seat at one of the outside tables shaded from the bright morning sun by a large yellow and lime-green striped umbrella.

A plump young waitress with pink hair pulled into four shining pigtails, incredibly long false eyelashes, brilliant orange metallic-toned lipstick and an irresistible smile welcomed her, presented her with a menu, hurried back inside and returned within two minutes asking, 'What can I get for you on this beautiful day, Miss Wilder?'

Brynn raised her eyebrows. 'You know me?'

'Oh, for sure. Well, I'd know you from the picture on your book covers even if the whole town wasn't buzzing about you being here. I'm Mindy. Are you back for the festival?'

'Uh, yes.'

'Great! Wonderful! I'm a huge fan of yours. Do you think I could have your autograph before you leave today?'

'Sure, Mindy. I'm always happy to accommodate fans.'

'Fabulous! I just knew you'd be nice.' Mindy glanced back at the middle-aged man staring at her through the front window. 'That's the manager. I'd better take your order before I get fired.'

The whole town is buzzing about me being here? Brynn thought as she scanned the menu. Judging from the number of people Garrett said had stopped in headquarters, a good number of people in town had been buzzing about Mark's presence, too. They hadn't wanted him in Genessa Point. Now everyone seemed to know he was missing and the police were searching for him. A lot of them probably thought he was on the run but Brynn knew better. Someone had hated Mark to the point of kidnapping him. But why? No demands for ransom had come. Why were they holding him? Or *were* they holding him? Was he actually . . .

Brynn couldn't finish the thought. In spite of the warm day, she shivered when she thought about the blood in his car – a car in which he'd gone missing on the day he'd told Cassie he'd found out something about their father's death. What the hell had he learned?

'Know what you want, Miss Wilder?' Mindy prodded gently.

'I'm afraid my mind was wandering, Mindy.' Brynn glanced at the menu again. 'I'll have this chocolate thing with all the whipped cream and sprinkles.'

'The Chocolate Dream. My personal favorite.'

'And a raspberry Napoleon.' Brynn frowned then grinned. 'I don't even want to know how many calories I've just ordered!'

Brynn looked around while she waited for her food. People armed with cameras, most accompanied by children, strolled past her, clearly tourists here for the festival and lured out early on this balmy day with its nearly cloudless powder-blue sky and lemon-drop sun. A lot of buildings had been renovated since Brynn had moved away, most of them sporting brick fronts with dusky blue or white shutters and doors, and lots of windows above boxes bursting with vivid petunias and marigolds. The look of Genessa Point had definitely improved, Brynn thought. Her feelings about the town had not.

Mindy hurried back with Brynn's order. She had just dipped her spoon into the heavily-sprinkled mound of whipped cream topping on her Chocolate Dream when someone said, 'Why, hello, Brynn.'

She looked up. Her father's best friend, Edmund Ellis, stood beside her, smiling but also looking slightly awkward. 'Doctor Ellis,' Brynn said in a neutral tone.

'May I sit with you?'

Here stood the man who'd sworn the knife bearing the DNA of three murdered children was her father's knife and he knew nothing of it being missing for years before Tessa used it to kill Jonah Wilder. Here stood the man who had never visited them after they'd moved to Baltimore, although at first he'd sent Christmas and birthday cards always accompanied by a gift of money – money which Marguerite had promptly returned. Here stood the man who'd called Marguerite only twice during the year preceding her death.

'Certainly.' Brynn motioned to the chair across from her.

'Thanks. And even when you were a child, you called me Edmund, not Doctor Ellis. When you were a toddler, it was *Ed-mud*. Remember?' He sat down, folded his hands on the table and looked at her with a benign expression.

'No, I don't remember calling you Ed-mud.'

'Well, you were only two or three.'

Brynn recalled Dr Ellis as tall, muscular and energetic. Even when he wasn't flashing his winning smile, his dark gray, gold-flecked eyes had always held a glint of laughter, and his face was tanned and cheerful. Now he looked slightly soft, as if he didn't get much exercise. Furrows dug into his high, pale forehead, and his eyes were shadowed and somber even though he smiled at her. Silver laced his dark brown hair, which was completely white at the temples.

'I heard you were in town,' he said finally.

'Yes. I got here on Tuesday.' Brynn searched for something else to say, struck with a sudden reluctance to talk to her father's friend who she used to see at least every two or three weeks. Then she remembered his recent tragedy. 'I'm so sorry about Joy,' she said sincerely. 'You know how silly kids are about their cliques – she was five years younger than me so I thought I couldn't let her be in my circle of close friends, but I liked her. She took piano lessons from my mother and Mom said she was very talented, even more in art than in music. When she was seven she started bringing her sketchbook to show Mom.'

A shadow seemed to pass over Edmund's face. 'I didn't know she'd been drawing since she was six. I should have. It must have been about the time my wife had the stillbirth. I started paying more attention to her than to Joy.' He looked away. 'Poor little girl. She deserved so much more than she got from her parents.'

Brynn softened toward him. 'I'm sure you and your wife gave her the best of care. She was a charming, well-mannered child. A *good* child.'

Edmund smiled tremulously.

'I would have sent flowers, but I didn't know about her death until I came here. Cassie told me.'

'You and Cassie stayed close?'

'Yes. I'm staying with her while I'm in town.'

Mindy appeared at the table, looking tragic. 'Oh, Doctor Ellis—'

'I know you're sorry about Joy. She enjoyed coming here and liked you very much.'

'Oh, dear.' Mindy's glittery green-shadowed eyelids batted away tears. 'She always brought her drawing book. She did my picture. Made me look lots prettier than I am. I put it in a frame beside my bed.' She sniffed mightily. 'Oh, gosh.'

'You sent a note telling her how much you liked the sketch. She was very pleased.'

Mindy sniffed mightily. 'Oh, my. I just feel so bad!'

'You mustn't be sad, Mindy,' Edmund said quickly, cutting off what Brynn knew would be a sob. 'Joy was resigned and I think she was relieved – breathing had become difficult. She went peacefully in her sleep. The flowers you sent to the funeral were beautiful. I saw you there. Thank you for coming.' Brynn saw Edmund's eyes focus on a tear running down Mindy's face. 'I'll just have a black coffee this morning.'

'How about a croissant? A muffin? *Anything?*' Mindy almost begged.

'OK, a walnut croissant.'

Mindy smiled shakily, as if he'd done her a favor by ordering food. 'The biggest, freshest one I can find coming right up!'

Brynn could tell Edmund couldn't bear talking about Joy any longer. He looked at her with false brightness. 'What do you think of Genessa Point after all these years?'

'It's bigger. So much of the business district has improved – new upscale stores, older ones looking better after face-lifts.' She paused. 'But it's still Genessa Point.'

'And you hate it.'

'Yes,' Brynn said firmly. 'I've spent eighteen years hating it. You can't expect me to roll into town and suddenly say, "Wow, this place is great!"'

'You came because of Mark.' Brynn looked at him steadily. 'I couldn't believe it when I saw him last week, yet I knew he'd come back eventually.'

Mindy arrived with Edmund's coffee and croissant. 'Your Chocolate Dream OK?' she asked Brynn.

'Great. I'm just taking it slow.'

As soon as Mindy left, Edmund said softly, 'I was sorry to hear about your mother's death last year.'

Brynn felt sympathy toward Edmund for the loss of his daughter, but she couldn't forget how quickly he'd distanced himself from her family after disaster and disgrace had struck. Remembering, she felt a cold lump form in her stomach as she looked at him squarely. 'In all the years after we left town, you never came to see her. Not once.'

'She didn't want to see *me*.'

'Do you blame her? You lied about Dad losing that knife.'

Edmund's gaze shifted. 'I don't remember Jonah losing the knife Mark gave him for his birthday.'

'Are you sure?'

Edmund's gaze sharpened and his eyebrows pulled together. 'I was sure your father used that knife when we went fishing just two weeks before his death.'

'Oh, you're absolutely certain it was the same knife.'

Edmund stared at her.

'You're absolutely certain Dad killed eight people with that particular knife.'

Anger flashed in Edmund's eyes. 'I did *not* tell the police your father killed *anyone*.'

'You might as well have.'

Edmund sighed. 'Brynn,' he said softly. 'Brynn.'

'What?'

'Do I have to go over this again? Your father's knife blade had a nick in the exact place as the knife used to stab Tessa Cavanaugh. The handle had the letters J.W. The DNA on the knife—'

'I don't care about DNA!'

People at other tables turned and looked at Brynn, who'd nearly shouted. She lowered her voice. 'Dad said he hadn't seen that knife for years. He'd bought a new one just like it. If you're not lying, then you made a mistake. You saw the new knife, not the old one!'

'I know Jonah said he bought a knife exactly like the one he lost, but there was no knife in his tackle box or in the woods where Tessa was stabbed. That's what the police kept stating. They only found one knife – the one that stabbed Tessa and killed your father had the initials J.W. on it and the DNA of some of the other murder victims.' Edmund's eyes closed tiredly. 'I'm not going to argue about this with you. I've been over it a hundred times with the police, with myself, with other people.'

'But the knife used to kill him disappeared nearly two years—'

'I told you I'm not going to argue with you anymore, Brynn,' Edmund said quietly but with a whiplash finality.

Brynn turned her attention back to her food, shocked by his stunning change of tone. She tried to compose herself as she sipped hot chocolate and took a bite of her Napoleon. 'You said you saw Mark last week,' she said finally.

'Yes. He came to visit me.' His voice had calmed. 'He talked mostly about Joy. He was very kind – not lingering on the subject too long or asking too many details. He talked about how proud he was of you. He mentioned his divorce but didn't act broken up about it. And we talked about his mother and my wife.'

Cassie had told Brynn about his wife's death two years earlier from cirrhosis. The woman who'd once been Marguerite's friend had started drinking heavily before the Wilders moved away. Edmund had sent seven-year-old Joy away to boarding school as her mother spent two stints in rehab and endured a failed liver transplant. After graduating from college, Joy had moved to another state. Then, a year after her mother's death and as her own health took a steep decline, Joy had come home for good.

Brynn chewed thoughtfully on her pastry before asking, 'Did Mark talk about Dad?'

Edmund flinched. 'No.'

'Are you sure?'

'I think I'd remember.'

'He didn't say he'd found out something about my dad's murder?'

Edmund shook his head.

'But he told Cassie he had. Now he's gone and no one has heard from him for days. Don't tell me you didn't know he's missing.'

'I knew.'

'Don't you find that coincidental?'

'Maybe.'

'*Maybe?* Do you also know that the police found his car with blood on the seats and the floor?' Edmund's face blanched. Obviously he hadn't heard about the car. 'I'm so frightened for him,' Brynn said flatly. 'Why can't you be honest with me about Mark?'

Edmund suddenly leaned forward, his voice deep and fierce. 'You want honesty? Well, here it is. I'm frightened, too, both for Mark *and* you. You shouldn't be here, Brynn. Please, for the love of God, leave Genessa Point before you go missing, too.'

After Edmund left, his coffee and croissant barely touched, Brynn lingered, feeling desolate. She used to love Edmund Ellis and think of him almost as a second father. How could she have been so cold, so unrelenting, so severe? She hadn't been able to stop herself. For the last eighteen years he'd been an enemy, the person who'd damned her father by not affirming he'd lost the knife that someone twisted beyond humanity had used to murder children as well as Jonah Wilder.

Maybe what's devouring you, Brynn, is that *you* are afraid Dad didn't lose the knife, she thought guiltily. She remembered one night in the basement of their house watching Mark frowning ferociously as he worked. 'Are you sure you should be carving J.W. into that pretty wood handle?' she'd asked.

'They're Dad's initials. He'll really like what I'm doing,' Mark had answered confidently. 'Nobody'll ever get his knife mixed up with theirs. They'll know it's his.'

Mark had been pleased with himself, never guessing what a curse those initials would be one day for his father.

'Doctor Ellis didn't eat much.'

Mindy had reappeared and stared at Edmund's croissant and half cup of coffee.

'He was in a hurry.'

'Oh. I was afraid he didn't like the food, although he stops by here every couple of weeks. In the spring, he and his daughter ate here on the patio at least twice a week. She was so pretty and sweet, even when she was getting sicker. I could tell. She was so thin and pale it just broke my heart.' Mindy looked like she was going to cry again.

'I'm sure seeing you every few days cheered her up. Joy must have really liked you or she wouldn't have done a sketch of you. But I'm sure everyone likes you. You're so good with your customers and act like you love what you're doing,' Brynn said, smiling.

'Well, I like people. Most people, that is. The manager says I get too familiar, but I never ask personal questions. I just try to let them know that I remember them.'

'That's an excellent trait in a waitress and I'll tell your manager so if he ever gives you trouble.' Mindy looked pleased and Brynn suddenly had an idea. She reached in her bag and pulled out her wallet. She flipped to a snapshot of Mark taken just a year ago and held it out to Mindy. 'Did you see this guy last week?'

Mindy leaned close and scrutinized the picture. 'Yeah, I did. He's handsome – he looks a little bit like you. Not that you're handsome. You're really pretty.'

'Thanks. Anyway, did you talk to him?'

'Ummm . . .' Mindy stared into the distance. 'Just to say hi and take his order. She scrunched up her round face in ferocious thought. 'Darn! It was near lunchtime and we were getting busy so I don't remember what he ordered. I'm sorry.'

'It doesn't matter. Did he look calm and happy, or maybe worried?'

Mindy's bright orange lips tightened as she thought. 'It seems to me he was OK.' Then she snapped her fingers. '*Now* I remember! Oh, how could I forget?'

'What was it, Mindy?' Brynn asked urgently.

'A woman came by and sat down with him. He looked kind of surprised. They were arguing. She got, well . . . loud is the polite word. She said something about making him pay. I thought, pay for what? You didn't order anything. Then she jumped up and took off in a hurry. Everyone was staring at them! The manager had started to come out just as the handsome guy left, too. He went in the opposite direction of the woman. He left money on the table for his meal and a big tip for me.'

'That must have been bad,' Brynn said quietly, shocked. 'Do you know who the woman was?'

'I don't know her name, but she's tall and slender and has long auburn hair.' Mindy got that strained, thoughtful look again. 'She works at Love's Dress Shoppe and she's been here before with that nice Cassie Hutton.'

EIGHT

'Is something wrong, Miss Wilder?' Mindy asked.

'Yes.' Brynn looked at Mindy's anxious face. 'I mean no – I was just surprised. I think I know who the woman is, but I didn't know my brother did.'

'He's your brother? Oh. Well, maybe I shouldn't have said anything . . .'

Brynn was already standing up, laying down money on the table just as Mark had done last week. 'I'm glad you told me.'

'My boss won't like it – he says I talk too much.'

'Your boss won't know you told me anything.' She smiled at Mindy, who gave her a worried smile in return. She began edging away from the table. 'See you in a day or two.'

Brynn barely remembered driving to Love's Dress Shoppe. At eleven o'clock, the parking lot was already half full but she didn't care about interrupting a busy work day. She needed to find out about Rhonda's public argument with Mark.

Two years ago, over the course of several phone calls, Cassie had told Brynn about her store renovations. Still, her description hadn't prepared Brynn for the shock of seeing neat but uninspired Love's Dress Shoppe turned into a beautiful upscale boutique.

Inside, James Blunt's 'You're Beautiful' played softly. Maple veneer floors gleamed, accented with three large oriental rugs in muted colors, pale lavender walls, ivory damask upholstered chairs and couches, glass-topped tables, and track lighting shining down on artfully displayed merchandise.

Cassie was walking toward the door with a casually elegant middle-aged woman as Brynn hurried inside. 'Brynn!' she said in surprise. 'How nice to see you! I didn't know you were stopping by this morning. Mrs Levitt, this is my friend, Brynn Wilder.'

The name clearly meant nothing to Mrs Levitt, who murmured a polite greeting, then left holding two familiar ivory and gold shopping bags. As she closed one of the double doors behind her, Cassie beamed at Brynn. 'Come back to my office and let's have a cup of coffee. The girls can take care of things without me for a while.'

Brynn cast her gaze over 'the girls,' who consisted of a tall blonde, a short brunette and a woman with salt-and-pepper hair and thin-rimmed glasses.

Cassie shut the door to her sizeable office and motioned Brynn onto a comfortable chair beside her white L-shaped desk littered with stacks of papers, fashion magazines, African violets in a lavender bowl near a window and two framed pictures – one of her parents and one of her and Brynn, arm-in-arm, grinning, at age ten. A laptop computer was pushed aside.

'I hear you eat at Cloud Nine sometimes with an auburn-haired employee.'

'Oh?' Cassie looked at her curiously. 'Hmmm. Well, I suppose that would be Rhonda Sanford. I told you about her. Who said I've been there with her? No, let me guess. Mindy.'

'Yes, Mindy of the shocking pink hair. She's a nice girl.'

Cassie sat down. 'I agree. So, what's the big deal about me being there with Rhonda?'

'I thought she wasn't your friend.'

'She's not. I mean, we're cordial, but that's all.' Cassie paused. 'I try to keep a good relationship with all of my employees, Brynn. I take each one to lunch about three times a year. Always something casual.' She frowned. 'Why are you so interested in Rhonda? Because she used to date Garrett?'

'Garrett! What does he have to do with this? I couldn't care less who Garrett Dane dated.'

'OK, *ok*, I'm sorry I even hinted at such a thing. Geez, Brynn.'

Brynn realized her voice had risen. Embarrassed, she overcompensated by speaking in an almost hushed tone. 'I'm interested in Rhonda because Mindy said one day Mark was having lunch at Cloud Nine and a woman with auburn hair who works for you stopped by his table, sat down and started an argument. It must have been Rhonda, and I'd like to know how she knew Mark and why the hell she attacked him.'

'*Attacked?*' Cassie asked cautiously.

'Oh, not physically.' Brynn paused. 'She started a quarrel.'

'Yeah, but was Mindy sure Rhonda started it?'

'Yes.' Brynn waited a beat. 'I think. She was busy.'

Cassie sighed. 'We got in a new shipment today and Rhonda's in the storeroom, organizing things. She's much better at organizing than I am. Do you want me to call her in?'

'I'd appreciate it, Cassie. I promise not to be antagonistic. I'll just act . . . curious.'

'You might get Mindy in trouble with her boss for gossiping about customers.'

'No, I won't. Cass, please.'

Without a word, Cassie left the office. In five minutes, she returned with the tall, slender woman whose features and slightly tilted cool gray eyes could have gotten her a photo in *Vogue*. Brynn guessed her to be in her early thirties.

'Rhonda Sanford, this is Brynn Wilder,' Cassie said, smiling.

'We've met,' Rhonda said tonelessly. 'Briefly.'

'Oh, yes, she did mention that.' Cassie's voice sounded high and unnatural. She's afraid one of us is going to cause a scene, Brynn thought.

'Brynn and I have been friends since we were about three years old,' Cassie went on. 'I'm sure you've heard of her wonderful books.'

Rhonda appeared to be thinking before she said, 'No, I haven't, but I'm sure the books are entertaining. Hello again, Miss Wilder.'

'Please call me Brynn. Cassie's told me a lot about you.'

'Oh, really?'

'I mean that you're a great employee. A master salesperson, wonderful at organization, a real asset to Love's . . .' Brynn ran down. Rhonda raised an eyebrow. 'She values your work.'

'I'm glad. Is that why you wanted to talk to me?'

'Well, no. Of course not. I wanted to talk to you about something in particular.'

'I think I'll see how things are going in the showroom,' Cassie said hastily.

Rhonda still stood, gazing at Brynn without blinking. 'Please have a seat, Rhonda. This might take a few minutes.' The woman crossed the small room, sat down gracefully in Cassie's desk chair, crossed her long legs and folded her slender, manicured hands in her lap. 'I want to talk about . . . well . . . a quarrel you had with a man at Cloud Nine last week.' Rhonda's expression didn't change, but her eyelids fluttered. 'That man was my brother, Mark.'

'Yes, I know. Mark Wilder, the son of Jonah Wilder.'

The son of Jonah Wilder. Just the way Rhonda emphasized Mark's identity angered Brynn, although she'd been certain the argument had been to do with her father. Still, she sensed the woman sitting calmly in front of her wouldn't respond to a demand for information. She had to tread carefully.

'May I ask what you and Mark quarreled about?' she asked, thinking she sounded stiff and old-fashioned but polite.

'Who said we had a *quarrel*?' Rhonda was subtly making fun of Brynn's choice of words, amping up Brynn's antagonism. Brynn tried to keep her voice neutral.

'You were on the patio of a crowded restaurant. Quite a few people saw and heard you, Rhonda. You know how word travels in this town.'

Rhonda gave her another long, steady look, as if sizing her up. Brynn fought the impulse to shift positions or smile, something to break the tension. Finally, Rhonda began slowly and distinctly. 'I had a cousin named Frankie Gaines. My aunt Miranda didn't have him until she was forty-five. He was her only child. She worshipped him. I was like his big sister. My mother was single and we spent every holiday and most of every summer here in Genessa Point with my aunt and uncle and Frankie. Twenty years ago, when Frankie was eight, the Genessa Point Killer murdered him. My uncle had a fatal heart attack after the police found Frankie's body.'

After a short pause, Brynn said softly, 'I'm very sorry, Rhonda.'

'Aunt Miranda still lives here. She was never the same after her husband's and son's deaths, though. She's in her seventies, frail and sickly,' Rhonda continued in a monotone. 'Mark Wilder had the nerve to come back to this town, still banging away at clearing his father's name. He went to see Miranda. She called my apartment when I got home from work. She was terribly upset. The next day, I saw him at Cloud Nine and told him I wouldn't stand for him harassing my aunt. I told him I would have Garrett Dane, our sheriff and *my* lover, run him out of town.'

'You're sure he tried to talk to your aunt?'

'Of course I'm sure and I knew he wouldn't stop. I know he's your brother, Lynn, but I also know he was his father's partner in the killings, or it's possible he might have murdered Frankie all by himself. Garrett thinks so, too. Mark knew I saw right through him and that I would *not* let him hurt anyone else, certainly not my aunt! Afterward, I left him to think long and hard about everything I'd said.' Rhonda paused. 'Does that answer your question, Lynn?'

'It's *Brynn*,' she hissed as red hot fury erupted in her. She could barely stop herself from lunging across the room and grabbing

Rhonda's long, slender neck. Which is exactly what people would expect from the daughter of Stone Jonah Wilder, Brynn thought. Instead she stiffened, holding herself as rigid as possible, and tried to push down her volcanic anger. Still, it took nearly fifteen seconds before she could speak with near-calm.

'That was an extremely succinct account, Rhonda. It sounded almost rehearsed.'

'I've been through the story before. With Garrett. Sheriff Dane.'

'I know who Garrett is. I've known him since he was twelve,' Brynn snapped. 'What was his reaction?'

'He's always concerned about keeping peace in town. However, he was more concerned about me.'

'He wasn't mad at you?'

'Mad that I'd had the nerve to confront Mark Wilder? No. He was just—'

'Concerned about you. So you said. Did you tell Mark you'd make him pay?'

Rhonda raised her thin, penciled eyebrows. 'I don't remember. I was furious. Maybe I did. Probably not.' She uncrossed her legs and her expression hardened. 'I don't have any more to tell you about my encounter with Mark. I haven't seen him since that day.'

'And he didn't try to see your aunt again?'

'No. I've heard he's disappeared.' She shrugged. 'Good riddance.' Rhonda stood up. 'I really have a lot of work to do unless I want to stay past closing time, which I don't. I have a date.'

As she walked out the door, Brynn restrained herself. She wouldn't let the woman goad her into a nasty retort, although a dozen flashed through her mind. Of all the nerve, the insolence, the gall! She should tell Cassie, but Brynn wouldn't put her friend in the position of possibly firing her best employee. Besides, the idea that she'd needled Brynn into 'tattling' to Cassie would just be another triumph for Rhonda.

So, enraged as she was, Brynn merely sat still, replaying Rhonda's conversation. Was she lying? Had she really said all of those things to Mark? Had she accused him of killing her little cousin, Frankie? Had she threatened him and told him she'd make him pay? Brynn didn't think Mindy had lied – and if she'd been serious about making Mark pay, of seeking retribution, just how did she intend to do it?

Also, Brynn couldn't stop herself from wondering whether, as of last week, Garrett Dane had still been this chilly, unnervingly composed woman's lover.

'Going out for lunch today, Sheriff?'

Garrett Dane looked at the eager new deputy standing near the front doors of headquarters. 'Yeah. Lunch will be short, though. I've got a lot of work.' Garrett decided he really needed to get out of this building and clear his head. He couldn't remember the guy's name. 'How's it going?'

'Fine, sir. Just fine.'

'Good.' Garrett searched for something else to say. 'Glad to hear it.'

As he walked down the steps to the sidewalk, Garrett drew a deep breath. The air felt especially clean and refreshing. Either that, he decided, or he was spacey from lack of sleep and growing uneasiness about Rhonda. At midnight, she'd called him on his cell phone, counting on privacy from Savannah, whom she seemed to blame for what she termed their 'breakup.' She always acted as if they'd had a long and loving relationship instead of a four-month affair that, for Garrett, had nothing to do with love. Attraction, yes. Passion, yes. Love, no.

Often he told himself he shouldn't feel guilty about Rhonda. He'd never said he loved her. He'd never hinted at a future together. He'd spent so little time with her he could remember every date – three movies, two dinners in nice restaurants, a birthday party Savannah and Grams had planned for him, the wedding of a friend, three home-cooked meals at her house. Four of those dates had been followed by an hour or two of lovemaking. Although at first the sex had been pleasurable, the last two times he'd left her house feeling as if ivy were twining around him, tying him to her, trying to pull him back. The illusion was right out of a fairytale book that had belonged to a young Savannah, but he couldn't shake it. That's when he'd begun trying to put distance between them.

In May, when Savannah's great-grandmother died, Rhonda had forced herself deep into his world, trying to plan the funeral, prying into details about the dispensation of the estate, exerting authority over Savannah as if she were Garrett's wife. That's when he knew he'd let their 'relationship' go on too long. He hadn't meant for it to happen; he hadn't fully realized it *was* happening, but in Rhonda's mind, he was hers. Even worse, her possessiveness of him caused her to resent Savannah. At first she'd tried to hide it, but toward the end it grew more evident every day.

A week after the funeral, he'd given Rhonda a kind but firm goodbye. She'd turned to stone when he said he'd decided they weren't right for each other, which, at the time, he'd thought was good. Only two weeks later, he'd realized that stoniness had been a sign of her unrelenting resolve that he would be hers, body, soul and wedding.

Garrett felt guilty. Certainly he'd done *something* to make Rhonda behave the way she had at the end, the way she was acting now. She managed to run into him at least three times a week. She called his home in the evenings and talked, argued and pleaded until he finally told her goodnight and unplugged the landline phones in the house so Savannah could sleep. Then he'd gotten an unlisted number for their home phone.

Until last week, Rhonda hadn't known his cell phone number. She'd managed to find it out, though, and she'd called four times in the past five days. And now she'd finally called headquarters. Less than an hour ago, she'd phoned to report that Brynn Wilder had ambushed her at work and grilled her 'unmercifully' about Mark. When Garrett had cut off her rant by hanging up, he'd rushed from the building, as if being outdoors could quiet his growing uneasiness. God, he was beginning to feel like the guy in *Fatal Attraction*, he thought in despair.

He headed to Savannah's temporary place of employment. About thirty feet ahead a big red and white umbrella shaded a large aluminum portable hot dog cart. A cluster of people dressed in vivid summer wear stood in two lines, some of the younger children laughing and roughhousing until called down by their parents. Garrett took his place in Savannah's line, watching his daughter work even more efficiently than Mrs Elbert yet never forgetting to smile at the customers.

Finally his turn came. 'Hello, madam. I'll take two of your finest hot dogs.'

Savannah glanced up and laughed. 'Dad! I didn't even really look at you!'

'I'm just another face in the crowd, huh? And after all the years I've devoted to you – changing diapers, calming temper tantrums, putting Band-Aids on skinned knees—'

'Enough!' Savannah giggled. 'You said you want *two* hot dogs?'

'No breakfast. I was running late.'

Savannah lowered her voice. 'That's because you spent half the night on the phone with Rhonda.'

Garrett's expression grew serious. 'Were you eavesdropping?'

'No! I'd never do that. You got kinda loud a couple of times.' Savannah's beautiful blue eyes lowered. 'What toppings do you want?'

'Ummm, ketchup and relish. No onions. And a large Coke.' While Savannah went to work, Garrett looked down at Henry, who sat obediently by her side, panting. 'You brought Henry?'

'Did you expect me to desert him?' she asked, appalled, as if he'd suggested leaving a two-year-old child home alone.

'I'm sorry. I forget what a protective mother you are,' Garrett said dryly. He paid for his hot dogs and then gave the real canine a last glance. 'Honey, I think Henry could use a walk and I could use some company. How about letting me take him across the street to the park? I'll sit on a bench and he can wander around, sniff everything, confide secrets to me.'

Savannah grinned. 'I think he'd like that.' She put the hot dogs and drink in a box. 'And I hope you like your hot dogs, sir.'

'I'm sure I will.' He balanced his lunch in one hand and took Henry's leash in the other. 'We both promise to behave.'

'You'd better. I have connections in the police department,' Savannah told him ominously.

In Holly Park, Garrett let Henry lead for a few minutes before he sat down on a bench, holding his hot dogs absently as his thoughts took a dismal turn. So, last night his precious daughter had overheard him talking to – maybe shouting at – Rhonda after midnight. She'd sounded slightly drunk at first, then become increasingly loud and irrational until he'd hung up on her. He didn't remember her having more than a glass of wine when they'd first begun seeing each other. When had things changed? He couldn't remember. He'd liked her at first and even thought maybe there was potential for a romance. Then she'd slowly become possessive, demanding and erratic. They'd been apart for weeks but she still called his home. What next? He regretted ever dating – even meeting – Rhonda Sanford.

'You look like you've got the weight of the world on your shoulders, Sheriff.'

Garrett looked up to see Nathan Cavanaugh, smiling, slim, tanned and still boyishly handsome at thirty-five. 'Nathan! I haven't seen you for over a year.'

'Would I miss the One-Hundred-and-Fiftieth Festival? My sister would have killed me.'

'Have a seat. Want one of my hot dogs?'

'I'm meeting Tessa for lunch. I wanted to take her to a restaurant, but she tells me she always make sandwiches and eats here in the park. She's bringing enough for two.' He made a face. 'That means two cold sandwiches, two apple juice boxes and, if I'm lucky, an extra Twinkie.'

'When did you get here?'

'Last night. I've been in Rio de Janeiro the past few weeks.'

'You poor guy. Must be hell developing software and hardware technologies for maritime training systems, traveling all over the world teaching your brilliant inventions. Did I get that right?'

'Partly. My systems *are* brilliant. But I don't get to go all over the world. Only the places with major shipping ports.'

'Sounds like a snooze to an exciting guy like me.'

Nathan grinned. 'So how's life as the sheriff of Genessa Point?'

'Non-stop action. Danger every day. They should make a TV show about my life.'

Nathan burst into laughter. 'Your sense of humor often went unappreciated back in the day, Garrett. However, I have a feeling you're not as bored as you pretend. You wouldn't want to live my life and also bring up a twelve-year-old girl.'

'She's thirteen. And you're right. Savannah and I have a good life here – quiet, but good.'

'Anyone special in your good life besides Savannah?'

Oh yeah, Garrett thought. Rhonda Sanford. What more could a man want? ''Fraid not, Nate. Not a lot of single women around here.'

'There's always my sister.'

Garrett searched wildly for something appropriate to say until Nathan reached out and nudged his arm.

'Don't look so scared of saying the wrong thing! I'm kidding,' Nathan laughed. 'I love Tessa, but I know she's an acquired taste.'

Garrett relaxed, trying for a natural smile. 'How is she these days?'

'About the same as always.' Nathan's laughter died and he gazed into the distance. 'Since she was a little kid, she was never like other girls. Really shy, overly sensitive, always living in her head. She didn't have any close friends – didn't seem to want any. She was happy with solitary stuff like reading and puzzles.' His mood changed and he suddenly laughed. 'God, I thought she'd drive us nuts with those huge jigsaw puzzles – you know, the kind that have a thousand pieces and take up a whole tabletop. Then she got interested in photography and we were all relieved. But after Jonah Wilder . . .' Nathan suddenly looked uneasy. 'Well, she was never the same. She started acting *really* different than other girls. She's not crazy like a lot of people think,' he clarified immediately. 'She's just . . . different.'

'Well, that's understandable,' Garrett said mildly. He knew he should say more, but once again, he found himself short on words. To his relief, Nathan smiled and said, 'Speaking of Tessa, here she comes with our gourmet lunch.'

Tessa moved in her usual slow, slightly aimless way across the park until she spotted them and almost stopped, looking uncertain. 'Look who I've found, Tess,' Nathan called. 'The sheriff is going to share lunch with us.'

'Oh,' she said doubtfully, drawing nearer. 'I'm not sure I brought enough for three.'

'I already have my lunch,' Garrett said, holding up a hot dog. 'Courtesy of my daughter. She's working at the hot dog stand across the street.'

'Savannah. She's a lovely girl – careful with the books, and so quiet in the library.' Only Tessa Cavanaugh could make 'quiet in the library' a compliment, Garrett thought. She sat down cross-legged on the ground in front of him and Nathan, spreading her full skirt carefully over her legs. 'I see you've brought her dog with you. Harry, is it?'

'Henry. Savannah named him for her maternal great-grandfather.'

'I hope he appreciated the honor,' Nathan laughed as he petted the dog.

'He did,' Garrett smiled. 'He's dead now.'

'What a shame. And your father?' Tessa asked. 'Wasn't his name William?'

'Yes. William Bale Dane,' Garrett said flatly. 'He's dead, too.'

Tessa gave him a tremulous smile. 'He was good to me after the . . . accident in the woods.' She blushed and said quickly, 'I'm sure Savannah loved him.'

'She didn't know my father.' Thank God, Garrett thought, remembering his frustrated, lightning-tempered father. He wouldn't have wanted Savannah to know him. 'He died before she was born.'

'What a shame,' Tessa mourned as she pulled sandwiches from a paper sack. She glanced at Henry, then handed a foil-wrapped antiseptic towelette to Nathan, who rolled his eyes at Garrett as he obliged. Henry then nosed at Tessa, who cringed away from him.

'Back, Henry,' Garrett said. 'Not everyone loves dogs.'

'Oh, I like dogs,' Tessa said solemnly. 'I'm just a little bit afraid of big dogs, even if they seem well-mannered.' She brushed crumbs from her old-fashioned pink gingham dress with a slightly scooped neck. The sun that turned her brother's hair golden emphasized the gray in her own. Her lackluster, dull blonde hair was pulled back, as always, with a ribbon. Her skin looked pale and dry, the light shone harshly on the narrow scar running from the top of her ear down her neck and collarbone and her sparse blonde lashes were untouched by mascara. The years had blessed Nathan but not Tessa. She glanced at Garrett with candid blue eyes. 'Is something wrong?'

'Not at all,' Garrett said too quickly.

'Sheriff, some people have told me that Mark Wilder came to town last week. Is it true?' she asked.

Garrett glanced at Tessa, whose hands had begun to tremble. 'He's gone,' Garrett said firmly. He wasn't going to discuss an ongoing case with them. He also wasn't going to make Tessa more anxious. 'He left on Saturday.'

'He did?' Tessa asked in a small voice.

'No one's seen him since then. The motel manager last saw him Saturday evening. His motel room hadn't been used Saturday night. I guess he didn't feel welcome here.'

Tessa looked at Garrett doubtfully. 'You're sure he's gone?'

'I've looked for him,' he said truthfully. 'I can't find a trace.' Except for his car with bloodstains inside, Garrett thought, and I'm sure as hell not going to talk about that.

'But Brynn's here.' Tessa wasn't going to let the subject go. 'Don't you think she came with her brother or maybe to meet him?'

'I know she didn't come with her brother. Cassie Hutton's been her friend all these years and she wanted Brynn to come to the festival. Brynn is staying with Cassie.' He paused. 'Mark left before Brynn even got here.'

'Oh,' Tessa murmured. Then she surprised him. 'Do you know I used to have a crush on Mark?'

'Uh . . . you did?' Garrett was flummoxed. She was talking about once having a crush on a guy who now terrified her.

'Yes. I think I made a fool of myself. I never knew how to act like the other girls – pretty, feminine girls.'

'You were just young, Tessa,' Garrett answered off-handedly. 'All girls go through an awkward stage.'

'Not Savannah.'

'Oh, yes. She just never shows it in public.' He winked at Tessa. 'Very aware of her image and all that. But she's not what she calls one of the "cool girls."' He paused. 'I think she'd like to be Taylor Swift.'

Tessa smiled at Garrett. He caught Nathan's sharp, knowing glance that said he realized how uncomfortable Mark Wilder's visit to Genessa Point made his sister and he was grateful for Garrett turning the subject light. Garrett focused on Tessa.' 'The festival's bigger than ever this year. We're having a carnival, fireworks displays over the bay every night, boat rides on the bay, an outdoor play—'

'Tessa wrote the play and is directing it,' Nathan interrupted with pride.

'Oh, I know all about the play. Savannah's in it. She's rehearsed so much you'd think she was making her debut on Broadway.' Garrett looked at the faded woman sitting on the grass like a little girl. 'Tessa, you've been busy! Writing and directing.' Garrett hoped he didn't sound too amazed that reclusive Tessa Cavanaugh was so involved in the play. 'I had no idea you were so talented,' he added heartily, wishing he could shut up.

Tessa didn't seem to notice, though. 'I have been busy. At least, busy in a different way than usual,' she said diffidently. 'I've always tended to all my outdoor flower gardens. Father loved my flower gardens.'

Nathan gave her a disbelieving look before he said, 'He griped about you always "messing with those damned flowers" as he put it. Remember that year he dug up all those pansies you'd planted and threw them all over the yard? You were so upset.'

'Nathan, please!' Tessa's cheeks turned red as she looked at Garrett. 'That was just two years ago. Father wasn't well and resented the world for his illness,' she said regretfully. 'Also, he was annoyed with me about something – I don't recall what it was now.'

'So he tore up your pansies?' Garrett asked. 'Did you plant new ones?'

'They were petunias and no, I didn't plant anything in that garden. Nothing would have grown.'

'Why not?' Garrett asked.

Tessa shrugged. 'Because it was a graveyard.' She looked at Garrett again. 'Some people think I'm strange, but I know flowers have feelings. If I'd planted new ones, the sadness of that garden would have caused their death.'

They're right – you are strange, Garrett thought, but gave her a smile. 'Maybe so.'

'That was an unfortunate incident I don't like to remember. It certainly wasn't Father at his best,' Tessa said gently. 'In earlier years, he was always proud of how I maintained all of our home's gardens and grounds.'

'We only have three acres, Tess, and a couple of buildings for yard equipment and your gardening stuff.' Nathan suddenly sounded irritable. 'It's not an estate, for God's sake, and we have people to do most of the lawn work. You only planted a few flower gardens.'

Tessa's gaze dropped. 'Five, Nate. Five large gardens. Last year I won the Good Gardener Award from the Garden Club.' Her voice dipped to a mournful whisper. 'I was so pleased and proud. I'd never won anything in my whole life before then.'

Garrett thought she was going to burst into tears. His spirits plummeted. God, all he'd wanted was a peaceful lunch. Was he going to end up with a sobbing Tessa Cavanaugh? Then Nathan looked at his stricken sister. A mixture of pity and frustration crossed his face and he managed to rescue the moment. 'I just think it's time for men to be bringing you flowers instead of you raising them, sis.'

Tessa sniffed, her eyes still downcast.

'Savannah and I walk Henry every evening. We usually go down Oriole Lane, but after you won that award, Savannah insisted we see your flower gardens,' Garrett said.

'You did?' Tessa asked.

'Sure. You live near us. It was a nice change from our usual walking route and the gardens were beautiful. Savannah was dazzled. Well, we both were.'

'How about Henry?' Nathan asked seriously.

'He barked three times then howled,' Garrett returned just as seriously.

'Oh, you two,' Tessa said, finally almost smiling.

'I didn't mean to hurt your feelings about the flowers,' Nathan said to Tessa, then looked at Garrett. 'I have to leave next week and I'm taking Tessa with me. We're going to Casablanca, Morocco.'

'Oh, dear,' Tessa uttered, as if afraid.

'You haven't been away from this town for so long, you've dug in roots deeper than your cherry trees,' Nathan went on, undaunted. 'But just wait until you see a completely different part of the world.' Once again he looked at Garrett. 'And she's not just going for her two-week summer vacation. She's taking a leave of absence from the library. We're not sure for how long, yet, but I'm not going to let her leave Genessa Point just to come running back in fourteen days or less. After Casablanca, we'll travel for a few weeks and have some fun.' He leaned down and tilted his head at his sister, giving her that movie-star smile. 'You promised me, didn't you?'

'Y-yes. It's just that . . . well, it's so far away and Dad hasn't been gone for very long. There's still estate business we must attend to and . . .'

'And you're just scared. I'm going to see that you have the best time of your life, though, Tess.' Nathan nearly glowed as he talked to her. 'Honest, cross my heart, Scout's honor—'

'All right.' Tessa finally giggled like a little girl. 'We'll go and I'll have a wonderful time!'

'You sure will because I make every day a joy, Tess,' Nathan joked. 'You know I do. Garrett knows, too, from the old days when we were lighthearted teenage boys.'

Garrett said dryly, 'Yeah, sure. In the old days, we both caused trouble and I always got the blame.'

'We weren't the only troublemakers.' Nathan grinned. 'Mark Wilder was the worst,' he said, then looked as if he could bite his tongue.

The levity of the moment died again when Tessa quickly asked, 'What did Mark do?'

'Oh, just his fair share of troublemaking,' Nathan answered with false easiness.

Tessa seemed to know her brother too well. 'You might as well tell me. I'll keep pestering you until you do.'

Nathan sighed. 'I guess letting Garrett take the blame for something fairly bad that *he* did was the worst.' Tessa raised a pale eyebrow and Nathan went on. 'Mark got a mannequin from the store where his mother worked and threw it on the highway late one night. A car ran over it and slammed to a halt. The wife and one of the kids in the car were hurt pretty bad. Anyway, Mark told Sheriff Dane that Garrett threw the mannequin on the highway and the sheriff gave Garrett worse than hell for it.'

'My goodness, how awful!' Tessa exclaimed.

Scalding fury flashed through Garrett at the memory of his father's belt hitting him until it drew blood. It hadn't been the first time that belt had struck him – only one of many times – but it had been the worst. His back and legs had hurt so badly he couldn't walk normally for over a week. After all these years, though, he was able to keep his outward expression benign no matter how vividly he remembered the pain.

'You must have resented Mark so much!' Tessa said, looking at Garrett with deep understanding.

'Oh, I was mad back then, but it was nearly a lifetime ago. Besides, Mark was a year younger than me and terrified,' Garrett said calmly. 'I didn't suffer any permanent damage, so it's all water under the bridge.'

'But what he did later . . . what people said he did, helping his father murder those kids. How did you feel then?'

Garrett paused. 'I don't remember how I felt except that maybe he was being blamed for something he didn't do.'

'You don't think he was his father's accomplice?' Tessa asked in surprise.

'The police never found any evidence that he was, which doesn't mean it didn't exist.' He could feel himself beginning to sweat. 'It's a beautiful day. Let's appreciate it and not talk about the past.' He flashed a smile at Tessa. 'Hey, do you happen to have an extra Twinkie for a hungry sheriff in that bag?'

NINE

Brynn waited a few minutes after Rhonda left Cassie's office before she walked out of the store at a leisurely pace. Brynn didn't want any of the other saleswomen to tell Rhonda that she'd seemed flustered or upset. Nevertheless, she merely gave Cassie a casual wave, which looked natural considering that Cassie was helping a customer.

Once in the car, though, Brynn sat drawing deep breaths until her heart slowed. That insufferable bitch! How could Garrett have been her boyfriend? No, correct that. 'Lover,' she'd said aloud. Who referred to someone as their *lover*? Someone wanting to make a point. Someone who didn't know that Savannah had already confided that her dad no longer wanted Rhonda's company. Not that I care, of course, Brynn reminded herself. She didn't care how many girlfriends Garrett had. It was only the term *lover* that had—

That had what? Annoyed her? Embarrassed her?

Made her jealous?

Brynn felt color rush to her cheeks. Jealous! Jealous of a boy she'd found mildly intriguing when she was twelve? Jealous over a man she wasn't even sure she liked? How ridiculous!

She threw the car into reverse and zoomed out of her parking space, narrowly missing a passing car. The other driver hit the horn, glaring at her. I deserved that, Brynn thought, glad she was wearing her sunglasses. She took two more deep breaths and crept from the parking lot, a model of careful driving.

Back on the highway, Brynn couldn't decide where to go next. She berated herself for not having a plan, then eased up. How could she have a plan of action when she had no idea where to look for Mark? She didn't even know exactly where his car had been found other than behind a cluster of trees about ten miles south of town. *About* ten miles. And how far off the road? Why hadn't she asked Garrett for more details when she'd been at headquarters this morning? Because she'd been too busy ranting about her mother's compact being left on Cassie's porch. And after that scene, she certainly couldn't return to Garrett's office now.

Disheartened, Brynn turned on the CD player and the car filled with the discordant sounds of a jazz number. Jazz? Cassie hated jazz. Then Brynn remembered – this had been Ray's car that he'd lost in the divorce. Brynn quickly turned off the music. She didn't like most jazz any better than Cassie did. Besides, it reminded her of Ray O'Hara, whom she also didn't like. What had Cassie ever seen in him besides his good looks?

Over Fifty Years of Service
Fenney Realty

The billboard words stood out in bold red against the blues, greens, tans and yellows of the Chesapeake Bay. Beneath them in slightly smaller letters was the address of the company and beside them beamed the face of Sam Fenney as it must have been at least fifteen years ago. In his dreams. Brynn couldn't help laughing. Who would have thought Sam Fenney would stoop to photoshopping? But the sign had been exactly that – a sign of what she needed to do next.

Twenty minutes later, Brynn parked, fed the meter and began walking. The sun felt softly warm on her neck exposed by the heavy hair she'd pulled up in a ponytail. She liked the rustic look of the new brick sidewalks and tree borders, and the old-fashioned globe street lights that gave this section the look of a quaint, picture postcard town. If Genessa Point had no history for her, she would like it, she mused. She would find it picturesque, the atmosphere slow and peaceful. Experience had taught her, though, that Genessa Point was not peaceful. Brick sidewalks and old-fashioned lampposts could not hide the ugliness bubbling beneath the pretty surface.

Brynn was so lost in thought she almost walked past Fenney Realty. She backed up two steps and entered a cool room decorated in tones of lime green and beige. A pretty young blonde sat behind a large desk scattered with at least a dozen folders and a flourishing philodendron. 'Hi!' Bright tone, and an even brighter smile accented with sheer red lip gloss. 'Can I help you on this beautiful day?'

'I hope so. I'm Brynn Wilder and—'

'Oh! Brynn Wilder!' Her lovely blue eyes lit up. 'I heard you were in town. I read your books. I helped my niece do a report on you. What an honor!'

'Thank you,' Brynn said, slightly embarrassed by the gushing, although the waiting room was empty. 'I hope the teacher liked your niece's report.'

'Oh, yes! She got an A!' By now the young woman had risen and was partially leaning across the desk to shake hands. 'Could I get your autograph? Oh, that would just make my niece's whole year!'

'Lexa, what's all the fuss out here?'

'Oh, I'm sorry, Mr Fenney but Brynn Wilder is here! She's an *author*! Her books are published all over the world—'

'I know who Brynn is.' Brynn turned to see Sam smiling. 'I've known Brynn most of her life. Do you think we could get Miss Wilder some coffee or a soft drink?'

'Oh, sure. I didn't even think to ask. Miss Wilder?'

'Call me Brynn, and I'd like some black coffee.'

'I'm with a client right now,' Sam told her as Lexa hurried to the coffee maker, 'but we should be finished very soon. Mind waiting?'

'Not at all. I'll stay with Lexa until you're finished.'

Lexa returned, beaming. 'It's a good thing I put on a fresh pot of coffee ten minutes ago. Is it all right?'

Brynn took a sip. 'Perfect.'

She and Lexa were laughing over some of the off-the-wall comments people wrote to Brynn about her books when Sam ushered out Edmund Ellis. Brynn's eyes widened in surprise but Sam had obviously told Edmund that Brynn was in the waiting room.

'Hello, Brynn,' he said easily with a smile that didn't reach his eyes. He looked slightly wary. 'Stopping in to see Sam for a tour of your old house?'

'I've heard it's on the market again but I don't have any particular desire to see it. How about you?'

Edmund flushed. 'Do I want to see it? No. I'm here on business. I've decided to sell my house.'

'Really?' Brynn was surprised. 'But it's been in your family for what – two generations?'

'My grandfather built it back in the twenties.' Some of the guardedness left Edmund's tired eyes. 'Frankly, I've never really liked it. He's probably turning over in his grave right now, but it's the truth. Aside from not liking it, my wife died in it three years ago and my darling Joy less than two weeks ago and—' His voice thickened. 'I've been offered a partnership with an old friend who's opening a clinic in San Francisco and I think it's the perfect opportunity for me to move on. I need a complete change of scene.'

Although Brynn had harbored a resentment of Edmund for eighteen years, her throat tightened. This man had been her father's best friend. Long ago, the families had enjoyed picnics together and occasional birthday dinners. They'd been fun, Edmund usually the life and soul of the party, his wife amusing and pleasantly gregarious until the stillbirth of their second child had turned her somber and remote.

'This town will miss you,' Brynn said quietly.

'Maybe. I hope I touched a few lives for the good.' He gave her another one of his empty smiles. 'I wish you all the best, Brynn. You and Mark.'

Then he was out the door.

A few minutes later in Sam's office, she said, 'I can't believe he's selling his house.'

'It's just a house now that he has no family. An empty house. It won't be easy to get rid of – it's big and dated – but the market's picking up. Besides, I don't think Edmund is in immediate need of money.' He gave her a warm look. 'What can I do for you, Brynn?'

'Maybe the same thing Mark asked you to do. Give me information about our old house.'

Sam's smile faded as he walked behind his desk and sat down. 'I've told you it's for sale. Been sitting empty for six months. Mark wanted a tour of the inside. Do you want to see it?'

'I want more than that.' And I'm sure Mark did, too, Brynn thought. 'Our house sold less than three months after we left town. That was a godsend. We had a savings account and Mark's and my college funds, but still – well, I don't have to tell you how things were for us financially. Selling that particular house so quickly was beyond lucky. What was the appeal? Don't tell me it was its background.'

'The buyers knew the history of the house but that had nothing to do with their interest.'

'Then what was it?'

Sam didn't answer. Instead, he began typing on his computer, and in a moment had an answer. 'The house wasn't sold to a family, Brynn. Farrah-Stef Realty bought it for a very reasonable price.'

'Who's that?'

'It's a company owned by Kalidone Corporation.'

'Kalidone Corporation? I never heard of them. What do they make?'

'They're a widely diversified corporation. Apparently they make a lot of things.' Brynn stared at him for a moment. 'These details can be very boring and frankly, I'm no computer whiz, but maybe I can be of more help.' Sam began pecking clumsily at keys on his computer. 'Umm, I'm afraid I'm not finding much,' he mumbled, still tapping keys and peering at the monitor. After mumbling, 'Well, hummm,' and 'That's frustrating,' twice, he looked up and shook his head. 'Not much luck, I'm afraid.'

'I thought you said Kalidone was widely diversified.'

'It was, but we're talking about eighteen years ago, Brynn. You know the shape the economy's been in during all that time. Mergers. Corporate takeovers.'

'Yes, I do, but for a major corporation to vanish with no information on the internet seems strange.'

'I doubt if it just vanished. Kalidone probably merged with another corporation and they changed the name. Or it could have been bought by a larger corporation. Absorbed, sort of.'

'Absorbed.'

'Yes, when it became part of the larger business—'

'I understand what "absorbed" means, Sam.' I don't understand why you're talking to me like I'm a child, she thought. 'Never mind Kalidone. What about the realty company? Feron-Step?'

'Farrah-Stef.' He spelled it.

'Well, what's going on with Farrah-Stef?'

'Let's seeeeee . . .' Sam's forehead wrinkled. Again he poked at keys, muttered 'oops' a couple of times and finally peered at the monitor. 'Well, shoot,' he said finally. 'There's nothing.' He looked up and smiled. 'Nothing.'

'Nothing,' Brynn repeated flatly. 'Did Mark ask you these questions?'

'Some of them. I told him the same thing. It's frustrating.'

Yes, Brynn thought. Damned frustrating. And odd. So is your lack of reaction, the carefully empty look in your eyes, the frozen smile on your face. She stared at Sam. His smile didn't waver. Obviously time to give up.

'Well, thanks so much for your help, Sam.'

'Do you want to tour your old house?'

'Maybe another day.'

'Fine, but I have a client who's extremely interested. I think he might make a good offer soon, so if you do want to see it, let me know, day or evening.' Sam paused, frowning at her. 'Brynn, are you going to keep up this search for the original buyers?'

Was she imagining the trace of anxiety in his voice? Brynn decided to be careful. 'If you can't find anything about those companies, then I'm sure I can't. I'm no computer whiz, either.' She laughed. 'I don't even remember the companies' names, anyway.'

'Farrah-Stef Realty, Kalidone Corporation,' she said to herself for the fifth time as she climbed into her car and waved gaily at Sam, who stared at her thoughtfully from his office window.

It was nearly five when Brynn pulled onto Cassie's driveway. She felt like she'd run a marathon although she'd accomplished little in terms of finding Mark or even tracing his footsteps since he'd arrived in Genessa Point. Distracted, she fished in her oversized bag for the house keys when the front door swung open and a man said, 'As I live and breathe! If it isn't the famous Brynn Wilder.'

Ray O'Hara – Cassie's ex-husband – stood in front of her: tall and muscular, with longish, coarse rusty-brown hair pulled back in a ponytail and slightly bloodshot olive-green eyes regarding her with a self-satisfied smirk.

After a shocked moment, Brynn managed, 'What are *you* doing here?'

'I live here,' Ray answered smoothly.

'Oh, really? Does Cassie know?'

Ray laughed. 'You always were a smart alec.'

'Funny. That's what people say about you.' Although she'd never thought of Ray O'Hara as a danger in the past, circumstances had changed. Now she wasn't so sure of his harmlessness. He'd acquired a toughness over the years. Brynn knew he'd gotten in trouble for bar brawls and he'd dabbled with drugs before Cassie had divorced him, a divorce he'd fought. He had no business in Cassie's house and Brynn suddenly felt fiercely protective of her friend. Even if Ray wasn't looking for trouble, she didn't want Cassie walking in alone to find Ray here.

Brynn remembered how her friends used to praise her bravery, drew on her childhood resources and looked at Ray steadily. 'Would you mind stepping aside so an *invited* guest can enter?'

'What makes you think I haven't been invited?'

'Intuition.'

'Things have gotten better between Cassie and me.'

'Not that I've heard.' They exchanged unflinching stares. 'Well, are you going to let me in, Ray, or do I have to call the police?'

'Come right in. No one's stopping you.' Ray took one step back. Brynn had to squeeze past him. He snickered when her thigh touched his. 'Welcome, Miss Wilder. Or may I still call you Brynn?'

'I'm sure you'd rather call me something less polite than Brynn or Miss Wilder, but Brynn will do.'

Ray tossed back his head and laughed. Cassie used to think his laugh was sexy. Brynn had always found it loud and raw, like he had an inflamed throat. 'The years haven't changed your sense of humor, *Brynn*.'

'I don't think you meant that as a compliment,' she said flippantly, although his authoritative stance and the arrogant look in his eyes made her nervous. 'You never told me what you're doing here, Ray.'

'I left a few things behind when I moved out. Cassie won't mind me being here.'

'Did she know you were coming today?'

'No, but this *is* my home.'

'This isn't your home.'

He dug in his jeans pocket and came up with a key. 'Would Cassie have let me keep a key if she wanted to keep me out?'

'I know she doesn't want you here.'

'She doesn't care.'

Brynn sighed. She couldn't shake Ray's confident, domineering manner and she couldn't stand his eyes roving over her body a second longer. 'We could argue that point all day, Ray, and I'm tired. And thirsty. Why don't you just sit down in *your* living room and I'll get something to drink?'

'Can't have you accusing me of being a bad host. *You* sit down and I'll get you a drink.' He walked into the kitchen. 'Coke?'

'Wine.'

'I forgot. Cass told me you drink like a fish these days.'

'Oh, she did not. I'd like sweet white wine. I know she has some.'

He clattered around in the kitchen for a few minutes, then brought her a brimming glass. 'M'lady.'

'I didn't ask for the whole bottle,' Brynn said, trying not to spill wine as she took the glass.

'No fun today, are you? Things not going your way?'

Brynn ignored him and took a gulp of wine, wishing it were vodka instead. Vodka gave her courage. Ray sat down on a recliner across from her and lit a cigarette. He wore a small gold hoop in his left lobe, a scar bisected his right eyebrow, and the short sleeve of his tight white T-shirt exposed a large Aztec sun tattoo decorating one bulging bicep. He was still oddly striking, but he'd lost the handsomeness of his youth. His skin was weathered beneath its stubble and deep lines creased his forehead. He could have passed for forty-six instead of his thirty-six years, and the look from his once-mischievous eyes now showed disillusionment.

He leaned back on the recliner, crossed ankle over knee, sniffed and tried to look like the master of the domain. 'So, writing's been good to you, Brynn.'

'Yes.' She took another gulp of wine as his penetrating gaze never left her face. 'I wrote the first book with no expectations at all. Its popularity was a complete shock to me.'

'I've never read any of your books. Kids stuff, right?'

'Young adult audiences like it but it's doing even better in the adult market.'

'Well, will wonders never cease.'

'Everyone thought *you'd* be the bestseller.' She heard the waspish tone of her voice and tried to take off the edge. 'Cassie sent me some of the stories you wrote back when you were working at the newspaper.'

'I quit to devote myself to real writing.' He leaned forward and tapped off his unfiltered cigarette ashes in an empty Waterford crystal candy dish on Cassie's coffee table. 'I'm working on my novel and writing some other projects.'

'Like what?'

'Last month I was in California helping a friend put together a documentary, and I've just done a couple of articles about guys on death row. Face-to-face interviews.' Ray took a deep draw of his cigarette and breathed it out toward Brynn. 'Now that I've finally got a little time to myself, I'm going back to work on my book.'

'What's it about?' Brynn asked.

'Ah, Brynn, I know better than to divulge my topic too early,' he said cockily.

'I wouldn't steal your plot, Ray.'

'With the last name of Wilder, I'm not so sure.'

'What's that supposed to mean?'

Ray shrugged again and grinned as he scratched his neck lazily.

Brynn sat tightly holding her wineglass, wishing she could stand up, stride over to Ray and slap his face with all her might. Instead, as their gazes locked and burned, Cassie walked in gaily, then slammed the door and shouted, 'Ray! What the hell are you doing here?'

After five non-stop minutes of yelling at each other, Cassie and Ray froze at the sound of the doorbell. Their eyes widened and Cassie asked, 'Who's that?'

'The neighbors, no doubt,' Brynn said in relief. 'You should stop standing like a couple of statues and go to the door.'

Cassie hesitated, then walked to the front door and swung it wide open. Brynn could see Garrett Dane standing on the porch. 'Did I come at a bad time?' he asked wryly.

'I think you came at just the right time,' Brynn called to him. '*Please* come in.'

Garrett walked in, tall and slender in his uniform, his smile slipping while his laser-blue gaze darted between Cassie and Ray. 'Anything wrong here?'

Ray immediately became congenial, relaxing his posture as he laughed. 'Nothing except that I scared Cassie. She wasn't expecting me and she found me here with Brynn and, well . . . you know how women are!' He had the nerve to wink and grin as he extended his hand and boomed, 'How've ya been, Garrett?'

Garrett simply looked at the extended hand for a moment before saying, 'I thought you'd left Genessa Point.'

Ray's smile wavered but he answered heartily, 'I came back for the festival. Couldn't miss it now, could I? After all, I've lived here most of my life.'

'And you decided to visit Cassie unannounced?'

Ray's expression hardened. 'She's my wife and this is my house, Garrett. I don't have to explain myself to you.'

'I am *not* your wife and this is *not* your house,' Cassie blustered. 'Did Brynn let you in?'

'I certainly didn't! He has a key.'

'A key!' Cassie glared at Ray. 'Where did you get a key?'

'I had keys to all the doors when I lived here. I just forgot to give one back,' he said with maddening patience. 'What's the big deal?'

'I want that key!' Cassie demanded.

Ray huffed and handed it to her. 'Satisfied?'

'You kept that key on purpose,' she said as Ray shrugged again and sniffed. 'Admit it!'

'I need to talk to Brynn,' Garrett said calmly. 'We'll go out on the porch while the two of you work this out. Is that all right, Brynn?'

She stood up and walked out the front door without looking at Ray. She worried about leaving Cassie alone with him, but Garrett would only be a few feet away.

Garrett shut the door behind them and steered her toward the porch swing. They both listened as voices rose again inside.

'I hope he doesn't hurt her,' Brynn said.

'He won't.' Garrett sat a couple of feet away from her. 'He's not drunk and he's fully aware that I'm not only the sheriff, I'm armed.'

'Would you please go in and shoot him for me?'

Garrett grinned. 'Did he piss you off?'

'Royally.'

'Ray's always had a knack for rubbing people the wrong way. I couldn't believe it when Cassie married the jerk.'

'She thought he was *sexy* and *romantic* and an *intellectual genius*. Believe it or not, that's a direct quote from a letter she sent me.'

'Was she high? On crack?'

Garrett had managed to make her giggle. 'Just young.'

'I can't imagine a smart girl being *that* young.'

'Well, in a very few years you'll have to deal with a smart young girl's fantasies yourself.'

'Savannah will *never* be so . . .'

'Goofy? Wipe that smug expression off your face and trust me. Savannah's day will come.' Brynn smiled at him. 'Did you really want to talk to me, Garrett, or were you just looking for an escape from the melee inside?'

'I have some information about Mark for you. Well, not directly about Mark. It's about the car.'

'Oh.' Brynn stiffened. 'The blood.'

'I won't bother you with a lot of technicalities. The blood was Mark's type, but the techs didn't find enough to indicate serious blood loss in a grown male.' Garrett paused. 'Do you understand, Brynn? An adult, maybe not even Mark, lost O positive blood in that car, but not enough to cause death or even to indicate serious injury.'

Brynn finally let out her breath. 'Thank God.'

'They found Mark's fingerprints in the car, on the back and front seats, but that was to be expected. They found a lot of other prints, too, but no matches to IAFIS – Integrated Automated Fingerprint System. A background check had never been run on anyone who had those fingerprints. Also, there was no damage to the upholstery. In other words, no holes or tears caused by a bullet or knife.'

'So he wasn't injured in the car?'

'Well, there are other ways. He could have been struck over the head. Scalp wounds bleed like crazy.'

'His neck?'

'If so, the attacker didn't get a major vein or artery. Not enough blood was lost.'

'OK.' Brynn smiled weakly. 'I'm imagining the worst. Go on.'

'We wondered why the car was in the middle of nowhere,' Garrett said. 'The oil pan cap had come loose. We found it on the highway and a trail of oil ending not far from where we found the car. When the car ran out of oil it stopped. It doesn't show any signs of being moved by a tow truck so, luckily for the driver, the cluster of trees must have been nearby so he could push it to a hiding place.'

'You mean whoever took Mark didn't deliberately hide the car in the trees?'

'Doesn't look like it.'

Brynn frowned. 'Were there any buildings around where someone could have hidden Mark?'

'No buildings.'

'Then where—'

'I think a second car was involved, Brynn. When Mark's car broke down, one driver hid it and the victim was placed in a second car and taken away. Someone had to be driving that second car.'

'A second car,' Brynn said thoughtfully. 'Do you have any idea what direction it could have gone in?'

'It hasn't rained for over a week. The ground is hard and the grass growth is sparse in that area, so there are no convenient tire tracks to follow.' Garrett paused. 'I'm sorry I don't have more to tell you, but this has changed my take on the case. I thought one person kidnapped another. I thought the victim either died of blood loss or was murdered then buried somewhere near the car, even though we couldn't find any evidence of the ground being disturbed.'

Brynn looked at him. 'You keep saying "the victim" instead of Mark. You think Mark is the kidnapper.'

'Frankly, I'm not sure. I thought your brother had a nervous breakdown – something that sent him back to the past when maybe he *was* your father's partner. It seemed possible to me that he went into a spiral, came back here and kidnapped someone.'

'You mean you thought – think – he was my father's partner in the murders and he was reliving past behavior.'

'I thought it was possible. I wasn't sure what happened.'

'Your father didn't think in terms of possibilities. He thought he *knew*.'

'And I've told you, I'm not my father,' Garrett said, giving her a hard, steady look before he glanced away.

'All right. I'm sorry. This isn't about your father. But mine didn't—' Brynn broke off. 'This isn't the time to talk about your father or mine. It's time to concentrate on Mark. Do you still think it's a strong possibility that Mark kidnapped someone?'

'Well, I know that no one besides Mark has been reported missing.' He finally looked at her. 'And now I'm sure three people were involved – there were *two* kidnappers, Brynn. If your brother took someone, he didn't do it alone and I don't think he brought an accomplice from Baltimore.'

'And that means—'

'Someone else in this town is involved in a kidnapping and probably a murder.'

Brynn sat gazing at a beach she thought she'd never see again and looked up at the unusually bright full moon. Earlier, she'd told Sam she didn't want to tour her old house today. Now, she grew more anxious by the minute to see it inside.

A few hours ago, Ray had left under Garrett's steely stare, but Garrett had stayed for half an hour to make sure he didn't immediately come back. While they'd waited, Cassie had told Brynn that Sam's secretary had left a message at Love's. 'I was busy so she talked to one of my saleswomen. She wanted you to know that the person Sam hoped would buy your house wants to close the deal in a couple of days with a contract stipulating that, after signature, the house can no longer be shown.'

'Why did she call Love's and not me?'

'She said she doesn't have your cell phone number and my home number is unlisted. Sam told her you were staying with me and if she called the store, I'd pass on the message. Anyway, she said Sam's taking another client to dinner and will be out of town tomorrow, so tonight around nine will be your best, maybe last chance to go in the house. He can meet you there.'

Those were Cassie's last calm words. Once Garrett had left Cassie let loose her anger at Ray. When mad, she could talk for hours without a break. She'd started a rant session that Brynn knew would go on throughout the evening. She drank two more glasses of wine, which didn't take off the edge of her nervousness.

Finally, she'd thought about Sam's offer without enthusiasm. Then Cassie had angrily ripped open a package of individually wrapped butterscotch hard candies, dumping them all over the kitchen table. 'He acted so damned proprietary!' she'd fumed, still in the kitchen opening and slamming shut cabinet doors. 'He told me this was *his* house! I'm having the locks changed tomorrow – if he had one key, he could have more. I'm sure he has more!'

'Garrett said you could swear out a restraining order.'

'Oh, sure. That would just make Ray get drunk and more deter-mined than he already is to reclaim this as his home!' Cassie was almost shouting from the nearby kitchen. 'Besides, he'd think I'm scared of him.'

'Are you?'

'Not at all! Still, I feel violated knowing he was just strolling around this house like he owned the place. I threw him out of here almost a year ago and he hasn't been back, yet here he was today, acting like he just left yesterday, like he had a *right* to be here! Oh, I can't stand the thought of him snooping around in my house, the son of a bitch!' Cassie had stalked into the living room, chomping viciously on a piece of hard candy. 'Right now you don't know how much I wish I was on that Miami beach with you drinking tall, cold piña coladas with extra pineapple!'

The mention of piña coladas had sent Brynn's memories flying. Pineapple. Her father's fortieth birthday. She recalled it as if it had happened last week.

If there was ever a man who didn't like a fuss made over himself, it was Jonah Wilder. They held small birthday celebrations for Mark and Brynn, but Jonah wanted nothing more than a card. Everyone respected his wishes until Marguerite had decided his fortieth birthday was a landmark that demanded more than a card, so she'd planned a surprise party.

Brynn would never forget how shocked her father had looked when he'd walked into the house after a Saturday of fishing to find a group of ten friends all yelling 'Surprise!' They'd placed a gold foil-wrapped crown on his head and sung, 'Happy Birthday' before Marguerite presented two large pineapple upside down cakes – Jonah's favorite – both flaming with candles. He'd managed to blow out all forty. Later, Jonah had grudgingly admitted it had been one of the best evenings of his life. Brynn remembered it as one of the best evenings of hers, too. Meanwhile, between Cassie's non-stop talking and her flash of a good memory, Brynn had changed her mind about touring her old home, and she'd left Cassie's at around eight forty-five to meet Sam there at nine.

She looked at her watch. Nine-twenty. When she'd arrived at the house on the sparsely occupied Oriole Lane, it was empty and locked. Sam's dinner must be running longer than he'd expected, she'd thought. Always punctual, she knew he would be fidgeting by now.

Brynn looked at the beach from the top of the wooden steps leading down from the house. The house behind her was still dark – no Sam yet. Restless and enchanted by the moonlit beach, she walked down the steps, kicked off her shoes and pressed her feet into the soft sand, closing her eyes and taking deep breaths of the tangy bay water.

A sweet dampness blew in from the water, wafting her long hair, brushing her cheek and caressing her neck like a kiss in a dream – delicate, sensitive, full of promise. She suddenly felt as if she'd entered a mythical, romantic world removed from the everyday reality where she always tried to stay grounded. For her, the atmosphere turned heady and beguiling, and she allowed herself to transform from Brynn Wilder to the fairy-like, mystical character of Evangelista in her novels.

'You drank too much wine earlier,' she murmured to herself, but she didn't care. For the first time in days, her body relaxed, her worry about Mark dulled, and the tension that had preoccupied her for days snapped loose like a constricting band.

Brynn started walking on the stretch of beach leading toward Oriole Lane, feeling as if she were floating in the cool night, while she looked up at the stars glittering sharply silver against a black velvet sky. She dug in her jeans pocket, pulled out the MP3 player Mark had sent her for Christmas, and flipped on Rihanna's 'Diamonds.' Brynn twirled in the sand, feeling young and carefree. She turned up the music and began moving with abandon, extending her arms, letting the breeze catch the long, billowy sleeves of her chiffon tunic as she happily dipped and pirouetted.

Then, in the distance, she heard a dog barking, fast and loud, as if it were on the trail of something. Brynn stopped moving and listened. She could tell the animal was big from the deep bark and it seemed to be coming her way. She'd never feared a dog in her life. Still, alone on the dark beach, she felt a slight uneasiness. Maybe the dog wasn't harmless and she would need to find a place of safety.

The nearest building was her former home. She looked up at the two-story house. Three minutes ago it had been dark; now a dim, golden-toned light shone in an upstairs window. That window would be in my old bedroom, Brynn thought. But I didn't see Sam's headlights swing into the driveway. And why has he turned on only one muted light on the second floor?

While she stared at the house, she saw a figure standing in front of the window – a motionless figure that seemed to be staring at her. In spite of the bright, moon-silvered night, Brynn could tell nothing about its facial features or even hair, which could be short or merely pulled back. Was it Sam? No, he would have opened the window and called to her, or at least waved. Instead, she and her watcher stood frozen, gazing at each other while Rihanna sang with growing ecstasy in the background and the dog's barking grew louder. Brynn's anxiety about the dog heightened, but she couldn't move. For some reason, she felt she must stay still and try to remember every detail of this eerily suspended moment in time.

They stood motionless, looking at each other. Brynn couldn't see the eyes, but she could feel them, traveling up and down her body. Brynn somehow knew she was meant to make the next move. Trapped between the eerie figure and the dog, she now had no intention of running anywhere. But how long could she stand here?

The dog barked even louder, faster, nearer. Growing fear locked Brynn in place, but she turned her head and saw a large shape racing toward her, kicking up sand with big paws and a feathery, wagging tail. Before the dog reached her, she recognized it – Henry, emitting a flurry of whines, snorts and playful growls. He gamboled around her, letting out muffled barks, leaping on his hind legs, his ears flapping.

'Henry, what are you doing here!' Brynn cried in shock, as if the dog could answer. She kneeled and hugged him in relief. 'My God, I'm glad to see you!' He wallowed his big head in her hands. 'Don't tell me you've run away from home!'

Still hugging him tightly, she glanced up at the house's second-floor window. Although the golden light still glowed, the watcher had gone. Had he merely ducked away from the window, or was he fleeing the house?

'Henry Dane, you come back here right this minute!'

Savannah, Brynn thought. She was in hot pursuit of her dog and, a moment later, she ran up to them. 'Brynn!' she cried in surprise, then gave Henry a hard look. 'Henry, you ditched me!' she accused breathlessly. 'You know *I'm* supposed to be in charge.'

'I guess he doesn't,' Brynn said, standing up.

'Why are you here?' Savannah asked.

'I was going to see my old house before someone buys it, but Mr Fenney, the real estate agent, isn't here yet.' Suddenly she realized Rihanna was still singing into the night. She turned off her MP3 player. 'Actually, while I waited I decided to walk on the beach and listen to music and . . . well, dance.'

'Dance!' Savannah grinned. 'I should have known you like to dance. Me, too.'

Brynn tried to hide her uneasiness by keeping her voice light. She smiled. 'We're kindred spirits. Why are you and Henry out after dark?'

'It's his evening walk, only we're a little late. We only live a couple of blocks from here. We walk to the end of Oriole Lane on our usual route.'

'Do you come to this beach?'

'No, never. We stay on the street but I love the song "Diamonds" and Henry hears it all the time. I guess he loves it, too, because when he heard it, I lost control of him and he came flying this way. Now he's even more excited because he found you.' Savannah's eyes probed Brynn's face. 'I hope he didn't scare you. You look kinda freaked out.'

'No, I'm fine. Honey, are you by yourself?'

'Oh, no. I never bring out Henry for his evening walk by myself.

Dad comes with me. He's somewhere behind.' Savannah jerked her head over her shoulder and lowered her voice. 'He can't run as fast as I can, but don't tell him I said so. You know how men think they're better at everything than women.'

'I sure do,' Brynn answered, keeping her tone confidential although she was almost shaking with waves of delayed apprehension. Settle down, she thought sternly, more grateful than she could imagine. It's all right now. Garrett's coming.

'Hey!' Garrett called, trotting up the beach. 'Savannah, you know better than to run away from me!'

'I had to catch Henry!'

'That is no excuse for running away from me—'

'Look who's here!' Savannah interrupted brightly, clearly trying to save herself. 'It's Brynn! She was playing "Diamonds" and Henry heard and he came running 'cause he knows the song and when he got here, he found Brynn! Isn't that wild?'

'Truly wild.' Garrett had reached them and gave his daughter a hard look. 'He doesn't love the song. Dogs respond to familiar, repetitive noises.'

'No, he loves the song and he saw Brynn dancing on the beach—'

'Dancing on the beach?' Garrett turned his attention to Brynn.

'Yes,' she said, glad it was night and he couldn't see her blush.

'Is dancing on the beach alone at night a Miami thing?'

'No, it's a one-night thing for me. An impulse. I feel silly but . . . oh, well, it doesn't matter.' Brynn took a deep breath. 'I'm really glad to see the three of you.'

Garrett must have picked up on her tone because his anger seemed to wane. 'Mind if I ask what you're doing here tonight?'

'Someone is buying the house and will be moving in next week. Sam said he'd show me round. He was supposed to meet me here at nine, only he wasn't here, so I decided to wait. I got bored and came down here and put on the music and lost track of time and—'

'Slow down,' Garrett said, glancing at his watch. 'Brynn, it's nearly ten o'clock. If Sam was coming, he'd be here.'

'Maybe he forgot. Only . . .'

Garrett frowned at her, then looked at Savannah, who'd been listening avidly. 'Henry's getting too near the water. We don't want him to go swimming. Run and get him, honey.'

'He won't go swimming, Dad.'

'He'll wade. Now go.'

Savannah let out an exasperated groan and walked toward the dog, calling, 'Henry! Red alert! You're not allowed to wade!'

When Savannah was out of earshot, Garrett looked at Brynn with concern. 'Now tell me what's wrong.'

'It's so strange. I told you I came down here and put on the music. I suddenly felt sort of light-hearted and started dancing. I glanced up at the house every few minutes, though. I knew when Sam got here he'd turned on the inside lights. Well, that never happened. The house stayed dark except for one room.' She pointed up at the second-floor window where the golden light still glowed softly. 'That used to be my bedroom. All at once, I saw someone – probably a man – standing in the window watching me. At first I thought it was Sam, but he just stood there,' Brynn went on. 'Sam would have opened the window and yelled or waved when he saw me looking at him. The moon is so bright he had to see that I was facing him. Then I wondered why that was the only light on in the house.' She stopped. 'It wasn't Sam. I'm sure it wasn't. He stood absolutely still and kept looking at me. And I kept looking at him. I don't know how long we stared at each other, but the time seemed endless. It was like the world stopped.' She paused, then said in frustration, 'Oh, I sound crazy!'

'No you don't,' Garrett said reassuringly. 'Go on.'

'I knew I should leave, but my car is parked at the house. I wasn't going anywhere near it. I had a feeling if I left this spot on the beach, something would happen to me. I was getting so weirded out and that's not like me. Then Henry came rushing up. I bent to pet him – well, actually, to clutch him because he seemed so big and safe and like he'd come to rescue me – and when I looked back at the window, the man had vanished. The light's still on, as you can see, but the guy's gone. At least from the window. He could still be in the house.'

'Then he'll stay while I call for back-up and get you and Savannah to safety.'

'And please check on Sam. I have a bad feeling about him.'

'OK.' Garrett removed his cell phone and called the deputies on duty, who happened to be close by. 'Get here as soon as possible. Also, have someone call Sam Fenney's house and see where he is.' He ended the call, turned toward the bay and called, 'Savannah, time for all of us to go!'

'Brynn, too?'

'Yeah. Let's walk her to her car.'

Brynn had retrieved her shoes, and they'd reached the top of the wooden steps and started through the backyard when, suddenly, Henry froze. Then he began barking frantically and running at top speed toward the front of the house.

'What the hell?' Garrett muttered.

'A squirrel? A cat?' Brynn asked with tremulous hope.

Savannah stiffened. 'Henry likes cats. He wouldn't chase one like that. Something's wrong! He senses danger!'

'Henry, come back here!' Garrett yelled. The dog didn't respond and Garrett looked back at Brynn and his daughter. 'You two stay here.'

'I'm *not* leaving Henry!' Savannah shouted, running after the dog. Garrett took off right behind her.

Brynn wanted to stop still. After her unnerving experience with the man in the window, she didn't want to go anywhere near what the dog was chasing, but the momentum swept her up and she charged ahead with the other three. Besides, being left alone in the backyard might be even more frightening. Clouds had skimmed across the moon and the light dimmed. The stranger could come out of the rear door and be on her before she saw him and had a chance to cry for help.

They circled to the front of the dark house. The home across the street was also dark and the one next door barely lit. No porch light burned at the porch of her house and Sam's car wasn't around.

'Sam's not here!' Brynn called to Garrett. 'He never was. We have to leave *now*!'

Garrett didn't answer. Brynn glanced at her car sitting in the driveway. She wanted everyone to jump in and drive away fast, but Henry raced ahead, aiming for the front door that stood open about three inches. Savannah followed him. He skittered up the front steps, across the porch, hit the door with his head and knocked it completely open before plunging into the entranceway, shadowy with moonlight.

'Savannah, stop right now!'

Brynn didn't think the girl even heard Garrett. She guessed the dog dominated Savannah's concentration, both because of the teenager's love for her pet and from the excitement of the chase. Once inside, Henry slowed his pace but didn't stop, and Savannah dashed in behind him.

In the running tangle, Brynn somehow got caught between Savannah and Garrett. The dog nearly flew up the stairs, Savannah behind him, with Garrett pushing Brynn in his frenzy to catch his daughter. Along the way, Brynn began to hear music – an acoustic guitar and a male falsetto voice. The song was haunting and familiar. Chillingly familiar.

As they neared the top of the steps, the music grew louder, the golden light glowed brighter and Brynn's fear grew. In an instant, panic for Savannah flooded through her. She could hear herself screaming, 'No! Savannah, stop! Garrett, stop her!'

She heard him breathing loudly behind her, but he said nothing. Did he have a gun with him? Brynn wondered. Probably not. This was supposed to be a peaceful evening dog walk. He hadn't been expecting an attack on a calm residential street.

Brynn's bedroom was the first room on the right. Henry bolted inside then skidded to a complete stop. Savannah almost fell on top of him, barely catching herself before regaining her balance and going as rigid as the dog. The music washed over Brynn and she spotted an old boombox that looked just like the one Mark used to have. Steve Winwood's hauntingly forlorn voice sang 'Can't Find My Way Home.' With a growing sense of dread, Brynn glanced at the amber, yellow, blue and green imitation Tiffany dragonfly wall sconce emitting the soft golden light in her room. She remembered her delight when her father had installed it for her eighth birthday.

Now the light fell almost ethereally over the body of Sam Fenney. He rested peacefully on his back, his arms and legs splayed. Large lit candles surrounded him and a Bible was by his side. The neck and chest of his light blue shirt were covered with crimson and a knife was buried to the handle in the area of his heart.

TEN

B rynn wondered why in books funerals usually took place on dreary days. Was it to create a somber atmosphere? Or to cause foreboding? Of course, she didn't need to be told fiction didn't always reflect reality. Right now, for instance, she stood by a graveside on one of the most beautiful afternoons she could remember. A sun the color of a buttercup petal glowed against a cornflower-blue sky and only occasional clouds like huge dollops of fluffy marshmallow floated above the mourners.

The mourners. Brynn glanced around while the son of the new director of the family-owned funeral home conducted the service. He was very young, nervous, obviously did not know Sam and hadn't done any research on the man. Still, he haltingly plowed on with his uninspired speech, throwing in a grand gesture or a tragic facial expression for effect. Across from Brynn stood Sam's young secretary, Lexa, who dabbed at what looked like genuine tears.

Tessa, looking frail, swollen-eyed and even more washed-out than usual, clutched Nathan's arm. Brynn hadn't seen him since he'd come home. He was tanned and the ends of his dark blond hair had been bleached golden by the sun. He wore a charcoal-colored suit that looked as if it had been tailored especially for him, and once, when he glanced at her, she was startled by the brightness of his green eyes. How different would Tessa's life have been if she'd looked like her beautiful brother? Brynn thought, remembering the quirky, unkempt, friendless girl who'd taken a few disastrous piano lessons from Marguerite. Tessa's peculiar behavior, even her tacky appearance as an adult, couldn't all be attributed to the stress she'd suffered after the violent attack when she was fifteen. She'd been eccentric since she was a child.

Edmund Ellis stood alone. His tie looked as if he'd made his first attempt at a Windsor knot. His suit was too big and even his shirt collar was too loose around his corded neck. The Edmund she recalled would never have worn clothes that no longer fit. He'd never been vain, only scrupulous about his appearance. Even his thinning hair had gone too long without a cut. He kept brushing the top hair to the side to keep it out of his eyes – his eyes, which stared straight ahead and looked blank, as if no thoughts floated behind their once-warm dark gray that now looked the color of ashes.

'Samuel was a fine man, a regular churchgoer, a devoted father and the faithful husband of a loving wife who always stood by his side through this mysterious experience we call life,' the assistant funeral director droned mawkishly. Some of the mourners who were actually listening looked startled. A few exchanged meaningful glances with other attendees. Some blatantly cringed. Sam attended church twice a year – Christmas and Easter. He did not have any children. Most shockingly, his 'loving' wife had not even appeared at his funeral.

As far as Brynn knew, the only person Mrs Fenney had seen was the sheriff, who'd notified her of Sam's death. Garrett had told Brynn the woman who'd been Sam's wife for over thirty years simply asked how he'd died and then said, 'He was stabbed? On purpose? Murdered?' Garrett said that before he'd had a chance to say anything else, she'd commented tonelessly, 'How sordid.'

'I'm sorry for your loss,' Garrett told Brynn he'd said stiffly, appalled by her reaction to Sam's murder, even if she was odd.

'He did get a call last evening around seven . . . no, nearer to eight. He said he had to go out.' Garrett said she'd sounded completely casual. 'I don't know who called or where he went. He just wasn't here this morning. I slept late. I assumed he was at the office.' She'd looked at Garrett, showing mild agitation for the first time. 'Oh, dear, there will be so much legal mumbo-jumbo I'll have to deal with for his real estate business. There's also the motel and that little café.'

'Little café?' Garrett had asked.

'Why, yes. What's that silly name? Oh, Cloud Nine.'

'Sam owned Cloud Nine?'

'Yes. He also owned the Bay Motel.'

'He owned it? The whole motel, not just half?'

'Yes. It came as a surprise to me, too. You see, he'd told me he invested a small amount of money in the motel and the café. I suppose if I got out more, I would have learned the truth sooner, but as I'm sure you know, I'm agoraphobic.'

'I know you don't go out much,' Garrett told Brynn he'd said, trying to be tactful.

'I *never* go out. I . . . can't. But then, you aren't interested in my problems, only Sam's death. The last two weeks he was nervous, sleepless and absent-minded. For instance, he was usually so controlled, he always locked his desk and file cabinet in his study. One day he didn't lock either and . . .' Garrett said she'd given him a tight, forced smile, '. . . I snooped. I found the deeds to both the motel and the café. They were owned by a realty company called Farrah-Stef, which was owned by Kalidone Corporation. The knowledge that Sam owned the hotel and that café came as a tremendous shock.'

Garrett had told Brynn he must have a talent for acting, because he'd managed to keep his voice calm even though Brynn had already told him about Sam saying the real estate company Farrah-Stef, owned by the Kalidone Corporation, had bought the Wilder house on Oriole Lane only three months after Jonah's death. Brynn hadn't pretended her astonishment that Sam had a connection to Farrah-Stef and Kalidone, even though she'd known since that day in his office he wasn't telling her the truth. But she was also aware of Garrett scrutinizing her closely. She knew he could be giving her information police might usually keep confidential to get her reaction. She didn't have to feign shock with Garrett, though. She was genuinely stunned by Sam's tangle of business that had involved far more than the purchase of her old home.

Garrett continued to watch her closely as he proceeded with the details of his meeting with Mrs Fenney. 'Farrah-Stef? Kalidone?' he said he'd repeated to Mrs Fenney, trying to keep his expression blank as he wrote the names in his notebook. 'What makes you think they had anything to do with your husband?'

Garrett said her smile had grown more strained. 'Sam used to watch reruns of that ridiculous show, *Charlie's Angels*, and Farrah Fawcett was his favorite actress. When he was young, he loved a book with a magical hero named Kalidone. He got a hamster and called it that. He said he loved that hamster.' She'd paused. 'One day when he was at school, his mother beat it to death with a hammer and left it on his bed.'

'How . . . cruel,' Garrett said he'd stammered.

'Yes. Apparently she was a terrible woman. A psychiatrist would probably say her treatment of him might have accounted for some of the strange things he did later in life.'

'Such as?'

Garrett said her pale gaze had hardened. 'I knew a few things from Sam's past, but not much from the present. For instance, all of these assets of his that I had no knowledge of just show you how little I knew about my husband's life outside this house. I didn't really know him at all. Therefore, I can't even speculate about who would have killed him.'

Garrett told Brynn that while he'd sat stiffly on her couch, Mrs Fenney had looked vacantly around the room for a minute, then ended their meeting with, 'Is there anything else I can do for you, Sheriff Dane? Because I must take a sleeping pill and try to shut out this ghastly business until morning. I'm shaken to the core, and people will be expecting so much of me – a wake, and a reception after the funeral, all those arrangements, all that ceremony.' She'd sighed. 'I'm simply not up to it. Just thinking of it frightens me. But Sam was popular – I'm sure someone else will take over for me. Let's see . . . I can't ask Edmund. He just buried his daughter. I know! That girl who works for Sam – Elizabeth or something – will consider arranging the funeral as part of her job.'

'Lexa.'

'Pardon? Oh, the secretary. Lexa, you say? Well, I've never met her, but I've talked to her on the phone and I think she's fond of Sam. People always seem to like Sam.' Again a twitch of the face. 'Yes, she'll jump at the chance to take care of Sam all the way to the grave.'

Garrett said she'd fallen into a nearly ten-second silence. Finally, she'd said in a normal voice, 'Well, thank you for telling me, Sheriff. I'm sorry Sam has put you to all of this trouble.'

Two hours later he'd driven past Sam's house and spotted the gaunt Mrs Fenney walking past a lighted window, holding a phone receiver and smoking a cigarette. He'd said, 'Either I'm lousy at body language, or she wasn't a woman devastated by hearing her husband had just been murdered and who had to run for a sleeping pill and her bed.'

Brynn had known that even if Garrett had let the matter drop for now, he wouldn't let Mrs Fenney off the hook so easily. He'd have questions for her – many more questions – especially because she'd so recently found out about her husband's secret business dealings and because of her reaction – or lack of it – to his murder.

Now, after the speaker's last atrocious blunders about Sam, Brynn finally looked at Garrett. He was staring at her. He shut his eyes and subtly, despairingly shook his head. She felt as if she could read his thoughts: *My God, poor old Sam. What a circus.* It *was* a circus, Brynn thought and felt the dreaded, nervous giggle rising in her as it always did when she saw something meant to be dignified turned into the ridiculous. Cassie, knowing her so well and standing so close their bodies touched, must have felt Brynn's body beginning to vibrate. She jabbed Brynn in the ribs and frowned, helping her to swallow what could have been an appalling peal of laughter. Brynn sent Cassie a tiny, reassuring smile.

Garrett hadn't brought Savannah with him, Brynn noted while trying to ignore the pain in her side where Cassie had hit too hard. Brynn was glad the girl wasn't here. She couldn't know whether or not Savannah had wanted to attend the funeral, but even if she had, Garrett would have been right to refuse. Savannah's reaction to finding the murdered body of Sam Fenney had frightened Brynn. She knew the image of Sam surrounded by candles with a knife in his chest would be scorched into her brain for life.

After they'd found Sam in Brynn's old room, Henry's whine had turned into ferocious barking and he'd rushed past Savannah into the upper hall. His nails had scrabbled on the hardwood floor as he started down the hall, growling, lips drawn back to show his teeth. He'd passed four other open doors, reached the end of the hall and stopped, peering down the narrow back staircase leading to the kitchen. He whined. He turned in circles. He sent another growl down the stairway and then started moving backward.

'What's wrong with him?' Brynn had asked before suddenly her nose and eyes began to burn. 'What's that?'

'Pepper spray,' Garrett had managed, coughing, as she, Garrett and Henry had halted, driven back by a potent chemical cloud. Henry had followed the killer's scent down the hall to the narrow back stairs. The killer must have run down the stairs and then opened a complete canister of pepper spray, sending an acrid fog up the enclosed staircase. Garrett had squinted past Brynn, but he could barely keep his eyes open. Henry had whirled and run back down the hallway.

Suddenly, the color had drained from Garrett's face. 'He might still be in the house,' he'd ground out. 'Where's Savannah?' He'd pushed past Brynn and run back down the hall, bellowing, 'Savannah! *Savannah!'*

They'd found her in Brynn's room, standing stiffly over Sam's body. Garrett had rushed to her, wrapping his arms around her rigid body. She hadn't hugged him back. She hadn't spoken. She'd just stared at Sam.

'Honey, are you all right?' Garrett had asked, and Brynn heard the fear in his gritty voice.

Nothing.

'Savannah?' Garrett had pulled her against himself, squeezing her hard. 'Sweetheart, please say something. Please . . .'

'He's dead, Daddy,' she'd finally said in a dreamy, faraway voice. 'He got stabbed, just like Brynn's daddy.'

'Oh, Savannah,' Garrett had crooned, but she hadn't seemed to hear him.

'And that music playing is about somebody who's lost like Brynn's brother and you were playing that song over and over the other night and Mr Fenney was nice, I think, but look what's happened to him. *Look!* You're the sheriff and people say that's a dangerous job even in Genessa Point and that terrible Rhonda who hates me keeps calling . . .' The girl began to wail, tearlessly, sharply and shrilly. Savannah didn't sound completely human and chills had raised on Brynn's arms at the frightening sound.

Garrett had clutched her even tighter if that was possible, and she'd let out another almost animal sound of pain. Henry walked aggressively toward them, looked at Garrett and growled, low and warning. The dog thinks he's hurting her, Brynn thought. Henry would protect Savannah even from Garrett.

'It's all right, Henry,' Brynn had murmured, not approaching him, not touching him. After all, the protective, provoked dog didn't really know her. 'Henry, *no.*'

The dog had spun on her, teeth bared, and she froze. Abruptly, Savannah had stopped her eerie howl and commanded, 'Henry, don't!' Then, more softly, 'Henry, leave her alone.' She'd shrugged out of her father's arms and kneeled. 'Come to me, Henry. Everything's all right. Come!'

The dog had looked warily at Brynn, then Garrett, and after a moment trotted to Savannah, letting her wrap her arms around his neck. She'd hugged him fervently and he'd let out another whine, as if in sympathy.

Brynn had been dimly aware of sirens screaming in the distance shortly before someone began pounding on the front door. Garrett had looked at Brynn. 'It's the deputies I called earlier. Come downstairs. I'll fill them in before I get you and Savannah home.'

And so he had, although Savannah had simply clung to Henry, stared, and never made another sound.

Brynn's thoughts jerked back to the funeral service as the speaker's voice rose. 'And I shall close with lines from the twenty-third Psalm, which is one of my favorites,' he informed his audience. He bowed his head, as did all of the mourners. *'Surely goodness and mercy shall follow me all the days of my life; And I will dwell in the house of the Lord for ever.'*

The director raised solemn eyes, gazing meaningfully at the group. 'And I'm sure we all hope Samuel does get to live in that house forever. Amen . . .' He paused, then raised his voice to a loud, ringing tone as he lifted his hand and waved to the beautiful blue sky. 'Farewell, Samuel!'

Brynn wondered for a minute how Sam's wife could have allowed this travesty of a service. Then the answers came: because she chose to have no say; because she didn't care as long as Sam was in the ground and she could say he'd had a 'proper' funeral.

At the end of the service, some people moved forward toward the coffin and pulled flowers out of the casket spray and few wreaths, a custom Brynn hated. Let the dead have their flowers, she thought. You'll just throw them in the trash when you get home.

'Do you want to get a flower?' Cassie asked.

'No!' Brynn snapped just as she saw the gray gaze of Rhonda Sanford on her. 'What's she doing here?'

Cassie looked at Rhonda then back at Brynn. 'Maybe she knew Sam. What's the matter? Are you still mad at her for starting a ruckus with Mark? Because I told her he was a friend of mine and I didn't want to hear about anything like that happening again or else I'd have to let her go.'

'I didn't expect you to fire her for what she said to Mark, but I don't like her, and not just because of Mark. Something about her gives me the creeps.'

'Well, she *is* sort of a puzzle. She can be charming with a customer one minute and cold as ice to another employee the next. That's strange behavior and doesn't make her popular with the store's staff.' Cassie looked at Rhonda again. 'Uh oh. I think she came because she knew Garrett would be here.'

Brynn glanced at Rhonda. Sure enough, as Garrett spoke to an older man, Rhonda headed straight for him. She wore a tight, short black dress and a waterfall of pearls over a low-scooped neckline. She tottered slightly on the ground in her five-inch heels.

'Is she wearing enough jewelry?' Brynn asked sourly.

'Watch it, kid,' Cassie said good-naturedly. 'You sound jealous.'

'That's absurd. After all, according to her, Garrett is her *lover*. I guess he likes the way she dresses. Anyway, it's nothing to me.'

'Oh, sure it's nothing to you.'

Brynn looked at Cassie, who raised an eyebrow.

'Anyway, from the way he's watching her bearing down on him, Garrett is *not* her lover. In fact, he looks like he'd like to run a mile.'

Brynn stifled a giggle then turned to see Ray O'Hara, wearing dark jeans and a dark gray shirt, approaching Nathan and Tessa. He was smiling. They smiled back. In fact, even from this distance, Brynn could see Tessa's heightened color and a slight dipping of her head before her face turned almost girlishly flirtatious.

'Are you seeing what I'm seeing?' Brynn murmured to Cassie. 'Nathan looks like he's spotted his long-lost brother.'

Cassie stared hard as Nathan and Ray vigorously shook hands before Ray turned his attention to Tessa, who blushed, batted her bare eyelids and smiled coyly. 'I've seen her look at Ray that way before.' Cassie's whisper had a razor's edge.

'You have? *Tessa?*'

'Look, Brynn, I know you think everyone considers Ray an unattractive jerk, but—'

Lexa suddenly appeared and drew their attention away from Ray. 'Miss Wilder, Miss Hutton, we're having the post-funeral reception at the Fenney offices. Mrs Fenney said she didn't feel up to having a lot of people in her house. I know she's supposed to be agoraphobic.' Lexa's throat closed as she fought tears. The expression in her eyes said everything about her feelings for Mrs Fenney.

Cassie reached out and took Lexa's arm. 'We'll be there. And I'm sure Sam would appreciate all you've done for him, Lexa. You've been like a daughter to him.'

Lexa finally gave way to tears while Brynn's gaze strayed to Edmund Ellis edging away from the gravesite, a bundle of daisies in his hand, and headed toward the north end of the cemetery. Certain she knew where he was going, she excused herself from

Cassie and followed him. Sure enough, he went straight to what was obviously a relatively new grave, one with only a marker, not a granite headstone.

'I'm sorry I didn't bring any flowers for Joy,' Brynn said as she neared Edmund.

He took a daisy from the small bunch he carried and handed it to her. 'Daisies were her favorite flower. She'd be as touched by you giving her one daisy as she would if you gave her dozens of roses. She never asked for much from life.'

'If I'd known about her death in time, I would have attended her funeral.'

Edmund looked surprised. 'You would have? You'd have come back to Genessa Point for Joy? That would have meant a lot to her. Even when she was a child, she admired you, and the last year of her life she read your books. She said they were wonderful.'

Brynn felt her face color. 'I'm so glad she liked them.'

'She said you were born to write.'

Brynn smiled. 'I don't know about that, but I certainly wasn't born to be a musician. She played so well and never missed one of Mom's lessons. Kids were always canceling, but not Joy.' Brynn frowned. 'She had a lesson on the day my dad was killed, but Mom had to work at Love's and canceled all her lessons. I remember thinking she was so young and, with her heart condition, I was especially glad she hadn't been there to see what happened to my father.' Brynn looked into Edmund's eyes. 'I wished she was my little sister.'

Edmund quickly looked down at the other grave, that of his wife. 'Joy wanted a sister. The baby my wife lost at seven months was a girl.' His voice thickened. 'Joy was only five when that happened and it changed everything for us, especially my wife . . .'

'She and Mom were so close, but after she lost the baby, she seemed to drift away, shut herself into the house more often. We never heard from her after we moved.'

'I'm sorry about that. The circumstances became . . . strained.' Edmund seemed uncomfortable and looked down.

'The *circumstances* meaning my father being labeled the Genessa Point Killer. Isn't that what you mean? It seems to have been the case with all of our friends around here.'

'I meant things changed at home,' Edmund said softly. 'My wife . . . Joy . . .'

'Did your wife decide she wanted no contact with Marguerite Wilder anymore? At a time when Mom needed her most? And why did you send Joy away to boarding school? I know you sent her right after we left. Cassie told me. Were you afraid Mark would come back and kill her?'

Edmund looked at her tragically. 'Brynn . . . please.'

'Please what?'

'Please *stop*. I know you're furious with me for not telling the police your father lost that knife, but I couldn't . . . lie.'

'*Lie?*' Brynn hadn't known how bitter, how enraged she was until now. All her antagonism bubbled to the surface as she stood here with the man who was supposed to be her father's closest friend but whose defense of him had been weak and half-hearted, the man who stood over the lonely grave of the sickly, adoring daughter he'd sent away when she was only seven.

'Everybody in Genessa Point deserted us except Cassie!' Brynn nearly hissed, beginning to shake from the force of emotion.

'Brynn, you have to understand the situation we were all caught in—'

'The situation *you* were caught in? Well, maybe I didn't understand your situation eighteen years ago,' she said caustically, 'but tell me about another situation going on now. At Cloud Nine, you said you were worried about Mark *and* me. You told me to leave Genessa Point before I went missing, too.' She took a deep breath and went on relentlessly. 'You saw Sam in his office and a few hours later he was murdered. Mark came to visit you and, within days, he disappeared. I think you know who killed Sam, Edmund. I think you know what's happened to Mark.'

Edmund took a step back and slowly shook his head, but she saw fear in his eyes.

'If you know something, Edmund, you have to tell the police. If you don't, Mark might be murdered too!' Her voice broke and the day turned dark and cold for her as she choked out her greatest fear. 'Or is my brother already dead?'

Edmund closed his eyes. His face had turned pale as alabaster and his lips trembled. His legs began to shake, and his hands clutched at his chest. Instinctively, Brynn reached out. She managed to catch him just as his knees buckled. By the time she'd lowered him to the ground, Edmund was unconscious.

ELEVEN

In the privacy of his office with the door closed, Garrett Dane took a gulp of hot coffee, leaned back in his executive swivel desk chair and closed his eyes. Had Sam Fenney's funeral been less than twenty-four hours ago? It seemed like a week had passed – a week of questions, worries, tears and doubts. Thank God Edmund Ellis hadn't died at the foot of his daughter's fresh grave. Brynn Wilder had sat on the ground holding his head as she'd screamed for help.

And help had come fast. Within half an hour, Edmund had been loaded into an ambulance. In another hour, they'd learned he'd merely passed out from lack of food, dehydration and exhaustion – conditions that had been building for days, probably since Joy had died. Doctors told them Edmund would be in the hospital for at least another day – weak, confused and hooked to IV machines, but in no danger of dying. Brynn, who'd confided in Garrett all she'd said to Edmund at the gravesite, had sagged against him in relief, her own slender body badly in need of rest and food.

She'd leaned against Garrett as they left the hospital and slumped in her seat as he'd driven her to Cassie's house, where he'd let her best friend take over. Garrett hadn't wanted to leave Brynn. He didn't know why, he'd only known he'd wanted to stay with her, to make certain she was all right, to reassure her she hadn't been to blame for Edmund's collapse. Instead, he'd had to settle for a phone call from Cassie that came three hours later, telling him that Brynn had finally calmed, eaten a beef sandwich, drunk a tall glass of milk – complaining all the time that she hated milk – then, with the help of a tranquilizer, gone to sleep.

This morning Garrett had called the hospital and gotten an update on Dr Ellis. The man had no immediate family and identifying himself as the county sheriff had gotten Garrett the information he needed. Dr Ellis was doing better, but his doctor wanted to keep him in until tomorrow, even though Ellis already wanted to go home. 'He's still weak. We're hoping he'll fall asleep and not release himself from hospital care,' a senior nurse told him.

Garrett had then called Cassie's cell phone.

'I'm in the car on my way to the store – I wanted to stay home today, but Brynn wouldn't hear of it. She's worse than my mother!' Cassie had laughed. 'I'll call her and let her know about Doctor Ellis, though, unless you'd rather call her.'

'No, no, that's why I called you,' Garrett said quickly. 'I don't want to wake her up if she's still sleeping.' The truth was that he didn't want to talk to Brynn today, maybe because he'd felt so tender toward her yesterday as she'd poured out her guilt and shame for causing Ellis's collapse. Maybe because he'd dreamed of her half the night. He wasn't certain he liked the way his feelings were leaning. 'Just tell her Doctor Ellis is doing fine and they're going to keep him in until tomorrow. And reassure her that *nothing* she did caused this. He's just dehydrated and—'

'Hasn't been eating or sleeping,' Cassie interrupted. 'I know and I think when Brynn's more rested and calm today, she won't feel quite so guilty. Doctor Ellis probably should have been in the hospital anyway, but he wouldn't have gone.'

Twenty minutes later, Garrett started on a fresh cup of coffee, looked at all the papers spread in front of him on his desk, rubbed his forehead and groaned. Since he'd become sheriff three years ago, he'd dealt with several cases of domestic violence, five burglaries, one armed robbery, three car jackings, two rapes, a child molestation and even the murder of a man by his enraged, drug-addled wife whom they'd found crowing over his dead body that she'd finally gotten rid of the rotten, stupid, lazy drunk. Garrett had never been confronted by a true murder mystery, like something in a novel, and he was afraid that he wasn't up to the job of solving it.

But he'd try his damnedest, he told himself. He'd discover who killed Sam.

He picked up a clear sheet protector. The paper inside was labeled, 'Quote marked in Gideon Bible placed next to victim.' The Bible had been stamped BAY MOTEL and was most likely the Bible missing from Mark's room. Did this put Mark in the frame, or was the killer the same person who'd kidnapped Mark – someone who must have been in his motel room? Garrett noted that no fingerprints had been found on the paper or the sheet protector, and that an inside page bore an identification stamp: The Bay Motel, Genessa Point, MD. Then he read the marked verse, Hosea 4:2 O. T.:

By swearing and lying,
Killing and stealing and committing adultery,
They break all restraint,
With bloodshed after bloodshed.

Garrett frowned, wondering. Was the killer explaining why Sam had been murdered? Had Sam committed one of the sins? He'd probably sworn – most people did. Had he lied? Once again, it would be hard to find a person who'd never told a lie, no matter how they denied it. If someone told me they'd never told a lie, I'd know they were lying, Garrett thought.

"'Killing and stealing and committing adultery,'" Garrett read aloud. Killing? The first person who came to Garrett's mind was GPK. An image of the tall, slim man, usually smiling, spending his years chained to a peculiar, emotionless recluse seemed outlandish. If Sam was going to kill anyone, it would be his wife. Had there been a third person in the woods who'd attacked Tessa Cavanaugh? Few people still living in Genessa Point believed that story and they wouldn't have waited eighteen years to kill Sam. The only likely candidates were Brynn and Mark. No evidence pointed toward Brynn. And Mark? Maybe, but to Garrett, Mark was a cypher at this point.

Stealing? Sam's lifestyle had remained the same since Garrett was a child and no one had ever accused him of underhanded behavior when it came to business. Even his owning the Bay Motel and Cloud Nine weren't a mystery – Sam had always lived frugally. He'd saved his money and invested it. As for adultery, few people would have blamed him for affairs considering the woman who'd been his wife for over thirty years. Once again, though, Garrett had never heard a whisper about an affair. Even Sam's wife had only barely expressed resentment when talking about how Lexa, as so many other people did, liked Sam.

Garrett shook his head. Why had the killer put the Bible next to Sam's body? Why had he marked this verse? He'd have to be able to read the killer's mind to find the answer because nothing came to his own.

Already feeling slightly defeated, Garrett turned to the preliminary autopsy report he'd read carefully three times earlier. Some parts of it he could recite from memory and caught himself saying aloud, "'The patient was a sixty-five-year-old Anglo-American male with no significant past medical history . . . The patient was pronounced dead at 22:45 with fixed, dilated pupils, no heart sounds, no pulse and no spontaneous respirations.' Garrett sighed. Sam hadn't been pronounced dead until ten forty-five p.m. He, Brynn, and unfortunately Savannah had found Sam approximately forty minutes earlier.

The esophagus and stomach were normal in appearance without evidence of ulcers or verices. Garrett knew that verices could be the result of cirrhosis, but Sam never drank. Everyone who'd ever invited him to a party knew he always passed up alcohol, choosing a soft drink instead. But the next sentence had drawn him up short the first time he'd read it. Sam's stomach contained no pills and no other food stuff material.

No food. Yet Lexa had supposedly left a message at Love's saying that Sam couldn't meet Brynn at the house until nine o'clock because he'd be taking a client out to dinner.

His mind flashed back to when he'd questioned Lexa the day after Sam's murder. She'd seemed stunned as she tore at a tissue in her hands when she wasn't dabbing away tears. Her young face had looked bleached, her eyelids swollen, her blonde hair pulled back carelessly with a rubber band.

'Brynn Wilder received a message from you saying that her former house had been sold, and Sam said if she wanted to see it, she should meet him there at nine o'clock last night,' Garrett had said in a soft, non-accusatory voice.

Lexa's bloodshot, puffy eyes widened. 'I didn't call Brynn Wilder!'

'No, you didn't call Brynn. You didn't know her cell phone number. You called Cassie Hutton's dress shop and left a message for Brynn.'

Lexa shook her head vehemently. 'No, I didn't!'

'Cassie Hutton says you did.'

'Ms Hutton says I called her? I didn't! I *swear*, I didn't!'

'Cassie doesn't say you called *her*. You called the number of her store. She was busy, so you talked to one of the salespeople in her shop.'

'I've never called Love's Dress Shoppe, period,' Lexa said, her voice a tad less defensive. 'Who says I called?'

'One of the salespeople, as I said. I'd rather not get into names right now.'

'I think I have a right to know who's accusing me.'

'Yes, you do, and we'll get to that later. Right now I want to ask about Brynn's former house on Oriole Lane. I know it's for sale. How long ago did the owner move out?'

'I'm not sure. Seven or eight months.'

'Was there a potential buyer?'

'I probably shouldn't tell you this, but Ray O'Hara went through the house at least three times and took pictures. Mr Fenney didn't like it, but he couldn't refuse to show the house.'

'So Sam thought O'Hara might buy the house?'

'No. He said O'Hara was just being a ghoul wanting to see Jonah Wilder's home. He really didn't like Ray O'Hara. Neither did I.' She blushed. 'He, well, what they used to call "made a pass at me." More than one. He was very crude. Mr Fenney overheard him once and told him to never come back.' Lexa took a deep breath. 'But a very nice couple with two children looked at the house twice within the past month. Sam was certain the husband was going to make an offer within the next few days.'

'Was Sam going out to dinner with that man last night?'

'Not that I know of. In fact, at around two Sam said he felt sort of queasy and he had a headache. He left the office around four-thirty popping Tums in his mouth and saying he'd better skip dinner or just have toast.'

'I'm sorry to keep harping on this, Lexa, but I have to be sure. The potential buyer hadn't already made an offer on Brynn's old house?'

Lexa shook her head.

'Was he expected at the office the next day to sign a contract?'

'No. Sheriff, I told you that he hadn't even made an offer. Unless his offer had been accepted, there wouldn't be a contract to be signed. There was no offer and I didn't call Love's Dress Shoppe. I swear.'

Phone records were being checked as he talked to Lexa. Now, four days later, he knew one of Cassie's salespeople had taken a call at around four-fifty asking her to deliver the message to Cassie, who would know Brynn's cell phone number and pass along Sam's supposed offer to show Brynn the house. 'The woman – Lexa, you said – didn't leave a number where Sam could be reached,' the saleswoman had told him. 'We were busy and it didn't hit me for about ten minutes that I hadn't gotten Mr Fenney's cell number. By that time, the real estate office was closed. I simply told Miss Hutton what Lexa had said.'

'Miss Hutton went straight home and told Brynn,' Garrett told the woman. She'd told Brynn *and* Ray. 'Have you ever spoken to Lexa before?' Garrett had asked.

'No.'

'Was there anything distinctive about her voice?'

'She just sounded young, professional, a bit rushed,' the woman answered, then looked upset. 'I wish I hadn't been so distracted I didn't get Mr Fenney's cell phone number. Maybe that would somehow have prevented his . . .' She'd gulped. 'Murder.'

'It wouldn't have,' Garrett had said confidently, although he was fairly certain it would have screwed with the killer's plans. 'Don't worry. You didn't do anything wrong.'

And now the investigation had revealed that Love's received a call at four-fifty but it was untraceable, just like the call to Brynn at Cassie's house. If Lexa hadn't been the woman who made the call, they'd probably never know who had. They knew only one thing: Brynn had been lured to that house on Oriole Lane.

Garrett sighed as his headache intensified. Even his vision felt blurry. He leaned back in his chair, knowing he couldn't read the pages of the autopsy report again. He didn't need to read them again. He knew a massive blow to the back of Sam's head had driven bones into his brain. Probably that blow had come as a surprise and knocked him unconscious. At least, Garrett hoped so. Unconscious, Sam would not have felt a knife slicing the left side of his neck, severing the internal jugular vein and the superficial cervical artery. Crime scene specialists agreed that Sam had been lying on his back while his neck had been slashed. There was no blood splatter – all the blood lay in a pool beside Sam and under his neck. Finally, the knife had been driven into his heart. The only blood found on the knife was B positive and there was some fish blood.

There were stab wounds to the face, arms and hands, with the longest and deepest being one across the abdominal region. The fatal wound had been the slashing of the left external jugular vein, the internal jugular vein and the superficial cervical artery. A moment later, he found the apparent murder weapon listed: a Havalon Baracuta Edge Folding knife with a five-inch blade.

Wounds to the hands, arms, face, abdomen, the deep slash to the neck and, finally, a five-inch blade jabbed into the heart. This murder hadn't been committed by a person Sam had found spending the night in an empty house, even if that person had been a criminal on the run. Sam Fenney had been murdered by someone with a violent rage against him. No doubt the person who'd made the call to his house around eight o'clock.

The person who'd made the call they couldn't trace.

Later that evening, Garrett called. Brynn answered and, as soon as she heard his voice, she panicked. 'What is it? Have you found Mark?'

'No, Brynn. I'm sorry I scared you by calling.'

Brynn took a deep breath. 'It's OK. I'm just nervous in general.'

'What are you and Cassie doing?'

'Cassie and I?' Brynn asked, puzzled. He sounded so casual. 'Cassie's on the city council. She's at a meeting. I was watching a movie, or rather looking at it. I can't concentrate.'

'I hate to ask, but I need a favor from you.'

A favor? At first the word didn't register with Brynn – not coming from Garrett. Then, without thinking, she said, 'Anything.'

'Would you mind coming to my house for a while? Savannah's upset.' He lowered his voice. 'She's barely spoken since we found Sam. I've been getting really worried. Then tonight we were watching a TV show and she suddenly burst into terrible sobs. She's still not talking – except to ask for you.' Garrett took a deep breath. 'I think she's been silent because she was so horrified by Sam's murder she just went numb, but the trauma has broken through tonight. I'm obviously not handling things too well and I thought maybe you could—'

'I'll be right there,' Brynn interrupted. 'I know the street where you live, but not the house. I need the address.'

'Deputy Carder will bring you.' The day after Sam's murder, Garrett had assigned round-the-clock surveillance for Brynn and tonight Dwight Carder was on duty.

'Oh. Will he wait for me while I'm at your house?'

'No, I'll send him back to Cassie's while you're here. I don't want her to come home and find Ray waiting for her – she needs protection, too, even though she won't admit it. When you're ready to go home, I'll call for him to come back and pick you up.'

'Fine,' Brynn said. 'Does Savannah need anything? I mean, is she feeling well? Is there something from the drugstore I could get for her?'

'She just needs you.' She heard Garrett take a deep, relieved breath. 'Thanks a lot, Brynn. See you soon.'

Fifteen minutes later, Deputy Carder pulled up in front of a staid, two-story white Georgian house with black shutters. Brynn smiled when she knocked on the bright front door. Garrett opened it almost immediately. 'Hi,' she said. 'I like your door!'

Garrett grinned. 'This was Savannah's great-grandmother's house. The door used to be black. It had always been black, just like the shutters, but Savannah said all black and white made the house look "duller than dull." It wasn't easy because Grams hated change, but my daughter talked her into having the door painted what she called peony pink coral. Savannah could charm that woman into anything.'

'I like it. The color is more festive and distinctive than plain red.'

'Grams came to like it, too, although she wouldn't admit it. Anyway, be sure to tell Savannah *you* like it. She'll be pleased.' He smiled at her, then seemed to give himself a mental shake. 'I asked you to come over and then I keep you on the porch discussing the color of the front door. I don't mind admitting I'm shaken up. Come in.'

As Brynn stepped inside the house, Garrett nodded to Carder in the car, who pulled away from the curb. 'How's Savannah?' Brynn asked.

'Not good. She seemed to cheer up a little bit when I told her you were coming, though.'

'Well, that's something. I just hope I can help.'

As Brynn entered the house, she saw large, cool rooms decorated with pale walls, hooked rugs on hardwood floors and some blue and pink chintz upholstered furniture. As Garrett led her into the living room, though, she focused on the teenage girl who sat huddled in the corner of a long couch, sniffling.

'Hi, Savannah,' Brynn said softly.

In spite of the warm night, Savannah wore long jeans, heavy socks and a navy-blue hoody zipped to her throat, hood up. A moment passed before she raised her head to show a blotchy face, swollen eyelids and waxy-pale lips. Some tangles of her beautiful blonde hair peeked from beneath the hood and her nose was bright pink. Henry sat on the floor by her side and she kept a hand on his head.

'Hi, Brynn,' Savannah said in a flat, nasal voice. 'How come you're here?'

Savannah wasn't a child and she was extremely intelligent. Brynn decided excuses would only create distance between them. 'Your father called me and told me you weren't doing so well. He asked if I could come over and help you.'

'I'm sorry he bothered you.'

'He didn't bother me,' Brynn said sincerely. 'Even though I don't know you well, you mean a lot to me.'

Tears brimmed in Savannah's eyes.

'Besides, the movie I was watching on TV was lousy.'

Savannah finally smiled weakly. 'What was it?'

'Something with a ditzy girl trying to choose between two idiot guys. Cassie's at a city council meeting.'

Savannah abruptly burst into tears again and Henry moved closer to her, gazing at Brynn warily, protecting the love of his life. Brynn walked toward the couch while Garrett hovered in the doorway. 'Honey, what's wrong?' Brynn asked softly. 'Do you think it would be easier to talk if just Henry and I were here?'

Savannah raised her head and cast a guilty look at her father. 'Well . . .'

'I have to make a few calls,' Garrett said casually. He glanced at his watch. 'As a matter of fact, the mayor was expecting a call from me about half an hour ago.' He grinned. 'If I'm even ten minutes later than I am now, he'll fire me!'

He vanished and Savannah gave Brynn a shaky smile. 'Dad's a county-elected official – the city mayor can't fire him. Besides, they're like best friends.'

Brynn grinned back. 'You are too smart for your own good, Savannah Dane. Mind if I sit down next to you?'

Savannah leaned forward and patted the couch.

Brynn looked at the dog watching her warily. 'Will Henry mind?'

''Course not. Henry thinks you're cool.'

Brynn rolled her eyes. 'Oh, that's what *all* the dogs think,' she said insouciantly, shrugging her shoulder and earning a giggle from Savannah. She sat down on the chintz-covered couch about a foot from Savannah, who emerged slightly from her hoodie and began fidgeting with a chain around her neck.

'New necklace?' Brynn asked.

Savannah pulled out the chain. 'New dog whistle after Henry ran away from me the other night. Dad says it's not so powerful it will hurt his ears.'

'That's good.' Brynn smiled. 'OK, kiddo, tell me what's going on with you.'

An hour later, Garrett sat at his desk in a little room at the back of the house he used as an office. His back was to her and he jumped when Brynn appeared and spoke to him. 'She's so exhausted, she'll sleep through the night.'

He turned. 'Really? She's all right?'

'She's OK and Henry's with her. I'd say she'll be all right in the morning.'

Garrett looked at her searchingly. She looked serious but not grim. He took a deep breath before asking carefully, 'Would you be breaking a confidence by telling me exactly what's wrong?'

'Quite a few things are bothering Savannah.' Garrett felt himself tensing and Brynn said quickly, 'Wait, I phrased that wrong – made it sound more serious than it is.'

'Does she need professional help?'

'I'm not a psychologist, but I don't think so. Not at all. I think it's just a build-up of a lot of things – things that time and a few adjustments in her life can change. That's only my opinion, but—'

'I respect your opinion.' Garrett swallowed. 'Brynn, Savannah is the most important thing in my life. I'll do anything to see she grows up healthy and happy.'

'I know. And I want to help you, even if all I can do is calm her down by talking to her and maybe even keeping her entertained. After we talked, I spent about twenty minutes reading to her from one of my books.'

'I'll bet she loved that.' He stood up. 'Let's go in the kitchen and talk.'

The kitchen looked as if it hadn't been redecorated since the 1970s. The scrupulously clean gold and white vinyl floor had cracked in places, avocado-colored Formica covered the scratched oak cabinets and matched the refrigerator and stove. Two dim ceiling light fixtures gave the room a gloomy look.

Garrett noticed Brynn glancing around. 'I know. Dated. Grams wouldn't allow anything except Savannah's room to be redecorated. This is how the house looked when she and her husband moved in.'

'Except for the peony pink coral door.'

Garrett laughed. 'Except for the door!' He opened the refrigerator. 'Well, what'll it be? Coke, ice water, a glass of grocery store cheap wine, or lemonade Savannah made?'

'Lemonade, please. I haven't had a glass of homemade lemonade for years.'

Garrett motioned toward an oval table at the end of the kitchen. Beside the table was a wall covered with a glaring yellow and avocado wave-patterned paper.

'Wow,' Brynn murmured. 'I think I'm getting dizzy.'

Garrett burst into laughter. 'I told you Grams wouldn't let anything be changed. The house is almost a hundred years old and could be beautiful, but . . . well, Savannah wants some changes, thank God, and it's her house.'

'*Her* house. This house belongs to Savannah?'

'Yeah. Patty's father died and Patty's mother raised her. Needless to say, Grams wasn't impressed with her daughter's parenting skills.'

'I heard that Grams was Savannah's mother's mother?'

'Yeah. Most people assume she was my grandmother, but mine hasn't lived around here for quite a while. After Patty left, Grams opened her house to Savannah and me and I jumped at the chance. I sure didn't want Savannah raised by Patty's mother, not that she wanted to be saddled with Savannah anyway. Like mother, like daughter.

'Grams was horrified by Patty's desertion of her child and she wanted to make certain that her great-grandchild would own this house,' Garrett went on. 'Grams cared about me, but she thought there was a chance I might get married again and if she left the house to me, a second wife might cause trouble – splitting of assets and all that. She made the most iron-clad will in history leaving the house to Savannah, held in trust by me until Savannah is twenty-one. Patty can't possibly return to town and try to take it, although I've been steeled every day since Grams died for exactly that event.'

'Where is your ex-wife?' Brynn asked softly.

'I don't know. Her last Christmas card to Savannah came two years ago and was postmarked Las Vegas. We haven't heard from her since then. I don't think she keeps in touch with anyone else in town. All I care about is that she stays wherever she is and never bothers us again.' He hesitated. 'Does Savannah want her mother to come back since Grams died? Is that what's wrong with her?'

'Just the opposite,' Brynn said quickly. 'She's afraid her mother *will* come back. She's a savvy girl, Garrett. She knows her mother could try to get this house or, well . . . take *her*, not because Patty wants her, but because she has an ulterior motive.'

'My God!' Color flowed and ebbed in Garrett's face. 'I've been worried about the same thing but I had no idea it had crossed Savannah's mind.'

'Well, it has, and she doesn't feel safe, partly because she's spending her days with the woman next door – Mrs Persinger? The Doily Lady as Savannah calls her.'

Garrett closed his eyes. 'Of course she doesn't feel safe. Mrs Persinger is a retired grade school teacher. She loves children and she's especially fond of Savannah, but she's seventy-six and looks and acts ten years older. She means well but she's vague and frail. She lives alone and doesn't have any younger friends – not even middle-aged people.'

'The situation with Savannah's great-grandmother was different?'

'As different as possible. Grams was seventy-six too, but she could work me into the ground, and was one of those people who seemed like they could handle anything. She loved people in general and had them coming and going all day – even young women with babies and toddlers. Savannah loved to play with the kids. Grams was a widow, but she was rarely alone. That gave Savannah a sense of security. Grams had energy and strength and joy for life. She kept Savannah busy with a dozen hobbies and activities.'

Garrett stopped for a moment, his throat working. Finally, he said, 'I couldn't believe it when Grams dropped dead of a heart attack. We didn't even know she had heart trouble. I thought she'd live to be a hundred.'

'What a shock that must have been for both you and Savannah,' Brynn said softly.

'Yes. I think we were in a daze for at least a couple of weeks. Then I had to make some other arrangements for Savannah. Mrs Persinger really likes to look after her when I'm at work, but the poor thing rocks and crochets and maunders about the past all day. I haven't found anyone suitable and I've done a bad job—'

'Stop it,' Brynn said sharply. 'You haven't done a bad job. Savannah's great-grandmother has only been dead seven weeks. You're not a miracle-worker. You've done the right thing. After all, you couldn't drag Savannah to work with you.'

Garrett shrugged, not feeling better. I could have tried harder, he thought. I could have interviewed younger women who are more active, more fun, more . . . *something* . . .

'She worries about you,' Brynn said, breaking his train of thought. 'Of course, she worries because you're the sheriff and she thinks you're in constant danger.'

'I'm not. Things aren't always the way they've been lately.'

'But she worries about more than your job. She worries because you're alone.'

'I'm not alone. I have her.'

Brynn's gaze shifted slightly and she said quickly, 'She thinks you need, and I quote, "someone your own age." She wishes you had a girlfriend. Well, really, she wishes you had a wife. She's not one of those jealous, possessive little girls who wants all of Daddy's attention. She's afraid you're lonely. She wants you to find love. And, frankly, I don't think she'd mind having a mother.'

'A mother?' Garrett felt a shockwave go through him. He thought most girls Savannah's age resented their mothers who wouldn't let them wear what they wanted, or go wherever they wanted, or disapproved of any boy they had a crush on. 'A mother?' Garrett repeated. 'I never dreamed she'd want a mother. Am I stupid? I thought adolescent girls wanted as much freedom as they could get.'

'They think they do. When I was just twelve, I got frustrated with my father sometimes because he could be strict. But later, when I didn't have him anymore and my mother had to work, I realized how much I wished I had *two* parents who cared about what I did. I guess I decided freedom was overrated.'

'I can't say I've tried very hard to find someone. I've dated a few women through the years since Patty left, but that was such a bad experience . . .'

'You couldn't get over her?' Brynn finally asked.

Garrett looked at her in surprise. 'No! I mean, she didn't break my heart or anything romantic like that. I haven't been pining for her all these years. Hell, I was only twenty-two when I married her. She was twenty.' He lowered his voice. 'I'll be honest – Patty was pregnant with Savannah. She talked about getting an abortion, but I didn't want that. I wanted a family, especially because my own was such a mess.' He saw curiosity flare in Brynn's eyes. 'William Bale Dane was a good sheriff but he wasn't a good father. And my mother was too scared of him to do much except try to stay out of his way. Anyway, I had this crazy idea that I could turn everything around for myself. I thought I loved Patty. I thought I'd be a great father.' He shook his head. 'God, I was stupid.'

'You've been a great father. No one can doubt how much you love Savannah.'

'Maybe. But that's not enough. That's not all I wanted – want – for her. Patty and I weren't happy but I thought she cared enough about Savannah to stay around, even if we got divorced. Instead, she turned out to be the flake of all flakes and ran off with a guy. Don't think *that* didn't get the town talking.'

'I know all about small town gossip.'

'I guess you would.' Garrett tried to smile at her, but his face was tight with pent-up emotion. 'After I finally managed to divorce her, I tried dating, but I must have bad taste in women. Just lately I got myself entangled with Rhonda Sanford, a real head case.'

Brynn couldn't help smiling. 'So I heard.'

'From who?'

'It's "whom" and Savannah, for one.'

'Oh, God.' Garrett bent his head. 'I wish I'd never seen her, much less asked her out. Grams kept telling me I needed a woman in my life, though. I hadn't had a date for a year when I met Rhonda and at first she was fine. Pleasant, intelligent, good company.'

'And beautiful.'

'Well, yes. At least, that's what everyone said. I thought she was attractive but there was just something about her – maybe a coldness in her eyes – that never appealed to me. And I let things go on too long. It wasn't until I sensed that she didn't like Savannah that I knew I had to end things.'

Brynn hesitated. 'Garrett, from what Cassie's told me, Rhonda doesn't just dislike Savannah. It's worse than that. And Rhonda partly blames Savannah for your break-up. Maybe *partly* is too weak a word.'

'She hates Savannah?'

'I don't know Rhonda well enough to guess her exact feelings about Savannah, but I know she can be very aggressive. She was hostile toward Mark after he'd talked to her aunt, Miranda Gaines. Her son, Frankie Gaines, was a victim of the Genessa Point Killer.'

Garrett looked at Brynn solemnly. 'Mark didn't talk to Miranda Gaines. I called her. Mrs Gaines said Mark didn't come to her house and he didn't call her. She said there must have been a misunderstanding.' He paused, then decided to be completely honest. 'Rhonda also told me you'd been to Cassie's store and said awful things to her – frightened her.'

Brynn started to say something but Garrett held up his hand. 'You don't have to defend yourself. I know you saw her at the store and you wouldn't have said anything awful to her. You certainly didn't frighten her. No one frightens that woman. And she's a liar.'

'I think she's even worse than that, Garrett. Savannah is afraid of her. She won't come out and say it, but the calls at night, Rhonda's possessiveness of you, her attitude toward Savannah – yes, Savannah knows Rhonda really dislikes her – have her worried. She's only thirteen, Garrett, and Rhonda is—'

'Unbalanced,' Garrett said flatly. 'I don't know what she's like normally, but she's either drinking or doing drugs. She's gotten strange, unpredictable – scary.'

'You have to do something about her, Garrett. For Savannah.'

Garrett could feel his jaw tightening. 'Oh, I will,' he managed. 'You bet I will.'

'But here I am, blaming Rhonda, when I've frightened Savannah even more.'

'*You*? How?'

'How? As long as I'm in town, she can't forget that Mark's been kidnapped.'

Brynn began nervously rubbing the pendant on a necklace he'd seen her wear before. Savannah had told him the pendant was a dragonfly. Brynn had loved dragonflies since she was a little girl, Savannah said. Wasn't that cool?

'And what about Sam?' Brynn asked. 'Savannah would never have seen him dead, stabbed through the heart in my old bedroom if it hadn't been for me. I've done more to traumatize that girl than any fear of her mother or Rhonda could!'

Garrett leaned forward and said intensely, 'Brynn, you can't hold yourself responsible for what happened to Sam or for Savannah seeing him. You were trying as hard as I was to keep her from going into that house. And even if you hadn't stayed in town, I'd still be searching for Mark and she'd know about it.'

'You wouldn't be listening to "Can't Find My Way Home."'

'What does that have to do with anything?'

'She knows the song has something to do with Mark – Mark, who's missing, maybe dead. And then she heard it again, playing over and over on a boombox beside Sam's body.' She looked at Garrett, her hazel eyes brimming with tears. 'What in God's name does that song have to do with Sam?'

'I think there must be some connection between Sam's murder and Mark's kidnapping.' Garrett waited a beat, then said, 'Don't bite off my head, but did Mark have any special grudge against Sam?'

'No. He resented the way Sam dropped out of our lives after Dad's death, but if he had a special grudge, it was against Edmund Ellis. He's the one who claimed he didn't know Dad had lost the knife used to kill those children. He said he'd seen Dad use the knife about two weeks before Tessa killed Dad with it.'

'Actually, he said he was *fairly certain* your father used that knife.'

'In your father's eyes, *fairly certain* was as good as *absolutely certain*.'

Brynn was right, Garrett thought. He remembered with aversion his father blasting details about the case over dinner in the evenings, banging his fist on the table. His fragile mother would get so nervous, she could barely eat. Even then, Garrett hadn't thought everything was black and white concerning this case. He'd had questions, but he hadn't dared ask them. As if it was yesterday, Garrett could hear his father announce that Stone Jonah Wilder was definitely the Genessa Point Killer and his son Mark was his accomplice. There was no doubt about it . . . Well, Jonah had gotten what was coming to him. Mark hadn't. But he'd get him, William had declared viciously. One day, he would make Mark Wilder suffer, just like his father!

Brynn's cell phone rang. 'Oh, it's probably Cassie, even though I left her a note.' Without glancing at the caller ID, she said, 'Hi. I'm still at Garrett's.' Then her face went pale and she motioned for Garrett, who nearly turned over his chair in his rush to get to her as she held out the phone. His hand covered hers, steadying it as they both listened to 'Can't Find My Way Home.' The song ended and after a few moments of silence, a weak, gritty voice said just above a whisper, 'Help me. Please. But if you can't—' The voice scraped before dissolving into a dry, raking cough. 'If you can't, know that I love you, Dragonfly.'

The connection ended.

Garrett looked at a white, trembling Brynn. 'Was that Mark?'

She said nothing, still holding out the phone, her gaze fixed on the wall. Garrett took his hand off hers, moved it across her back and clasped her shoulder, drawing her close to him, hugging her gently. 'Brynn, could you tell if that was Mark?'

Finally, she whispered, 'It was Mark.' She raised her head from Garrett's shoulder and looked at him, pain clouding her eyes. 'He always called me Dragonfly.'

TWELVE

Garrett stopped shaving and looked in the mirror at himself. Brynn Wilder had cried in his arms last night. Mark's confident, beautiful little sister who'd always intrigued him. Even before she'd reached her teens, she'd seemed to look inside him, to discern the damaged spirit he tried so hard to hide from everyone. Sometimes he'd felt anger and embarrassment because he couldn't hide from Brynn what he was able to hide from everyone else. Not that she said anything revealing to him, but often when he glanced at her, he saw the knowledge in her expressive eyes. But she's a kid, he'd told himself back then. A smart kid, but just a kid who thinks she's a whole lot more perceptive than she is.

But he'd known he was only making up excuses. Being unnerved by a pre-pubescent girl had seemed almost perverted to him. But the truth was that she *had* shaken him. She'd also fascinated him. And now . . .

And now, what did he feel about Brynn Wilder? Last night he'd kissed her teary eyelids, held her close and finally pressed his lips against hers. At first he'd been almost unaware of what he was doing. He'd meant it to be a gentle, comforting kiss, like one would give a hurt child. But within a minute, his lips pressed harder and hers had responded. He'd held her tighter and she'd wrapped her arms around him, rubbing his back, touching the tender skin at his neck as he embraced her gently, then clutched her willing body against him, the urgency of their needs, their desires, overcoming all thoughts of what might be considered appropriate. Garrett had only known that this woman stirred feelings in the depths of him he'd never known existed, feelings that surpassed just the physical, feelings he couldn't ignore, feelings that churned whenever he thought about her—

'Dad, did Rhonda call again last night?'

Garrett jumped, nicking his cheek, and cursed.

'I'm sorry,' Savannah said, fear edging her voice. 'You never shave with the door open and I just thought I'd ask . . . Are you hurt?'

'Not at all. I was thinking of something else,' Garrett laughed, sticking a piece of tissue on the nick and turning to his daughter. 'I'm worried my hair doesn't look right today.'

Savannah smiled shakily. 'Your hair always looks wonderful, Dad. I'm glad I've got blonde hair like yours, not black like Patty's.' She always calls her mother Patty, not Mom, Garrett thought. She doesn't think of the woman as her mother at all. 'I'm sorry I asked about Rhonda. It's just that she calls all the time and last night I was coming downstairs to get something to drink and I heard a phone ring.'

Fear resonated in her voice and he put down the razor and kneeled in front of her. 'Rhonda won't call us anymore unless she gets our new phone number. And the call last night came on Brynn's phone.'

'Who called her?'

'I don't know,' Garrett said truthfully. Brynn had sworn that the voice that had asked for help was Mark's. Garrett might still have had doubts – it was easy to make a voice sound weak, dry and rough – almost unidentifiable. But even Garrett hadn't known Mark's nickname for his sister was *Dragonfly*. Brynn had told him it was a secret between her and Mark.

'She didn't tell you?'

Garrett's thoughts jerked back to his daughter, who was gazing at him quizzically. 'Uh, no. It was probably her friend Cassie. Brynn only talked for a minute.'

Savannah looked relieved. 'Oh, that's OK then.'

'That's OK? Why?'

'Well, I thought maybe Rhonda called her.' Savannah looked down. 'Sometimes she watches the house at night. She would have known Brynn was here.'

'Rhonda watches the house at night?' Garrett asked incredulously.

'Yes,' Savannah said just above a whisper.

'How do you know?'

'Well, sometimes I can't sleep since Grams died. She used to tell me that when I can't sleep, I should look out my window and try to count all the stars.' She paused. 'She said it was better than counting imaginary sheep. Anyway, I've been doing that a lot lately, or trying to, but I can't concentrate on the stars because I see Rhonda, just standing and staring at our house. She parks her car down the street. I guess she's afraid you'll recognize it.'

'Why didn't you tell me?'

'Because I knew you'd get upset or worried.'

Garrett felt a sinking sensation inside, almost a pain. His thirteen-year-old daughter shouldn't have a care in the world. Instead, she'd been protecting *his* feelings, looking after *him*. 'Was Rhonda outside last night?'

'I didn't look in case I saw her. I just thought that maybe she was outside and saw Brynn.'

Garrett tried to keep his voice even, but he was furious. 'How long has Rhonda been doing this?'

'Oh, I don't know. Maybe a month or a little longer.' Her gaze dropped to his hand. 'Dad, you're pressing your thumb on your razor! You're bleeding!'

'Damn it!' Garrett muttered, grabbing a tissue. 'I didn't feel a thing.'

Savannah handed him another tissue. 'It's going to bleed on your pants and your T-shirt. How can you stand wearing a T-shirt under your regular shirt? Anyway, do you think you need stitches?'

Garrett lifted the tissues he'd wrapped around his thumb. 'Doesn't look life-threatening.' He tried to make his voice light, unconcerned. 'I think some antiseptic spray and a Band-Aid will do.'

Savannah immediately gathered antiseptic spray and the box of Band-Aids while he kept wrapping tissues around his thumb until it had nearly stopped bleeding. Garrett pretended great pain when she sprayed on antiseptic, which made her laugh, and finally she applied the Band-Aid.

He smiled at his daughter. 'You're good at first aid. Maybe you'll be a nurse or a doctor.'

'No. I want to be an actress or a writer,' Savannah said firmly. 'You didn't forget that the carnival is tonight, did you?'

'Of course not,' he said heartily, although he'd completely forgotten. 'Are you still my date for the evening?'

'Sure. But I wondered . . . well, I'd like to ask Brynn to go with us. Would that be OK?'

Brynn. Garrett couldn't wait to see her again, but he managed to say casually, 'That would be fine, but you should ask Cassie Hutton, too. You don't know her, but it's the polite thing to do. Besides, she's fun.'

'Then I'll ask her.' Knowledge suddenly flashed in Savannah's eyes. 'You don't want me to ask Cassie Hutton just to be polite. If only Brynn goes with us, people will think she's your date, and I know you aren't supposed to date a client.'

'A client?'

'Well, someone who's part of a case you're working on. Or something like that.'

'Yeah, something like that.'

'So you can call Brynn and ask if she and her friend want to come with us.'

'Why don't *you* call Brynn and invite her and Cassie? Call her "Miss Hutton."'

'OK, Dad,' Savannah grinned. 'I'll do the asking. Only don't hurt yourself anymore. If you've got Band-Aids stuck all over yourself, Brynn will think you're a total geek.'

'Brynn! Brynn, wake up!'

'Go 'way,' Brynn mumbled, rolling over and pulling a pillow over her head. 'Sleepy.'

'I don't care!' The pillow seemed to fly off Brynn's head and light hit her swollen eyes. She scrunched them tighter. 'Brynn, this is important. You have to wake up!'

'Oh, damn,' Brynn moaned. 'I just got in bed.'

'You did not. You got in bed at eleven o'clock. I tucked you in myself.' Cassie shook her. 'I'm sorry you're still tired but—'

'I hafta wake up. I know.' Brynn moaned again and squinted at Cassie. 'What's wrong?'

Cassie pulled the sheet and light summer blanket off her and began tugging her toward the side of the bed. 'You have to get up and come see something.'

'Oh, Cass, can't you just tell me—'

'The police are here. They want you downstairs.' Cassie gave her a vigorous yank. '*Now.*'

Brynn tumbled out of the bed like a child, staggered, then got her balance and stood up, taking in Cassie's sleek beige linen dress, high heels, subtly sophisticated makeup and shining, smooth hair while aware that one of her own drawstring pant-legs had caught at her knee and her T-shirt was rolled up to her breasts. Half of her thick, tangled hair hung over her face. Brynn swept it back and repeated fearfully, 'The *police* are here? Is it about Mark?'

'No, it's not about Mark.' Cassie was already stuffing her into a white waffle knit wrap robe. Brynn couldn't untangle her thoughts enough to ask more questions as Cassie grabbed her hand and hurried her down the stairs. At the bottom, Brynn heard men's voices. Cassie led her into the kitchen, where she immediately saw Deputy Carder and another unfamiliar young man in uniform.

'Go outside and get a couple of pictures of this – no, three. One from each angle,' Carder told the young one, then looked at Brynn. 'Good morning, Miss Wilder. Sorry to get you off to such a bad start today.'

'It's all right,' Brynn said shakily. 'What's happened?'

'Nothing's really happened. Miss Hutton spotted this when she was getting ready to leave for work. Come look.'

Cassie led her to the kitchen window above the sink. Brynn looked out at the sunlight-drenched large backyard with lush fescue grass surrounded by a six-foot-high fence covered by a dense growth of English ivy.

'What is it you want me to see?' Brynn asked, mystified. Then she caught a small, bright flash a few feet in front of the kitchen window. She leaned forward and saw something sparkling as it dangled from a chain hung on the inside edge of the porch roof.

'What *is* that?' Brynn asked, although something already niggled in her memory. She padded barefoot out the back door and across the porch where a necklace hung. She reached up to touch it before Carder snapped, 'Stop!' Then: 'Sorry. Fingerprints.'

'Of course,' Brynn said vaguely, looking at the small imitation turquoise dragonfly decorated with two tiny glass beads cut to sparkle in the light. 'It's my necklace. Or *was*. I bought it when I was . . . nine, I think.' She looked at the worn twenty-inch chain that had once been silver tone and now looked dull gray and black in spots. 'I loved it. I wore it almost every day under my tops. That's why the chain is so long for a child's necklace. It was supposed to be a secret good luck charm.' She took a deep breath. 'I haven't seen it since I was twelve.'

Another missing item from her past in Genessa Point.

Cassie said she'd spotted it when she was rinsing out the coffee pot. Light had shimmered off the two beads of glass. She told Deputy Carder she'd gone outside and almost reached for it until she saw it was hanging from a clean, adhesive-backed plastic wall hook she hadn't attached to the porch rim. As she stared at it, she'd vaguely remembered something about Brynn losing the necklace not long before Jonah's death. 'Being cautious and suspicious has already become a habit, I guess,' Cassie had said, 'and I immediately ran outside to tell the surveillance guy.' He'd gone around the house and looked at it, then told her to get Brynn while he called headquarters.

Now the excitement was over and everyone had gone, except for the cop watching the house. Brynn's necklace had been taken away by a policeman wearing latex gloves who'd placed it conscientiously in a plastic bag.

Brynn smiled at the thought. Who would have thought that cheap little necklace would someday be treated with such care? She remembered saving the money her parents gave her: Mom for helping weed the flower beds and household chores; Dad for stuffing dead leaves into trash bags. Finally, one autumn she'd caught sight of the necklace in a little 'this and that' shop, as her mother called it. She'd thought silver plate and turquoise-colored Lucite was real silver and turquoise, bought the piece of jewelry and started wearing it every day. Then it disappeared. She thought the cheap chain had broken and the necklace had fallen off without her realizing just a couple of months before Jonah was killed. If so, someone had found it, kept it, and decided to 'return' it at a suspiciously significant time.

Determined to brighten her mood with anything – to begin with, clothes – Brynn was zipping herself into a bright coral and pink dress when her cell phone rang. She picked it up from the dresser top. After she said hello, a man said in a regretful, embarrassed voice, 'Miss Wilder? This is Jack Porter, the manager of the Bay Motel. I hate to bother you with this, but would it be possible for you to clear out your brother's room today? The sheriff has kept it closed since . . . well, for the last few days, but he said the police have gotten everything they need and now with Sam dead and us having to turn away people who'd like to rent a room . . . I talked to him this morning and he said it was OK for you to get . . . well, everything personal out of there.'

'Oh.' Brynn felt as if she'd been kicked. Mark's room isn't important to anyone anymore, she thought bleakly. Come get his stuff. Clear out the last traces of him. 'I can do that today.'

'How about this morning? Our check-out time is noon and I'd like to have that room in shape to rent out again by one at the latest. It's nothing personal . . .'

'Personal? How could it be? You don't even know me,' Brynn

snapped. 'I'll be there within half an hour. Will the room be unlocked?'

'Uh, yeah, if you're sure you'll get here pretty fast. I can't just leave a room unlocked, you know.'

'I know. Goodbye.'

'Good—'

Brynn cut him off and stood staring venomously at the cell phone. Then she closed her eyes, took a deep breath and counted to ten. She put down the phone and stared at herself in the mirror. 'So much for trying to look upbeat today,' she said, gazing at the cheery dress. She unzipped it, threw it on the bed and dug in her duffle bag for a pair of jeans with tears at the thighs and knees, a faded Rolling Stones T-shirt and a pair of worn sandals. Clothes for packing and moving, she thought. Work clothes. This is nothing but work. It has nothing to do with Mark.

As soon as she'd dressed and found an empty box in Cassie's basement, Brynn left for the Bay Motel. She turned into the parking lot and saw that the parking spaces across from Mark's room were occupied. 'Damn it,' she muttered, driving to the back of the motel. As she headed for an empty space across from the rooms, she caught sight of an auburn-haired woman stepping out a doorway, then turning and grasping a tall, beefy man and kissing him passionately. As soon as she saw the hair, she knew the woman was Rhonda Sanford. Brynn whipped into a narrow space, shut off the car, lowered herself in the seat and watched in the rearview mirror.

Rhonda's kiss turned from passionate to almost violent. She looked as if she were going to devour the man's face. He raised his arms and grabbed her hair, pulling back her head, and Brynn almost gasped to see Ray O'Hara. He said something to Rhonda, who laughed and pushed forward, groping him, holding up her face for another kiss. Brynn glanced at her watch. Ten o'clock. Rhonda should have been at work an hour ago. Had she been here all night? Her wrinkled dress and bare feet answered that question.

Finally, Ray took her arms, turned her around and propelled her forward. Her shoulder bag fell off her arm. She laughed, staggered, turned and started back toward him but he stepped into his room and shut the door. Rhonda stood weaving for a moment, then shrugged, picked up her bag and walked unsteadily toward Brynn's car, stopped, looked around in confusion, and staggered toward a sedan three cars away. After nearly a minute, she crept out of the parking place and started out slowly, nearly hitting the trash dumpster as she turned the corner and headed to the east side front of the motel.

Rhonda and Ray? Brynn thought, baffled. Since when? And why did Rhonda keep harassing Garrett if she was involved with Ray O'Hara?

THIRTEEN

Not many of Mark's belongings had been left in the motel. Brynn didn't look at anything closely. She didn't hold the shirts up to her nose and try to catch Mark's scent. She didn't inspect the condition of the clothes or search the room, looking for some important clue the police had missed like some genius amateur detective. She hummed and thought about the book she should be working on, trying to take her mind off what she was doing – sweeping away Mark's things as if he'd never occupied this sadly plain, anonymous room.

Brynn filled only two of the three boxes she'd brought. She made two quick trips to the car, hoping Ray wouldn't come out of his motel room and see her or that he'd already left for the day. Afterward, she drove slowly around town, gazing at everything, almost as if by looking hard enough, she'd spot him walking along jauntily, whistling. Mark loved to whistle.

At least he had before Jonah died.

Brynn squeezed her eyes tight for a moment then opened them, relieved that she hadn't swerved into the other lane. What was wrong with her? Did she want to die because she might never see her troubled, maddening, beloved big brother again?

Well, she wouldn't see him if the search for him had been called off. The possibility seemed strong if the police were no longer interested in the place where Mark had been just before he disappeared, and it had kept her in a daze since she'd gotten the call from the motel. She had to know what was going on. She needed to talk to Garrett.

She parked near the courthouse where police headquarters was housed. Brynn didn't want to see Garrett this morning. Last night was too fresh in her mind. She'd cried after hearing her brother's tortured voice on the phone. She'd clung to him at first in devastation, then in slowly growing desire, until finally her passion had taken control as she'd felt his passion for her. Brynn knew they could never go back to acting as if they were nothing except two acquaintances working together only because they were searching for her lost brother. They'd unmasked each other last night, the deep, fiery yearning between them showing in their kisses, their intimate caresses, their whispered expressions of pleasure . . .

'May I help you?'

Brynn realized she'd walked into the main room of headquarters without even realizing it. The craggy-faced woman she'd seen on her first visit here was looking disapprovingly at her over the rim of her glasses. Brynn glanced down at her ragged jeans and Rolling Stones T-shirt. 'I'm here to see Sheriff Dane.'

'Is he expecting you?'

'No. But it's important. I'm Brynn—'

'I know who you are,' the woman said in her grainy voice. 'You really should call before you just show up here. The sheriff is a very busy man.'

'But not too busy to see Miss Wilder.' Brynn looked up to see Garrett standing in the doorway. He didn't smile but walked slowly toward her. 'I've been expecting a visit from you today. Come back to my office.'

Brynn heard the craggy-faced woman huff in exasperation. 'Not one of my fans,' she murmured to Garrett.

'Not one of anyone's fans. Perpetual sense of being wronged by the world, but too organized and experienced for me to let go, much as I hate being greeted with that sour expression and sandpaper voice every morning.'

'Did you know I was here?'

'Yes. Carder saw you come in and headed straight back to tell me. He knew she'd give you a hard time.' He walked slightly farther away from her than usual and his voice sounded more formal. He opened the door to his office. 'Have a seat. Want coffee?'

'Not this morning. Especially nothing with caffeine.' She sank tiredly onto the hard chair across from his desk. 'I've just come back from the Bay Motel. The manager called me this morning and told me to clean out Mark's room before noon. They're ready to rent it out again.' She gave Garrett a hard look. 'He said you were through with the room.'

'We are.' He sat down in his comfortable executive desk chair. 'Did you think we'd keep it closed forever?'

'No, but it's so soon after Mark disappeared. You've stopped the investigation, haven't you?'

Garrett looked at her in surprise. 'God, no. We're just finished

with the motel room, which I told the manager, but I didn't say it
had to be cleaned out today. Apparently the manager just couldn't
wait to get someone else in there.'

'But why *today?* Why so soon?'

Garrett picked up a pen and tapped it almost nervously against
his desk. 'Look, Brynn, he's planning on pooling funds with some
of his friends and buying the place. He said he didn't want the room
getting the reputation of being the place where Stone Jonah Wilder's
accomplice lived for a few days before he disappeared.'

Brynn winced, then said, 'What about the former owner being
murdered?'

'I don't think he knew Sam was the sole owner. I'm keeping that
confidential.'

'Have you found out anything about Sam's murder?'

'You know I have to keep details about another investigation
confidential,' Garrett said.

'So details about Sam's murder, which took place in our former
house, is confidential and you haven't found out anything about my
brother.'

'Sorry, but I'm being honest.'

'I know. I guess I'm just not in the mood for so much honesty
at the moment.'

'You're always in the mood for honesty. You're mad at me.'

Brynn looked at him questioningly.

'I was out of line last night – so out of line I can hardly believe
it,' Garrett said stiffly. 'You're involved in a case I'm investigating.
We should have a professional relationship, nothing more. Instead,
I took advantage of your vulnerability. My behavior was unprofes-
sional, inappropriate—'

'Oh, be quiet, Garrett,' Brynn snapped. Last night had meant
more to her than she wanted him to know. She also saw that he felt
deeply embarrassed. The moment she'd seen him this morning,
she'd decided to act off-hand, even a bit hard-nosed about the whole
incident. 'I'm a woman, not a little girl. Nothing happened that I
didn't want to happen.'

After a moment, Garrett said, 'You don't know what you wanted
to happen. You were too upset and I was there, representing authority,
strength for you.'

Brynn laughed. 'I kissed the hell out of you because you repre-
sented authority? Garrett, I kissed you because I wanted to. In fact,

I think I've wanted to kiss you since I was twelve. Not passionately back then, of course, I was just a little girl, really, but now . . .'

'But now?'

'I'm not saying any more. You'll drown in guilt if I do. Either that or you'll think I'm half out of my mind because of Mark. Don't get me wrong. Right now, finding Mark is the most important thing in the world to me. But it's not the *only* thing that's important to me.' She looked at him. 'Stop gaping and blushing. You're acting like a teenage girl. And don't you dare imply that you haven't thought about me over the years, just like I've thought about you. I'm not an adolescent with a silly crush. I'm a woman, Garrett. I know what I want and I'm strong. I don't swoon into the arms of any man who comes to my aid.' She stopped until she was certain Garrett was too shocked to answer. He just stared at her. 'You said you were expecting a visit from me today,' Brynn finally said crisply, knowing she couldn't keep up this casual act much longer when what she really wanted to do was to wrap her arms around him and taste more of his kisses. 'So, did you want to see me about Mark's room?'

Garrett cleared his throat, shuffled a few papers, then met her gaze. 'Partly about Mark's room but mostly because I heard someone left another of your old possessions at Cassie's house this morning,' he said in an almost businesslike voice. 'Uh, a necklace? When did you lose it?'

'It was an imitation turquoise and imitation silver necklace I bought when I was nine or ten. It was very cheap. I used to wear it every day and then I got careless with it when the chain started turning my neck green. I guess my body chemistry changed. That was sometime when I was twelve. I didn't miss it immediately. One day I wanted to wear it but it wasn't in my little jewelry box. I couldn't remember when I'd worn it last and I thought maybe it had just fallen off and I hadn't noticed.' Brynn sighed. 'It wasn't something I really valued like Mom did her mother-of-pearl makeup case. I wasn't upset.'

'But somebody found it and cherished it enough to hold onto it all these years.'

'I guess.' Brynn felt a chill on her neck. She hadn't wanted to think about someone keeping that little piece of junk jewelry for eighteen years. 'The house was under surveillance last night,' she said vacantly.

'The front of the house. Carder wasn't circling the place once an hour and no one was watching the backyard with the fence covered in all that ivy. The necklace was hanging from a plastic adhesive hook?'

'Yeah. Brand new. Cassie said she hadn't put a hook there.'

'So someone probably sneaked in during the night and put up the hook directly in front of that window where it would catch the morning sun.'

'I guess.'

'You don't sound very interested.'

Brynn turned her head and gazed out the window. 'I'm tired,' she said flatly. 'Not just physically. Emotionally. And I feel like a failure. I pictured myself coming here, finding Mark in record time and taking him home. I *knew* something serious had happened to him, but I still kept that stupid super-girl fantasy in my mind like some kid.'

'Finding Mark is up to us, not you,' Garrett said mildly. 'I heard from the Baltimore police this morning. There's no sign of Mark being at his house for days. The neighbors haven't seen his car. He didn't seem to be close to any of them. They talked to the manager of the bank where Mark worked. He said Mark was fired for continually coming in late and not being in shape to work.'

'Hungover.'

'Well, yes. The manager gave him a couple of warnings, but he didn't improve. After nearly three months he let Mark go.'

'His wife left three months before he was fired.'

'The bank manager emphasized that Mark's . . .' Brynn looked up to see Garrett barely smiling, '. . . lackadaisical manner, poor deportment with customers and slipshod appearance were the reasons he was fired. God, this guy sounds like a barrel of fun. Anyway, there was no question of Mr Wilder doing anything dishonorable businesswise.'

Finally Brynn smiled. 'Was this manager from the nineteenth century?'

'Eighteenth, I believe. The cops in Baltimore got a kick out of him, too. They said he tried to get more information as to why they were concerned about Mr Wilder, but they gave him nothing. I'll bet he stewed over Mark all day. A young guy who works in the bank went on break just as the cops were leaving and told them he's a friend of Mark's. He said he knows all about the GPK murders and Jonah and how much it obsessed Mark, especially after his wife left. He said he and Mark and a couple of others play poker once a week, but none of them have heard from Mark for two weeks. Absolutely nothing. The friend said he was on the verge of calling you. He seemed really worried.'

'I'm glad Mark has at least one friend who cares so much. If the Baltimore police will give me his name and phone number, I'll call him.'

'Are you sure that's a good idea?'

'Why wouldn't it be? If this guy knows Mark and has been talking to him for months, he might know more about what's going on with him than we do. And if I was him, I might be more inclined to tell his sister than the police. He knows Mark doesn't trust the cops.' Brynn looked at Garrett imploringly. 'Please!'

'You need to do something else other than calling this guy, Brynn.'

'What?'

'Rest.'

'Rest? You mean go home and take a nap?'

'It wouldn't hurt you.'

Brynn's fist came down hard on the arm of the chair. 'Are you crazy?'

He paused. 'You're hanging by a thread today, in case you didn't know it.'

'So I'm not good for anything, right? Dammit, Garrett!'

Garrett stared at her for a few moments. 'OK. I'll get Mark's friend's name and phone number if you'll do something for me.'

'I will not take a nap!'

'You sound like Savannah when she was three. It doesn't involve sleep.' Brynn looked at him warily. 'I'd be grateful if you could go down the street to Mrs Elway's hot dog stand.' He glanced at his watch. 'Savannah's been working there for over two hours. I'd like for you to take her – and Henry – away from work for a while. She could use a break.' He hesitated. 'She also has something she wants to ask you. Will you do it?'

Despite Garrett's composed voice, Brynn saw the pleading look in his azure eyes. She felt embarrassingly surprised and touched, not just because she wanted the phone number or because she couldn't say no if Savannah wanted something of her – she already knew that – but because she'd just realized she couldn't refuse to do something that obviously meant so much to Garrett. He didn't have to know that, though.

'Well, OK,' she answered, trying to sound mildly agreeable. Brynn longed to see Savannah, but she didn't want Garrett to know how attached she'd become to the girl. She pretended to give it a moment's thought. 'I guess I can work it into my schedule,' she said casually. 'Anything in particular you'd like for us to do?'

'She and Henry might like a walk around Holly Park.'

'Fine.' She grinned at him.

Garrett smiled. 'I really appreciate this.'

'Oh, you should,' Brynn said, standing up. 'It's a terrible imposition.'

Ten minutes later, she was at the hot dog stand.

'Hi, Brynn. What can I get for you?' Savannah looked miserable.

'Nothing. You're due for a break.'

Mrs Elway looked slightly put out, but Savannah's face immediately brightened.

They crossed the street and wandered around Holly Park. Outside Painter's Cove, three artists drew chalk portraits of people. 'Want your portrait drawn?' Brynn asked Savannah.

She shook her head and whispered, 'Grams did one of me in January and she was a better artist than these people.'

Meanwhile, Henry drew a lot of attention, standing patiently while people petted him, sitting on command, striking seemingly endless poses for cameras and shaking hands with everyone while Savannah smiled like a proud mother.

Finally, Brynn said, 'I'm starving. How about you?'

Savannah nodded enthusiastically. 'I didn't eat any breakfast.'

'Me neither,' Brynn said. 'Let's go to Cloud Nine.'

They reached Cloud Nine just before noon. Brynn scanned the full tables beneath the bright umbrellas and saw a hand waving toward her. Her mouth nearly dropped open when she saw that the hand was attached to Tessa Cavanaugh, who was sitting with Ray O'Hara.

Savannah looked at Brynn, who said, 'I can stand it if you can.'

They both smiled for all they were worth and moved toward Tessa's table. 'Hi!' they blurted at the same time. Brynn added, 'We thought we were out of luck.'

Tessa smiled back, her long, shiny face almost pretty. Her pale blue eyes traveled up and down Brynn, taking in her torn blue jeans and faded Rolling Stones T-shirt. 'My goodness, Brynn, you're looking . . . casual today.'

'It's a casual kind of day,' Brynn returned easily.

'I think she looks cool,' Savannah piped up.

Tessa frowned slightly. 'Well, I've never understood wearing torn clothes, but then I'm set in my ways.'

Ray made an attempt at a smile. 'Hi, Brynn.' He looked at Savannah. 'Sorry. I've forgotten your name.'

'It's Savannah,' she said.

'Ray O'Hara. I'm a writer, like Brynn.'

'I've never read your books. Are they like Brynn's?'

'No,' Ray snapped before Tessa flew into sudden action, rising, moving to the chair next to Ray and motioning to the other two empty chairs. 'Please sit down. We're so glad you could join us.'

Ray doesn't look like he shares your sentiment, Brynn thought, trying to hide her smirk. Savannah looked at him tentatively, sensing he didn't really want them at the table. 'We've just about finished,' Tessa said. 'The food here is *so* good.'

'I thought you always ate lunch in the park,' Brynn said.

'I do when I'm working at the library, but I'm on vacation. My first vacation in years.' Her cheeks looked pink and she wore a bright blue short-sleeved blouse. 'Ray invited me to lunch.'

After spending the night with Rhonda, Brynn thought, unable to look at him. She felt as if Ray knew that she knew about Rhonda. Brynn wondered if he'd seen her at the motel this morning.

Mindy whizzed up to them, today's paprika-colored lip gloss gleaming over white teeth. 'Miss Wilder! Savannah! And Henry! What can I get you?' The dog held up his paw. 'Oh, sweetie, I'm not allowed to shake hands with dogs when I'm on duty.'

Savannah giggled.

'It's Brynn, Mindy, not Miss Wilder,' Brynn said, smiling.

'I'd like a Cloud Nineburger, please.' Savannah started fishing in her pocket for money until Brynn covered her hand.

'Luncheon is on me, mademoiselle and monsieur. I'll also have a Cloud Nineburger, please, Mindy.' Brynn looked at Savannah. 'And how about the Chocolate Dream?'

'Oh, wow!' Savannah uttered in ecstasy.

'Two Cloud Nineburgers and two Chocolate Dreams,' Brynn told

Mindy, then looked at Tessa. 'So, what are you and Ray up to today?'

They glanced at each other, then Tessa shrugged. 'I'm not sure. Maybe a walk.'

'What about you two?' Ray asked.

'I'm in the mood to see a movie,' Brynn said, as if the idea had just popped into her mind. 'I think there's an early matinee showing of the new *Transformers* movie downtown.' She turned to Savannah. 'Do you like *Transformers*?'

'Gosh, yeah!' Her smile faded. 'But I have to go back to work.'

Ray pulled out his wallet and put two tens on the table. 'Time for us to go,' he said brusquely, pulling a jacket off the back of his chair.

Tessa stood clumsily, pulling at a white, blue-pinstriped skirt at least four inches shorter than she usually wore. Her bony knees showed and she frowned. 'Clothes these days,' she said with one last tug. 'They're so skimpy.'

'I like your outfit,' Savannah said shyly. 'You look . . . cute.'

Tessa's eyes widened. 'Cute? Me?' She blushed. 'Well . . . uh, thank you, dear. Nathan bought me this outfit.'

The poor thing's not used to getting compliments, Brynn thought with an unexpected twinge of sympathy. Tessa had always lived in Nathan's shadow. Then she'd retreated even farther after the attack in the woods and begun dressing as plain and dowdy as possible.

Brynn realized she was staring. 'The bright colors are flattering.'

Tessa looked at Brynn suspiciously for a moment, as if she thought Brynn was making fun of her. Finally she smiled. 'I'll tell Nathan you liked the outfit.'

'OK, let's break up this love-fest.' Ray stood. He looked tired and grouchy.

'Tessa, Ray, have a nice day.' Brynn gave them a small smile before Ray grasped Tessa's arm and guided her away. He acts as if he really likes her, Brynn thought. But she knew better. Tessa wasn't Ray's type. Now, Rhonda . . .

'Do you really want to see the movie?' Savannah asked meekly.

'I sure do. And I'm sure I can talk your dad into letting you go.' Brynn pulled her cell phone from her tote bag. 'No one can resist my charm.'

Their food arrived just as Brynn said goodbye to Garrett on the phone. Brynn grinned at Savannah. 'The afternoon is all ours, kid.'

At three-thirty, Brynn waved to the policeman assigned to surveillance in front of Cassie's house and unlocked the front door. The new locks and keys still worked stiffly, but after some jiggling, the door swung open to Cassie's cool, bright living room.

She was tired but in a good way. She'd actually enjoyed the movie with Savannah as well as the dog that the manager had allowed them to sneak in through the side door. It's good to have contacts, Brynn had thought as Henry entered quietly, almost stealthily, and slipped into an aisle not far from the movie screen. This was obviously not his first time at the theater – perk for being the well-behaved dog of the city's well-liked sheriff.

Brynn tossed her tote bag on a nearby chair, headed for the stairs and suddenly stopped. She took a deep breath, her eyes darting around. She saw nothing, smelled nothing, heard nothing unusual.

But she was not alone. 'Cassie?' she called, although she'd called Cassie on her way home. Cassie said she'd be at the store for another hour. Besides, Brynn had always been able to sense when her best friend was near.

She'd also always been able to sense when danger was near.

She couldn't explain it. Her parents had always smiled at her indulgently when she used to talk about it. Mark had told her she was nuts. But Cassie had believed her. Cassie always believed her.

'Cassie?' she called again as the hair on her arms raised. It was just the change in temperature, she thought. It had been hot and humid outside. It was cool and dry inside.

Too cool. The air conditioner must be set on sixty degrees, she thought.

Brynn's rationality told her to go outside and talk to the policeman on surveillance. Ask him if anyone had come into the house. Even if he said no, she'd ask him to come inside and search the house with her because she had a sense that someone *had* been here. She started to turn around and go out the front door, then stopped abruptly. No one was allowed in the house except Cassie and Brynn. The cop would think she was a fool. After all, Brynn Wilder wrote supernatural fiction for a living. Now she couldn't tell the difference besides her stories and reality. That's the tale that would go around town. She could hear people laughing at her, even now, and she couldn't stand not to be taken seriously. She *had* to be taken seriously. Mark's life might depend on it.

Brynn looked to her left. The kitchen – the perfect place to find a weapon. If no one was in there . . . She took small, quiet steps to the doorway, standing sideways, and peeped around the doorframe at all four corners of the bright room. She saw no one and hurried to the drawer where Cassie kept the kitchen cutlery. She chose an eight-inch carving knife.

I'm being ridiculous, Brynn thought. There's something wrong with the air conditioner thermostat, I've got a case of the creeps because of the call last night, I should just go outside and get the cop . . .

She walked slowly out of the kitchen, holding the knife, and stood in the living room. She breathed deeply. A smell. Faint. Lingering in the cold air. Musk. So light as to be almost imperceptible. Could it be Cassie's Vanilla Musk cologne? Not unless it was still drifting around since this morning and Cassie had been wearing more than usual or had spilled some in her room.

Brynn made a quick search of the first floor. A bathroom. A bedroom that Cassie's parents once shared. Another room that now held a few shelves of books, and an antique desk bearing an old Remington typewriter Brynn knew had belonged to Cassie's grandfather. After his wife died and he'd broken his hip on the morning Brynn's father had been killed, he'd moved in with his son and this had become his bedroom until he, too, died ten years ago. The only sign of him now was the typewriter and an 8 × 10 double picture frame holding old photos of Mr Hutton and his wife, looking young and happy.

As she climbed the stairs slowly, holding the knife in front of her, the smell of musk grew stronger. She stood on the landing for a moment, then went into Cassie's bedroom. The bed was made. Only her robe lay across a chair near a window. The dresser was neat but a cloudy film obscured the mirror. Brynn touched it then smelled her finger. Dried Vanilla Musk cologne. She looked at the few items Cassie kept on a mirror tray on the dresser top, including her cologne. The bottle was missing.

She glanced in the bathroom, which looked exactly as it had this morning. Next she entered the room Cassie used as an office and upstairs den. Against one beige wall stretched a long, ginger-colored couch. Across from it sat a long cabinet with a thirty-two-inch HD television – smaller than the television downstairs – on top along with a Bose music system. Still feeling tense, Brynn looked around the office one last time, then moved down the hall. She took one step into her bedroom and froze.

After being awakened to see her old dragonfly necklace dangling on Cassie's porch, she'd gone back to her room and, out of habit, made her bed. She remembered trying to occupy her mind with being particularly careful to pull the sheets and the light green bedspread tight, smoothing out any wrinkles. Now the top sheet and bedspread had been tossed to one side, as if someone intended to go to bed. Instinctively, Brynn raised her knife and moved closer to the bed. The bottom sheet was slightly wrinkled and the down-filled pillow showed a dent the shape of a head. On the snowy white pillowcase lay three long, light auburn hairs.

FOURTEEN

When Cassie got home a little after five o'clock, she found three patrolmen and Garrett in her house. 'What's wrong?' she cried, dropping her heavy tote bag. 'Another necklace?'

'An intruder,' Garrett said calmly before a still shaken Brynn could blurt out something frightening. 'Nothing's been damaged. I don't think anything was taken.'

'But how could anyone get in when we have surveillance?' Cassie asked in disbelief.

'You have surveillance at the front of the house. Not at the back or the side,' Garrett said. 'You also have that six-foot fence covered with ivy. We're sure someone just slipped through the gate and then they were hidden. The lock on your back door has been picked. It wasn't an expert job, but it was good enough to get the lock open.'

Cassie still looked stunned before she asked, 'You said there was no damage. How did you know someone had been in here?'

'I came home around three-thirty and felt . . .' Brynn paused. She could tell Cassie she'd simply sensed someone had recently left the house and Cassie would understand. She didn't want to say it in front of the police, though. 'It was cold in here. It wasn't cold when I left. Then I smelled your cologne. It was fairly strong. Someone sprayed it all over your dresser mirror.'

Cassie wanted to see. Brynn and Garrett went upstairs with her. She looked at the clouded mirror. 'Guess I'll need to buy more cologne tomorrow,' she said, as if trying to rally from her shock. 'Is this all you found?'

Brynn said, 'Well, the air conditioning had been turned down to about sixty and whoever it was decided to take a nap in my room.' She told Cassie about the turned-back bedspread, the wrinkled sheets, the head imprint and the three long auburn hairs on her pillow. 'The forensics people have taken the bedding for evidence. The creepiest thing to me was the hair. It's sort of like that story by Faulkner, "A Rose for Emily" that you and I read over and over when we were twelve,' Brynn said. 'Remember it?'

Cassie said nothing, her gaze unfocused. Then she closed her eyes and sighed. 'I know who was here,' she said without opening her eyes. 'Rhonda. I fired her this morning.'

Garrett's attention seemed to sharpen. 'You fired her? Why?'

Cassie looked at him. 'Her work has been slipping for a couple of months. I've had complaints from customers about her. I wondered if she'd started drinking. This morning she turned up over an hour late. She was a mess, wearing the clothes she had on yesterday, no makeup, either drunk or flying high on something. Fifteen minutes after she arrived, I sent her out the door.'

Brynn said nothing about seeing Rhonda leaving Ray's motel room that morning. Later she would tell Cassie and Garrett individually, but she didn't think telling them together was a good idea, especially since Garrett had been involved with Rhonda up until a couple of months earlier. She didn't want to embarrass him. Instead she asked Cassie, 'How did she take being fired?'

'Like she thought I was joking. She laughed and told me to lighten up. I told her again that she was fired and that I meant it. She just stared at me. I told her a third time and she started yelling that I was making a mistake and that I'd pay. I guess breaking into my house was my payment.'

'I guess,' Brynn said, frowning.

'You don't think so?' Cassie asked.

'It seems if she was furious, she would have done more than spray cologne on your mirror and lie on my bed. And what does turning down the air conditioner have to do anything?'

'She always said I kept the store too cold,' Cassie said absently. 'I asked all the other salespeople. They said it was fine.' She looked at her blurry mirror. 'That's going to be hell to clean.'

'I think you'll only need soap and water,' Brynn said.

'And I just bought the large bottle of Vanilla Musk last week.'

Finally, Brynn's mouth twitched as she tried to hold back a smile. 'I think that'll set you back less than twenty dollars, Cass. It won't break the bank.'

'I guess not,' Cassie said disconsolately. 'But so much for our plans to go to the carnival tonight.'

Brynn's gaze met Garrett's. 'We don't have to stay here this evening, do we, Sheriff?' Brynn asked.

'No. I'm going to put a second surveillance car on the house – one parked with a view of the back gate. You can leave every light in the place on when you're gone if that'll make you feel safer.'

Cassie stood with her shoulders slumped, mute.

'Cass, I think it would be good for us to get out of here this evening – have some fun instead of just sitting here talking about my necklace appearing this morning and Rhonda breaking in.' She paused. 'Besides, Savannah asked me if you and I would meet her dad and her at the carnival tonight. It would be the four of us.'

Cassie said nothing for a moment. Then Brynn saw the gleam slowly returning to her eyes. She was a die-hard romantic and a poorly disguised tryst didn't stand a chance of getting past her. 'I guess it *would* be a downer to just sit here and watch TV. We planned on going to the carnival. I was really looking forward to it. And if Garrett and Savannah will be there . . .' Cassie looked at Garrett. 'I'd really like to meet Savannah. Brynn thinks she's wonderful.' She gave Brynn a wink which Brynn prayed Garrett hadn't seen, then said, 'I think going to the carnival with the three of you is exactly what I need tonight!'

'Rhonda's been acting strange, but this is crazy,' Cassie said as they drove to the fairgrounds just south of Genessa Point where the traveling carnival had been set up. '*I* fired her. What's she got against you?'

'Mark. She thinks he helped Dad murder her cousin.'

'Yeah, or so she claims. I think she just wanted to cause trouble, get attention. Garrett's romantic attention, and that's directed elsewhere.'

'Oh? Where?'

'Come on, Brynn. It's hard not to see how you two look at each other.'

'We hardly ever look at each other!'

'That's the telling sign,' Cassie said sagely. 'You two avoid eye contact. Maybe some people don't notice it. Rhonda would.'

'Rhonda's never seen me with Garrett.'

'She knew you were at his house last night. Garrett's house is on my way home from the city building where I had the meeting last night. As I drove by, I saw her car parked at the curb a couple of houses down. She was sitting in it, looking in the rearview mirror. She'd probably been out of the car and looking in Garrett's windows earlier. Or later. When I got home, you weren't back yet. Deputy Carder said he hadn't picked you up yet.'

'You should sell the store and become a detective.'

'I thought about it when I was about sixteen,' Cassie said nonchalantly. 'I think that's part of why Lavinia left the store to me – she was afraid I'd go through with it and get killed my first day on the streets.'

'You never told me in any of your letters.'

'Well, you weren't too fond of the cops at that time.' Cassie glanced at her and grinned. 'I think you're over that phase.'

'Cass, you'll never win any awards for subtlety.'

'Oh, look! We're at the fairground!' Cassie burst out. 'Gosh, I didn't know the travelling carnival was going to be so big!'

Night had begun to fall and against the darkening sky burst a maze of vivid color. As soon as Brynn opened her door, she heard the blare of carnival sounds – calliopes, cymbals, drums, trombones and the carousel organ. To her surprise, she felt excited.

'You look like a wide-eyed kid,' Cassie teased.

'I guess that's what I feel like,' Brynn answered, then became aware of Cassie's close scrutiny. 'It sounds like fun. And I didn't expect so many people to be here so early.'

'Uh huh,' Cassie drawled. 'That excited flush on your face wouldn't have anything to do with us meeting Garrett, would it?'

'Savannah will love this. I think it's just what she needs.'

'So your enthusiasm is all about Savannah. I suppose you took your second shower of the day and tried on three outfits before you decided on one before we came. It was all for Savannah. Whatever you say, Brynn.'

'Smart ass,' Brynn muttered and Cassie started laughing.

They parked and walked to the carnival entrance where Garrett and Savannah lingered, waiting for them. Garrett held a camera and Savannah beamed.

'Hi!' she called loudly and waved before Brynn and Cassie reached her.

'Hi, Savannah. Hi, Garrett.' Brynn gave Garrett a quick, almost shy smile before looking at Savannah. She was afraid she would blush or her gaze would tell the eagle-eyed Cassie all she needed to know. 'Savannah, I'd like you to meet Cassie Hutton. She's been my best friend since I was five.'

'Wow, what a *long* time!' Savannah realized she'd made a verbal blunder and turned pink. 'I meant a long time to be friends, not that you're old or anything.' She sighed, looked at Cassie and turned on all her charm. 'I'm really glad to meet you, Miss Hutton. I think your store is *so* great. Last year, a girl I know got to pose for an ad poster you put up in your store. She's fifteen. The ad was gorgeous.'

'I'm glad you liked it.' Cassie smiled at her. 'I think this year I might feature a fourteen-year-old in one of my autumn posters. Aren't you almost fourteen?'

'Me?' Hope shone in Savannah's eyes. 'Yeah. In October.'

'Are you booked up or do you think you might have time in late August for a photo shoot?' Cassie asked.

'Me? In a photo shoot for an ad?'

'Sure,' Cassie said. 'You're tall, slender—' She took Savannah's chin in her hand and gently turned her face side to side. 'Beautiful bone structure. Great hair. You're a natural model.'

Savannah looked as if she was going to jump up and down in her glitter mesh Rykas. 'I'd *love* to be in an ad. Wow!' She looked up at her father. 'Can I?'

Garrett grinned. 'Sure, honey, although I'm not ready to let my little girl go gallivanting off into the modeling world. Paris, Milan, London . . .'

'Oh, I won't gallivant. Not yet,' Savannah assured him.

'Fine.' Garrett glanced at Cassie. 'How're you doing, Miss Hutton? You look good.'

'Brynn talked me into wearing skinny jeans. I think they look better on her, but thank you anyway. You look good, too. Your shirt is the exact color of your eyes.'

Well, this is awkward, Brynn mused. Anything I say will be better than this. 'I went to an amusement park when I was six, but I don't remember much about it. I've *never* been to a carnival and I can't wait to see everything.'

The four of them stood still, smiles fixed, until Garrett took Savannah's arm and propelled her toward the carnival entrance. Cassie gave Brynn a sideways glance and winked, grabbed her arm and quickly followed Garrett and Savannah. At least they were on their way, the stiffness of their meeting over as they walked onto the midway, Brynn thought.

Brynn felt as if she'd stepped into another world full of light and color, noise and movement. And the smell of food. 'How long will the carnival be here?' she asked.

'Ten days,' Cassie answered. 'They're closing the night of the town play. The one Savannah's in.'

Savannah turned. '*Genessa Point: The Beginning.*'

'You have great hearing,' Cassie laughed. 'You're also great at advertising!'

'That's 'cause I'm the second lead. I've worked really hard and want everyone to come.'

'You can be sure Brynn and I'll be there,' Cassie answered loudly, then lowered her voice. 'Is this the play that Tessa wrote?'

Brynn nodded. 'I hope it isn't awful. Savannah will be crushed.'

'It doesn't matter if it's awful or not. The people of this town will cheer like crazy. I just can't believe Tessa wrote a play. It's so unlike her to do anything except run between the library and home.'

'Maybe she's changed since her father died.'

Two men dressed as court jesters danced around Garrett and Savannah, juggling balls. One tossed a ball toward Cassie. She caught it, threw it upwards, whirled around and caught it. The jester and a gaggle of onlookers clapped. Cassie giggled and flung it back to the jester.

'I didn't know you could juggle!' Brynn teased.

'I have many hidden talents,' Cassie returned, bowing to her small audience. 'Besides, that wasn't really juggling.'

Brynn looked to her right. Through the opening in a large black tent she saw flames blazing and flashing as the song 'Light My Fire' played loudly. 'Oh, fire-eaters!' she exclaimed, hurrying into the tent where people oohed and aahed as a man and a woman in sequined costumes twirled fire torches, tilted back their heads, put the torches into their mouths, pulled them out, flung the torches back and forth to each other and then sent them spinning high in the darkness and caught them with ease.

'How do they do that without burning their mouths?' Savannah asked in awe.

'I'm sure they have a few burns and blisters,' Garrett answered. 'Don't you try this, Savannah. It's dangerous.'

'Oh, Daaad,' she groaned. 'I'm not stupid.'

They watched for about ten more minutes. When they emerged from the tent, Brynn was overwhelmed by the smell of pizza, caramel apples, hamburgers, roasted chicken, peppers, coffee and soft drinks. 'I think watching all that fire-eating made me hungry. Actually, change that to *starving.*'

'I suppose you want a hot dog,' Garrett said.

Savannah made a face. 'I never want to see another hot dog in my whole life. Last night I dreamed I was being eaten by a giant hot dog!'

'Her job at Mrs Elway's hot dog stand has traumatized her,' Cassie said.

They all had sausage and pepper sandwiches, soft drinks, French fries, and then wandered down a few tents looking for something for dessert. Five minutes later, the four of them were seated at a picnic table, eating different flavored beignets and drinking cafe au lait. 'I've never had one of these,' Savannah said to Brynn. 'Mine's cherry. What's yours?'

'Spice. It's delicious.'

Brynn's good mood now overshadowed the break-in at Cassie's house. Cassie, too, seemed relaxed and happy. A warm sense of ease had developed among the four of them.

When they'd finished their food and set out to explore more of the carnival, Cassie now walked with Savannah, leaving Brynn behind with Garrett. Clever girls, she mused. They're both determined to encourage a romance.

When Garrett drew closer to her, his hand casually brushing her, she smiled. Against all odds, Brynn thought, this was going to be a nice evening.

FIFTEEN

Seeing that Savannah and Cassie were a safe distance ahead of them, Brynn said softly, 'I'm sure you heard that someone managed to get into Cassie's house today.'

'Sure. Seems like it was Rhonda. I called her next-door neighbor at her apartment complex. She's a stay-at-home mother of a baby. She said she didn't see Rhonda come in today, so I talked to Mrs Gaines, Rhonda's aunt. She claims Rhonda was with her from before noon until around four o'clock.'

'Do you believe her?'

'She sounded sincere. She told me Cassie had fired Rhonda. She said Rhonda was upset and didn't want to go back to her apartment to be alone.'

'But the auburn hair on the pillow . . .'

'A lot of people have auburn hair.' Garrett looked at her. 'Well, not a lot of people have *long auburn* hair. But there were no roots on the hair, so a DNA match is impossible. Given the circumstances, I'm fairly sure those were Rhonda's hairs on your pillow.'

'But when was she there? Cassie didn't fire her until around eleven-thirty and Mrs Gaines says she was at her house until four. I got home at four-thirty. That doesn't leave much time for Rhonda to have broken in.' Garrett said nothing. 'What are you thinking?'

'About Cassie saying Rhonda showed up over an hour late wearing the clothes she did yesterday and acting bizarre. High on something. We don't know where she was last night.'

After a moment, Brynn said, 'I think I know.' She told him about seeing Rhonda and Ray at the Bay Motel that morning. 'It was ten o'clock so she was already an hour late for work. She was barefooted and clinging to him, trying to kiss him. He finally just pushed her away and closed his door in her face.'

'Did she see you?'

'I don't think she or Ray did. She was holding him, groping him. He was too busy trying to shake her loose to look around.' Brynn took a breath. 'I'm sorry.'

'About what?'

'Well, you dated her.'

'So you think I'm jealous? God, no. I just wonder why she won't leave me alone when she has Ray.'

'Maybe Ray isn't the guy she really wants. I'm surprised she even knows him.'

'Ray grew up in Genessa Point and Rhonda and her mother spent a lot of time here with the Gaines family. She could have known him for years.'

'Have you known Rhonda for a long time?' Brynn couldn't help asking.

'Me? No. I met her in Cassie's store when I was looking for a Christmas gift for Grams. Her last Christmas. Rhonda helped me pick out a long burgundy velvet robe with gold embroidery.' He smiled. 'Grams said it was so beautiful, she was going to wear it everywhere instead of a coat. Savannah believed her and was horrified, explaining that this was supposed to go over Grams's pajamas, not a dress she'd wear to church. Grams finally confessed that she was joking. We all ended up laughing. That was a good Christmas.' His smile faded and he went silent again. 'Anyway, Grams *and* Savannah had been telling me I should be dating, so at the end of January I asked Rhonda out.' He shook his head. 'What a mistake I made.'

'You didn't know her,' Brynn said mildly. 'You couldn't have known she had problems.'

'And they didn't show up until spring, although I think Grams saw them before I did. She started talking about Cassie a lot, steering me in that direction. It's just that I've always thought of Cassie as a good friend. I was afraid that if we dated and things didn't go well, I could lose that friendship.'

'That's true.'

Garrett grinned and stepped closer to her again. 'It might interest you to know that as early as March my daughter started showing me your picture on your book jackets, mentioning that you used to live in Genessa Point and asking if I'd ever known you. She was elated when I said I did know you. She started harping on how pretty and nice you were.'

'Nice? She'd never met me. What made her think I was nice?'

'Your books.' Garrett looked deeply into her eyes. 'And she said she had a *feeling* about you.'

Brynn was glad all the bright, flashing lights of the midway hid the color rushing to her cheeks. 'She's a sweet girl,' she managed. She wanted to reach out and take Garrett's hand, to rub it along her cheek like she'd done last night. But they weren't alone. And everything was happening too fast. She knew it. She was frightened for her brother and certain Garrett was the only person who could save him. She changed the subject. 'After what happened this afternoon, I told Cassie I think I should move out of her house and go to a motel. She said she didn't want me to, of course, but I think it's best.'

Garrett turned his head, looked straight ahead and after a moment said curtly, 'I don't.'

'Why?'

'Because we have surveillance on Cassie's house – more surveillance now than we did earlier today. It's easier to watch one house than a motel with people coming and going all the time. Also, she just had all of her locks changed—'

'She did that after Ray's visit.'

'You didn't let me finish. She's having deadbolts added this evening. Didn't she tell you?' Brynn shook her head. 'Well, whoever picked the lock on that back door today wasn't a professional and they aren't going to get through a deadbolt. You're safer at her house.'

'But she's not safer with me there.'

'What happened today could have been directed at her, not you. As for Ray's visit, he didn't use his key so he could hang out and wait for you. You know he was waiting for Cassie.'

'Yes, and my heart's broken that I'm not the girl of his dreams.' Brynn realized she'd answered flippantly because Garrett sounded as if his concern about her well-being was strong. The intimacy they'd shared last night frightened her and she'd wanted to return to their earlier, light tone. Punishing him for her own feelings, though, was wrong and she regretted it. Still, she couldn't make herself sound warm. 'So if I move, you'll call off the surveillance?'

'Maybe.'

Brynn took a breath to say something – anything – to brighten Garrett's sudden coolness when he said, 'Well, speaking of Ray, there he is.'

'With Tessa?' Brynn blurted before she realized how close Ray was to her.

'Not with Tessa,' Ray said, smirking, knowing he'd surprised her.

'Tessa's with Nathan right now, but the three of us are here together.'

Brynn caught herself before asking why he wasn't with Rhonda. Instead she said clumsily, 'I didn't know you liked carnivals.'

'You don't know much about me at all, Brynn, except what my loving ex-wife's told you.' Ray looked at Garrett. 'As soon as Cassie saw me, she darted into that tent with your daughter, in case you even care to know where Savannah is.'

'I saw them go in,' Garrett nearly snarled. 'I don't let my daughter out of my sight.'

'Well, that's an exaggeration if I ever heard one,' Ray drawled. 'Seems to me she's on her own a lot, Sheriff. Better keep a closer eye on her or you never know what might happen.'

'What does that mean?' Garrett demanded, but Ray simply walked by him, whistling tonelessly. 'That son of a bitch,' Garrett mumbled.

Brynn forced herself to put her hand on his arm. 'He's only trying to rile you up. Deep down, Ray's mostly talk. He doesn't have it in him to do something truly dangerous.'

Garrett looked at her solemnly. 'Do you really believe that, Brynn? Because if you do, you might get a surprise.' She opened her mouth to say something, but he cut her off. 'I have to find my daughter.'

Garrett plunged into the Maze of Mirrors, Brynn close behind him. Everywhere they looked, they saw distorted images of themselves until finally Garrett called out, 'Savannah!'

'Over here, Dad.' They followed the voice until they found her and Cassie standing in front of a mirror that made them appear over seven feet tall. They held hands and laughed, Savannah standing on her tiptoes so she was slightly taller than Cassie. When Garrett stepped in front of the mirror, he looked like a giant.

The mirrors had been placed in a convoluted puzzle that Cassie, a carnival fan, declared the most complicated she'd ever seen. The four of them rambled through the labyrinth, catching sight of themselves looking short and fat, skinny with huge heads, and almost frightening with wide, vertical faces and bulging eyes.

Brynn was smiling when long auburn hair and porcelain skin flashed in the mirror. She heard a woman laugh, husky and dark, the voice full of malice. Whirling around, she saw no one except a thin teenage boy and his clinging girlfriend. 'Did you see an auburn-haired woman?' she asked them.

'Uh, nope,' the boy said as the girl hugged him tighter. 'Did you lose someone?'

'Maybe.'

Brynn stepped aside so the couple could look at themselves in the mirror. 'Rhonda?' she called.

In less than a minute, Garrett appeared. 'Did you see Rhonda?'

'I'm fairly certain I saw her and heard her laughing.' Brynn shivered. 'I didn't like the sound of that laugh.'

'Stay here and keep Savannah and Cassie with you.' Garrett barged past a gaggle of people, looking determined and uneasy.

Cassie and Savannah appeared and, before even looking in the mirror, Cassie glanced at Brynn's face and burst out, 'What's wrong?'

'Nothing. I just got lost in the crowd.'

Savannah inserted herself into the giggling group of teenagers gazing at themselves in the mirror but Cassie moved deftly through them to Brynn's side and whispered, 'I'll ask again. What's wrong?'

'I thought I saw Rhonda,' Brynn said softly. 'I'm not sure – I just caught a glimpse – but she was laughing and it wasn't a happy laugh. When I said her name, she vanished.'

'Well, that's bad news.' Cassie grimaced. 'A carnival doesn't seem like Rhonda's idea of a good time.'

'She'd know Garrett would bring Savannah, and Garrett is certainly her idea of a good time.'

Cassie looked alarmed. 'Oh, God, she wouldn't follow him *here*, would she?'

'Who wouldn't follow who here?' Savannah asked, startling both Brynn and Cassie.

'Uh, someone that someone else doesn't want to see,' Brynn stumbled.

Savannah's smile disappeared. 'You mean Rhonda. Is she here?'

'I'm not sure,' Brynn said. 'I thought I saw her . . . well, just her hair . . . it probably wasn't—'

Garrett's image appeared in the distorted mirror and Savannah let out a small squeak that set the other teenagers laughing. Her face reddened. 'Never mind them,' Brynn said, then looked at Garrett, now standing in front of her. 'Find her?'

'No. She had a head start and a lot of people are here tonight.'

'It may not have been her.'

Garrett sighed. 'That's too much to hope for, Brynn.' He looked at his daughter. 'But we're here to have a good time and that's what we're going to do.'

Savannah let out her breath. 'Great. I was afraid you'd want to go home.'

'Not on your life. I'm in the mood to go on a ride. Who else wants to go?'

'Depends on what it is,' Cassie said. 'Anything except the Ferris wheel. Ferris wheels scare me to death.'

As soon as they stepped out of the Maze of Mirrors, Brynn's gaze shot around the midway, looking for a tall woman with long auburn hair. She couldn't get the sound of the woman's laughter out of her head. It was like something from a horror novel. No, it was worse because it was real.

'Are you OK?' Savannah asked.

Brynn realized her face was tight, grim. She forced a smile. 'I'm fine.' Then she brightened and turned to Cassie. 'Hey, Cassie, is the merry-go-round too scary for you?'

Cassie made a face at Brynn. 'Bring it on!'

'I love the merry-go-round!' Savannah exclaimed. 'C'mon, everybody!'

'Why don't you and Cassie go ahead,' Garrett said. 'Brynn and I'll take pictures.'

'But Brynn doesn't have a camera—' Savannah broke off, a knowing smile appearing on her face.

Cassie took Savannah's hand and they ran toward the carousel. They got on and the carousel started turning, the horses dipping up and down. Savannah waved and Garrett took a picture.

'Do you have a secret to tell me?' Brynn asked. 'I love carousels.'

'Sorry. You can ride the next time around. I wanted to tell you that I talked to Mark's friend in Baltimore.'

'And?'

'He said Mark began drifting away from his small group of friends before the wife took off, but afterward he cut himself off from just about everyone. This guy, Greg, said he'd been closer to Mark for longer than any of the others, so he hung on. He could tell Mark really needed a friend.'

'I'm glad Greg stuck with him. What was Mark's emotional shape?'

'Bad. It wasn't good before his wife left and much worse after. Greg said he didn't know why Mark cared so much – the wife was hardly ever around and she'd been taking little vacations for a few months. The strange thing was that Mark didn't seem to love her anymore – he just didn't want her to leave.'

'He felt deserted again, just like when he lost Dad and then Mom.' Brynn paused. 'And me. I should have stayed in Baltimore, not moved to Miami.'

'Don't blame yourself. You have the right to a life, too. Anyway, Greg said that about a month after the wife's desertion, Mark started dragging out all of his files on your father's death and the Genessa Point Killer. He reread everything. He drew time charts. He started putting pictures from the newspapers up on his walls. He was drinking more and more and every time Greg went to see him, he seemed more lost in the past. Then he was fired from the bank, but he didn't care. He said now he had time to do what he couldn't do when he was a teenager.'

'What was that?'

'He didn't tell Greg, just said that the answer was in Genessa Point. He was going back to get answers, no matter what the risk.' Garrett shrugged. 'Sorry. I thought you knew the path Mark was on. You just didn't see it firsthand, like Greg did.'

'I felt it. I just didn't want to believe it,' Brynn said slowly. 'Will you give me Greg's full name and phone number?'

Cassie and Savannah passed again. Garrett took another picture. Then he reached in his pocket and pulled out a piece of paper. 'I didn't tell Greg you'd be calling. In spite of everything I told you, he's not very forthcoming. I had to pull out the information and he didn't say anything that would help us. I got the sense that he wanted to help, but he didn't know much and he was afraid that he might be making things worse for Mark.'

'How could he be?' Brynn asked as she put the paper in her pocket.

'By sounding like Mark had gone off the deep end. Like he wasn't quite rational and might do something that would only make things worse. I think he was worried about Mark.' Garrett looked solemnly at Brynn. 'I think he wasn't too sure what Mark might be capable of at this point.'

'Capable of? Like what?'

Garrett paused, then, after taking a final picture, he said, 'Like hurting someone to get information he wanted.'

When the merry-go-round stopped, Savannah slid gracefully off her horse and stood while Cassie clambered off hers. Savannah rushed to her father. 'So, did you get pictures?'

'Fifteen.'

'Really?'

'Well, maybe three.'

Cassie walked slowly to Brynn. 'If I ever try to ride a horse in skinny jeans again, knock me unconscious.'

'It wasn't even a real horse!' Brynn laughed.

'If it had been, I'd be dead.'

'Cassie's just teasing. She's really the outdoors type,' Brynn said to Garrett.

'I could tell. Let's plan a camping trip. Cassie can pitch the tent and shoot something for our dinner.'

It was almost nine o'clock and the carnival was in full swing. The sound of carnival music – heavy on calliopes and drums – children giggling, hawkers, screams and laughter from people on rides or games of chance winners swirled around Brynn. Gold, blue and red lights flashed, reflecting off dozens of large, metallic silver balloons. Brynn tried to look for Rhonda, but there were too many people, too much distortion caused by the lights, for her to scan the crowd well. She noticed Garrett doing the same, although he never ignored Savannah, whom he kept close by his side. Was Rhonda really here? Brynn wondered. If she was, what might she do?

Not much, Brynn reassured herself. After all, what had she done so far? Followed Garrett, sat outside his house spying, broken into Cassie's house, sprayed cologne on a mirror and lain down on Brynn's bed. Rhonda seemed capable of only small, non-dangerous acts of revenge. Just because she had such an icy, intimidating demeanor didn't mean she was a true menace.

Cassie and Savannah ran off to get glow sticks, and Brynn smiled after them. 'Looks like those two have really taken to each other,' she said with pleasure.

'I'm glad Savannah has another friend. I just wish she had some her own age.'

'She said the same thing about you, remember. She thinks you're lonely and that you worry too much about protecting her.'

Garrett looked down at her. 'All good parents try to protect their children.'

Brynn smiled into his eyes. 'Mine certainly did. Mom and Dad were wonderful parents, Garrett. Both of them.'

'Is that right? I didn't know serial killers made good fathers.'

Brynn jumped as Rhonda's voice came from behind her. She whirled around to see the woman standing casually, smirking at her. She wore tight black jeans and an unlined black lace top over a demi cup black bra. Her lips shone with bright red gloss and she'd gone heavy with silver eye shadow and black liner. Garrett turned and reached for Brynn's arm, pulling her closer to him. 'What the hell do you want, Rhonda?' he said in a soft, grim voice that was more unnerving than a shout.

She blinked. His anger had registered, but she quickly pulled herself together. 'I was just strolling along, watching you two love birds in action.' She raised a penciled eyebrow. 'Believe me, Brynn, he's capable of much more action than he's showing with you. Maybe he's not as hot for you as you think he is.'

Garrett started to answer but Brynn was quicker. 'Go away, Rhonda. No one's interested in what you have to say.'

Surprised by how calm she'd sounded, Brynn continued to look Rhonda in the eye, keeping her face expressionless. Garrett's arm tightened around hers.

Rhonda tilted her head. 'You haven't heard all I have to say, Brynn. But I applaud your composure. You're a good actress.'

'I'm not acting. I don't care about you.'

'Garrett does.' Rhonda took a step toward Garrett. 'You care about me. The way you made love to me—'

'Go to hell, Rhonda.' Garrett drew a breath and spoke sternly. 'I don't want to talk to you now, but later I will. You broke into Cassie Hutton's house.'

Rhonda gave him a brief, startled look. 'Cassie Hutton's house? Why would I break into her house?'

'Because she fired you. Seems you been acting strange lately, insulting customers, and today you turned up late and a damned mess.'

'Or so she says. I think it's because Brynn said she'd seen me with Ray.' Her gaze sliced back to Brynn. 'I saw you at the motel. You didn't think so, but I did.' Rhonda stepped closer to Garrett. 'I don't care about Ray O'Hara.'

'Ray O'Hara?' Cassie and Savannah suddenly arrived, both bedecked with glow sticks, necklaces, and bracelets. 'Ray O'Hara?' Cassie asked again. 'What about him?'

'Can't hold onto your man, Cassie?' Rhonda asked venomously, her hands beginning to shake. 'Is that why you fired me? Or did your best friend here ask you to fire me and tell Garrett about Ray? Is that why Garrett's acting so mean tonight? Well, it won't work. Garrett's just pretending to care about Brynn. How could he? Her father was a murderer – a murderer of children like his own little girl. His dear little Savannah. Besides, Garrett can't let go of me, Cassie.' She turned cold, glittering gray eyes toward Brynn. 'Poor Brynn. Dead daddy and lost brother. Can't find your brother, so close and yet so far . . .'

'What?' Brynn asked loudly. 'What do you mean?'

Rhonda seemed to coil. 'I know you're famous and think you're beautiful and act like you're in love with his little brat, but Garrett's *mine*.' She glared at Savannah, looking as if she was going to strike. '*Mine!*' She turned and ran.

For a moment everyone stood still, silently watching Rhonda push her way through the flock of people who'd begun to gather around them. Then she disappeared down the crowded midway. 'What did she mean about me not being able to hold onto my man?' Cassie finally asked Garrett.

Garrett shrugged. This morning Brynn had told him about seeing Rhonda and Ray, but she would wait until tomorrow to tell Cassie. Meanwhile, Savannah stood with her mouth slightly open, her eyes fearful.

'Forget about Rhonda, honey,' Garrett said to his daughter. 'She's drunk or something.'

'Or something?' Savannah asked tremulously. 'Crazy?'

'Drunk,' Garrett answered definitively. 'She'll get sick and go home. Don't worry.'

Savannah still looked fearful. 'She looked crazy. She said crazy things.'

'Drunk people do that.'

'Oh, forget her. Did you and Cassie buy all the glow stuff for yourselves?' Brynn asked lightly, trying to act as if nothing mattered but the luminous handful of items Savannah and Cassie held. 'I like glow bracelets and I know your dad wanted something.'

When Savannah didn't answer, Cassie said, 'Uh, we got something for everyone.' She glanced at Savannah. 'Didn't we? Show your dad what you got for him.'

Savannah looked absently at all the glowing objects in her arms and said in a small voice, 'I got Daddy a red glow stick.'

Daddy, Brynn thought. She'd never heard Savannah call Garrett

Daddy. She'd become a scared little girl. She even looked as if she'd shrunk in on herself, trying to look like a child.

Garrett held out his hand. 'Great! I was afraid you'd buy me a necklace.' He took the glow stick. 'If this was a little longer it could be a lightsaber like the ones in *Star Wars.*'

'It would have to be a *lot* longer and you'd need a blue one if you want to be like Luke Skywalker, the good guy. Darth Vader's lightsaber was red,' Brynn laughed. The laughter was strained, but Garrett played along.

'Does this woman know her *Star Wars* movies or what?' he asked Savannah.

'I guess she does,' Savannah said without enthusiasm. 'Three bracelets for you, Brynn.' Savannah held them out. 'I thought you'd want bracelets because you've already got that cool dragonfly necklace. For me, I got one bracelet and two necklaces. I'm going to wear both necklaces tonight, but when I get home, I'll give one to Henry.'

'With all that light, he'll never go to sleep,' Brynn said. 'He'll stay up and read all night, which is fine as long as he reads one of my books.'

Savannah finally smiled. Cassie encouraged her, modeling her own five bracelets, two necklaces and two glow sticks. 'How do I look?'

'Like you're in no danger of getting lost,' Brynn said as Garrett snapped a couple of pictures of Cassie. Then Brynn's smile failed and her stomach clenched as she thought, You're not in danger of getting lost, like Mark. Oh, Mark, where are you? How can I be here laughing, almost having a good time, when you're God-knows-where?

Cassie, who knew her every facial expression, stopped posing and said loudly, 'I'm ready to go on another ride! How about you, Savannah? And this time, Brynn's going with us!'

As they walked toward the Tilt-a-Whirl, Savannah ahead of them with Cassie, Brynn asked Garrett, 'What are you going to do about Rhonda?'

'We have no evidence that she's done anything against the law,' Garrett answered in a low voice. 'But I'll have a deputy pick her up and bring her in for questioning. That's the best I can do right now.'

When they reached the ride, they could see that the cars held three passengers each, so Garrett said Cassie, Brynn and Savannah should ride in one while he took pictures. A minute after the three had gotten settled, the cars began spinning in different directions and at different speeds. Up, down, around and around, faster, slower, faster. Brynn noticed Cassie gripping the seat, her eyes closed, her lips clenched. Savannah, sitting between them, was laughing and waving at her father as they passed him dutifully taking photos.

At the end of the ride, Cassie sat still and announced, 'I might be sick.' Cassie swallowed a couple of times. 'I need to sit here for a few minutes.'

'You can't,' Savannah said. 'We have to get off so other people can ride.'

Cassie climbed shakily out of the car, her face pale and sweaty. Brynn, seeing that Cassie wasn't just scared or dizzy, took hold of her arm and led her away from the ride, Savannah following them anxiously. 'What's wrong?' Garrett demanded when they reached him.

'I think all that spinning around got to Cassie,' Brynn said. 'She doesn't feel so well.'

Savannah pointed. 'There's a bench. Cassie can sit down and I'll go over to that concession stand and get her something to drink. Would you like a Coke or 7Up or just water, Miss Hutton?'

'I'd love a 7Up, thanks.' Cassie smiled at Savannah.

Brynn looked around. She couldn't shake the disturbing feeling that they were being watched. She wondered if Rhonda would dare to suddenly show up and create another scene. Her gaze searched the crowd, looking for a tall, slim woman with auburn hair wearing a black lace top and a black bra. Her mind was so consumed with Rhonda, she didn't see Nathan and Tessa approaching the bench.

'Oh, Cassie, are you all right? You look terrible!'

'Thank you,' Cassie said dryly to Tessa. Nathan looked impossibly handsome next to his plain, long-faced sister in her pleated waist baggy jeans teamed with a cardigan set that looked like it had come from the fifties and her thin hair pulled back in the ever-present white ribbon. 'Actually, I have an upset stomach. The Tilt-a-Wheel was too much for me,' Cassie managed.

'You don't look terrible. You just look like you're not feeling up to par,' Nathan said quickly, smoothing over his sister's unflattering comment. 'Some of those rides can do a real number on your stomach.'

'Where's Ray?' Brynn asked. 'We saw him earlier and he said he was with you two.'

'We lost him at one of the game of chance tents,' Nathan said with an edge to his voice. 'He's a real gambler.'

'Oh, he's just having fun and not spending much money.' Tessa sounded defensive. Brynn immediately wondered if Nathan didn't approve of Ray dating his sister and was relieved to see Savannah and Garrett approaching them.

'Here's your 7Up,' Savannah, clearly sensing tension, said hesitantly, handing the giant cup to Cassie.

'Oh, thank you, honey.' Cassie immediately took a gulp. 'That feels better already.'

Savannah smiled, then looked at Tessa. 'Hello, Miss Cavanaugh.'

'Hello, dear. Playing nurse tonight?'

'I just got Cassie a drink. No big deal. Are you having fun?'

'I suppose it's amusing. I just can't stand all the noise. I hate loud noises.' Tessa stared at the beautiful girl and Brynn was sure she saw jealousy flicker in her pale eyes. Then she smiled. 'I don't think you've ever met my brother. Savannah Dane, this is Nathan Cavanaugh.'

'Hello, Mr Cavanaugh,' Savannah said.

Nathan held out his hand and flashed his dazzling smile. 'Not so formal! We have met, but you were only about three years old. I'm Nathan – or Nate – and I've been friends with your dad since we were kids.'

'Oh.' Even though Nathan was over twenty years her senior, Savannah responded to his knockout face and warm voice. She smiled beatifically and said in a melting tone, 'I'm very pleased to meet you. Sorry I don't remember meeting you before . . . Nathan.'

Brynn could hardly suppress cringing for Savannah as Garrett loudly stepped in, all fatherly protective of his little girl. 'You were just a baby, sweetheart. You're still my baby.' Savannah blushed furiously as Garrett wrapped his arm around her and squeezed. 'Hello, Tessa, Nate. Enjoying the carnival?'

'It's nice. I was just saying it's a bit loud,' Tessa said. 'And I don't like rides.'

'Tessa's just not used to being out so late at night around a bunch of people. When I'm home, I always drag her out of the house. She'll have to change her ways when we go to Morocco.'

'Morocco?' Savannah echoed.

'Casablanca in Morocco,' Nathan said. 'I have a job there starting next week. I've talked Tessa into taking a leave of absence from the library to go with me. After I'm done, we're going to travel some more. It's time Tessa had some fun in her life!'

'My life's been fine,' Tessa said softly.

Nathan frowned playfully at her. 'Maybe your idea of *fine*, not my idea of *fun*.' He smiled at Savannah. 'She'll be a different woman when she gets back to Genessa Point.'

'I don't know exactly where Casablanca is, but I'll look it up. We'll miss you at the library, Miss Cavanaugh,' Savannah said graciously.

Tessa looked startled. 'Why, my dear, what a sweet thing to say.'

'Well, I think I've recovered.' Cassie stood up. 'I don't want to ruin the evening for everyone.'

Brynn stood up. She hated the thought of spending the rest of the evening with Tessa, of all people, but she also didn't want to be rude. Tessa would probably burst into tears and Savannah's evening had already suffered enough drama. 'Tessa, Nathan, why don't you hang with us for a while?'

'Hang with you?' Tessa asked in confusion.

'Oh, Tess, really,' Nathan said in exasperation, then caught himself. 'We'd be glad to hang with you guys if we won't be a drag.'

A man walked past selling balloons and Garrett bought eight, Savannah picking and distributing colors with ceremony that left Tessa looking baffled but made Nathan smile. She gave her father one metallic gold one and Brynn metallic silver. 'You're the sun and Brynn's the moon,' she said before handing Cassie another in metallic copper, explaining, 'You're a comet.' She chose blue for Nathan, 'because Dad told me you work with the ocean,' and Tessa another 'white as snow.' For her and Henry, she picked out two in yellow, 'for happiness.'

'Where is your dog tonight, Savannah?' Tessa asked, clenching the string on her white balloon as they began walking again.

'Henry's at home, watching *Animal Planet* on TV. I wish I could have brought him.'

'You should keep what's important to you as close as possible.' Tessa had said this before at the wishing well, but tonight her voice had a distant, eerie tone. She stared vacantly ahead. 'If it's important enough, though, you can find a way.'

Savannah's gaze met Brynn's for an instant, almost as if she was afraid that Tessa was going to fall into one of her 'freaky' spells. 'All the noise might have gotten on Henry's nerves,' she said quickly. 'And he couldn't have ridden on anything or eaten most of the food they have here. He's probably happier watching *Animal Planet*. Do you ever watch it?'

'*Me?*' Tessa looked as if Savannah had asked if she ever jumped off the roof. 'No. Is it about all kinds of animals?'

'Well, yeah. It's real educational. Last week I learned—'

'There's Ray.' Tessa was peering ahead and stiffened suddenly. 'He's holding a gun.'

SIXTEEN

'What?' Cassie cried in alarm.

'It's a fake gun at a shooting game,' Brynn answered calmly, spotting Ray holding his replica Winchester rifle and looking as intense as a real sniper although the gun shot either air or corks. She turned to Garrett and Nathan. 'Ray's shooting up the place. You two should step in and show him a thing or two.'

'I'll give it a try, but Garrett's the marksman,' Nathan said. 'Garrett, get in there before Ray wins all the toys.'

'Looks like Ray's having a good time. Let him enjoy it for a while.' He snapped a photo of Ray.

Nathan ignored Garrett. 'Hey, Ray, the sheriff's here to give you some competition.'

Ray looked around, obviously annoyed. People nearby looked in Garrett's direction and most seemed to recognize the county sheriff. In a moment, they began moving back, making way for him.

'You must have quite a reputation,' Brynn murmured, feeling a wave of affection when she saw how many people smiled at Garrett. Nobody had given his father genuine smiles, she recalled. People treated William Dane with respect, but not an ounce of true friendliness, much less fondness.

'Brynn, anyone home in there?' Brynn looked up at Garrett. 'I asked if you want to go first.'

'She can't shoot,' Ray almost growled. 'This isn't a woman's sport.'

'This isn't a sport, Ray, it's a game,' Garrett snapped, then looked again at Brynn.

'Thank you, sir. I'd be glad to go first.'

Brynn took the gun and pointed. She ended up with enough points to prevent humiliation and win a small toy.

'You did good,' Savannah told her as Ray pushed back to his spot and picked up the gun, placed his feet shoulder-width apart, bent his head down to the rifle, gripped it and held it firmly, pressed the butt of the gun against his right shoulder and yelled, 'Start!'

'Yes, sir,' the game operator said, hiding a smirk. Nathan and

Garrett exchanged looks. The trail of tin wildlife began their march toward certain death accompanied by music. Ray fired, fired, fired. Ray missed, missed, missed. Occasionally he hit something and whooped with glee. When he finished, his score was less than Brynn's.

Cassie looked at Brynn and rolled her eyes. Then she said, 'Garrett, your turn.'

'Oh, no,' Garrett laughed. 'I'm not going to compete with Ray.'

'C'mon,' Cassie urged. 'We'd like to see someone who knows how to shoot.'

Ray cast her a murderous glare, but her attention was focused on Garrett. 'Garrett, for Savannah?'

'For Savannah?' She looked at her father expectantly and he pretended to think it over. 'Well, OK.'

Ray relinquished his spot. Garrett handed his gold balloon to Savannah and stepped forward, picking up the replica rifle. His stance looked entirely different than Ray's. 'OK,' he said, and the death march began. *Pop, pop, pop*. Garrett missed only once. While everyone clapped, Garrett was informed his score had won him three toys. He asked Savannah what prizes she'd like. She picked a stuffed pink teddy bear, a stuffed elephant and a stuffed giraffe, then gave both Cassie and Tessa each a toy.

'All right, Nathan, time to face the music.' Cassie's voice was loud yet somehow intimate. Nathan protested but Cassie insisted he do it for Tessa.

'Well, I can't say no to winning a prize for Tessa,' Nathan laughed. He assumed the same stance as Garrett, and managed to hit half as many.

'Don't feel bad,' Cassie said. 'After all, Garrett shoots rifles for a living!'

Nathan gave her a cocky look and didn't lay down his harmless rifle. Instead, he told the man behind the counter he'd go again, moved the butt of the rifle to the pocket of his shoulder formed by his left arm. Brynn frowned. Then, close to her ear, she heard Garrett murmur, 'I forgot – Nathan's ambidextrous.'

Nathan as well as the crowd whooped when he hit more targets than he had the first time. He turned to the clapping crowd and bowed. Then he collected four toys and distributed them among Tessa, Savannah, Brynn and Cassie.

'I thought you'd grow out of that ambidextrous trick,' Garrett teased. 'Show off.'

Nathan laughed. 'They tried to break me of it in school. One teacher even paddled me for it because I wouldn't use only my right hand, but I stuck to my guns, pardon the pun.'

'It makes you very special,' Tessa said formally. 'Thank you for the hippo. It's lovely.'

'What're you gonna name it?' Savannah asked.

Tessa studied the stuffed animal. 'Thaddeus,' she said, looking around as if she dared anyone to laugh. 'It was our great-great-grandfather's name, wasn't it, Nathan?'

'Hell, I don't know, Tess. You're the one who's into geneaology. I just hope our great-great-grandfather Thaddeus didn't look like the Thaddeus you're holding! Smile, little sis. Garrett, take a picture of Tessa and Thaddeus!'

Nathan was clearly having a good time even if his sister wasn't. She barely smiled at the camera. Then she began walking slowly and the vertical creases between her eyebrows dug deep in the skin. To make matters worse, Ray was distancing himself from her with every step he took. He looked at each pretty young girl who walked by and said nothing to Tessa. Brynn thought no one would ever guess he was with their group.

Garrett seemed to notice Ray's rudeness and, as if to take control of an uncomfortable moment, he said excitedly, 'I think I see a Ferris wheel!' He cast a sideways glance at Cassie. 'Wanna ride?'

Brynn looked at the giant vertical ring of brilliant gold, red, green and blue lights revolving in the darkness as people riding in the passenger cars whooped and screamed and laughed, then jerked in surprise when Rhonda appeared. Her long hair was tousled, her lip gloss smeared, and her gray eyes wide and bloodshot. 'The gang's all here! Including the brat, of course,' she ended, giving Savannah a threatening look as her hands clenched.

Brynn could see Garrett struggling for patience. 'Rhonda, I think you should go home,' he said evenly. 'You don't look well.'

'*I* don't look well? I look fabulous! It's your girlfriend Brynn who doesn't look well. Probably been losing sleep because she knows no one in this town wants her here.' Rhonda ran a finger under her nose, then glanced at Cassie. 'And you look crappy in those skinny jeans! Your store is a piece of crap, too! I'm glad I don't work there anymore!'

Garrett took a step toward her. 'OK, Rhonda. *Enough.*'

Rhonda ignored him. 'And there's poor little Tessa Cavanaugh with the sad, pasty face! Tell me, what brings you out with all the normal people tonight?'

Tessa's lips parted. She looked like she'd been slapped. 'I . . . I . . .'

Rhonda's attention had returned to Garrett. 'C'mon, sweetie. Go on the Ferris wheel with me? *Please?* Hold me like you used to do.' In a flash, she was right in front of him, rubbing against him, running her hands through his hair, trying to kiss him.

'I'll have you forcibly removed if you don't stop,' Garrett managed around kisses while he gently tried to push her away.

'No you won't. You still want me. You know you do. My love, *mon amour . . .*'

Garrett looked like he was going to lose control and slap her when Nathan came up behind her and wrapped his arms around her waist, pulling her a couple of steps backward. 'You're gorgeous. You don't want to ride the Ferris wheel with Garrett. You want to ride with me.'

She struggled in his arms. 'No! I want—'

Nathan whirled her around to face him. 'Garrett doesn't deserve you. How dare he turn you down! He's nothing. A little-town sheriff.' He hugged Rhonda, whose resistance slowed. 'I'm Nathan Cavanaugh. My father was the richest man in this town. I'm fairly well-off myself. Make my dreams come true. Ride with me, Rhonda.'

Rhonda nearly sagged against Nathan as he pulled her toward the ground level of the Ferris wheel. Meanwhile, he tossed a glance over his shoulder at Garrett. Garrett nodded, already reaching for his cell phone.

The Ferris wheel stopped, a laughing couple emerged quickly from their passenger car and Nathan pushed Rhonda onto the vacated seat, sitting down beside her and talking to her, smiling, touching her hair. Within moments, the Ferris wheel spun again, bright lights glowing in the dark night. Brynn looked at Nathan. He'd draped his arm around Rhonda's shoulder. The higher they climbed, though, the more it seemed as if he were almost clutching her. His expression was serious; Rhonda's flippant smile had vanished.

Savannah hurried to Brynn, trying to take her hand even though Savannah was still holding her balloons and stuffed animals. 'I'm scared of Rhonda. She hates me. And now she probably hates Dad. When she gets off the Ferris wheel—'

'When she gets off the Ferris wheel, there will be people to take her away. Your dad's taking care of that right now. Don't be scared.'

Cassie sidled up to Brynn on the opposite side of Savannah. 'That bitch,' she murmured in Brynn's ear.

'She's on something,' Brynn whispered back. 'I don't know what, but did you see her eyes?'

'Not up close.'

'Bloodshot with dilated pupils. She was rubbing her nose. Don't tell me you haven't seen someone else with those symptoms.'

'Ray!' Cassie blurted, then lowered her voice. 'Ray when he was using cocaine!'

Brynn nodded.

'Should you tell Garrett?'

'I'm sure he knows. He got a closer look at her than any of us. I think he's calling the cops to come and get her for disturbing the peace.'

Cassie raised her eyebrows. 'She's going to do something bad before this is all over if she's not taken away from the carnival.'

All of the group concentrated on the passenger car carrying Rhonda and Nathan, although they could barely see them. They reached the top of the sixty-three-foot wheel, then started downward. Only eight cars were ahead of them. Now what? Brynn wondered. When the ride is over, can Nathan and Garrett control her until help arrives?

Suddenly, the wheel stopped. The passenger cars swung. The couple in the lowest seat sprung out, quickly followed by the two guys in the second seat. Those in the third were too high. Within seconds, people had begun to yell. Two operators of the wheel ran toward the electric motor. In a moment, they yelled something to the man opening and closing the doors of the passenger cars. After they finished, the man nearest the crowd yelled upward, 'Nothing to worry about, folks. Just a little glitch in the motor. Hold on for five minutes. Enjoy the view.'

A woman shrieked. Her husband put his hand over her mouth. Some teenagers began to sing 'Rocky Mountain High.' Here and there came a loud curse or a soaring yodel.

'Is this really dangerous?' Cassie asked Garrett.

'I don't think so. The men working on the motor don't look overly concerned.' He glanced at Cassie and grinned. 'Don't worry. Rhonda will be back soon.'

'Oh, hooray.'

They all kept their gazes fixed on the car halfway down the wheel. In spite of the multi-colored lights, Brynn saw Rhonda run a hand under her nose and then stare at it. She moved close to Garrett and muttered, 'I think Rhonda's nose is bleeding.'

'Too much coke,' he said abruptly.

'You knew she did coke?'

He shook his head. 'If she did when we were seeing each other, she never used it around me. I wouldn't have stood for it, especially because she was around Savannah, too.'

Brynn looked up at the passenger car holding Rhonda and Nathan. She seemed to be moving around in the car, fighting to push open the door, flinging her hands and elbows at Nathan, who was trying to hold her still. 'Is Rhonda having a panic attack?' Brynn asked Garrett.

'God, I hope that's not what's wrong.' He frowned up at them. 'Nathan's in good shape, but if she's wired on cocaine, she could be stronger than normal.'

'I wish they'd get that motor fixed,' Brynn said tensely.

Rhonda leaned over the side of the car. Nathan pulled her back as she fought him, then began screaming, high and loud, dimming the noise made by the other passengers.

Savannah's grip tightened on Brynn's hand and she quavered. 'Daddy?'

'It's OK, honey,' Garrett answered. 'She's just scared.'

'I don't think so, Daddy. There's something else wrong with her.'

Brynn scanned the crowd, wondering if Ray had pulled himself away from the games of skill and could see his 'girlfriend.' He might know if she was suffering a coke overdose, but Brynn didn't spot him in the crowd.

Without a word, Garrett strode toward the guys working on the motor. Brynn knew he was asking what was wrong, if they could fix it quickly or if there was any other way they could quickly get the woman down. They shook their heads and began working feverishly.

Suddenly, Rhonda began to arch, her chest and neck rising, her head dipping backward, her beautiful hair hanging long over the back of the seat, her face contorting. Nathan seemed stunned for a moment, then wrapped his arms around her again, holding tight although she didn't relax. She looked as if she were going to snap in two.

'Help!' Nathan yelled desperately. 'Somebody help us!'

Brynn didn't know Tessa now stood beside her. 'She's going to hurt Nathan,' Tessa grated out. Brynn looked at Tessa's face bleached white in spite of the colored lights, her eyes wide with fear. 'Don't let her hurt Nathan!'

'They're trying, Tessa,' Brynn said, although she knew Tessa wasn't listening.

Rhonda's body relaxed slightly but she grabbed at her throat. 'She can't breathe!' Nathan shouted as she heaved, gulping for air that wouldn't come. 'Help us! She can't breathe!'

Rhonda's mouth seemed to snap shut. Her body heaved, arched violently, and finally went limp. She crumpled against Nathan. In a minute, the Ferris wheel started. It made no stops until Nathan and Rhonda's car reached the platform. Garrett reached it first. Brynn thrust Savannah's hand toward Cassie and said, 'Keep her here.'

But Cassie couldn't hold onto the panicked girl. She caught up to Brynn and screamed when she saw Nathan, sweating and pale, pushed to the side of the car with Rhonda lying against him like a broken doll, blood pouring out of her nose and mouth.

Brynn looked away to see Tessa's white balloon floating gracefully up to the starless black sky.

SEVENTEEN

'**R**honda snorted cocaine cut with strychnine,' Garrett said tonelessly.

Brynn sat straighter on Cassie's couch. She hadn't slept all night, but she felt alert. And shocked. 'Strychnine! Are you sure?'

'The medical examiner is. He hasn't had time to determine exactly how much she had, but depending on the amount, the symptoms of poisoning usually show up in fifteen to forty-five minutes.'

'Do you think it was an accident?' Brynn asked hollowly, knowing the answer.

'No. Someone wanted to kill Rhonda.'

Brynn went quiet for a moment. 'Who? Why?'

'I don't know much about Rhonda's background. She was always dodgy if you asked questions about her past. I'll talk to her aunt, but I don't count on getting much information. Mrs Gaines is very protective of Rhonda.'

Brynn hesitated, not wanting to bring up the subject but unable to avoid it. 'Did Rhonda ever talk to you about her cousin Frankie's murder?'

'A couple of times.'

'Did she want to know about my father and Mark? Did she ask what they were like?'

'She had her mind made up about what they were like, Brynn. She hated them, especially Mark.' Garrett went silent for a moment. Then he said, 'She knew him.'

'Rhonda *knew* him? Personally? She made it sound as if she only knew who he was when he came back to Genessa Point! Why didn't you tell me she actually knew him?'

'I didn't want to make matters worse. She was already getting out of control. I wanted to keep her away from you.'

Brynn took a minute to digest this news. She didn't know whether or not to be mad at Garrett for withholding information. She decided that before she made up her mind, she'd ask more questions. 'How well did she know Mark?'

'Not well. It was through Nathan. They went out a couple of times.'

'Really? She acted like she didn't know him!'

'Brynn, she was too out of it to know much of anything. Besides, they only went out a couple of times. They were both sixteen, she was pretty, and Nathan's always been every girl's dream. I think they just went to see a movie and maybe spent an evening at that year's festival. Nathan didn't like her.'

'Why?'

'He said she was weird.'

'Weird? How?'

'At sixteen we weren't into analyzing girls' personalities – looks, yes, personalities, no. He said she was weird *and* nosy. She asked too many questions about his life, his sister – pretty much how much money he'd inherit someday.'

'How much money? That was tactful.'

'Yeah, it pissed him off. She was fairly persistent, though. He was glad when summer was ending and she went home with her mother.'

'If you knew all of this, why did you start a relationship with her?'

'Because it happened a long time ago. She was so young.'

Brynn thought Garrett sounded defensive. 'She was single and she acted perfectly normal when I started dating her – at least for a couple of months. Then I started seeing trouble. She got possessive . . . Well, we don't need to go over all that again.'

'No, we don't. She was obviously troubled.' Brynn hoped that sounded polite. Just because Rhonda was dead, Brynn couldn't manufacture kind thoughts for her. She asked, 'How's Nathan?'

'Stunned. Shaken to the core.' Brynn could picture him shaking his head. 'God, what a thing – stuck on that Ferris wheel with Rhonda convulsing, bleeding, choking to death in his arms. And he took her up there to get her off my back.'

'It's awful, but at least he's all right.'

'I heard Tessa was having heart palpitations, her lips turned blue and she almost fainted. They had to sedate Tessa and Nate insisted she be kept at the hospital all night. He stayed in her room with her.'

'He shouldn't have bothered. Tessa's indestructible.' Brynn realized how acidic she'd sounded and was embarrassed. She'd always tried to keep her dislike of Tessa a secret. She had no reason to hate someone for defending herself. But Tessa had killed Brynn's father, and nothing could ever convince Brynn that Jonah Wilder had tried to murder her. She quickly changed the subject. 'Garrett, Cassie told me Ray used to do a lot of cocaine. I have a feeling that's why Rhonda was with him – he was her supplier.'

'Did you tell Cassie about Ray and Rhonda?'

'Yes. Last night. She wasn't surprised that they were together and she'd already wondered if Rhonda was doing coke. Garrett, where is Ray now?'

'We haven't found him yet. His car isn't at the Bay Motel and that can't be good. We've put out an APB for him.'

'You think he murdered Rhonda?'

'I think he gave her that cocaine, and she certainly didn't put strychnine in it.'

'Why would he kill her?'

'I don't have any idea. Certainly not because she was giving him too much business.'

'How's Savannah?'

'I'm not sure. First there was what she saw last night, then this morning I told her she can't be in the play tonight. There's too much going on in this town. I want her safe at home.'

'I can't believe the town's still having the play!'

'The mayor says townspeople will be disappointed if the play is canceled. What he means is that a lot of people have bought tickets. He doesn't want to refund the money.'

'Savannah must be heartbroken.'

'She is. After I told her, she stomped off to her room and went to bed. She won't get up. I had to ask Mrs Persinger – better known as the Doily Lady – to come sit with her at our house. I also talked to Savannah's great-aunt in Ohio. I'm sending her there until things settle down around here.'

'Oh. Does she like her great-aunt?'

'No. But she'll be safe.'

Brynn sighed. 'What a shame. I know how hard she's worked on her part in the play.'

'She has an understudy.' After a moment, Garrett said, 'She'll just have to be a grown-up and accept this even if it makes her hate me for a few months.'

'She'd never hate you, Garrett.'

'Maybe, but she can resent me. It doesn't matter, though.' Brynn heard the steel in his voice. 'Given what's been going on in Genessa Point lately, I have to protect her no matter how she feels about me.'

By early afternoon, Brynn's nerves were getting to her. She wanted to take a long walk, but Garrett still had surveillance on Cassie's house. After thinking it over for a few minutes, she decided to tell the policeman posted out front she'd like to walk around the block a couple of times, thinking he wouldn't believe that was too dangerous for her to do on her own.

'You walk, ma'am, and I'll creep along behind you,' the young cop had said with a friendly smile. 'You won't even know I'm here.'

Brynn started out with high hopes, but by the time she'd passed four houses, she realized she'd glanced back at her guardian twice. Once she'd smiled, once she'd waved. This wasn't going to work, she told herself. She was too self-conscious. But she also couldn't just sit in Cassie's house.

Brynn considered going to Garrett's house and visiting Savannah, but she was afraid the girl might see a visit as a vote for her being allowed to participate in the play. She didn't want to come between her and Garrett again, as she'd done on the day she'd met Savannah and allowed the girl to be her sightseeing guide when she knew Garrett didn't want Savannah to go with her. Besides, she agreed with him. If Savannah had been her daughter, she wouldn't want the girl to be out in public surrounded by so many strangers.

She also wouldn't want Savannah to be in this town – a town where a man had been stabbed through the heart and left in a vacant house, a town where a young woman had been given cocaine heavily cut with strychnine, certainly meant to kill her. Brynn closed her eyes for a moment, picturing Rhonda flinging her arms, arching her body and gasping for air before she died on a beautiful Ferris wheel. She hadn't liked Rhonda. She'd thought Rhonda might be dangerous. But had she deserved such a gruesome death? Had she deserved death at all? Someone had thought so. But who?

Someone who'd given her cocaine laced with strychnine. How long had the strychnine-laced cocaine been in her body? Garrett had said symptoms of strychnine poisoning would begin to show within fifteen to forty-five minutes. It was obvious now that Rhonda had been using for a while. Her suddenly erratic behavior at Cassie's store now made sense. Had rejection by Garrett caused her to start? Probably not. She could have had a history with the drug. But what drove her to snort so much cocaine the night of the carnival? And who could have laced it with strychnine? Was she already so high that all of her senses were dimmed? Brynn sighed. Rhonda had wanted to dull the pain, but she was certain Rhonda hadn't wanted to die.

As Brynn walked in the well-maintained neighborhood of two-story homes built mostly in the seventies and eighties, she abruptly felt a gaze fixed on her. She slowed down and looked at the house to her left. Every window showed only the edges of opened draperies. The same with the next house. That didn't mean no one was peeking at her, she thought. No one else was walking the neighborhood with a police car trailing behind them.

Her cell phone rang and she jumped. She fished in her purse until she found it and glanced at the caller ID. G. Traymore. She didn't know anyone named Traymore. She hesitated, then answered.

'Miss Wilder? Brynn Wilder?' asked a pleasant, young male voice.

'Yes.'

'I'm Greg Traymore in Baltimore. I'm a friend of Mark's. I've talked to the Baltimore police about him and the sheriff in Genessa Point, but I know how much Mark cares for you and I think I should talk to you, too.'

Brynn stopped on the sidewalk. The patrol car stopped, too, so she decided walking was better. She didn't want to answer questions from the patrolman.

'I'm so glad you called,' she exclaimed. 'I knew Garrett – Sheriff Dane – spoke to you but I wanted to talk to you myself. He gave me your phone number. I was going to call this evening.'

'Mark gave me your number a couple of weeks ago.' Greg paused. 'He said if things didn't go the way he planned, I might want to talk to you.'

Brynn felt as if a lump of ice had settled in her stomach. 'If things didn't go the way he planned in Genessa Point?'

'Yes.' He paused. 'I know the whole story about your father, Miss Wilder. I didn't think it was a good idea, but there was no talking him out of the trip. He's been drinking a lot lately, he lost his job . . . well, I guess you know all that.'

'Unfortunately, yes.'

'Well, there's something that's been bothering me. I didn't tell the Baltimore police or Sheriff Dane because I thought they'd ignore it. But I can't stop thinking about it.'

Brynn turned a corner, seeing the sidewalk stretch before her but not registering. She was aware only of a strong, cool breeze whispering through tree leaves, blowing her hair, freeing a piece of silvery paper from beneath a fence and sending it across the street.

'Brynn, are you there?' Greg asked.

'Yes,' she said. 'I'm outside and a chilly breeze came out of nowhere. Go ahead.'

'Well, both my wife and I were friends of Mark's. We were worried about him and she suggested she bake some lasagna as an excuse to go check on him. When we got to his apartment, he was half-drunk and looked like hell – sorry – and newspapers and clippings were scattered all over the place.'

'Oh, no,' Brynn said, thinking that while she'd been walking along the beach in the evenings, dreaming up the plot for her latest book, Mark had been on a steep emotional decline. 'I wish I'd been there.'

'I don't think he would have let you do anything for him. He talked about you a lot, Brynn. He loved you, but he also admired and respected you, talked about how much stronger you were than him. He wouldn't have let you into his apartment. Anyway, my wife and I nearly forced ourselves in and we all ate. Then we went in the living room,' Greg went on. 'Honestly, it was hard to find a place to sit. Mark was beginning to sober up and I got him talking about the Orioles – he's still interested in baseball. While we were talking, my wife glanced around at the newspapers. She didn't try to straighten them – Mark had them in some kind of order. She saw one with a headline about another murder in Genessa Point.

'She said that on the opposite page was a follow-up story about a car wreck that had happened two days earlier. A car had swerved to miss what the driver thought was a person but was in fact a mannequin. Two people were hurt. When my wife asked Mark about it, he got this distant look on his face. He didn't say anything for a couple of minutes. Then he started shouting, "The mannequin! Not me . . . not Garrett." He smacked himself on the forehead and said something about how stupid he'd been and maybe what she'd written was true.'

'She? Who?'

'I don't know. I was afraid to start asking questions because he'd get rid of us. My plan didn't work. About ten minutes later, he asked us to leave. He was polite and thanked us for dinner, but he said he had work to do. Does any of that mean something to you?'

Brynn paused. 'I remember something about a car wreck caused by a mannequin from the store where my mother worked. Does your wife recall the date of the newspaper?'

'I asked her. She doesn't. She also said the number of victims wasn't in the headline. Sorry.'

'That's all right. Sounds like it was a hectic evening.'

'It sure was. We were being so careful not to upset Mark. The next day I called and Mark said he was going to Genessa Point to find out the truth about his dad. Remembering that car wreck set him off. That and whatever *she* had written. I thought you might have the answers. I didn't want to bring it up to the Baltimore police or to Sheriff Dane because I thought maybe Mark had something to do with the wreck.'

Brynn stopped walking, feeling tears rising in her eyes. 'That was very thoughtful of you, Greg. I really appreciate you not dragging the police into it.'

'Hey, Mark's my best friend. And that newspaper was old. The wreck happened a long time ago and no one was killed.' Greg went silent for a moment. 'And the guy I know wouldn't have anything to do with a prank like that.'

'I can't imagine my brother ever doing such a thing, either, and not just because I love him. He was a good kid, Greg. Always.'

'That's what I figured.' She could feel, even if she couldn't see, Greg's smile. 'It's been nice talking to you, Brynn. Let me know just as soon as you find Mark. The Orioles had a great game last week. He'll be ecstatic.'

EIGHTEEN

Twenty minutes later, Brynn was pounding up the stairs in Cassie's house, headed for her second-floor office. The computer, which Cassie rarely used, seemed to be calling Brynn's name. 'Thank God you're not still sitting in the computer shop "on the blink" as Cassie says,' Brynn murmured, as if the machine could answer her. She turned the computer on, went to the internet and searched for the *Genessa Point Gazette*. On their webpage, she searched the archived articles for 'mannequin.' Disappointed, she found nothing. She thought of trying 'car wrecks,' but that was too generic. Even in a town of twelve thousand people, not counting the tourists in the summer, wrecks happened all the time. Besides, she didn't know the year of the wreck or the names of the people involved.

Letting out a huge sigh, Brynn glanced through the email subjects. She'd expected to see ads for fashion, colognes and shoes, but Cassie must have a different address for her store computer to which those emails were sent. Most of these seemed personal. And there were few of them. Brynn felt guilty that she hadn't emailed more regularly.

Finally she saw a subject that made her sit up straight: Pics from Mark. These had to be the pictures Mark had taken on the Saturday Cassie and Mark had walked around town together early in the day. Later that same day, he'd disappeared.

Brynn clicked on the email and saw that there were five photos attached. The first showed Cassie wearing dark wash jeans and an ivory short-sleeved tier top. She stood in front of a rail fence beside a garden of sunflowers. In the next photo, Cassie leaned against her sonic orange Hyundai Coupé, wearing sunglasses with a sunflower tucked behind her ear. She was laughing and the sun glistened on her reddish gold hair.

They'd ventured away from Cassie's house for the third photo, with Cassie sitting at a Cloud Nine table holding out a delectable Chocolate Dream. Cassie posed on a park bench, probably at Holly Park, in the next photo. Brynn was about to open the final photo when her cell phone rang. She answered without looking at the caller ID and was silent for a moment when an unfamiliar female voice asked, 'Miss Wilder? Brynn Wilder?'

Brynn hesitated, catching her breath, before she answered, 'Yes?'

'This is Miss Kern, Doctor Ellis's nurse.'

'His nurse? I thought he'd retired?'

'His private nurse, Miss Wilder. Maybe you didn't know, but for the last few days he's been confined to bed rest in his home. I'm taking care of him.'

'Oh, my, I didn't know.' Brynn felt a wave of guilt, remembering his collapse at her feet when she berated him at his daughter Joy's grave. 'Is he improving?'

'Not really. Frankly, I don't think he wants to recover.' The nurse's voice was low. She doesn't want Edmund to hear her, Brynn thought. 'He asked if he could see you this afternoon.'

'This afternoon? Could it wait until tomorrow?'

Miss Kern hesitated. 'Well, possibly, but . . . well, it's just a feeling I have, but I think if you wait, he may not be able to speak to you. He's very weak and he's adamant about seeing you.' She lowered her voice even farther. 'He says it's a matter of life and death.'

'Do you think he's . . . well . . .'

'In his right mind? Yes, Miss Wilder. He's perfectly lucid.'

As angry with Edmund Ellis as she'd been for years, she couldn't forget his gray and dying look the last time she'd seen him; she couldn't forget how harsh she'd been to him; she couldn't forget how she'd once cared for him – almost as much as she'd cared for her father.

'Tell Doctor Ellis I'll be there within an hour,' she said. 'Be sure to tell him I'll come.'

'I'll tell him. And thank you, Miss Wilder. I just have a feeling that . . . well, that it's vitally important he sees you as soon as possible.'

Brynn turned off Cassie's computer, hurriedly left her office and ran out to the patrolman, asking him to take her to Doctor Edmund Ellis's home. God only knew why he was so insistent about seeing her, she thought, her hands trembling, but she knew it had to be something important.

When Brynn dashed out of Cassie's house, she once again had that strange feeling of being watched, and not by the surveillance cop.

She looked around and saw hardly anyone. Festival activities were taking up the time of kids who would usually be seen on the sidewalks and she pictured women starting dinner for their husbands. She smiled. Most women had full-time jobs nowadays. Her imagination was hopelessly locked in the past, playing over and over images of her mother who only worked part-time so she could always fuss over the big dinners she fixed for her family every evening.

When she reached the Ellis home, Miss Kern took her upstairs to Edmund's room. He was sitting up in his bed, looking alarmingly thin and ashen. He ordered Miss Kern to leave and asked Brynn to sit on the bed so they could talk quietly. He sneezed and reached for a bottle of pills. Brynn handed him a glass of water and he swallowed four of them.

'Do you need so many?' she asked.

He smiled at her. 'They're just antihistamines. They help this damnable cold I can't shake, but I've built up a tolerance to them. Don't worry – I've been a doctor long enough to know what I'm doing.'

'You don't look well,' Brynn said gently.

'I thought you were too mad at me to care how I looked,' he said without rancor.

'So did I,' Brynn answered. 'I guess I don't know myself as well as I thought. I loved you when I was young, almost as much as I loved my father.'

Edmund winced. 'I know. I loved you, too. I still do. That's why I have to tell you the truth about something. The time's finally come.'

Oh no, Brynn thought. This is about the Genessa Point Killer. She reached in her purse and turned off her cell phone. He's going to tell me what I've wanted to know for so long, she thought, but suddenly I'm not sure I want to hear it. She said nothing, frightened into silence, her cold hands clenched, her face feeling frozen.

'You know, my wife Iris had a stillborn baby when Joy was five. Iris was seven months pregnant and it hadn't been an easy pregnancy. I'd told her to just rest until her labor started, but she had a compulsion about cleaning. She climbed halfway up on a stepladder to dust the top of a bookshelf and fell. The bookshelf turned over on her. Her leg was broken, she had a concussion and . . . and the baby was born dead. In spite of the fall, the baby could have been saved, but Iris was unconscious and hemorrhaging until Joy found her when she got home from kindergarten.'

Brynn had been eight when Mrs Ellis lost her baby. She remembered crying because she loved the Ellises and couldn't wait for them to have another baby. Her mother hadn't told her how the baby died, though. She'd said that sometimes these things just happened.

'I wasn't perfect, but I tried not to blame her for the baby's death,' Edmund went on. 'After all, I should have gotten a private nurse for her, someone to keep her from being reckless. Iris's own mother came to help, though, and never let up on her. She piled on the guilt. I couldn't understand it until my mother-in-law told me Iris had a drinking problem before we got married – no one had mentioned it to me because they were afraid I wouldn't marry her. She said she was sure Iris was drinking again – that's why she'd climbed up on that ladder. All I know is that after the stillbirth, Iris started sneaking in bottles of liquor. She wasn't careful about hiding them and sometimes I found them.' He turned his head and looked into Brynn's eyes. 'My mother-in-law was a destructive woman. I banned her from the house, but Iris was emotionally fragile. After the baby, after the drinking started, she was never the same.'

'Is that why she pulled away from my mother? They used to be best friends.'

Edmund nodded.

'I asked Mom why she never came to visit anymore. Mom told me that Iris was very busy and couldn't visit as much as she used to do. I missed her. I know Mom did, too, but looking back, I think she suspected the drinking.'

Edmund nodded again at Brynn, sneezed then pointed to his water glass. She handed it to him and he took two more pills. 'Had them in my pocket,' he said and winked.

'Maybe I should call Miss Kern.'

He shook his head. 'She's a tyrant. Besides, this is important. I have to say it now.'

Edmund swallowed more water, then stared ahead again, as if he was gathering his thoughts. 'The day your father . . . died, Joy was supposed to have a piano lesson. I'd gone to the hospital early for an emergency. After I left home, Marguerite left a message on the answering machine saying she was canceling Joy's lesson.' He went silent again for a moment. 'Iris later admitted she'd had a sip of bourbon for breakfast. She didn't know how to have a sip of anything alcoholic. Anyway, she didn't play the message. She took Joy to her lesson and didn't walk the child to the door. She just let Joy out of the car, told her to go knock on the door and she'd be back in an hour to pick her up.'

'I'd spent the night with Cassie, Mark was on a school trip, and Dad was fishing,' Brynn said softly, almost as a way of delaying what she thought she might hear.

'I know. Joy said no one came to the door. She thought she was too early and went into the woods. She didn't know you'd come home. She was bending down, picking a bouquet of wild violets for your mother, when she heard someone scream.' He swallowed hard. 'Joy saw a girl with her back turned toward her. Joy was frightened and flattened herself into the high grass and vines. She was such a little thing, you remember . . .'

'Yes,' Brynn said tremulously. She could hardly breathe.

'Well, she just lay there, literally scared stiff, but still watching. After the second scream, your father ran into the woods. Joy said the girl was still standing and, when your father reached her, she stabbed him in the neck. Once. Twice. Then they began to wrestle for the knife. The fight spun the girl around and Joy recognized her.' Edmund looked at Brynn, his cloudy gray eyes filling with tears. 'There was a third person in the woods that day, but not a killer. It was my little Joy and she saw Tessa Cavanaugh murder your father.'

NINETEEN

Brynn felt as if she couldn't get enough air to breathe. She made a couple of strangling noises until her lungs seemed to inflate, filling her with startling, dizzying oxygen. Edmund reached out and took her arm, asking, 'Should I call for Miss Kern?'

Brynn shook her head. She couldn't stand a barrage of questions about how she was doing, someone taking her pulse, someone looking into her eyes with a tiny light. When she felt she could speak again, she asked, 'Joy was certain she saw Tessa stab my father? No one else was there? Dad just ran into the woods after she screamed and Tessa stabbed him?'

Edmund nodded. 'Joy was a very truthful little girl. She would never have claimed to see Tessa stab your father if she hadn't. She said after they started fighting, they fell on the ground. Then she said everything got "mixed up." That's what she called it. Jonah got the knife – that must have been when he managed to stab Tessa just above the kidney – and then they fought some more and finally Tessa stopped fighting. Your father left the woods before Tessa did, according to Joy.'

'I saw Dad come out of the woods and then Tessa.' Brynn swallowed hard. 'I was so shocked I ran to him. I thought he was already dead. Tessa was crying, begging. Then I called the police, so it was probably fifteen to twenty minutes later before they arrived. I never saw Joy, though, and she didn't come to the house.'

Edmund closed his eyes and tears ran down his cheeks. 'That was part of the trauma. Iris went to sleep and didn't go back for Joy in an hour. I got home four hours after Iris should have picked her up and found Iris passed out. Drunk. At first she kept claiming she'd picked up Joy. I couldn't find her, though. I was frantic. I called your house. A man – probably a policeman – answered the phone. I heard a lot of hubbub in the background. I was startled and, before I could say a word, Joy stumbled into our house. She'd hidden in the woods until she heard what she said were "a lot of men" coming. That must have been the police and she was frightened, so she finally took off for home. She'd dodged and hidden all the way. She was nearly hysterical and exhausted.'

'Didn't you call the police then?'

'As I said, Joy was almost hysterical and so weak. All I could think about was her. I had to get her calmed down – her heart, you know. I didn't even risk taking her to the hospital – I had everything I needed at home. While I was taking care of her, she babbled out the story. When she was finished, she didn't speak again for three days.' He asked for his water again, but this time he only sipped without taking any pills. 'After Joy had told me what she saw, then went silent, I called someone and asked what was going on at your house. They told me Tessa Cavanaugh had killed Jonah Wilder when he attacked her. I knew that's not what had happened, but I didn't say anything.'

'Why not?' Brynn demanded.

'Shock. Confusion. Mostly concern for my child. I sat up all night deciding what I should do. Joy was only seven, Brynn. I could picture her telling a story about a fifteen-year-old girl killing a grown man – a badly injured fifteen-year-old girl, no less.' He looked at Brynn. 'Would you have believed Joy?'

Brynn thought about it for a moment, then said, 'I don't know.'

'I couldn't take the chance that the police wouldn't believe her and, even if they did, I could not put my little girl in a courtroom. She would have been more traumatized emotionally and the risk to her heart – well, it would have been bad enough for a healthy child, but Joy was so delicate.'

'But she had to tell the truth, Edmund! Did you think it was better for her to keep it bottled up inside for the rest of her life? And didn't you feel any obligation to us? My God, Dad was your best friend. What about Dad?'

'What about Tessa?' For the first time, Edmund's voice sounded almost normal. 'What if no one believed Joy and Tessa was left free? Don't you think she would have retaliated against Joy?'

'Not if she wanted people to believe *her*, not Joy!'

Edmund had gotten so agitated, his breath grew ragged and his hands shook. Brynn raised his arm and held it softly against her chest. 'Give your voice a rest. Do you want more water?' Edmund shook his head. 'Then just lay quietly for a few minutes. I won't leave.'

'I don't have time to rest. Not yet.' Edmund looked at her beseechingly. 'I did your family a terrible wrong. I said I didn't know anything about Jonah losing that knife with his initials. But I did. I knew it had been gone for a couple of years before he was killed with it.'

Brynn stiffened. 'Why did you lie?'

'Because I had a little girl to protect. That's why I sent her away. When she started talking again, she described the stabbing, over and over. She drew pictures of it . . . all the time. All the time . . .'

Edmund seemed to be slipping away. Brynn shook his arm. 'Edmund, I understand that you wanted to protect Joy, but you should have told the truth!'

He looked at her and she could see the pain behind his eyes. 'Dear, telling the truth wouldn't have brought your father back. All it would do was put you and Mark and Marguerite in the same danger as Joy. I did all I could think of – I bought your house three months after you moved to Baltimore. Sam Fenney and I came up with a corporation and a real estate company. The real estate company supposedly bought the house. Your mother would never have let me buy it outright, but I knew how desperately the three of you needed money.

'As for not telling the truth about that knife, the case was closed even though a lot of people didn't think Jonah was the Genessa Point Killer. Sheriff Dane wouldn't have listened to what I had to say anyway. It didn't amount to much and certainly wouldn't have counted as evidence. Dane had his mind made up about your father after Tessa. He'd always hated your father, but Tessa gave him a reason to say that he hated Jonah.'

'Why did William Dane hate my father?'

'You don't know? No, of course you don't. Your mother would never have told you. William Dane fell in love with her when they were teenagers. At least, he loved her as much as he was capable of loving. That's not saying much. They went out a few times and suddenly he was determined they'd get married. He asked her and she said no, but she didn't tell me about it – Iris did. When your mother was twenty-one, your father came to Genessa Point. Your mother played piano in church. That's where they met. Six months later, she married him. It was obvious she adored Jonah. William Dane was so furious I thought he'd kill your father. Instead, he married a sweet, diffident little widow ten years older than he was and he completely dominated her. They had one boy – one hand-some, intelligent son – and William made his life miserable. Garrett hated his father with good reason, but Garrett's a fine person, Brynn. He's nothing like his father.'

'Then when he became sheriff, why didn't you tell him your story?'

'It had been so long ago. I didn't think he'd believe me. I'd never left Genessa Point and didn't move near Joy because it was bad for the child to be near Iris. My wife was so conscience-stricken she'd always retreat into booze when she was near Joy. It upset Joy terribly, so I kept Joy away as much as possible and tried to rehabilitate Iris, but it was useless.

'Finally, about six months after Iris died from cirrhosis, Joy's health began declining. She couldn't work anymore and she'd never married, so last year she came home. I thought I could make her comfortable and happy, but she'd felt so guilty all those years that, right before she died, she sent a letter to your brother telling him all about Tessa killing your father. That's why Mark came back. Joy died four days before he arrived, and he might have thought she hadn't been in her right mind, but *I* told him the truth.'

Edmund's jaw clenched. 'That devil found out Mark was here. Watched him come to this house, figured I'd told Mark the truth, and kidnapped him. Called me and told me if I said anything to police, Mark would be dead like his father. So I've waited. I didn't go to the police. I've tried to get you to leave so the same thing doesn't happen to you, but you won't go. Stubborn. Stubborn like your brother. Jonah's children, almost like my own, and I let them down.' Edmund's voice became even weaker and thinner. 'Let both of you down.'

'Do you know where Mark is?' Brynn almost shouted. 'Who's the devil? Tessa?'

But Edmund was barely breathing. Brynn called for Miss Kern. Within ten minutes the nurse had checked Edmund, sternly told Brynn he'd been taking sleeping pills, not pills for a cold, and was searching for the cord she'd taken from the landline phone beside Edmund's bed. 'I didn't want him making calls or getting calls. He needed rest!' Miss Kern told Brynn.

The cord had slipped under the bed and while Miss Kern tried to reach it, Brynn grabbed her cell phone out of her purse, turned it on and dialed 911. She then handed the cell phone to the nurse so Miss Kern could give details of the patient's condition and the address.

How stupid she'd been, Brynn condemned herself. She would

have known Edmund wasn't taking pills for a cold if she hadn't been more concerned with getting information about the past than concern for the sick man right in front of her.

When the EMS squad arrived, Edmund looked dead but the paramedics assured her he wasn't. They moved him from his house to an ambulance as fast as possible and took off, Miss Kern riding in the back of the ambulance with Edmund.

Brynn walked to the patrol car and tried Garrett's phone. He answered. 'Oh, Garrett,' Brynn nearly sobbed. 'I'm at Edmund Ellis's house. He's in a very bad way.' She heard a low beeping sound. 'Is that your phone battery?'

'It's low. Too many phone calls this last hour.'

'Where are you?'

'Brynn, I want you to stay calm. Don't call Cassie immediately. Promise me.'

'Cassie? OK, I promise.'

'I'm about fifteen miles north of town. We found Ray O'Hara's truck. He went off the road and rolled over a steep embankment. The truck wasn't spotted until a couple of hours ago.' Garrett took a breath. 'He's alive in spite of some serious injuries from the wreck, but he's unconscious. We've found a lot of cocaine in his truck and the paramedics say he shows evidence of having been on coke. That's probably why he wrecked it.'

'He left the carnival like a bat out of hell after he saw Rhonda die on the Ferris wheel, Garrett,' Brynn said slowly. 'I *know* he was her supplier. That's why she was sleeping with him. Sex for drugs.'

'I think so, too. If Cassie knows about his wreck now, she'll probably get in the middle of things. Let's keep this between us until he's settled at the hospital.'

'Good idea.'

'What were you trying to tell me before my battery beeped?'

'Edmund told me something about Tessa. And I talked to Mark's friend in Baltimore. He said something about a car wreck caused by a mannequin.' Her voice was shaking. 'But Garrett, listen, Edmund told me that Tessa—'

'A mannequin? Yeah, I remember that. What about Tessa?' The beeping sound again. 'I don't have time now.'

'But—' More beeping.

'Later. I should check on Savannah. Mrs Persinger is staying with her at our house.'

'I'll check on Savannah. Garrett, Tessa—'

'Take care of yourself, Brynn. Besides Savannah, you're the most important—'

The phone went dead.

Brynn asked the young patrolman to take her to Cassie's. She needed to calm down and then call to check on Savannah rather than face the girl now. Brynn realized her hands were trembling and she looked drained. Savannah didn't need to see her this way. A block from Cassie's house, Brynn glanced at her watch. 4:45 p.m. Cassie had told Brynn she'd be staying an hour late at the shop this evening. That was a relief. By the time she got home, Ray would probably be in the hospital.

Still, these thoughts only skimmed over the deeper knowledge that Tessa had deliberately lured Brynn's father into the woods to stab him. But why? Brynn hadn't realized until now that she'd been certain Tessa had deliberately stabbed Jonah. She'd told everyone, including herself, that a third person had killed her father. But deep in her mind, she hadn't believed it. And she'd been right. There hadn't been a third adult in the woods – only a terrified seven-year-old girl.

'We're home, Miss Wilder,' the patrolman said. 'You OK?'

'Oh, uh, yes. Just upset over Doctor Ellis.'

'Maybe you should call someone to be with you for a while. Don't mean to insult you, but you're pale.'

'Cassie will be home soon. I'll have a glass of wine and be fine.' She looked at him and tried to smile. 'Want me to bring you some wine?'

He grinned. 'I'm more of a beer man when I drink, but I'm on duty.'

'A soft drink? Coffee?'

'Coffee'd be nice, if you don't mind.'

'Not at all. I'll be back quick as a bunny, as my mother used to say.'

Another smile, this one even wider. 'I say the same thing to my little girl.'

Brynn didn't realize how tired she was until she climbed Cassie's porch steps and used her two keys, one for the door lock, one for the deadbolt. She went in and carefully relocked the doors. On her way to the kitchen, her cell phone rang again. Maybe Garrett with more news about Ray, she thought.

Instead, she heard the quavering voice of an older woman. 'Miss Hutton?'

'No, she's still at her store. I'm Brynn Wilder.'

'Oh, I'm Mrs Persinger. Savannah talks about you all the time. I'm at her house today. That's what her father wanted because she was so upset about not being in the play she wouldn't come out of her room. So I said I'd stay here and watch her. I'd take good care of her . . .' The woman suddenly sobbed.

'Mrs Persinger? What's wrong?' Brynn anxiously asked the woman who'd been taking care of Savannah during the day for months since Grams died.

'She's gone! I dozed off – oh, I'll never forgive myself – but I did and when I woke up, I went to check on her. She wasn't in her room. I've searched this whole house. The dog's here, but she's not.' Mrs Persinger's voice raised to a wail. 'Savannah's gone!'

TWENTY

Brynn felt a dark flutter of fear in her stomach, but her voice emerged even and strong. 'Calm down, Mrs Persinger. If Savannah has run away from home, she'll have taken Henry. She was determined to be in the play tonight. She was supposed to be there by five-thirty for last-minute directions, a costume check, several things. I'm sure she's on her way to the amphitheater. I'll have the patrolman outside take me there right now. If she's not there already, we'll look all around for her.'

'Should I call her father?'

'He's at a crime scene and his cell phone is running low.' Garrett doesn't need to hear this right now, Brynn thought. 'The policeman outside and I will find her, I promise.'

'Are you sure?' Mrs Persinger was crying. 'I mean, if that dear child is lost because I fell asleep, I just won't be able to stand it. Sheriff Dane trusted me and I let him down!'

'You didn't let him down,' Brynn said. 'Savannah took advantage of you. She knew she wasn't supposed to go to the play, so you stop worrying. Everything will be fine. As soon as we find her, I'll call you. I know the Danes's phone number. You just stay there. Don't go out looking for Savannah. We don't want to search for you, too!'

'No, I guess you don't.' Brynn heard the attempt at lightness in Mrs Persinger's voice, followed by a note of hopelessness. 'I'll be here until Savannah comes home.'

No time for wine or coffee, Brynn thought. They had to find Savannah. She was certain her explanation to Mrs Persinger for Savannah's absence was right. Well, almost certain. Still, the thirteen-year-old girl shouldn't be on the streets alone, much less heading toward the amphitheater. It was at least two miles from her home. Would she accept a ride from someone?

'Oh, God,' she murmured, feeling a migraine start behind her eyes. No time to go search for her migraine pills now, she thought. Brynn was heading for the front door when she first felt she wasn't alone. Instinct made her stop and look around the living room. It was bright with sun. Nothing was out of place. 'You're giving yourself the creeps over Edmund's story and Savannah running off,' she told herself aloud, rubbing a hand across her forehead.

Her hand, damp with sweat, trembled and she dropped her tote bag, spilling a few items. 'Dammit,' she muttered. She thought she heard a noise – a sigh, for God's sake, close by. She kneeled, grabbed her tote and reached for her keys and cell phone. In less than a second, from the tail of her eye she caught a flash of movement. She jumped up and started to turn, lifting her tote bag like a shield, but before she could make a sound, something crashed down on her head. Brynn stood long enough to feel blood flowing from her scalp down to her right eye before the world went dark and she wilted onto the floor.

Garrett walked up and down a hall at the hospital. He'd tried some of the foul coffee from the machine, eaten what tasted like a slightly stale candy bar but was actually considering another one. Eating was better than smoking, he thought. He'd started smoking when he was sixteen because he thought it made him look badass. He'd given up the cigarettes three months before Savannah was born. Patty had smoked even more after having the baby, in spite of his lectures about the dangers of second-hand smoke.

But now he wanted a cigarette. He couldn't remember the last time he'd craved one. He also couldn't remember the last time Genessa Point had seemed in such danger, even when the GPK was murdering two or three times a year.

Ray's doctor came out of his room and slowly walked toward Garrett. He's dead, Garrett thought. Ray didn't make it, the jerk.

'Sheriff Dane?' the doctor asked, knowing very well who Garrett was. Garrett nodded. 'Mr O'Hara has a broken left femur, broken left radius and ulna, broken clavicle, and a grade-three concussion. Grade three is the most serious form of concussion. All of the broken bones will require surgery. Oh, he also has cocaine in his system.'

'Just cocaine?'

The doctor frowned.

'I mean, it isn't cocaine cut with anything fatal?'

'You're thinking of that young woman who died on the Ferris wheel from snorting cocaine laced with strychnine.'

'That wasn't supposed to be public knowledge yet.'

'Well, it's knowledge in this hospital where she was brought DOA.'

Garrett nodded. 'Sure it is. What about Ray O'Hara?'

'If he had cocaine laced with strychnine in him, he'd probably be dead. The cocaine he'd had might have been laced with something like baking soda, but nothing dangerous. What worries me the most about his condition is the concussion, but I don't think it'll kill him.' The doctor looked at him and finally gave him a small, tight smile. 'I know you want to talk to him and he's conscious right now. He might lose consciousness any time, so you should probably question him as soon as possible. Just don't be surprised if he's muddled. If he is, I have to insist you let him rest. No more questions.'

'OK, Doctor. I'll be gentle.'

'I don't think this guy's used to gentle,' the doctor said. 'The X-rays show a lot of old breaks, and he has a lot of body scars. Maybe he was abused.'

'Bar fights,' Garrett said. 'Cops have broken up quite a few of them. Ray wants to be a tough guy.'

'The moron,' the doctor muttered, then motioned toward Ray's room.

Garrett walked in to see Ray lying lifelessly on the bed. His body was hidden beneath a sheet and blanket, but as Garrett drew nearer he could clearly see the scrapes and bruises all over Ray's face. His left eyelid was swollen. The right was shut, but Garrett saw the lid flutter. 'Hey there, Ray,' he said cheerfully. 'Don't pretend to be asleep – the doc told me you're awake and looking forward to answering all my questions.'

Ray's right eye opened but he said nothing.

'You were at the carnival last night,' Garrett said, standing over Ray. 'You ran off when you saw Rhonda die.'

'Rhonda's dead? How?'

'Don't give me that crap, Ray. I know you too well. She was connected to you – literally – at the Bay Motel. A witness saw her leaving your room the morning of the day she died. Do you know how she died? Overdose of cocaine laced with strychnine.'

Ray's one good eye widened. 'Strychnine?'

'You were supplying her, weren't you?'

'No.'

'*Ray!*'

'All right. I gave her some coke. It wasn't like she'd never had it before. She's been on and off it since she was a teenager.'

'I don't care how long she'd been using. I care about where she got the coke cut with strychnine!'

Ray's eye widened even father. 'Yeah, yeah, sure you are. But I didn't give it to her. God! Why would I do that?'

'You wanted to be rid of her?'

'No. Not yet.'

'Not *yet*? Tell me the truth, Ray. Why did you and Rhonda hook up? And what's going on with you and Tessa Cavanaugh? Is she buying coke from you, too?'

'Tessa! She doesn't even drink!'

Garrett gave Ray a long, hard stare, then stepped closer to the bed. Ray cringed slightly, then winced from the pain. 'Tell me the last time you sold Rhonda cocaine.'

'I didn't *sell* it to her. I gave her some this morning.'

'And did you use any of the cocaine you gave her?'

'No. I used some before the carnival, but just a little from a different stash.'

'Were you together just for sex and cocaine?'

'No!' Ray managed to look deeply offended. 'She was helping me with research for my book!'

'Your book?'

'Yes, dammit, my book! I've been saying for years I'm gonna write a book but no one pays attention to me. They all bow and scrape to Brynn Wilder because of that silly junk she writes but no one recognized the serious material I intend to write.'

'And what serious material would that be?'

'The truth about the Genessa Point Killer!' Ray sounded triumphant.

'You know the truth?'

'I know more than you do. I know more than anyone . . . except for Rhonda. That's why she was . . . killed.' Ray's eyelid was beginning to droop. He looked like he was losing focus. 'Her cousin . . . Frankie. She never got . . . never got over him. She blamed Mark but always had her . . . suspicions. Just like me.'

'What suspicions?'

Ray swallowed, his eyelid closing.

'What suspicions, dammit!'

'We knew. We *knew*. They found out we knew because Rhonda

wasn't careful enough. She and I saw the pictures on Cassie's computer. If I'd seen the pictures of Cassie and Mark sooner . . . I tried. Went in her house and it . . . was gone. Something wrong with it and she'd taken it to a computer shop. I tried to be careful but I got outsmarted. Too sneaky. Too evil . . . that's it . . . too evil for Rhonda and me. Killed Rhonda. He would have killed me . . . would have killed me . . .'

'Ray!' Garrett said loudly as Ray drifted off. 'Ray! What are you talking about? Who knew?' His voice rose. 'Who wanted to kill you and Rhonda?'

The doctor burst into the room. 'Sheriff, you're shouting at him.'

'I wasn't.'

'You *were*. Maybe you didn't realize it.'

Garrett stepped away from the bed, feeling his heart pounding, his breath rapid. He had been shouting, he thought. 'I'm sorry. He just said something important. If I could just have a few more minutes . . .'

'He's unconscious, Sheriff,' the doctor said evenly. 'He can't tell you anything right now. He might come to before he goes into surgery. I doubt it, though. We have the operating room scheduled for ten minutes from now.' The doctor, so young yet with such a look of calm and knowledge about him, gave Garrett a look of regret. 'I'm sorry, Sheriff.'

'So am I.' Garrett looked at Ray, then started for the door. 'He just might have had the secret to the chaos that's rocked this town for the last two weeks.'

Pain. Sharp pain in the right side of her head. Brynn put her hand to her head and felt a lump rising. She tried to open her eyes before realizing she wore a blindfold. She was on her abdomen lying on a cool concrete floor.

'How do you feel?'

'Like crap,' Brynn returned to the distorted voice. 'Where am I?'

'Some place safe. Some place . . . private.'

Brynn rolled on her side, facing the voice. 'Are we alone?' she asked.

'Thinking if there's just one person watching you, you might be able to escape?'

Brynn said nothing. That's exactly what she'd been thinking.

'Dream on. We're not alone.'

'Will you untie my feet so I can sit up?'

'And run?'

'And sit. You can move my legs in front of me and tie them again at the ankles.'

'Well, well, aren't you a cooperative hostage?'

I'm a *terrified* hostage, Brynn thought. But she could still think clearly, which amazed her. Maybe she was having a delayed reaction to her plight. In that case, it was best to take advantage of it. If her captor untied her bare feet and touched her ankles, she might be able to tell if she was dealing with a man or a woman. The robotic voice created by the distorter told her nothing. 'Please untie my ankles and let me sit up. I won't run.'

'Ummm . . . I don't think so. I like looking at you the way you are now.'

'Do you? Why?'

'Because you look helpless.'

And so I am, Brynn thought. She couldn't use her eyes, her hands, her feet. But she could still use her mind. 'Is Savannah here with me?'

'Why, yes. Good guess, Brynn.'

Brynn waited for Savannah to say something, but she didn't. Her mouth might be bound. Or the silence might mean Savannah wasn't really here. She took a deep breath, her heart pounding, and asked, 'Is my brother here? Is Mark with me?'

Silence. She heard nothing except the sound of her own blood pounding in her body. She went cold all over, the warmth of hope draining away in the silence. Then, finally, in a ravaged voice, Mark said, 'I'm here, Brynn. B-been here for days.'

'Would you mind if we stopped and checked on Savannah before we go back to headquarters and start on Ray's paperwork?' Garrett asked Deputy Carder, who rode with him. 'I've got a funny feeling about her.'

'Sure,' Carder said affably. 'Kind of strange about both our phones running low this afternoon.'

'Kind of a pain,' Garrett answered irritably. 'This is not a good day.'

'Don't tell me you're all broken up about Ray O'Hara.'

'I couldn't care less about Ray, but what happened to him is part of a pattern. I mean, no one did anything to him – he caused that wreck. He was reacting to Rhonda Fleming's death, and someone else caused her death. Why? Why did someone want Rhonda dead?'

Dwight Carder looked at him, his eyes narrowing. 'Isn't *who* more important?'

'Who and why. That's what we have to figure out and we're getting nowhere,' Garrett said seriously.

'It all started with Mark Wilder coming back to Genessa Point. I'm not saying he's done anything wrong,' Carder said carefully, 'but he's at the center of it.'

'I know.'

'And his sister. What about her, Sheriff? Do you think she's part of it all?'

Garrett thought a minute. 'Yes. This isn't just about Mark.'

'Do you think she's safe?'

'You know she isn't. She came here looking for her brother. I'm not sure she'll find him without getting hurt or worse.'

'Then shouldn't you make her go home?'

'Carder, I can't *make* Brynn do anything. She's strong-willed and determined. Those sound like good qualities, and sometimes they are, but this time they might be her undoing.'

'She's close to Savannah. Don't you think she might try to influence your girl?'

'Try to make her do something dangerous? No. Absolutely not. Savannah idolizes her and if Brynn was a different kind of person, that would worry me. But Brynn's a good influence, not bad. She'd never try to talk Savannah into doing anything that's not safe or something that's not in her best interest.'

'Like refusing to go to Ohio for a while till all this trouble blows over? You know, maybe taking off on her own?'

'Taking off on her own? No! Savannah's always been an obedient child. She's strong-willed, just like Brynn, and she's made mistakes, but Savannah wouldn't deliberately disobey me or do something she knows is wrong.'

'Oh. It must be hard raising a thirteen-year-old girl. I wouldn't know how to do it.'

'With a lot of patience and a lot of love,' Garrett said. 'Besides, she always sees herself as the heroine who does the right thing. Savannah would never run away.'

'Savannah's run away!' Mrs Persinger wailed when Garrett and

Dwight reached Garrett's door. 'I fell asleep. I didn't sleep well last night and today I just drifted off and when I woke up, she was gone! I've looked everywhere and called the friends you have listed on that white board beside your kitchen phone. Nearly half an hour ago, I called Brynn Wilder. She thinks Savannah decided to be in that play anyway. Brynn said that if Savannah had really run away from home, she would have taken her dog. Henry and I are nervous wrecks. I've had so much coffee I can't stop talkin', and he's had half a box of dog treats.'

Garrett looked down at Henry, whose gaze slid away. No doubt he'd taken advantage of Mrs Persinger's anxiety to get as many dog treats as possible.

'Brynn said she and that patrolman you have taking care of her would go right out and start lookin' for Savannah. They'd start by followin' the route Savannah would have taken to the amphitheater. She said she'd call me as soon as she found *any* trace of Savannah, but I haven't heard from her for fifty minutes. I tried to call her again five minutes ago. My call went to voicemail. Oh my God, sheriff, I love that little girl with all my heart. I'm *so* sorry. I just don't know what to do—'

Garrett enfolded the small, shaking woman in his arms while Henry looked up at him, whining pitifully. Garrett was furious with Savannah for sneaking out, but so scared he felt as if he had a chunk of ice in his stomach. He patted Mrs Persinger comfortingly while Dwight petted the worried Henry.

'What are we gonna do, Sheriff?' Mrs Persinger sniffled. 'I'll go out and walk the streets and yell for her until I don't have a voice. Ohhh, this is all my fault!'

'It's not your fault,' Garrett said, still holding her. 'Savannah knew better than to leave. She's usually fairly obedient, but today isn't one of those times.' And today of all days she'd decided to be a brat, he thought, wondering what her punishment should be after he'd found her and nearly hugged her half to death in relief. 'I'm glad you called Brynn. That was smart because she's got a deputy with her.'

Dwight Carder stood up. 'But you called and she didn't answer her phone?'

'No, she didn't. Like I said, my message went to voicemail. Oh, I *hate* voicemail!'

'At least you got to leave a message for her. She was probably out of the car and left her cell phone behind,' Garrett said, knowing that if everything was all right, Brynn would never have left her phone in the car. Mrs Persinger was so upset, though, he had to calm her down. 'I'm sure she'll be getting back to you soon, and then you can call me. The battery in my cell phone is running low and keeps cutting out, so only call me again if she calls you or it's urgent. I know how devoted you are to Savannah. You weren't negligent and you're helping me tremendously by staying here, waiting for Savannah or Brynn to call.'

Garrett tried to sound strong and reassuring, but he wasn't at all certain Savannah or Brynn would be able to call Mrs Persinger. He knew something was very wrong. They were in trouble.

TWENTY-ONE

'Mark? Mark is that really you?' Brynn asked desperately.

'Yeah. What's left of me. Don't think you'd recognize me.' He started coughing.

'What did you do to him?' she demanded of the person who spoke through a voice distorter – the same voice that had spoken to her menacingly on the phone.

'Nothing too bad.'

'Put that damn distorter down, you coward! What have you done to my brother?'

'He's alive, isn't he?' Still, the distorter. 'You're lucky I didn't kill him, so you should be a lot nicer to me. A *lot* nicer.'

'What does that mean? That you're going to rape me? Well, bring it on, you wimp!'

'Brynn!' Mark rasped. 'Don't!'

'No, let her rave, lying there on the floor, terror wiping away the loveliness of her face, that beautiful cinnamon-brown hair all tangled up. No one thinks you're a winner now!'

Brynn went silent, her mind working furiously. *'You're lovely like your mother, cinnamon-brown hair, Brynn's always been a winner.* She'd heard those phrases a few days ago. In Holly Park. Leaning over the wishing well.

Tessa!

'Where's the patrolman that was posted at the front of my house?' Brynn asked.

'Probably still just sitting there like an idiot. You were taken out the back.'

'Another patrolman was posted there. What happened to him?'

'I went up to him looking meek, almost apologetic. His car window was down – such a help! All I had to do was say, "Can you help me . . ." as I got to within inches of him, and I whipped out a hypodermic and gave him an injection to make him go to sleep. Fast. He'll live. However, he didn't see you being taken out the back door.'

'And you got in the house while I was gone this afternoon.'

'While you were at Doctor Ellis's. Poor Mark – visiting Doctor Ellis didn't do much for him, either. Just a few hours after he left the doctor's house, your brother ended up here.'

'I suppose you know what Doctor Ellis told me, Tessa,' Brynn said.

Silence vibrated between them for a couple of minutes. Then Tessa spoke to Brynn without the voice distorter.

'Well, aren't you the clever girl, knowing to whom you were speaking.'

'I didn't have to be very clever to figure that out, Tessa. What I want to know is why you got so nervous about Mark being back in town. After all, you'd gotten away with murder for eighteen years.'

Although Brynn was still blindfolded, she could sense rather than hear someone walking around on the concrete floor. 'Do you think that after eighteen years he suddenly decided to come home?' Tessa asked. 'He was lured here.'

'Lured? By you?'

'Don't act stupid,' Tessa said sharply. 'By Joy Ellis. At the end of her life, she got so worried about her soul she wanted to atone for her father's sin. The sin of silence. Edmund Ellis was Stone Jonah's best friend, but he lied about the knife. You'll never convince me your dad didn't tell him about "losing" the knife Mark gave him. But Ellis claimed he didn't know anything about a lost knife.'

'Don't call my father "Stone Jonah,"' Brynn said grimly.

'Oh, that's right. You're sentimental about your father.'

'And you aren't about yours?' Brynn asked, picking up something in Tessa's voice.

'We're not talking about Earl Cavanaugh right now. We're talking about *your* father and Edmund Ellis, and their good friendship that accounts for Ellis lying about your dad's knife.'

'What happened to the knife Mark gave Dad?'

'It ended up *in* Dad.' Tessa giggled snidely. 'Don't you remember? I'm sure you do. You saw him after the knife went in time after time after time—'

'Shut up!' Mark yelled in his gravelly voice. 'Shut up!'

'Mark, are you blindfolded?' Brynn asked.

'No.'

'Is Savannah here?'

'Yes.'

'Is she all right?'

'Tied up but I don't think she's hurt.'

'Are *you* all right?'

'I'm . . . OK.'

Tessa laughed. 'Satisfied, Brynn? The girl who idolizes you is alive. For now.'

'For now?'

'Savannah's life will depend on how things go in the next few hours.'

'It was a good idea to bring Henry, Sheriff,' Dwight Carder said. 'He can follow Savannah's scent better than any of the police dogs who've just taken a whiff of her T-shirt or something.'

'That's what I thought. Nothing against our dogs,' Garrett half-smiled. 'But when it comes to Savannah, no one knows her better than Henry. She's had him since he was a puppy. They're quite the couple.'

Dwight slanted a look at Garrett, then smiled. Dwight had worked for two years under Garrett's father. If Garrett had been anything like William Dane, Dwight would have transferred. William Dane had been condescending, swaggering, insulting and had absolutely no sense of humor, even if he did know his job.

When they reached the amphitheater parking lot and parked near the stage, Garrett led Henry by a long leash toward the back of the stage. A fussy little man rushed toward them. 'Sorry. The play doesn't begin for another hour.'

'I'm Sheriff Dane and this is Deputy Carder,' Garrett said in a stern voice. 'My daughter, Savannah Dane, is playing second lead in the play. I'm looking for her.'

The jittery man seemed to notice their uniforms for the first time. 'Oh, oh, Sheriff Dane, I'm sorry I didn't recognize you.' He walked forward, right hand extended. Garrett shook his hand. 'Your daughter is quite a good actress.'

'Thank you. Is she here?'

'Here? She isn't with you?'

'No. Actually, I'd told her she couldn't be in the play because of . . . unavoidable circumstances. I said her understudy could take over for her. She was really unhappy, though, and now she's not home. We don't know where she is. I thought maybe she'd decided to perform in the play in spite of my decision.' Garrett was aware he sounded stiff and formal, but the man didn't seem to have much of an attention span. He wanted to make him understand this was a serious matter. 'Have you seen Savannah Dane?'

'N-no!' The man put his hands to his cheeks. 'Oh, my! She might turn up any minute, though.' He looked sharply at Henry. 'We don't allow dogs back here.'

'He's a police dog,' Dwight put in sternly. 'He's part of the unit.'

'Oh, all right,' the man said with a trace of contrition. And maybe fear. 'I didn't realize he was official.'

Thank God Henry didn't raise a paw to shake hands, Garrett thought. Perceptive Henry had recognized that this nervous little man wasn't a potential friend. 'Are you *sure* you haven't seen Savannah?' Garrett looked over the man's shoulder. 'You have quite a few people running around backstage here.'

'I haven't seen her. That doesn't mean she won't turn up, although she's always on time.' The man rubbed his neck. 'Oh, I thought this would go so smoothly, but with Savannah gone and Miss Cavanaugh, too—'

'Miss Cavanaugh was supposed to be here this early?'

'It's not early, Sheriff,' the man cried. 'We go on in an hour and a half. Miss Cavanaugh called two hours ago and said she's sick. She sounded miserable – husky-voiced, nasal. I'm certain she's ill. She's so conscientious she would never make an excuse not to come. And this play means a lot to her.'

Garrett wrote his cell phone number on a card and handed it to the man. 'If either of them shows up, call me immediately.'

Dear God, Garrett thought as they walked away. A woman and a girl missing. Not just *a* girl. Savannah.

'We'll find them, Sheriff,' Carder said confidently.

'I hope so.'

'Don't hope. Believe. I do.'

Brynn couldn't see, the temperature had not changed, yet she felt evening coming. She was frightened and disoriented, she wanted to scream out of sheer frustration and terror, but some fragment of reason kept her under control. She had to save her strength. At least, she hoped she had to save her strength for a battle to save herself, Mark and Savannah. It might be pure delusion, but it was the only thing keeping her steady. Hang on, she thought. Hang on.

'Tessa, you said at the time you didn't understand why Edmund

Ellis lied about my father losing the knife Mark gave him. Why did you think he lied?'

'Oh, that puzzled me for almost a month. Then he sent his daughter away. I thought that was strange – he was crazy about her and she was sickly. Also, he never raised hell about his good friend being innocent. He just went along like nothing had happened. That wasn't like him. When he saw me or Nathan on the street, he used to just nod or say, "Hi" to us. Afterward, he was much friendlier. Particularly to Nathan.'

'And that seemed odd to you.'

'Very odd. At first. Then I thought about it. I must admit, that day in the woods when I stabbed your father, I felt like we weren't alone. I looked around before and after he staggered toward the beach, although afterward, my vision wasn't too clear. When we both made it out to the beach and you were there, I *almost* convinced myself it was you I'd sensed. You, running around looking for your daddy.

'Later, I remembered Mrs Ellis always taking Joy to her Saturday piano lessons, only I was told there hadn't been any lessons that day – the day I finished off your father. But by that time, Joy had gone away to school. I asked myself, why was she sent away to school when she was so young? It didn't make sense to me, unless her father had a reason for not wanting her to be in town. I thought it was possible she could have been there, in the woods, but either she didn't see anything or, if she had, she wasn't going to say anything. I could relax. After all, your father was out of the picture and if Edmund Ellis knew anything, he was going to keep his mouth shut. So, I ended up with a lucky stab your dad got in that almost pierced my kidney and a lot of sympathy. I felt triumphant.'

'You bitch!'

'My, that was eloquent, Brynn. With your command of the language, no wonder you're a bestselling author. By the way, I hate your books. They're pure tripe.'

She's having fun with this, Brynn thought in amazement. Quiet, awkward, downcast Tessa Cavanaugh was having fun talking about a murder she'd committed. She was the center of attention for once.

'Then, when Joy was about to die, she had to clear her conscience. She wrote me a letter.'

'Joy wrote to *you*?'

'Stupid of her, wasn't it, to put her father in danger. She told me she'd written to Mark, too, saying that she'd seen me stab Jonah Wilder.' Tessa shook her head. 'People thought she was so pretty and sweet and talented, but she was *stupid*!'

'Not stupid,' Brynn said coldly. 'Eaten up with guilt and not thinking clearly because of all the medication she was taking.'

Tessa shrugged. 'You're like everyone else. Making excuses for her. Just remember – neither your brother nor you would be here now if it weren't for her clearing her simple-minded conscience.'

Brynn absorbed this for a minute. In one way Tessa was right, but Brynn couldn't work up any anger to the girl who'd lived alone, silent with her awful secret for so many years until she couldn't bear it anymore. 'Why did you kill my father?' she finally asked.

'Ah, that's the *real* question, isn't it? Don't you agree, Mark? He knows the reason. Are you going to tell her, Mark?'

A long silence frightened Brynn. Had he slipped into unconsciousness? She'd no idea what he'd been subjected to the past few days. To her relief, he finally mumbled, 'N-no.'

'Yes!'

'T-too thirsty. Can't t-talk.'

Tessa sighed. 'I guess I have to do everything. I have been for years since Nathan went away. I've been Daddy's pet. And I've played my part. He needed me. But Father's gone now and I want you people who feel so wronged to know what *my* life has been like.'

Brynn felt someone coming near her. Fingers dug under the blindfold and yanked it off. Then two hands grabbed her shoulders and pulled her to a sitting position. Blinking furiously from the pressure of the tight cloth on her eyes, Brynn looked around. Tessa kneeled beside her, wearing tawny lip gloss, dangling earrings, hazel-colored contacts, false eyelashes and a wig with very long, cinnamon-brown hair. Brynn gazed at her in shock.

'Don't you love it?' Tessa asked, flipping a lock of the hair. 'Now I look just like you.'

TWENTY-TWO

Brynn raised slightly from the waist, searching the gloomy room for her brother. Only three light bulbs hung from the ceiling and her eyes hadn't adjusted to the dim light. She squinted into the direction from which Mark's voice had come, but she didn't see him and he made no other sound.

'Where are we?' Brynn asked.

'Oh, you don't expect us to tell you that, do you?' Tessa asked.

Us? But Savannah began to cry – quietly and hopelessly. Brynn squinted hard and could see that the girl was tied to a wooden post that went from floor to ceiling in the middle of the room. She hung her head, her long blonde hair falling around her face.

'Don't act like you're blind, Savannah,' Tessa snapped. 'You love the way Brynn looks. Now I look just like her – not like freaky Miss Cavanaugh from the library.'

'Leave her alone,' Brynn snarled. 'Don't torture her.'

'Oh, looking at me is torturing her? That wasn't very polite, Brynn. Besides, I'm not the Cavanaugh who enjoys torturing a kid.' Tessa looked toward a shadowy corner. 'I leave that to Nathan.'

Brynn followed Tessa's gaze. She saw the vague figure of a man sitting on a wooden chair, one leg crossed over the other at the ankle. He looked relaxed, Brynn thought. The longer she looked at him, though, the more she thought he merely looked resigned. 'I don't torture people,' he said calmly. 'I never have.'

'But we've been tortured, haven't we? Shall I tell everyone about our past, Nathan, or do you want to do the honors?' Tessa sounded completely different than her usual soft-spoken self. Her voice was strong, almost aggressive.

'You're having the time of your life,' Nathan said in a bored tone. 'Be my guest.'

'Tessa!' Brynn yelled. 'Let me go! Let me go, dammit!' By now she was nearly shrieking. 'Let me go! Let me go! Let me go!' Tessa stared at her with wide eyes. Brynn began to throw her head backwards and forwards and to writhe.

'Is she having a seizure?' Tessa asked no one in particular, but clearly stunned by Brynn's violent movements.

'I want to be *moved*! I want to sit beside Savannah,' Brynn screamed. 'Let me sit by Savannah and I'll be quiet.'

'You'll sit where I tell you,' Tessa snapped.

Brynn started screaming. On and on. Her voice wasn't used to the strain and she knew it would give out soon, but she remembered that Tessa couldn't stand loud noises. Besides, even though she didn't know where she was, maybe there was the danger of being overheard. All she needed was another minute or two. That would get her what she wanted.

'All right, all *right*, you damned lunatic!' Tessa screamed back, her voice sounding exactly as it had on that sun-drenched beach eighteen years ago when she'd killed Brynn's father. 'Nathan, you're stronger than I am. You move her over to that post.'

Nathan got up, his movements slow, and came up behind her. Brynn couldn't get a good look at his face. He bent down and dragged her to a splintery wooden post, picked up what looked like a nylon stocking and tied her hands to the post right below Savannah's.

'Are you sure she's secure?' Tessa demanded.

'Her hands are tied behind her back, and both hands are tied to the post. Would you like to come over and sign off on the quality of my work?'

Trouble in paradise, Brynn thought, then wondered why that phrase had popped into her head at such a serious time. Still, her body was beside Savannah's, and she curled her right hand up until her fingers touched the girl's flesh. Savannah sighed and seemed almost to lean against Brynn. Almost. She wasn't quite close enough. Brynn wanted to move nearer, but she didn't dare as long as anyone was looking at her.

'You haven't killed us so we're obviously waiting for something,' Brynn said, her own voice raspy from the screaming. 'I'm guessing it's your life story.'

Garrett called Brynn. When there was no answer, he got in contact with the patrolman posted at the front of Cassie's house. 'I can't get Brynn. Is she home?'

'I'm sorry, Sheriff,' the young man said. 'I took her to Doctor Ellis's house, waited for her, then brought her home. She went in the front door. I could tell when she came out of the Ellis house that something had shaken her up, but she said she was OK. I brought her home and she said she was going to make some coffee for me. When she hadn't come back with the coffee after twenty minutes, I got worried,' he went on. 'No one came to the door. I called the house. No answer. I headed toward the back of the house and found our guy Simpson unconscious. The EMS just picked him up and I called headquarters. You'll be hearing it on the radio any minute. I asked for back-up. Someone might have been in the house. More likely, though, someone got in the house while Miss Wilder was at Ellis's and I was waiting for her. They took her out the back door.'

'Dammit!' Garrett almost shouted.

'Sorry, Sheriff, but everything looked fine from out front. A back window's been broken out, so I'd say whoever took Miss Wilder knocked out Simpson before entering the house.'

'Is he OK?'

'Don't know yet. Like I said, EMS just left with him. I'm sorry.'

'It's not your fault. Is Cassie home?'

'Not yet.'

'Don't let her enter the house until we've had a chance to go over it.'

'Right.'

'You said Brynn seemed upset when she came out of Edmund Ellis's house?'

'Yes, sir. And an ambulance came for him.'

Edmund told me something about Tessa. That's what Brynn had said when she'd called earlier and the battery in his cell phone was dying. What had Doctor Ellis told her? Did it have anything to do with someone taking her when she got back to Cassie's?

Garrett called Savannah's cell phone again. Voicemail. Garrett cursed a few times. Then he said, 'We're going to the Cavanaughs' house.'

'How much did your father love you, Brynn?' Tessa asked. 'Enough to have sex with you?'

'*No!*'

'How about Mark? Did he prefer a young, fresh guy, preferably his son?'

'That's sickening,' Brynn spat.

'No, no, it isn't.' Tessa spoke in a sweet, crooning voice. 'It's smart. For one thing, your father, who gives you a roof over your head, food on the table, nice clothes and even cars if you want them, deserves to have sexual partners who are *quality*. He needs partners who are young and clean, unsullied by other people, preferably of his own blood. It's a fair exchange. Our father taught us this.' She sounded as if she were repeating a memorized part. 'I suppose Stone Jonah was too uptight to even discuss sex. He probably rarely had sex with your mother. I mean, she was beautiful and sweet and acted like she adored him, but after she'd given him two children, she had nothing left to give.' She opened her hands, turned the palms upward and lifted them wide. 'It only makes sense, Brynn. She'd done her job. But your father probably continued to have sex with her. He didn't give her the rest she deserved after having two children. Our father was different. Considerate. He would have been even if our mother hadn't gotten sick. Your father wasn't. If he really loved your mother, he would have turned to Mark and you for his sexual needs.'

'Tessa, do you have to go on like that in front of Savannah?' Brynn asked quietly, although she seethed inside.

'Yes. Savannah's of age. Her father isn't even married. He should turn to her for the satisfaction a man needs.' She paused. 'He may have already.'

Savannah moaned.

'Oh, I see that he has,' Tessa said, pleased.

'My dad would *never* touch me that way!' Savannah suddenly shouted. 'I hate you for saying he did!'

'I didn't say he did. I just said he may have. Pay attention, Savannah. I'm the director, as I am in the play. You must listen to me *closely*, not insult me by twisting my words or not listening carefully. Understand?'

Savannah nodded pitifully. Brynn felt as if something was squeezing her heart.

'My mother had a difficult pregnancy with Nathan,' Tessa went on in a flat, narrative voice. 'Almost immediately, she became pregnant again. She lost that fetus. A little over two years later, I was born. My father went through such misery, with my mother being pregnant twice in so short a time. I believe he saw other women during those years. Not prostitutes or sluts.' Tessa stroked her wig hair, showing a crystal dragonfly-shaped ring on her middle left finger. 'Women like your mother, Brynn. In fact, I think he was involved with your mother for a short time, particularly during and after Mother's second pregnancy.'

Brynn was so furious she went silent. Then she said unsteadily, 'That is a lie.'

'Don't be so sure.' Tessa stroked her hair again. 'Just look at our resemblance.'

Brynn tried to stare at Tessa with no expression in her eyes – no anger, no desire to fight, absolutely no feeling whatsoever. Tessa gazed at her closely and Brynn felt triumph at the disappointment on Tessa's face.

'My father started turning to Nathan for sexual satisfaction when Nate was five. Nathan didn't like it. My father told me. Nathan began to fight Father when he was eight. By then, Father was spending part of his time with me. He said I was more docile, more appreciative.'

'More *appreciative*?' Brynn echoed.

Tessa tilted her head. 'I don't remember those years very well, but I assume I fought less and I wasn't as strong. Father didn't ignore Nathan, though. He had sex with Nathan until he was in his early teens. He told me Nathan wasn't always cooperative, particularly as he got older. Father would tie Nathan's hands to that wooden post. That very rough wooden post over there. If you fought, it would make you bleed. Finally, Nathan fought too hard and Father kicked him. Nathan made an awful fuss, but Father couldn't take him to the hospital because he was afraid Nathan would say how he'd been injured and Father knew that people at the hospital wouldn't understand. He recovered but the injury caused another problem – Nathan was impotent.'

'Tessa!' Nathan barked. 'They don't need to know everything!'

'Well, you were. You are. And very angry. *Livid.* But you didn't dare take out your anger at home. You took it out on other people. Kids. No one could really blame you,' Tessa said sweetly to Nathan. 'I understood.'

After a short silence, Nathan said in a lifeless voice, 'I killed a five-year-old boy when I was fourteen. He was my first.'

'He was fascinated by serial killers,' Tessa went on as if Nathan wasn't in the room. 'He read about them and copied some of their techniques and learned all about DNA. He would keep the kid a prisoner for a while. Then he'd kill it, scrub it with bleach, and leave it someplace where it would be easily found.'

Brynn noticed that Tessa referred to the victim as it. Didn't she *want* to think of Nathan's victims as people? Or did she simply have no empathy for them?

'I never hurt them before I killed them,' Nathan said defensively. 'I just drugged them to keep them still. Then I told them my troubles – I couldn't tell my friends. When I'd told them all there was to tell, I had to do away with them so they'd never tell my secrets.'

Brynn's thoughts spun. She remembered that the victims of GPK had no signs of torture or sexual molestation. Now she knew the reason they hadn't been sexually abused.

'You didn't really keep them alive just to talk to them, did you, Nathan?' Brynn asked. 'You had another reason.'

Nathan finally stood up and sauntered toward her. Even under these lights and these conditions, he was handsome. No wonder some of the kids went with him, especially the girls when he flashed that devastating grin. 'Whenever someone went missing, everybody talked about it. It was all over the news – parents crying, saying the kid's name over and over to "humanize" the victim, begging. There was all this talk about the *monster* out there, roaming the streets.' Nathan laughed. 'You would have thought Jack the Ripper was on the loose. And here I was, just a fourteen-year-old kid. God, what a rush that gave me!'

And you didn't feel helpless anymore, Brynn thought. Your father had terrorized you, beaten you, resulting in an injury that left you feeling less than a man. But you showed that you *were* a man, didn't you? When you took those kids, you held all the cards.

Savannah had begun to cry again, silently, her body shaking. Brynn slid her tied hands up the support post, seeking the girl's hands again. This time the stocking holding her hand to the post had caught on something. She rubbed her hands up and down slightly so she wouldn't be seen. And that's when she realized what she'd found . . .

A screw that stuck out of the post at least two inches – a screw with threads sharp enough to tear nylon.

TWENTY-THREE

'Where are we?' Brynn asked.

'Where no one will ever find you,' Tessa replied.

'The place where Nathan kept his prisoners?' Brynn persisted. 'Have you stashed us in that same place?'

'No.' Nathan's voice was sharp as a knife. 'That place doesn't exist anymore. I'm using a different place for you. You drove us to it, Brynn. If Mark hadn't come here and you'd stayed in Miami and minded your own business, none of this would be happening. Tessa said she could scare you off with phone calls and returning some of your old stuff she'd stolen, but I knew she was just having fun. She shouldn't have made that first phone call to Miami, dammit! That's what got you stirred up. That's what made you come here!'

'My brother told me he was coming to Genessa Point. Then he disappeared. I would have come here phone call or no phone call.' Nathan glared at Brynn, then at his sister, who ignored him. Brynn had a feeling she needed to keep talking, though. Nathan had looked at his watch four times. He was waiting for something or he had a plan for a certain time. She wanted to distract him as much as possible.

'My father's knife,' she said suddenly. 'How did you get hold of my father's knife and why did you use it?'

Nathan turned and began restlessly walking around the room. 'Your father never liked me.'

'That's not true. You were friends with Mark.'

'When we were young. When we hit our teens, the friendship started falling apart.' Nathan stopped suddenly and looked at her. 'I don't like being watched and your father had his eyes on me all the time. Him and that friend of his, Doctor Ellis.'

That devil. Brynn recalled Doctor Ellis's words. Had he been talking about Nathan? 'You mean he was suspicious of you?'

Nathan began walking again. Everyone's gaze followed him so Brynn started rubbing the cloth over the threads of the screw. 'I didn't know why they kept looking at me at first.' He laughed. 'Hell, for a while I thought your dad was gay and I was his type. Or . . . that he was like my father.'

'You think what your father did to you was a result of being gay?' Brynn burst out.

'It was!'

'He was guilty of sexual assault! That has nothing to do with being homosexual!'

'Where did you read that, Brynn? Some book published by homosexuals?'

'It's common sense, Nathan. I'm always hearing about how smart you are. Couldn't you figure that out when your father wanted Tessa just like he'd wanted you?'

'You don't know what you're talking about,' Nathan said dismissively. 'You didn't live my life. But I endured it. And then, I began to enjoy the benefits of it. Dad let me do just about whatever I wanted, gave me plenty of money to spend and never nosed in my business, even though I think he might have guessed I was the infamous Genessa Point Killer. Tessa was such a sneak, following me all the time, she found out, but she adored me. She'd never have told the police. Anyway, I was doing just fine until I was almost sixteen and your father caught me with that coach. He was giving me copies of tests. That's all. There wasn't anything sexual between us. I didn't even like the guy.'

'But he liked you or he wouldn't have given you copies of the tests.'

Nathan shrugged. 'Maybe.'

'And maybe you took advantage of his feelings for you so you could get hold of those tests.'

'Yeah, but big deal. A few lousy tests and your father throws a hissy fit and gets the guy fired and me a suspension! Everyone thought the coach and I . . . well, you know.'

'Oh, yes, I know,' Brynn said with a touch of drama that enabled her to move, to slide the nylon bond on her wrists back and forth across the screw threads. 'I remember.'

Nathan winced. 'I *had* to get him back. I never went to your house again, although Mark and I were still sort of friends, but Tessa took a few more piano lessons. She was always quick on her feet, stealthy, good at stealing.'

Tessa beamed as if Nathan were complimenting her beauty and intelligence.

'Mark had told me about the knife he got your father, about carving the initials. I told Tessa it would be in his tackle box, where he kept it, and to get it. When your mother went outside for a few minutes during the lesson, Tessa swiped the knife and hid it under her clothes. I intended to use it on the next kills and finally kill your father with it to pay him back for what he'd done to me.'

'Except that *you* didn't pay him back. That's not why I killed him, anyway,' Tessa taunted Nathan, then turned to Brynn, as if they were good friends sharing gossip. 'Nathan wouldn't believe me that Stone Jonah was suspicious of him. I saw it in Jonah's eyes. He was getting too close. So the day when Nathan was on that school trip to Baltimore, I came to your house and did what needed to be done. I'd been there with my camera a couple of times before so it didn't seem as if I'd just turned up out of the blue. That day I insisted on taking a couple of pictures of Jonah. Then I *tripped* over his tackle box and went into a flurry of picking up everything and replacing it – except his knife. He didn't notice. I went into the woods with two knives. The knife I used on Stone Jonah was the knife Mark gave him. I dropped Jonah's knife in the knot hole of a tree. I didn't go near your house and the woods to retrieve the knife for over almost a year. I was careful.'

'You used the knot hole in a tree as a hiding place? Inspired by *To Kill a Mockingbird*, were you, Tessa?' Brynn asked with a disconcerting smile. Her desire was to keep Tessa and Nathan at least semi-surprised.

Tessa looked at Brynn searchingly for a moment, then leaned back her head and laughed. 'It was a deeper knot hole than the one in the novel, but I'm surprised you actually know literature! You'd never know it by reading your books.'

'You've hurt my feelings, Tessa.' Brynn had noticed that Savannah stopped crying when Brynn traded insults with Tessa, as though Brynn was so strong she felt no fear, no intimidation. Actually, she'd never been so frightened in her life. 'Why don't you like my books, Tessa?'

'I only read the biographies of women I admire.'

'Such as Lizzie Borden?'

Tessa laughed, low and husky. 'Oh, Brynn, you're on a roll, aren't you? Well, have fun now, dear, because your good times won't last for long.'

Garrett pulled up to the large Cape Cod home belonging to the Cavanaughs. 'I used to think this was the grandest house I'd ever seen.'

'It's impressive,' Carder said.

'From the outside. I have a feeling things aren't so impressive inside.' Garrett opened his door and let out Henry. If Tessa was home, he thought, she'd probably faint if he managed to talk his way in and brought Henry with him.

Garrett rang the doorbell. They waited a minute and he rang again. Another minute went by. This time he knocked loudly on the door. He noticed Carder standing back and scanning all the front windows and knew he was looking for the movement of a drapery. Garrett knocked again. Finally he abandoned the door. 'If someone's home, they don't want company.'

'I didn't see anyone at a window,' Carder said. 'Seems if Tessa was sick, she'd be home. Maybe she wouldn't come to the door, but her brother would.'

'If he's home tending to his sick sister like a good brother should. Wish we could go inside and look, but we don't have a warrant and no probable cause to get one. Let's take a walk around the property. I think it's about three acres.' Garrett looked down. 'Henry, keep your nose to the ground.'

They saw well-tended, brilliant-colored beds of marigolds, impatiens, petunias, pansies, and zennias arranged in artful designs. 'Sure are pretty flowers, Sheriff.'

'Tessa won the Good Gardener Award from the garden club last year,' Garrett told him, thinking about how Tessa had almost cried over winning the award. And now she had her petunias like the ones her father had destroyed in a fit of temper.

'The Good Gardener Award?' Carder repeated. 'I never heard of it.'

'I don't think a lot of people have, but Tessa was proud of it.' He sighed. 'I guess she was trying to create something beautiful outside because I have a feeling the atmosphere in that house wasn't so beautiful.'

'I wouldn't know.'

'I'm just going on a feeling,' Garrett said. 'I was friends with Nate for years, but I only set foot in that house one time. Nate's dad descended on me like I was a thief sneaking around. He actually scared me. After living with my father, I didn't think anyone could scare me, but Earl Cavanaugh did. Later, Nate told me his father was just really overprotective of his wife because she had cancer and was in a lot of pain and easily disturbed and blah, blah,

blah. I didn't believe it. Oh, Mrs Cavanaugh had cancer, but that wasn't the reason Earl didn't want outsiders in his home.'

'Then why didn't he?'

'I'm not sure, but something was wrong in that house. I don't know what, but I feel like I should have taken a closer look at the Cavanaughs a long time ago.'

'Why did you kill Sam Fenney?' Brynn asked Tessa.

'*I* killed Sam,' Nathan said.

'And it was unnecessary!' Tessa barked. 'You made such a show of it! It scared everyone and made things hotter in this town than we wanted.'

'He blackmailed Father!' Nathan shouted. 'Father stopped using this building after Mother died. You two were going at it in the living room and the son of a bitch looked in our windows and saw you. He held it over Father's head for years! Every month Father had to pay him! You knew what was going on and you didn't tell me. If you had . . .' He glared at his sister. 'We wouldn't have been left with nothing while Sam Fenney built the Bay Motel and Cloud Nine!'

So that's where the extra money came from, Brynn thought. Sam probably laundered it through the corporations Kalidone and Farrah-Stef. Edmund's name must have been removed from the corporations so he didn't know what was going on. She knew he wouldn't have been part of such a disgusting scheme.

'Besides, you went along with it,' Nathan accused. 'You're the one who called the dress shop pretending to be Sam's secretary and left the message for Brynn telling her if she wanted to see that house one last time, she had to meet him there that night.'

'But the rest of that nonsense was all *you*,' Tessa said scathingly. 'Candles. An open Bible with some verse about thievery marked. You were planning what you were going to do with Sam after I'd knocked the hell out of Mark in his car and you went in his room to get all his electronic stuff. You picked up the Bible. You thought it might come in handy to use against Mark, to send the police on the wrong trail. Then you paid that slut he kept on the side to call Sam and meet her in that house. You had her tell him it would be kinky. You're such a child sometimes, Nathan!'

'*I'm* a child?' Nathan yelled. '*You're* the one who wanted to keep playing games with Brynn, trying to scare her out of town. As for Mark, we took him in to question him about how many people he'd told about you killing Stone Jonah. He didn't have much time after his visit to Ellis's, but he could have told Cassie or a friend.' He smirked at Tessa. 'The main reason Mark's been here so long, though, is because you wanted it. You've never gotten over your teenage crush on him. You've spent a lot of time here with him, Tess. What have you been making him do?'

'Nothing!' Tessa stormed. 'We just talked!'

'Uh huh,' Nathan, still smirking, murmured. 'Sure you did.'

'You're ridiculous sometimes, Nate. But you're my brother. And we're going away together – away from this town, away from that house where Father—' She got a distant look in her eyes. 'All these years I stayed here and kept him company while you traveled the world doing God-knows-what. I know you didn't stop killing. And you won't have to stop killing now. I'll be around to take care of you like I used to do. I killed Stone Jonah for you, didn't I? And I almost died doing it. You owe me for what I did then and for what I've done since you left. But we won't think about that. You'll just consider me your loving sister. Your protector. I'll guide you. I'll always be by your side.'

That's exactly what Nathan doesn't want, Brynn thought, wondering how Tessa could be so blind. Nathan resents you for killing my father. *He* wanted to do it. As far as he's concerned, you jumped the gun and he had to be a good boy throughout until he left for California Maritime University or else destroy the illusion that Jonah Wilder was the Genessa Point Killer. She looked at Nathan, with his good looks and easy grace. He's been free of you for years, Tessa. He left you here to satisfy your father, Brynn thought. And you did it out of some sort of perverted love of your monster brother and loyalty to your monster father. But those days are over. Now you want him to pay you back. How will he like dragging you around like an anchor?

He won't, Brynn thought. As soon as Nathan's safe, he'll murder Tessa. She means nothing to him. Nobody means anything to him. He's a psychopath.

Suddenly Tessa picked up a silver-backed brush and held it up for Brynn to see. Then she ran it gently, almost sensuously through the long, lush wig hair. 'I never needed a fancy brush before. I do now. I saw that flash of recognition in your eyes as soon as you saw it. Years ago I took this because it had some of your hair in it – hair like I wanted.' Tessa smiled. 'Nathan told you I was a good thief.'

'How often do you use that brush, Tessa?' Brynn asked. 'How often do you get dressed up, put on your makeup and the wig, then stroke the hair with *my* brush in front of the mirror? You can't tell me this is the first time.'

'I don't dress up like you all the time,' Tessa flared.

'I don't believe you. You were such a gawky, bug-eyed little girl with baby-thin hair. I've seen pictures of your mother – she was so pretty. My mother was beautiful. And even when I was twelve, I wasn't bad. Not like you. No wonder you wanted to look like me.' Nathan started laughing and Tessa whirled on him, shouting that she hardly ever wore the wig.

'Oh, and then there was Rhonda,' Brynn went on relentlessly. 'She was tall and sexy and had all that long, auburn hair. I know you're the one who broke into Cassie's house and left the hairs on my pillow. When we found the hair, I said it reminded me of the story "A Rose for Emily." Rhonda had probably never read the story, but you have and you'd be certain I'd read it, too. You gave my knowledge of literature *some* credence.'

Tessa shrugged.

'It was real hair. It didn't come from a wig – the police lab said it had roots,' Brynn lied. 'Where did you get Rhonda's hair?'

'From the back of Ray's jacket. They were a team, you know. I remember how Ray was always talking about writing a true crime book. Then suddenly, after Cassie had kicked him out of her life and he'd left town, he came back at the same time Mark did. And he just happened to drop by the house, admiring my flower gardens, asking me out on a date. *Me!* He thought I'd be so bowled over by his charm I wouldn't put his sudden interest in me together with the fact that Mark Wilder had been in town. And Rhonda had been obsessed with the Genessa Point Killer ever since Nate murdered her cousin. I followed Ray and sure enough, they were seeing each other. Rhonda must have let him know Mark was in Genessa Point. That's why he came tearing back, only to find Mark gone. I knew Ray was only using me as a front, maybe even guessing that Nathan and I had something to do with Mark's disappearance or even the old killings. Then, when I was at Cassie's making a mess with the cologne, I looked on her computer and saw that fifth photo of Cassie and Mark with Nathan in the background, and the date. It was taken on the Saturday morning when he supposedly hadn't arrived in Genessa Point until Wednesday. I knew they were sniffing round, so I decided to take care of both of them.' Tessa looked at Brynn earnestly. 'I always keep strychnine for garden pests. When Ray got high on cocaine, he was very careless with his stash. Finding it was no trouble and I simply mixed it with strychnine. I thought it would take care of both of them.'

All the while Tessa had been explaining, almost bragging about how clever she'd been with Ray and Rhonda, Brynn had been rubbing her bound wrists against the screw. She felt the sharp metal threads scraping her wrist, but she also felt them tearing her cloth handcuffs.

Suddenly, Nathan glanced at his watch and said, 'Look, these explanations are entertaining, but we have a plane to catch in three hours, Tessa. We have to go soon. Let's wrap this up.'

They're going to kill the three of us, Brynn thought, rubbing the nylon wet with her blood against the bolt's sharp threads. We're running out of time. 'Where are you two going?'

'Why would I tell you?' Nathan asked.

'Oh, please, don't I get a few answers to a few questions before we all die?' Brynn asked.

'Seems to me you've gotten plenty of answers.' Nathan winked at her. 'And no one said you're *all* going to die.'

Suddenly, stifling a gasp of relief, Brynn felt the bolt cut through the last few fibers of nylon around her wrists. In spite of her surge of hope, she made her voice tremble. 'You're right, Nathan. No one said we're all going to die. Not all of us *have* to die.'

He looked at her suspiciously. 'What do you mean?'

'It could mean that you could spare one of us.'

'Savannah,' he said sarcastically.

Brynn smiled. 'No, Nathan. Me.'

TWENTY-FOUR

Garrett and Carder looked into the windows of a cement block storage building near the back of the Cavanaugh lot. All they saw in the fading light were two ride lawn mowers, a manual mower, clippers and other gardening equipment. 'That doesn't look like much of a prison,' Carder said, then glanced over at a cheerful-looking building with leaf green vinyl siding and white shutters. A tall rooster weathervane stood on the peaked roof. Red barberry shrubbery surrounded the building. 'Wonder what that is?' Carder asked.

'Never know until we look.'

They walked to the structure and Garrett carefully separated a few branches of the barberry with its thorns. He stepped closer to the building, cupped his hands and looked in one of the windows. He drew back. 'There's a metal grill over the window and insulation over the grill.'

'Insulation over the window?'

'Foil-backed insulation. Take a look.' Carder jabbed a thorn into his finger as he spread the branches. 'This barberry sort of discourages you getting too close,' he said, sucking on his finger. He managed to reach a window, peered in and drew back. 'What the hell? Insulation over the windows?'

'Let's look at the one toward the front.' Garrett handed the dog's leash to Carder and looked in the window, which was also insulated like the back window. 'I've heard of being energy conscious, but insulation over the windows? No natural light?'

Carder, still holding the dog's leash, looked at the orange-streaked gray sky for a moment, frowning, then said, 'Maybe the insulation isn't used just to conserve heat. Maybe it's also used to contain noise.'

'Noise caused by what?'

'Got me, Sheriff.' Suddenly, Henry jerked at his leash and barked. 'What's up, guy?' Carder asked as the dog pulled forward. He held back on the leash while Henry pulled harder.

'Let me have the leash,' Garrett said, taking it from Carder. He stopped pulling Henry back. 'Go where you want, boy.'

The dog nearly lunged ahead. He barked until Garrett picked up his pace, jogging behind Henry. The dog reached the front of the building and stuck his nose into the shrubbery. Garrett spotted the object of Henry's quest – a ragged piece of pink cotton stuck on a thorn. He stared at the cloth, noticing that it looked new, before Henry plunged away from the building and went closer to a narrow back road running along the rear of the property. He rubbed his nose in the grass, sniffing frantically, breathing hard, pulling to the right and then slightly to the left. Finally he stopped, barking at something in the grass.

Garrett approached Henry slowly and looked carefully at the grass where the dog's nose nearly touched the ground. Running his hand over the area, Garrett's fingers tangled in a chain. As he lifted it, Henry's head rose, following the scent on the object.

It was the dog whistle Savannah had worn around her neck for the past few days.

Tessa looked at Brynn in amazement. '*You?* Why would Nathan take *you* instead of me?'

'Take a look in the mirror, Tessa,' Brynn said with what she hoped was annoying confidence. 'Who do you think Nathan Cavanaugh would want by his side? You or me?'

'You're out of your mind,' Tessa stated.

'*I'm* out of my mind? Really, Tessa, I thought you were so smart.'

Nathan laughed softly. Two women fighting over him. He must love this, Brynn thought just as she heard a dog bark. Tessa and Nathan heard the bark, too, but Brynn knew it wasn't familiar to them. It was to her. It was to Savannah, who'd lifted her head slightly.

'What about your brother? What about Savannah? You want them to die? No, no you wouldn't. Never. The selfless Brynn Wilder wouldn't want Nathan to choose her life over theirs,' Tessa blustered.

'He can't let all of us live. As for the *selfless* Brynn Wilder, I'll tell you a secret. You're not the only actress here.' Brynn hoped Savannah would pick up on her reference to acting and not show any recognition of the dog's second bark. She kept talking, louder than earlier. 'You acted like the wounded bird for eighteen years, but you weren't wounded – not mentally. I understand you because that's something we have in common – acting hurt, acting gentle, acting like what we aren't deep inside.'

'Nathan wants *me* with him,' Tessa said, regaining her composure.

'He's gotten by without you for almost eighteen years.'

'All right, ladies,' Nathan said affably. 'Quarreling over a man isn't attractive. Complimentary, but not attractive. I'm going to pull the car around. Some of us will get in it. Some won't.' He handed a gun to Tessa, then picked up one for himself. 'I'll be back in a few minutes.'

As soon as Nathan opened the insulated steel entrance door and stepped outside, Carder took a shot, barely missing Nathan's body. Nathan whirled and raised a gun. Carder shot again, this time hitting Nathan's hand. Nathan yelled, grabbing his right hand with his left and falling down. Garrett charged between Nathan and the doorway, pointing his gun into the building.

Garrett blinked, his eyes adjusting from the fading daylight to the even dimmer building. He heard Brynn yell, 'Garrett – Mark, Savannah, and I are here!' He rushed into the building, blinked again, and saw Tessa holding a gun to Brynn's head.

'I'm here, too.' Tessa's voice was steel. 'You come any farther and I'll shoot Brynn and then your daughter.'

Garrett had called for back-up less than five minutes earlier. Neither he nor Carder had expected the door of the building to open so soon, certainly not before night. Instead, they'd had even less time than they thought.

'Daddy?' Savannah whimpered.

'Don't move, Savannah, or I'll shoot Brynn in the head,' Tessa snapped.

'Please don't shoot her. I can't move. I'm tied to the post.'

'Brynn acted like she was tied to the post, too,' Tessa said. 'But she's standing right here beside me. Now shut up before I kill her just because I've always dreamed of it.'

Savannah subsided with a choking sound. Suddenly, Henry ran into the building and straight to Savannah. Tessa moved the gun away from Brynn's head and aimed at the dog. Brynn jerked as if she were trying to pull free of her captor, and Tessa whisked the gun back to Brynn's head.

'Nate!' Tessa yelled. 'Are you all right?'

After a minute, his voice floated into the building. 'Wounded! Right hand!'

Garrett kept his own Glock 9mm aimed at Tessa. 'Back-up will be here any minute, Tessa. Put down the gun.'

'No,' she said flatly.

He took another step into the room. 'What do you plan to do, Tessa? Shoot your way out of here?'

'If I have to.'

'I thought knives were your specialty, not guns.'

'I like knives. I like cutting into people's necks with knives – slicing the carotid and the jugular. I did it to Stone Jonah. I did it to Sam, too, because Nate was too busy watching Brynn dancing on the beach like a fool. But I like guns, too. I'm a good shot, Sheriff Dane.'

Brynn glanced over and saw Henry licking Savannah's face, licking away the tears, snuffling lovingly at her neck beneath her hair. 'Good, Henry,' Savannah murmured. 'Stay, Henry. Stay.' The dog sat down beside her, his eyes fixed on Tessa, guarding Savannah with every fiber of his being.

'Got a proposition for you, Sheriff!' Nate yelled.

'Are you in a position to bargain?' Garrett yelled back.

'Yeah, as a matter of fact, I am.' In a moment, everyone in the room flinched at the sound of another shot. 'Just did away with your deputy, Garrett. He got careless because he didn't know I'm ambidextrous. Came near me to kick the gun away but I grabbed it with my left hand.' He waited a second. 'He doesn't look too good.'

'Damn you, Nate,' Garrett said grimly as he looked at Tessa. 'I'm lowering my gun.'

Brynn expected Tessa to say, 'Put it down,' but Garrett dashed into the room straight to the support pole and Savannah, then raised his gun again before she could get out a word. At that exact moment Nathan came in, his own gun raised. He held the gun with both hands, the right dripping blood below his trembling arm. He seemed unaware of pain as he scanned the room with slightly wild eyes.

'I'll say it again.' Nathan's eyes narrowed. 'Let Tessa and me go, and we'll let your daughter live.'

Garrett was silent for a moment. 'Nate, I have a gun aimed at you.'

'And I have a gun aimed at you. If I move it slightly, it'll be aimed at Savannah.'

'Where do you think you and Tessa are going?'

'I told you that day in the park. Morocco.'

'Nate, you're not going to Casablanca in Morocco. I realize you emphasized it too much. You're going somewhere else. I can easily check with your company.'

'Go ahead,' Nate answered nonchalantly.

'And what if I take you up on your deal?' Garrett went on as if he hadn't heard Nathan. 'What if I let you go so you won't kill Savannah? You'd take her with you when you leave Genessa Point, but you'd get rid of her before you board the plane for wherever you *are* going.'

'No, I wouldn't. You know I always make careful plans. I did this time, too. Just in case something like this unfortunate circumstance happened, I've made arrangements to take Savannah with us. That way I can be sure that if in the next half hour you find out where we're going, you won't notify all the airports in the area to have us stopped. If you do, I don't have anything to lose by killing Savannah. One knife slash across the neck and you wouldn't have a daughter anymore.'

'You son of a bitch,' Garrett hissed.

'Actually, our mother was a very nice lady, wasn't she, Tessa? A little dim-witted even before she got cancer and had to be kept doped up on drugs all the time, but nice. One of those idiots who sees the best in everyone. She had no idea what kind of man she'd married. She had no idea what her children were like because of him. He even convinced her this was our "playhouse."' Nathan looked around and shuddered violently, his memory obviously travelling back to his childhood days. He wasn't focused on anyone. He was seeing a different time, when he was young and terrified and tortured.

Garrett took advantage of the moment, taking a shot that hit Nathan in the side. Nathan made a high, squealing sound that didn't sound human and fired toward Garrett. As the bullet slammed into the concrete block wall, Savannah screamed, loud and unbelievably shrill, while Tessa shrieked and slightly loosened her hold on Brynn. The gun was still aimed toward Brynn's head, though. Brynn ducked and with all her strength, jabbed Tessa in the ribs with her elbow. Tessa shrieked again but this time the gun, unsteady in her hand, went off and caught Nathan in the throat, tearing it half away. He looked at her in utter surprise before he raised his left hand, pressing his gun to his chest and fell to his knees, blood pouring from his neck. Tessa ran to Nathan, sobbing wildly, yelling his name. She grabbed him as he fell forward, pressing his bloody body against hers.

And then everyone in the building heard the slightly muffled sound of Nathan's gun going off as it pressed against Tessa's heart.

EPILOGUE

'A re you sure you have to leave tomorrow?' Garrett asked Brynn. Surrounded by the softly warm summer night, they sat close together on folding chairs in Cassie's backyard, waiting to see the last and largest Holly Park fireworks display of the Festival.

'I need to get back to my book. I'm already behind schedule.' Brynn paused. 'And I want to get Mark away from Genessa Point.'

Brynn thought of her brother emerging from the dim cement block building – thin, pale, his lips parched and slightly bloody, his eyes surrounded with dark circles, his wrists bruised by the steel handcuffs he'd tried to escape, his legs shaky. With Garrett's help, he'd walked out of the building and taken three steps before collapsing. Afterward, he'd spent two days in the hospital being treated for abrasions, dehydration and the deep cut on his scalp delivered by Tessa, who'd hidden on the floor of his car's back seat as he'd started off for Cassie's one night and never arrived.

'Is Mark going back to Baltimore?'

'Absolutely not. I'm putting my foot down and he's too trauma-tized to argue with me.' A firefly blinked its small gold light in front of Brynn's face as if in agreement and she smiled. 'He's coming to Miami to stay with me for as long as he likes. I hope he'll fall in love with the city, like I have, and make it home. I know he can find a job eventually.'

'In spite of the glowing recommendation he'll get from that prissy bank manager?'

Brynn laughed. 'You mean about Mark's "lackadaisical manner," "poor deportment" and "slipshod appearance"?'

'What a memory!'

'Who could forget the insults of a bank manager from the 1800s? Mark had other jobs before that one, and he always performed well. He'll get some good recommendations.'

'The same can't be said for Ray,' Garrett said dourly. 'He's never had a steady job and I'm not expecting the next great true crime novel from him. He's lucky to be alive.'

At that moment they heard Mark yell, 'Hooray,' from inside the house where he was playing a game with Cassie and Savannah.

'I assume he won again,' Brynn said dryly. 'He's always been great at Scrabble.'

'If Mark won, it's only because Henry opted out of the game.' Garrett was silent for a moment. 'If it hadn't been for that dog, we might not have found you.'

'I don't know why you even thought of looking at the Cavanaugh place.'

Garrett took a sip of beer from the bottle. 'At the carnival, I heard Tessa say you should keep things that are important to you as close as possible. Savannah heard it, too, and she told me Tessa had said the same thing to her at the wishing well. She said it must be Tessa's mantra. I thought about the changes in Tessa – her dating Ray, the long trip planned with her brother – then her remark about keeping things close. I admit it was *a very* thin lead pointing toward Tessa – a change of behavior at the same time Mark went missing – but it was all I had. I thought that if the Cavanaughs had somehow taken Mark, it made sense that they'd keep him close enough to keep an eye on him most of the time.

'Still, we might have left if Henry hadn't found that scrap of Savannah's blouse and the dog whistle she lost when she managed to fight her way free from Nathan for a minute. We might have walked away from that building before Nathan walked out of it. We couldn't see in the windows or hear anything. Old Earl Cavanaugh had three acres and he put the building in a spot where no one from the streets or nearest houses could hear much, then he must have spent a fortune on insulation.'

Brynn recalled Nathan's shudder when he'd looked around what his father had called 'the playhouse.' Even if Nate had lived to be eighty, she thought, he wouldn't have been able to forget the abuse he'd endured there at the hands of his own father.

'Nathan said Sam Fenney saw Mr Cavanaugh raping Tessa in a downstairs room of the house.' Brynn could hear her voice hardening. 'I resented Sam for not standing by my mother after Dad died, but I never dreamed he was so vile! He blackmailed Earl Cavanaugh all those years to keep his mouth shut about the abomination he saw and used the money to build a motel and a restaurant!'

'Sickening,' Garrett nearly spat. 'Nathan came back to settle his father's will so he could later collect the money he thought was waiting for him and Tessa. Or rather, himself. I'm sure he planned to get rid of Tessa as soon as they reached South America. He'd chartered a plane to JFK Airport in New York and then a flight to Caracas, Venezuela. You can be sure Nathan wouldn't have dragged Tessa around with him. She probably would have been his first adult victim.'

'What about his wives?'

Garrett looked at her in surprise. 'I thought I told you. After his death, I checked into his background. He never had any wives. He had Tessa spread the word that he was married and divorced twice. That's why he never brought one home to meet the family. Whenever he came back, he was between wives.'

'Why keep up the charade of being married?'

'Because he was paranoid that people might think he was gay. You know how he hated homosexuals.' Garrett shook his head in disgust. 'He wanted everyone to believe he was a real stud with the women.'

'Instead, he was a serial killer.'

'God knows how many victims he's racked up over the last eighteen years,' Garrett said. 'I'm sure he didn't stop during his college years. Afterward, the maritime computer company kept him on the move. My research revealed that everywhere he was sent, at the time he was present, there were two or three murders that fit his M.O.'

After a long moment, Brynn said, 'My father was suspicious of him when he was just a teenager.'

'Kids were being killed. Your father was cautious about his children's friends.'

Brynn watched a firefly blink green twice before she asked, 'What happened to your friendship with Mark?'

'Oh, long story.' He paused and Brynn thought he was going to close the subject, but he finally began talking. 'You said Mark's friend Greg in Baltimore mentioned Mark looking at a story in the newspaper about a car wreck caused by a mannequin lying on the highway.' Brynn nodded. 'Because the mannequin was from Love's Dress Shoppe where your mother worked, Mark was the most likely suspect, but my father said Mark had told him that I did it. Dad took his belt to me. It was bad. I was furious with Mark, first because he told my dad I did it and second because I thought Mark did it. We never talked about it.'

'If you had, you would have figured out Nathan was responsible.'

'My father should have suspected Nathan, but he didn't want to – I was always his target. Not too long after that came the scandal about Nathan and the coach. Nate brushed that off and his father gave him a new Corvette. He was made of Teflon.'

'Speaking of cars, Mark's car being left out of town behind those trees was a set-up.'

'Yeah. Mark and I put it together. Tessa waited for him at the motel in his back seat and Nathan was in Tessa's car. When Mark got in, Tessa bashed his head and they put him in the back seat. Scalp wounds bleed like crazy. Mark came to after a few minutes. He was in a lot of pain but conscious enough to semi-know what was happening. They each drove a car and not too far from those trees, they stopped and Nathan unscrewed the cap on the oil pan. There was just enough oil left to get the car to hiding place, put Mark in Tessa's car and drive him back to their house.'

Brynn shook her head. 'What a remarkable amount of planning went into all of this.'

'Nathan and Tessa were a smart pair.'

'Well, excuse me for not admiring them.' Brynn took a drink of her own beer in a bottle. 'At least Dwight Carder will be all right. And Edmund Ellis is "in a better place" as the minister said at his funeral. I'm not sure that's true. I mean, I understand why he kept his mouth shut about Dad, but still . . .'

'I don't know how I feel about what he did, either. I'd give my life to protect Savannah, but I don't think I could stay quiet for so many years while your family suffered, especially Mark. No wonder Ellis left two-thirds of his estate to Mark.'

'I'm not sure Mark will accept the money under the circumstances. He's in sort of a moral quandary about it.' She paused. 'Besides, some of Edmund's distant cousins are crawling out of the woodwork to raise hell that he didn't leave them a dime. He didn't have a fortune, of course, but his giving two-thirds of what he *did* have to Mark is incomprehensible to them, especially because no one wants to tarnish Edmund's memory by telling them why he wanted Mark to have it.'

'He didn't leave anything to you?'

'He knew I didn't need it because I'm doing very well with the books. Mark has nothing left.'

Cassie, Mark, Savannah and Henry all poured out of the house at the same time. 'What's going on out here?' Mark demanded. 'You two are having way too much fun!'

'You've got a grudge against fun now?' Brynn asked archly.

'Not at all.' Mark came over and kissed her on the forehead. He was still too thin and had hollows around his eyes and a stitch in his lower lip, but he was also still handsome. And for the first time in years, he looked truly happy.

'We played Scrabble old-fashioned style with a cardboard game-board and little wooden squares with the letters,' Savannah announced. 'Mark won. He spelled words I've never even *heard* before!'

'Like doily?' Brynn asked, grinning.

Savannah rolled her eyes. 'Not only can I spell it, I can make one!'

'Then your time with Mrs Persinger wasn't wasted, although you gave her the scare of her life when you sneaked away, heading for the amphitheater,' Garrett said.

'I'm sorry I did that, Daddy,' Savannah said forlornly. 'Don't know why I did that.'

'OK, drama queen.' Garrett didn't smile. 'You did it because you were determined to be in the play, even though I told you that you couldn't. I had a very good reason for wanting you to stay safe at Mrs Persinger's, not sneak out and then accept a ride with a stranger.'

'Nathan wasn't a stranger. At least, I didn't think he was. Wow, was I wrong! I'll never do anything like that again, Dad. I promise, cross my heart, pinky swear.'

'I guess you learned your lesson,' Garrett said grudgingly.

'I'll say,' Savannah said enthusiastically as she came to sit on the grass beside Brynn with Henry beside her.

Cassie had brought out chairs for her and Mark. 'I wish you two weren't leaving tomorrow, Brynn.'

'The sooner we get back to Miami, the sooner you can come for your vacation.' Brynn pretended to look alarmed. 'You haven't changed your mind, have you, Cass?'

'No way. I can't wait to stretch out on a beach with you and a piña colada.'

'And me,' Mark put in quickly. 'My sister says I'm too pale. She prescribes lots of sun along with a beautiful companion – one about five foot two with shoulder-length hair and brown eyes and a heart big enough to still care about an old, beaten-up guy she knew when she was a kid. And I love piña coladas.'

Brynn glanced at Garrett and whispered, 'Sparks are flying.'

'I believe you're right,' Garrett answered, grinning.

'Didn't you say something about us coming to see you this summer, too?' Savannah asked Brynn tentatively.

'I'd be devastated if you didn't come.'

'Me *and* Dad *and* Henry?'

'What would a vacation be without the three of you?' Brynn frowned. 'You'll have to get some flip-flops for Henry. The sand would burn his bare paws but he'll love the ocean.'

A loud popping sound preceded the appearance of a huge white and red column shooting into the sky, then splaying out like a hundred spouts from a fountain. Savannah clapped and Henry barked. Garrett reached over and took Brynn's hand. 'Are you sure you want us to come and see you?'

'More than you know,' she said before a boom announced the launch of a huge green and blue blossom of lights. While everyone else clapped and 'oohed' and barked, their gazes fastened on the fireworks, Brynn drew Garrett's hand to her lips, kissed it gently and mouthed again, 'More than you know.'